TWISTED MAGIC

BY
JEFFE KENNEDY

Their love makes them stronger together… Unless the world rips them apart

Jadren El-Adrel knows he's a mess. He's a cobbled-together monster pretending to be a wizard, still unable to master the magic that makes him pretty much immortal and is useless for anything else. Though he's tried to learn to work with his familiar, Seliah, he's still terrified to discover what might happen if he gives himself full access to the depths of her powerful magic. Some questions should never be answered.

Seliah Phel got her happy ever after. Jadren loves her; they're together in a safe and beautiful place; and they're finally learning to work together as wizard and familiar. But even she must recognize that Jadren continues to stew in his black moods, brooding that only worsens when he receives a missive from home, his horrible family demanding the unthinkable: that they both return to House El-Adrel.

As the denizens of House Phel fight an increasingly pitched battle against the enemies determined to destroy them forever, Jadren and Selly fight their own war—against the past and to overcome their own failings. To become truly stronger together.

DEDICATION

To Minerva Spencer,
for the rapid reads, proofing, savvy insights, enthusiasm,
cackles and cocktails.
I'm still waiting for my Halloween cupcakes though.

ACKNOWLEDGMENTS

Many thanks to the readers who patiently waited for this book with excitement, always being so careful and generous not to pressure me about it, even when I admitted I was writing something else, the book I wasn't supposed to be writing.

As always, immense gratitude to Carien Ubink and Sullivan McPig, for reading, catching weird colloquialisms, and All The Assisting.

TWISTED MAGIC

BY
JEFFE KENNEDY

~ I ~

"**M**ISSIVE FOR YOU, Lord Jadren."

Jadren turned from his contemplation of the annoyingly serene view of the valley that comprised the heart of House Refoel lands and took in the page bearing the sealed scroll with some bemusement. When he'd arrived at Refoel—as a prisoner, not incidentally—he'd been universally addressed with contempt, labeled a rogue wizard and violent murderer. He'd also been facing imminent execution, so how people talked to him had been the least of his worries.

Still, it never failed to amuse him that, during the months he and Seliah had been living at Refoel, he'd gone to being called "Lord Jadren," which was a far sight better, if not necessarily correct. The community of healers had implemented the peculiar honorific as a way of acknowledging his status as a scion of another high house while discretely refraining from mentioning the name of House El-Adrel. He'd become somehow both a product of the house of his birth and severed from it in one fell moniker and he wasn't quite sure what to make of it. But then, he'd been turned so inside-out from the Refoel wizard-healers torturing him in the name of mental health and attempts to teach him to be a proper wizard, that he wasn't sure what to make of most anything.

It would bother him that he couldn't trust his own mind, except that it was the story of his life. He was used to it, which also said something.

"A missive," he repeated, eyeing the page. "For me?" He didn't usually clarify information that was already abundantly clear. In fact, he'd normally take the opportunity to mock someone who felt the need to be so irritatingly redundant. Still, considering that he was supposed to be in hiding with no one outside a select few knowing where—or who—he was, receiving correspondence seemed... questionable.

The page nodded, earnest in her youth, extending the expensive-looking envelope, magically shimmering with the seal of some house or other. Jadren seriously doubted he wanted to know which one. "Delivered by a Ratsiel courier," the page added. "Lord Refoel bade me bring it to you with all haste."

Only in the blissful, non-political, and almost oppressively quiet environs of House Refoel would a missive delivered via Ratsiel courier be treated with such reverence. At House El-Adrel, Ratsiel couriers came and went in a blizzard of activity, sent and received by wizards of all echelons. Even House Phel, backward upstarts that they were, employed Ratsiel couriers to communicate with the other houses in the Convocation with enough regularity that there were always a few rats—as Jadren and his siblings had nicknamed the magical constructs that could resemble bizarre beasties—roosting in the rafters of the library.

Jadren really didn't want to know who'd sent him a message, especially now, after all these months of silence, and especially since the potential list of senders was so short. Seliah had sent a message to her brother, Lord Gabriel Phel, the master they both looked to, when the two of them first decided to extend their stay at Refoel. "Decision" being a euphemism as it hadn't been entirely up to them. The good healers at Refoel weren't enthused about unleashing the monster that was Jadren on an unsuspecting population. Still, Jadren's status had been upgraded from prisoner to quasi-guest, allowing Seliah to finally contact Phel, reassuring him that they were safe, together, and would be staying put for a while.

Jadren didn't know what didn't know what details Seliah had shared in the letter about the events leading to their capture by the Refoel wizards or how they'd come to be part-boarder, part-patients at the house, though she'd offered to let him read it. He did know that Seliah and Gabriel had traded semi-regular correspondence ever since. Probably Lady Phel, Gabriel's wife, Nic, was in the mix, too. Jadren assumed Seliah was keeping House Phel abreast of their progress in healing from extensive trauma (mostly him), physical deprivation (mostly her), mental and emotional instability (both of them), learning to use their magic (both of them, but mostly him), and training in using their wizard–familiar bond (both of them, though they mostly sucked at it so far).

"Lord Jadren?" The page's outstretched hand sagged a little, her round eyes glistening in concern. "Don't you want it?"

"No," he replied honestly. Nothing good could be in that

missive. Why couldn't whoever sent it have continued to correspond with Seliah and let him continue happily with his head buried in the sand?

"Bu—but..." she stammered. "Lord Refoel bade me to—"

"I know, I know. All haste. Blah blah blah. Listen, you tell Lord Chaim Refoel that he can suck my enormous—"

"I'll take it," Seliah said, striding out to the terrace and plucking the envelope from the girl's hand. "Thank you, Pinny. Please tell Lord Refoel that I'll see to it that Lord Jadren reads this."

The page smiled at Seliah, gave Jadren a last, alarmed look, and fled back inside, the doors to the rooms he shared with Seliah closing with a thud.

"Do you know the name of every cursed robe-wearer in this valley?" Jadren asked her.

"No, only the people I see on a daily basis," Seliah retorted. "Pinny is in and out of our rooms all the time and she's the one who keeps you in endless carafes of wine and clean towels. You should know her name."

"I don't know the name of the wizard-nanny who spoon-fed me and wiped my hiney either," he pointed out. "That doesn't mean I should."

Seliah gave him a long, simmering look. With her brown eyes such a light golden color they resembled flawless amber, the glare imparted considerable impact, like a focused ray of light. And, like the lightning bolt emblem of House El-Adrel, that ray struck hard, piercing him to the bone with how much he loved her. He wasn't the kind of guy to fall in love. With the exception of his father, he'd never loved or been loved in

4

all his benighted life. Among all his other failings, he didn't know how to *do* this. If he had any choice in the matter, he wouldn't.

But he didn't have a choice. Not in having Seliah as his familiar, an irreversible bond, nor in loving her to the point of insanity.

Of course, it didn't help that she was infuriatingly gorgeous, in her own unique style that shouldn't work, but did. Her odd assembly of features, none of them pretty on their own, somehow combined into an original beauty infused with her strong-willed personality. She looked absurdly lovely in the golden Refoel robe, the silky material clinging to her lean figure in all the right places. Her glistening black hair fell to below her waist, long and loose, the way she knew he liked it. He liked it *too* much, immediately assailed by smoldering memories of being veiled in that hair as she rode him, rising above him, slender, tawny, and suffused with animal sensuality. Something he'd like to do, but had not yet tried, involved wrapping that hair firmly around his fist and—

"And what has crawled up *your* hiney?" she asked with false sweetness, startling him out of the lurid fantasy. She raised one black-winged brow as she tapped the missive against her thigh. Seliah had gained weight during their stay, thanks to the assiduous attention of the Refoel nutritionists, losing the gauntness from starving in the swamps during her magic-induced madness, but she would always be lean, all tensile strength and wiry muscle. "Did the session with Liat go badly?" she asked more gently, eyes filling with that compassion he both loved and loathed.

5

"Depends on what you consider to be bad," he answered, trying to sound flippant and turning back to the view, so he wouldn't have to see the sympathy in her gaze. He'd come out on the terrace with the half-formed thought of soaking in one of their three private pools of varying degrees of heat, with an eye toward unknotting some of the tension sending spikes up and down his spine.

Then it had seemed like too much effort to even get undressed and he'd ended up broodily staring into the distance like some damaged hero from a novel, full of existential despair and dreary self-involvement.

"I'm no closer to being able to consciously wield my healing magic—on myself or anyone else," he reported. "I suspect Liat is contemplating breaking all of her precious healer's vows by deliberately wounding me to determine if I even *can* heal. I'm not sure she believes me."

"You can't expect to solve a lifelong problem in a month," Seliah said, moving closer.

That was rich, coming from her. He cast her a scathing glance over his shoulder. "Weren't you the one to give that big speech about not liking when people tell you what you can expect of yourself and how important it is to you that I do expect you to step up and handle your shit?"

She actually rolled her eyes at him, coming up beside him and gazing out at the stupidly pretty valley. Unlike him, she looked peaceful and lovely, not tortured at all. "So, what's the letter about?"

"I don't know, do I?" he snarled. "You snagged it before I could even look at the cursed thing."

Giving him the side-eye, she blew out a huff of exasperation. "You're telling me that you were giving poor Pinny grief, refusing to take the missive from her, and you don't even know who it's from or whether it's good or bad news?"

"Oh, it's definitely bad news." No question of that.

"Jadren, you don't know that until you look," she said in her all-patient-and-reasonable tone that made him perversely want to be even more exasperating.

"Seliah, darling." He rounded on her. "Haven't you learned by now that it's *all* bad news? People don't pay for Ratsiel couriers and expensive stationery to send happy chirpy thoughts. People only invest time and coin in enterprises they expect will deliver even greater benefit in return, which is always at the expense of someone else."

"Hmm." She pursed her full lips, amber eyes brightening. "Perhaps I should start sending you happy, chirpy notes."

"With what coin?" he retorted, pointing out the obvious. "You and I are the impoverished charity cases living on House Refoel's good will, shamelessly exploiting their guilt and repressed desire. I doubt your admirer, Chaim, will extend his generosity in paying for you to correspond with House Phel to sending your wizard—with whom you share a bed nightly instead of with him as he so longs for—unnecessary love notes."

She frowned, narrowing her eyes. "Why do you assume they'd be love notes?"

Amused by her despite himself, and annoyed that she didn't dispute the bit about Chaim, he decided not to touch that one. "Fine. Who is the missive from?"

She turned it over in her hands. Deliberately, he didn't look at the thing, watching her face instead. "It's sealed with the El-Adrel crest."

No wonder Chaim had been so fired up to get the letter to him. No doubt the lecherous wizard was chortling with joy at the prospect of the El-Adrel claw poised to yank Jadren back to the house of his birth and his sadistic mother. Jadren's stomach curdled with dread. "Burn it," he advised.

"What? No!" Seliah danced back and held the envelope away from him, above her head, as if that would do anything to keep it from him if he should take the perverse notion to lay hands on the thing. Probably the magic seal was keyed to him and who knew what vile flower would blossom from it should he touch it. "It could be important." Seliah's eyes were wide with alarm.

"I don't care." He didn't even have to fake firmness in that statement. To his amazement and relief, he found a core of certainty in himself about the decision. Liat might be frustrated with their lack of progress in untangling his scarred-over psyche, but apparently he had made some sort of incremental recovery after all. He could make at least one decision. "Burn it," he repeated, pointing at one of the fire-elemental-crowned torches ringing the terrace. "Do it, Seliah."

She got that stubborn line between her brows. "No. You don't order me around, Jadren. If—"

He lunged for her and she shrieked, mostly in surprise, moving fast but not fast enough to evade him. Grabbing her with one arm around her slim waist and seizing her wrist—she was tall, but not taller than he was—he levered her arm down and toward the nearest torch. She fought him, of course, but this wasn't the first time he'd had to wrestle a crazed Seliah for her own good. Except this time she wasn't crazed at all. She fought him with slippery determination, twisting nearly out of his grip and using every dirty move she knew—including a few he'd taught her—to escape his grip.

But he'd contained her before, and at times when she was far more volatile than this. In her feral and demented state, she became wildly unpredictable, but in her right mind, she was a calculated fighter, applying rational choices and a smidge less conviction. Only the truly crazed would attempt to injure their loved ones, and Seliah loved him, despite all good sense. She didn't want to hurt him and that hampered her. She'd also forgotten about his magic.

He might be shit at healing on command, or doing any fancy enchantments, but he still possessed his fundamental wizardry. He didn't even need to employ any El-Adrel tricks or be all that skilled at manipulating elementals. Any wizard worth their salt could instruct a tame elemental that was already bound to a task. Reaching out with a lick of magic, he commanded the closest fire elemental to abandon its torch and leap onto the scroll Seliah desperately tried to keep out of his reach.

She emitted an ear-splitting shriek at a volume he hadn't known her slim body could produce, shocking him enough that he flinched—and she wrested herself and the scroll away. Then, arms cartwheeling, an almost comical look of surprise on her face, Seliah fell into the nearby hot pool.

~ 2 ~

THE WATER CLOSED over Selly's head, filling her nose and ears, stinging her eyes, flooding bitter into her mouth before she belatedly thought to close it. Thrashing, she righted herself from the shocking immersion—then battled the strong hands grappling her.

"No!" she yelled at Jadren, the obstinate idiot. She clutched the scroll, holding it away from him. "I'm not letting you burn this message."

"I won't need to," he retorted, hanging onto her, "as its impromptu drowning will have no doubt finished the job the fire began. Now stop behaving like a lunatic and let me fish you out of there, you half-feral swamp creature! Are you hurt?"

She shoved drenched and tangled hair out of her eyes with the crook of her elbow, which worked about as well as you'd think. "I can stand up in this pool. It's not as if I could drown."

Jadren scowled at her, wizard-black eyes stark and glittering in his pale-skinned face, auburn hair and beard catching the firelight from the torches and echoing the fiery streaks in the sunset sky. "You could have hit your head," he insisted, yanking on her arm. "Stop being a fool and let me see to you."

Calculating, she put on a pained expression. "Oof, maybe I

did hit something. I feel all weak and dizzy."

He cursed, a frantic light in his eyes, and he gentled his hold, reaching with both hands for her. "I knew it. Let me—"

Flipping her grip, she yanked him into the pool, delighting in his garbled shout of surprise as he tumbled in head-first beside her. He surfaced immediately, glaring daggers at her and sputtering in a most inelegant fashion. "You infuriating minx!" he snarled. "You wretched, ungrateful, traitorous Familiar."

He lunged at her and, shrieking with laughter, she attempted to evade him. No such luck in such a confined space. She did manage to hurl the scroll out of reach, however, sending it soggily skidding across the patio, where it fetched up against the low garden wall, safe from Jadren's unreasonable vindictiveness for the moment.

"You'll pay for that nasty trick," Jadren declared, pinning her to the low, prettily tiled ledge over which a clear sheet of water tumbled into the pool. He wound his other hand into her hair, holding her in place with a firm grip in the sodden mass at the base of her skull, levering his weight against her, their bodies pressed together. The hot and hard portions as well.

Oh, yes. She shivered, making a production of it, since she wasn't the least bit cold in the very warm water. It said something that Jadren still felt hot in contrast, his wizard's magic shimmering along her skin like miniature lightning bolts, firing her already aroused nerves. She met his gaze eye for eye, lifting her chin defiantly. Well, as best as she could with his iron grip in her hair. "I'd like to see you try, Wizard," she hissed.

His magic flared, along with his palpable desire. "I'm going to make you apologize," he informed her, "and beg for my forgiveness."

"Never. I won't—" She lost the words as his demanding lips closed over hers, fastening on with all the passionate energy that simmered through him. That brooding anger, and the very real fear she'd glimpsed in him as he'd regarded that missive like it might be a venomous serpent poised at his throat, transformed into greedy desire she was delighted to sate. Selly couldn't claim that she'd deliberately refocused his pent-up emotions into sex, but that's how it had worked out and she couldn't be happier. The care and feeding of wizards was how Nic referred to this sort of thing, and Selly could see her sister-in-law's point. It wasn't strictly a Familiar's duty to redirect the monumental powers their wizards wielded into avenues where they wouldn't cause collateral damage.

But it was decidedly a privilege of the job.

Still gripping her hair, Jadren plundered her mouth with barely restrained violence, and Selly opened to him gladly. He tended to be careful of her still, always worried about her health—physical, mental, *and* emotional, she'd been that much of a mess—and treating her with solicitous care. She appreciated his concern for her and frankly reveled in all the small ways he showed his love for her, especially since he never said as much, not in so many words, instead coating himself with a thick layer of sarcasm. But she'd also had a bellyful of being treated as fragile. Ever since she'd lost her mind to stagnant magic, everyone danced around her as if she were a rabid kitten. Delicate enough to require careful handling; dangerous enough to infect the unwary.

Only when Jadren lost himself in the fulminating desire between them did he forget to monitor his every touch. Murmuring encouragement and defiance in equal measures, Selly fought to remove Jadren's soaked clothing. He still wore his fighting leathers every day, all in black, along with weapons and the various metal implements he transformed into gadgets with his El-Adrel magic. He stood out amid the pastel-robed healers' community like a bloodied sword thrust though a bouquet of wistful blossoms.

He already had her robe open—the loose-fitting garments were comfortable and Selly did her part to blend in with the community, not only to make up for Jadren's determined and distanced enmity—leaving her mostly naked. One of the many advantages of the robes was their easy removal. Jadren's clever fingers raked down the center of her body, brushing the inner curves of her breasts with teasing lightness, before his hand settled low on her belly. Closing her eyes in sensual anticipation, she arched into the rough caress, releasing a gasp and shuddering for real, parting her thighs for him.

He didn't move. She squirmed invitingly. He laughed, low and ever so slightly cruel.

"Oh, no, my delectable familiar. Surely you didn't imagine I would satisfy you so quickly and easily."

She cracked her eyes open, finding him looming close, wizard-black gaze glittering. "Please?" she asked hopefully.

"That doesn't sound like an apology at all."

She attempted to look remorseful, something she didn't at

all feel, especially given her current most-rewarding circumstances. "I'm sorry, Jadren."

His intent gaze drilling into hers, he shook his head slowly. "Not even close, liar."

Heaving out a sigh, she wriggled, her taut, wet nipples chafing against his sodden leathers. His hand settled more heavily to hold her in place. "How can I apologize when I wasn't in the wrong?" she asked plaintively.

"Aha." He chuckled softly, tugging inexorably on her hair to tip her head back, then nibbling along her jaw. "That, at least, is honest. You can apologize for disobeying me."

She groaned, both at what his lips and teeth were doing to her and at his irritating words. "I don't have to obey you," she ground out.

"In point of fact, you do. It was part of the wizard–familiar bonding ceremony." He slid a leather-clad thigh between hers, just enough to tantalize, not enough to give her any friction where she needed it most.

She tried to think back to that ceremony, not easy with his teasing clouding her mind on top of her confused memories of that day. Their entire sojourn within the confines of House El-Adrel had the flavor of a protracted dream, complete with the occasional nightmare. Generations of El-Adrel wizards tinkering away at their proprietary area of magic had turned the entire, sprawling manse into a giant enchanted artifact that seemed to possess its own level of sentience. Being forced to bond with Jadren to save their lives had been only one bizarre experience in a gamut of them.

She did remember the words of the vow, however: *Take*

my power with the severing of my hair, wizard, so that I may be bound to you while you live. The magical gong that had reverberated through her, sealing the bond, echoed still. The living bond between them tingled with it, energized by their erotic embrace. "I know I never promised to obey," she protested.

"It's implied," he insisted, his hand traveling slowly up her ribcage to cup her breast, squeezing lightly so she whimpered. "You're mine, Seliah. I gave you a chance to be free and *you* are the one who came after *me*. It's far too late to protest your bondage now."

She stared fiercely up at the darkening sky, disappearing beyond the firelit ring of the terrace. "Because you're mine, too."

"Oh, yes," he agreed, sounding wry and rueful. "Duly captured, but not tamed." He moved down her throat, rolling her nipple between thumb and forefinger. "Apologize."

"It would be a lie." Despite the game, despite it all, she didn't like being untruthful with him. "I won't lie to you."

He lifted his head, eyes stark black pools in his pale face, hair sleek from the water. "Fair enough. Then begging for my forgiveness will suffice."

"What should I ask you to forgive me for?"

"For being so fucking beautiful."

"I'm not, though, I—" She gasped as he pinched her nipple, sending an exquisite bolt of pleasure-pain through her. "Jadren."

"Arguing with me is counterproductive to the point of this enterprise," he said smoothly, holding her in place, face set in a ruthless expression that shouldn't be so arousing, but was. "I'm setting the terms of the apology. Do you yield?"

Did she yield? Her pride wanted to say *no*, but her body was all *yes*. She dug her fingers into his leather-clad shoulders, wanting to rake him with the claws she wished she possessed. "This is unfair," she snarled, writhing between the twin pins of his grip on her hair and nipple.

He smiled, a thin slice of cruel desire. "I never promised to be fair, sweetheart. In fact, quite the opposite, as I believe I warned you numerous times. You wanted me anyway."

Oh, she had and still did. Always would. Her sex ached for him, desperate for his touch. "I apologize," she breathed, caught and held by that raptor-sharp gaze.

"I couldn't hear you." His smile widened at her groan of dismay, his thigh nudging high enough to brush her swollen nether lips.

"I apologize," she said, louder, through gritted teeth.

"For what?" he prompted.

"For... being beautiful." She blushed as she said it, unaccustomed to saying any such thing about herself.

"For being *so fucking beautiful*," he reminded her. "And say it louder."

"I apologize for being so fucking beautiful," she nearly yelled at him. It felt oddly transformative to shout those words.

"Apologize for being so irresistibly sexy." He released her nipple and took it into his mouth, laving the stinging with his tongue, cupping her breast gently.

She moaned, having to close her eyes to the intensity of it. "I apologize for being so irresistibly sexy."

"Louder." He moved his thigh higher, giving her the pressure she craved, and she ground her sex against the hard muscle. So close.

"I apologize for being so irresistibly sexy!" She'd lost herself to it now, happy to shout out whatever he liked so long as he kept going.

"Say that you beg my forgiveness for being such an amazing woman that you forced me to fall for you." He dropped his hand to tangle in the curls of her mons, and pulled his thigh out of her reach. "Say it, Seliah, and I promise to reward you. Look at me and say it."

She opened her eyes finding him close, watching her with glittering intent. "Please forgive me, Wizard," she said, not needing to fake the pleading edge to her voice. "Please forgive me for being such an amazing woman that I forced you to fall for me."

"Good girl," he murmured, making her wait just a beat longer, before he fastened his mouth over hers and pinched her clit, hard.

She came with a scream of completion, which he drank in, holding her close, his body plastered to hers. Clinging to him, she rode out the incredibly intense waves of pleasure, shuddering with it, calling his name as he showered her face with kisses, saying sweet nothings that he'd normally never be caught dead thinking, much less speaking. She'd learned this about him, that he dropped his impenetrable walls during sex with her, his caustic protective shell cast aside, if only for that short time.

As she caught her breath, he finally released her hair, startling a yip from her as he lifted her from the tumbling water and set her on the ledge of the pool. Seizing her knees, he spread her legs wide and dove between her thighs, avid mouth fastening on her oversensitized sex, applying suction that rocketed her into another screaming climax. Unable to do anything else, she clutched his hair and held on, spine bowing into an almost unsustainable arch, the firelit night sky a blur through the tears of extremity squeezing from her eyes.

He gave her no time to recover, pressing a firm hand to her lower back and driving two fingers into her throbbing passage, thrumming her clit with his tongue so she thrashed and sobbed, coming again or still, she wasn't sure. "Please, Jadren, please," she begged him, further words escaping her.

He took his time, but finally relented, backing off and gazing up at her, looking like some sort of wicked selkie with his hair sleek and black from drenching, wizard's eyes sparking with magic.

"I want you inside of me," she told him, trying to make it sound humble instead of the demand she wanted to voice.

"Do you?" He sounded dangerous.

"Yes."

"Yes, what?"

"Yes, please, Wizard."

"I want to show you something first," he purred, his voice full of sensual menace.

"I can't take anymore," she protested, trying to close her legs.

He held them firmly apart, shaking his head and tsking. "You can and you will take it," he said darkly. "You're still being punished."

"But I apologized." She didn't know if she wanted to cry or plead for more.

"Taking responsibility for your crimes and apologizing to me is only the first step. You must make amends."

"H-how?" She couldn't quite catch her breath, aquiver with anticipation and trepidation. What exactly was he going to do to her?

"By being a good girl and holding still. If you do, I promise to fuck you senseless."

She laughed a little, a watery sound, at his reminder of the promises he'd made her and broken. "I think you already have."

"Oh, no, my sweet, innocent familiar. You have no idea." He placed a kiss high on her inner thigh, the touch as electrifying as if he'd kissed her directly on her sex, chuckling as she moaned. "Will you behave?"

She could call a halt to this and he'd comply. Jadren loved to tease and push, but he always listened when she told him to stop. "Yes," she breathed, trying not to be so pleased when he smiled approvingly.

He let go of one knee, pausing to see if she'd stay in place, then glided his fingers up her inner thigh, taking his time as she trembled. "Wider," he instructed as he reached the hollow at the top of her leg, his proximity to her swollen sex excruciating.

"Jadren..."

"Wider," he commanded again, voice sharp enough to make her shiver.

She complied, biting her lip as she watched him lightly caress her spread lips with a fingertip, his magic shimmering under the surface of his skin. "What are you—?"

"Shh." He grinned up at her. "This will be fun."

"Jadren, I—" She shrieked, convulsing, as a tiny bolt of lightning leapt from his fingertip and shot into her clit and through her entire body. It kept going, lighting her up from within, all of her being shuddering with the intense pleasure.

Before she could register the change, Jadren had flipped her over onto her stomach, her legs dangling into the water. He slapped her bottom, the sting adding to the ongoing sparking through her body and she cried out wriggling, emitting a choked squeal when he did it again. Next, he had thrust inside her, filling her deeply, and she clawed at the smooth tiles, slicked from their splashing, trying to find purchase to ground herself.

To no avail. She was at his mercy and could only take it, his cock driving deep, the visceral punch of pleasure a dark counterpoint to the brighter, sharply sparking ecstasy still rocketing her nerves. He gripped her hips in vising hands, thrusting hard enough to make her see stars. Then, just as she was about to come yet again, he paused, and withdrew from her.

When a slick finger caressed her anus, she jerked in surprise and heightened arousal. He tickled her, making her moan, then pressed in. "Yes?" he grated out.

She nodded, bracing herself, and he worked his finger into her most private orifice, the sensation unlike anything else, intensifying the rest. Quivering with erotic tension, she held still. Slowly, he entered her again, his cock widening her sex as he drove that finger deeper into her remarkably sensitive rear passage. Doubly penetrated, she writhed, taking more than ever, blood roaring in her ears, full to bursting as he pounded into her.

Jadren came with a shout and she climaxed again, impossibly, her body blazing, bloodred surging through her vision as she fell gladly into sweet surcease.

~ 3 ~

S ELIAH WENT LIMP beneath him, passing into unconsciousness, and Jadren allowed himself a moment of smug, masculine triumph—mitigated somewhat by his own shuddering and the aftermath of a truly bone-watering orgasm. Still, he'd finally made good on that old boast. From someone decidedly terrible at following through on the words that came out of his big mouth, that was saying something.

It was all he could do to slide both of them back into the warmth of the pool and keep their heads above water. Tipping his head back to rest on the tiled rim, he held Seliah close and drew ragged breaths into his aching lungs.

A clearing of someone's throat, however, had him nearly lunging out of the water.

"Peace, Lord Jadren." Chaim Refoel emerged from the shadows beyond the torchlight, coming from the direction of their rooms, his dark-skinned, handsome face blandly neutral. He carefully averted his gaze as he spoke, fortunately for him. Otherwise, Jadren would've had to beat the intrusive healer to a bloody, whimpering mass of regret, which would create a significant mess and lead to a political catastrophe of monolithic proportions. "My people reported, ahem, screaming. They were alarmed."

Jadren couldn't help smirking. "I'd think your people would know the difference between sounds of ecstasy versus anything *alarming*."

Annoyed enough to lock gazes with Jadren, Lord Chaim Refoel opened his mouth to deliver a no-doubt blistering retort. Seliah stirred just then, however, and his expression contorted into something Jadren recognized very well. Chaim's mouth settled into sour and rigid jealousy. Seliah snuggled sleepily closer to Jadren. Nuzzling his neck, she made a low purring sound like a satisfied feline. "That was amazing," she murmured.

All right, it was petty of him, but Jadren had never claimed to be a decent human being. Quite the opposite, in fact. "We have company, darling," he replied, kissing her forehead. "Apparently Lord Refoel feared I was slaughtering you."

"Oh!" She spotted Chaim half in the shadows and, charmingly, slid deeper into the water, her chin skimming the surface. "I'm perfectly fine," she told Chaim. Then giggled, a sultry, pleased sound. "More than fine."

"Good," Chaim managed, looking determinedly away. "We were concerned."

"Why are you always running your own errands, Refoel?" Jadren asked, thoroughly enjoying the man's discomfited envy, not at all above poking at him further.

"You know I take a personal interest in Lady Seliah's well-being," Chaim answered stiffly.

Yeah... didn't he just. "So do I," Jadren drawled. "In truth, I just spent a considerable amount of time taking a very personal and intimate *interest* in her being."

Seliah emitted a mortified little squeak. *"Jadren."*

He kissed the top of her head. "I love it when you say my name. Or scream it." He raised his brows at Chaim. "Is there anything else or can you leave us to our privacy?"

"I apologize for disturbing you both, Lord Jadren, Lady Phel." Chaim turned away, rigid as a frostbitten corpse, then paused. Before Jadren could wonder what caught his attention, Chaim had retrieved the charred and soaked missive that had somehow ended up against the garden wall. Holding it up with disdainful fingers, Chaim leveled a reproving frown on Jadren. "And you call yourself a wizard," he chided, thoroughly enjoying himself now. "The scroll is warded against destruction. Attempting to destroy it will yield you nothing. Be a man and read the cursed thing." He dropped it again to the ground, curling his lip at Jadren. "You can't run away forever, wizardling."

At least having a grand exit line made the annoying man actually *leave.* Jadren fumed silently, trying not to show it. Fucking Chaim and his superior attitude. Jadren wasn't running away. He was in hiding, learning new skills, healing up his shit—a totally different thing.

"I'm surprised you didn't have the rooms warded," Seliah commented.

Yeah, big miss there. "I was waiting for you to get home, and then I forgot, in the ensuing argument," he replied, hearing the irritation in his own voice. Deliberately turning to her, he kissed her lingeringly, stroking her lovely body under the water. "Now, where were we?"

"We were done with putting off reading that missive."

"I don't *want* to read it," he protested. Not whining at all.

"I'll read it," Seliah said, slipping out from under his arm, brushing him off when he tried to tug her back. "Chaim is right," she told him firmly, not without compassion, but no longer in sultry purring cat mode. "Putting it off won't change anything."

Jadren mentally put 'destroying our afterglow' on the list of Chaim's many crimes. "We can read it in the morning," he grumbled.

"*Or*, we can read it now." She levered herself out of the water and onto one knee, giving him a glorious view of her long body and narrow ass, along with the crevice between. Only having to reach a short distance, she remained on her hands and knees, giving him all sorts of ideas. She scooted backward into the pool, scroll in hand, and waded across to him. "It's my turn to ask if you're going to behave."

He managed a saucy grin, throttling the urge to use magic to destroy the ill-omened thing. He might not be much of a wizard, but he was willing to pit some lightning against the spell supposedly warding it. Seliah gave him a narrow glare, knowing him far too well. "I'll be disappointed in you if you try anything."

"Fine." He wasn't pouting, he really wasn't. "I won't."

"And don't pout. It's unattractive."

"So much for your promises of undying love," he muttered sullenly. Why bother pretending to be chirpy if she was going to call him on it anyway?

"I can love you to my dying day, which I will, and still call you on your shit, just as you call me on mine," she replied evenly. Holding the scroll firmly on each end, she presented the middle to him. "You have to unlock the seal. It's keyed to you."

"Oh, give me that." He swiped the thing from her, savagely pleased by her startled yip—she'd underestimated how fast he could be—and hauled himself out of the water. "I'm not sitting here in wet leathers, boiling in this pool, while I read whatever vicious bit of extortion my mother has settled upon to make me do her bidding." It was definitely from her hand. His monstrous mother's magic was all over the scroll, like a poisonous fungus that would infect everything it touched.

Going inside, he tossed the scroll on the small table where he and Seliah sometimes shared meals and began yanking off his soaked leathers, not easy as they seemed to have shrunk to his skin. Seliah strolled in, gloriously naked, hair hanging in wet coils, her nipples taut on her full breasts, all of her as enticing as ever. "You look like a drowned rat," he told her, just to be mean. Served her right for pushing him.

She rolled her eyes, grabbing a towel and using it to wring out her hair. "So much for sex improving your foul mood."

"It did," he bit out, yanking away her towel to dry himself. "Temporarily. Until you and Chaim ganged up on me."

Taking up another towel without comment, she resumed working on her hair, standing hip cocked and bent sideways, methodically working her way down the tangled length of it, then dropping the towel to the floor and using her foot to scootch it around, mopping up the fallout. Throughout the process, she moved with sinuous sensuality, drawing his eye though he tried to ignore her.

"Chaim has good intentions," Seliah finally said, after he'd donned a soft pair of pants and shirt, and seated himself at the table. Not yet touching the ominous scroll.

"Chaim would cheerfully toss me off a cliff and bond you as his familiar if he thought you would cooperate," Jadren said, telling himself that Seliah had made her choice and that she would never do such a thing. Would she?

"Someone already tried tossing you off a cliff, but it didn't stick," she reminded him. "Immortality comes in handy that way."

"Relative immortality," he corrected, biting his tongue on pointing out that she hadn't reassured him that she didn't want Chaim for her wizard. Not that he needed to be reassured, but she could have said *something*. "Liat believes my ability to heal myself has its limitations. I just haven't reached them yet."

"Well, let's not explore those limitations," Seliah replied with a shudder, eyeing him darkly as she seated herself and began combing out her hair. "And quit stalling. Read the cursed thing."

"Aren't you going to put something on?"

"My robe is drenched," she answered sweetly.

"You have others. Dark arts know they practically grow them on trees here."

"I'm comfortable. Still hot from that... extended soaking." She shrugged, making her pretty breasts bounce, and he wrenched his gaze away, looking deliberately at her face which held a too-innocent expression. Yeah, she was doing this on purpose.

"You exhausted me sexually," he informed her bitingly, "so there's no point in trying to seduce me again."

"Just doing my part to distract you from your concerns," she replied in a soothing tone that he recognized as Seliah emulating Nic's technique for managing Gabriel.

"Don't do your care-and-feeding-of-wizards thing with me." He pointed a finger at her. "I don't care what Nic Elal taught you. It's not your job to manage me. Don't be all subservient."

She widened her amber eyes and combed her hair. "You seem to have a difficult time deciding which aspects of my traditional role as your familiar I should observe. You want me to obey, but not be subservient?"

Growling under his breath, he transferred his glare to the still-sealed missive. She was far too clever. Why couldn't he have bonded a feather-brained familiar? Someone nice and biddable, thoroughly conditioned to go along with whatever their wizard wanted. No, *he* had to fasten upon a rogue familiar and feral human being. Never mind that his controlling and monstrous mother wouldn't have allowed him to bond any familiar who wasn't as much of a social pariah as he was. In that way, he and Seliah were a matched set.

Still, he could have stuck to his resolve not to bond a familiar at all. If he had, then he wouldn't be undergoing this daily torture with Liat to learn to control his healing ability. Back when he'd healed only himself and affected no one else, he hadn't had to worry about draining someone else dry of magic—not incidentally, also killing them in the process—nor about what having a human battery connected to his twisted and powerful ability would do if unleashed upon the world.

But Seliah was his, for better or worse, so he'd better learn that control. As unlikely as that eventuality seemed, given his progress thus far. Somehow, he suspected the missive glaring menacingly at him bore news that spelled the end of their recuperation and learning time.

"Are you sure you don't want me to read it?" Seliah asked softly.

"I'm doing it," he snapped, and touched his finger to the seal. It sent up a spark, a small, three-dimensional illusion of a lightning bolt, gold on a field of purple, a showy bit of El-Adrel magic. The scroll unrolled itself with a flourish and an echo of invisible trumpets, all of it screaming his mother's adoration of everything glamorous. She played Lady El-Adrel to the hilt, especially when it came to manipulating her progeny.

Except the letter wasn't from his mother.

Oh, her magic had sealed it, as only a wizard could do, but she hadn't written the words.

His father had.

Emotion could be a funny thing. For weeks Jadren hadn't thought about his father, and yet now it felt as if Fyrdo sat in the room with them—and Jadren's eyes stung sharply, pricked with invisible needles. Suddenly, and ridiculously, it seemed he might break into unmanful tears at any moment and weep like a child, just from seeing his father's elegant handwriting. Leaning his head on his hand, Jadren blinked rapidly, willing his eyes to clear enough to focus on the message.

"Jadren?" Seliah asked tentatively, leaning across the table to fold her fingers around his wrist. Her cool-bright magic waited for him, deep pools of moon-silvered water. Though he didn't need to draw on her, just the sense of her magic, freely offered, helped to soothe the ragged edges of the wound abruptly rent open by receiving a letter from his father.

Fyrdo had been made to do it, of course. That much was obvious, especially since Katica wasn't the sort to let her familiar do anything without her knowledge, and Fyrdo wouldn't willingly apply emotional pressure to any of his children. Where Katica El-Adrel arguably didn't know how to love, Fyrdo possessed all the ability she lacked. He loved all of his progeny, awful as they were—which included Jadren—and had always done his best to protect them from their criminally ambitious and morally corrupt mother. Fyrdo had been the one to free Seliah and Jadren from their cage in the testing labs. He'd said goodbye to Jadren using their old code: three taps for I love you.

Jadren hadn't had any way to know if his father's complicity had been discovered, though it almost certainly had, nor what the punishment had been, though certainly it had been horrible. Katica understood pain very well. She'd made a science of it.

And now she'd made her familiar write this letter.

"It's from my father," Jadren managed to tell Seliah, his voice as creaky as his heart.

She gasped in delight that quickly morphed into fear. "Fyrdo—is he all right?"

"We can't know, can we?" Jadren retorted drily, finding more certain ground in scratching at her. "My mother will have supervised every word."

Seliah nodded in rueful understanding, dropping her hand. "Will you read it to me?

He cleared his throat and read aloud.

My Dear Son,

I hope you and Seliah are well. I mean that in every sense. We have been so terribly concerned about you both since House Phel reportedly lost you. When we recently learned that you'd been at House Refoel for most of the summer, we could only think the worst. Please write and reassure your family of your health—or inform us of your needs so that the house of your birth may do whatever is necessary to ransom your freedom. Particularly as it seems that your contracted house is disinclined to take action. You will always be an El-Adrel, and so should call upon us for anything at all.

You must come home.

Come home and bring the lovely Seliah with you. We are aware that she is the key to your happiness. We are reassured that you did not take drastic measures there, as an Elal might.

All is forgiven. And I do mean all. Your mother asks me to tell you that you've made your point. You need not seek training and succor among the healers, if you are indeed there of your own free will. El-Adrel will defend you against all grievances. Just come home, as soon as you can manage it. Reply to this missive and we'll send transportation for you. It would arrive faster than you might think.

Your mother sends her love and deepest concern. As always, mine is written between every line.

Father

~ 4 ~

S ELLY WAITED A beat—in case there was some sort of postscript, and in case Jadren had a comment. But he just sat there, staring at the scroll, his pale complexion so drained of color that the scattering of freckles high on his cheekbones showed as starkly as stars in the sky, making him look young and vulnerable. Truly, she wished he'd offer some sort of acerbic remark.

"I suppose there's a lot encoded in that message besides the emotional leveraging?" she finally asked.

Jadren lifted his gaze to hers, haunted and so black that his eyes looked like the pools of tar that lurked in the marshes of Meresin, from which nothing escaped. "What?" He sounded almost surprised to find her sitting there.

Feeling like her nakedness would only distract them both, and not in a good way, she got up and put on one of the several robes Refoel had gifted her. Chaim had been generous. A bit too much so, but Selly knew her own heart and mind. She wouldn't be swayed by all the charm and gifts Chaim could muster. She was apparently just perverse enough to crave Jadren's jibes and sly insults over all the compliments in the world.

"*Written between every line*," Jadren finally said, sounding annoyed enough to give her heart. She turned around to find him eyeing her with a sardonic half-smile, black eyes glittering with irritation. "Unfortunately, I don't know the code to read what might be there," he added. "Another chapter in the pitiful and twisted story of my life."

"Tell me what you *do* know," she prompted, pouring them both wine. An excellent Elal vintage, too. "Perhaps, together, we can puzzle it out."

"Stronger together?" he asked wryly, referencing her impassioned speech convincing him to stop fighting their relationship and take advantage of it instead. Though he gave her a cutting look with it, a softening in his magic revealed his true feelings. They *were* stronger together, in every way.

"Absolutely." She handed him the wine and took the missive. "Let's take the low-hanging fruit. They want us both back at House El-Adrel."

"That fruit hangs so low it's rotting on the ground."

She raised her glass. "I'll cross out those lines. We know Katica wants us back. That's why she sent Ozana. Addressing the next part, the 'all is forgiven' bit refers to our escape, surely, but also references Ozana?"

"Possibly," he allowed, his expression carefully neutral. Jadren had categorically refused to discuss his feelings—even more than Jadren categorically refused to discuss his feelings in general—about murdering his sister. He'd had to defend himself against the murder charge, the violent act witnessed by Refoel wizards, which had led to their plan to execute him. A judgment he'd narrowly escaped, mainly by revealing himself as a scion of the powerful House El-Adrel. No one liked to interfere with the internecine squabbles of high-house heirs, even when that sibling rivalry ended in death. In return, Jadren had agreed to learn from Liat Refoel and be studied in turn, with the aim of controlling his unprecedented abilities.

Ozana had been intent on dragging them back to House El-Adrel, resorting to torturing Selly to ensure Jadren's compliance. *We are aware that she is the key to your happiness.* Surely that line referenced El-Adrel's willingness to use Jadren's attachment to Selly against him. She in no way thought Jadren bore any guilt or shame for killing his sister, even if he had gruesomely exploded the woman. He hadn't had a choice. "Do you think they know *how* you killed Ozana?" she asked.

Jadren met her gaze evenly, hand going to toy with the brass tube hanging from a chain around his neck. Selly doubted he was aware of the gesture. He tended to fidget with it when his thoughts went elsewhere and refused to have the thing any distance from his person, ever since he'd discovered the enchanted artifact—a widget his mother had created and attempted to implant in him—enabled him to heal people besides himself. When reversed, it had allowed Jadren to use his healing magic to destroy, obliterating Ozana.

"They can only know if Refoel told them and so far this pompous house's clinging to their absurd code of honor means they've kept our secret," Jadren replied.

"That code has worked to our benefit," Selly felt compelled to point out. "They won't let anyone, even the Convocation, take us from here against our will. All right, let's assume El-Adrel doesn't know *how* you killed Ozana, only that somehow you did. What does it mean that they say you've made your point?"

Jadren heaved a sigh and rolled his head back, staring at the ceiling. "Any number of things. If I were to hazard a guess, which I apparently am being coerced into doing, I'd say that my dear maman thinks I ran away only as a bargaining chip. She won't believe that I don't truly want, in the charred cinder of my withered heart, to be Lord El-Adrel after her. Katica can't conceive of anyone not wanting her power. She's used that to play her heirs against each other all these years."

"Do you?" Selly asked.

He lifted his head and gazed at her. Blinked, long and slow. "Do I want to be Lord El-Adrel? Dark arts, no! What would possess you to even ask such a question?"

"It's a reasonable question," she answered, studying him.

"Not unless you think I'm enough of a monster that I want to become my mother," he spat back.

"See, that's not a reasonable *answer*. You can head your house without becoming your mother."

"Oh, and I suppose you believe I should follow the example of the pure-hearted Gabriel, Lord of House Phool?" he sneered. "If my choices are to become a tyrannical megalomaniac, an idealistic idiot merrily leading my house to doom, or a conniving wannabe like Chaim Refoel, then I'll take option D: none of the above."

"*Or*," she retorted, "you could make the role your own. You're not one of your mother's automatons, plodding along mindlessly in the footsteps of others. If you became Lord El-Adrel, you could make the house over into what you want it to be."

He curled a lip. "Why, Seliah—have you been harboring a secret desire to become Lady El-Adrel? Perhaps all that half-feral swamp-beast behavior of yours has been a cover for a heart that quietly yearns for the power and glory of a high house."

"Be nice," she warned him. "You know I don't care about heading a high house and, for the record, I don't care if you are Lord El-Adrel or not. But I think your people deserve better. And," she added after a moment, "the house deserves better."

"The house is a house. She doesn't deserve anything. She can't, because she's not a person."

"Then why do you talk about her like a person instead of an 'it'?"

"Because she's a right bitch," he observed without rancor. "You saw what she did to us."

"She helped us escape," Selly replied remorselessly. "Besides, I think she wants you to be Lord El-Adrel."

He rolled his eyes. "I'm not letting an over-magicked dwelling make life choices for me. Besides which, you're forgetting a key point here: House El-Adrel already has a head."

"That could change," Selly said, letting the words settle with their own weight, but Jadren was already shaking his head.

"That would change only if my powerful wizard of a mother, who also shares an uncanny resistance to death, were to drop dead in the bloom of health and youth." He pinned her with a pointed look. "And do not say that I could kill her.

There's no way I could defeat her in a duel, even if I wanted her job, which I don't. Even then, I have several other siblings far more powerful than I who *do* want the job and would fight for it."

"But Jadren..."

"No, and that's final. Let's stick to the topic at hand. Cross out the line about me making my point."

Selly wasn't convinced, but she complied. "The bit about training implies that she knows that you're seeking to understand your healing ability."

"No surprises there. The secrets surrounding my magic are ones she weaponized against me. They enabled her to wield power over me. She knows I want that knowledge to escape her grasp."

"Is this implying that she will share that knowledge if you go home?"

Jadren barked out a laugh, short and bitter. "Even if that is the bait so temptingly dangling from this hook, I'm not so much of an idiot that I'll bite on it. My memory isn't that short. My mother never met a promise she didn't break."

"So, that could be what a lot of this repetition is—promises to protect you, to defend you against all the allegations against you, that they can fulfill all of your needs." When he didn't comment, letting his head fall back again, she continued scanning for potential clues. If Fyrdo had embedded a code, she couldn't discern it. "He uses the phrase 'come home' three times. In old stories, three times is a charm."

"The old stories, as you so quaintly put it, knew shit about how magic actually works," Jadren replied wearily, his eyes closed, face lined with grief. "The only rule of three I can think of is this thing where… no, it's silly. A private joke, in a way."

"Tell me," she coaxed, aching for him. She'd had her troubles, but at least she'd had a good family who loved her. "A private joke would be part of a code."

"Not this. It's not even a joke. It's just that…" He trailed off, his eyes popping open to bore black holes in the ceiling. "When I was little, Maman didn't like it when Fyrdo told me he loved me, so he would tap me instead, three times, for I. Love. You."

A frisson ran down her spine. "That's a definite code then."

Jadren cracked one eye open, glaring at her balefully. "Don't get all sentimental. If it is a code, it tells me nothing I didn't already know. He tapped me three times like that when he helped us escape. It's sweet, but all the I love you's in the world won't protect either of us from her."

"But what if he—"

"This is pointless," he snapped out. Moving fast as a snake, he sat up and snatched the letter from her hand. "I know what Maman wants: me, back in her control, and you with me. It's not going to happen. You should've let me burn the thing." Scanning the letter, he mumbled under his breath. "*Terribly concerned, reportedly lost, disinclined to take action.* Nothing, nothing, nothing." He paused. "The only interesting bit is this: "*We are reassured that you did not take drastic measures there, as an Elal might.* Possibly in reference to you. Any idea what that might mean?"

"Not at all," she answered. Then the meaning hit her, lodging further words in her throat.

"No?" Jadren pinned her with a glittering black stare to her. "You seem like you thought of something." His voice remained smooth, but she caught the edge of suspicion in it.

"No." The denial came out as a squeak, as Selly fought to look puzzled, even as her mind raced. Surely they weren't referring to Alise Elal's newly discovered ability to sever the wizard–familiar bond. That was a secret, one only a few in House Phel knew about. Gabriel had offered the solution to Selly when Jadren abandoned her, an offer she'd adamantly refused. The bond was one of the few points of leverage she had on her wizard. If Jadren knew severing the bond was possible, he'd snap up the option, sacrificing himself to free her of him. She couldn't let him find out.

"Are you sure?" he prodded. "You mentioned that Nic taught you all about being a familiar and she's an Elal by birth. Maybe she said something relevant."

"But how would anyone at El-Adrel know about anything Nic taught me?" How could they know Alise's secret, for that matter? Except that Alise had used that skill to separate Lord Elal from his familiar, saving their mother from his vengeance. Selly didn't know enough about it, but she did know that Alise had been able to do the severing as part of her Elal magic, being a wizard who could bind spirits and otherwise manipulate them. Obviously Alise and Nic's father—sent back to House Elal wounded, missing an eye and a familiar—would know the bond had been severed and would likely guess how. Put that on top of Jadren's suspicion-bordering-on-paranoid-certainty that Elal had been collaborating with El-Adrel to bring down House Phel, and it seemed quite likely that Lord

Elal had recovered enough to tell Katica El-Adrel about the severing.

"You're thinking awfully hard, poppet," Jadren observed, getting to his feet and moving with liquid grace around the table. Standing behind her, he shifted her drying hair back from her shoulder, then trailed his fingers down the side of her throat. She shivered, both at the arousing touch and the feel of his magic sliding under her skin. Could he read her mind? Sometimes she wondered, though he denied it. "You can tell me," he coaxed.

"There's nothing to tell," she said, croaking slightly, and swallowed hard. She tipped her head back to smile up at him, and he slid his fingers along the grooves of her throat, twin pressures of thumb and forefinger, light but firm. Under the thin robe, her nipples peaked. She shouldn't find the possessive way he touched her so erotic, but she did. "Nic only taught me what I'd have learned at Convocation Academy if I'd attended. Nothing secret." There, that was true.

"I didn't say anything about a secret, nor does the letter," he mused, feathering fingertips over the hollows of her collarbones. "Why did your mind immediately go to a secret?"

"I—it didn't." She swallowed hard again, and he smiled, bracketing her throat with his hand. "Because we thought there might be a code, in the letter, and..." She couldn't think.

"Nic told you a secret," he prompted. "I can feel it in you."

"She didn't," Selly gasped, concentrating on sincerity. It was true. Nic hadn't told her; Gabriel had.

"Seliah," Jadren crooned. "I think you're lying to me." He eased the robe off her shoulder, baring one breast, her nipple going almost painfully taut. Still holding her throat, he traced the round of her breast, descending concentric circles that tantalized her, never quite touching her nipple, which ached for more. He stopped. Placed a flat palm over her heart. "Your pulse is pounding. What are you so afraid of?"

"I'm not," she denied, voice shaky, body trembling. "It's desire."

He pursed his lips, studying her, nudging the robe open to bare her other breast. "Oh, Seliah, you are such a terrible liar."

She was. It went against her nature to be anything but her authentic self. She'd spent too much time not knowing who she was to risk losing that again. And with Jadren... she loved him to an agonizing degree. Keeping anything from him was painful, but if she told him this, she could lose him forever. That mattered more than any of the rest.

"I'm not lying," she lied, the words acid on her tongue. Meeting his gaze boldly, she made herself stare him down. "You can torment me all you like, but I can't tell you something I don't know."

He stilled, cocked his head, then dipped his chin in a nod. Removed his hands and stepped away. "So be it," he said, his voice clipped and cool. "We should sleep. Liat will be at us early tomorrow."

Stunned, feeling more than a little abandoned and considerably sexually frustrated, despite having literally passed out from his attentions earlier, Selly sat there a moment longer, listening to him prepare for bed. Then, as if suddenly unfrozen, she pulled her robe together and stood, finding him across the room, turning down the covers. "That's it?" she demanded.

He threw her a perfectly neutral glance. "That's what, pet?"

"You're just going to freeze me out now." She stalked toward him and he deftly avoided her, slipping away like a shadow under too-bright light.

"I can't imagine what you're talking about." He dropped his robe, standing before her naked, supremely unaroused, and gestured to himself. "I'm tired. With all your care-and-feeding-of-wizards knowledge, I'd think you'd be sympathetic to that." His wizard-black eyes glittered, hard, unyielding. "Though I suppose there's all sorts of privileged information that you aren't at liberty to share with me."

It was a challenge, the implication clear. She sputtered mentally, trapped and unable to see a way out. She couldn't even tell him it had nothing to do with him, because it did. It was all about him and her selfish need to keep him tied to her. *Just a little longer,* she told herself. *We need more time together, for him to realize how much he needs me. That he loves me too much to let me go.* "Jadren, this is not an adult way to handle this problem."

He cocked an auburn brow, sardonic and mocking. "I told you I don't know how to be in a relationship. Apparently I should have had you sign a disclaimer. Of course, it seems I can't trust you to be honest with me, so it wouldn't matter."

And there it was, the deep pain of betrayal throbbing beneath his icy demeanor. She hadn't meant to hurt him. That was the last thing she wanted. Well, not the very last thing, as she wanted to keep him even more. Did this make her a terrible human being? Probably so. Trust didn't come to Jadren easily, not after he'd been lied to, manipulated, and tortured all his life by the very people who should have protected him.

"You can trust me," she said, though the words seemed far too weak and tepid to penetrate that wall of reserve he'd pulled around him like an invisible cloak.

"Can I though?" he retorted and got into bed, yanking up the covers to his chin and firmly turning his back to her. "When you're ready to tell me the truth, we can revisit that assumption. Until then, all bets are off."

"Jadren..." She trailed off uncertainly, wanting to beg, wanting to pummel him with her fists.

"Make sure to turn off the lights," was all he said.

Numb, with no idea how to dig herself out of this pit, she moved around the room, sending the fire elementals to sleep with the magical triggers even a familiar could use. The El-Adrel letter lay on the table, accusing, discarded.

She should've let Jadren burn it.

~ 5 ~

JADREN WAS STILL pissed. He'd slept pissed, dreamt pissed, and woke up pissed. Up for hours now, laboring under Liat's remorseless tutelage, he still couldn't shake the grinding anger. How *dare* Seliah lie to him? How could she keep a secret from him, after all they'd been through together?

"Calming breaths," Liat instructed, "as I count backwards, allow your breathing to deepen, your thoughts to settle. One-hundred, ninety-nine, ninety-eight. Make of yourself an open channel for the magic to flow. Ninety-seven, ninety-six…"

A pissed channel, Jadren thought uncharitably, trying to fake the breathing enough to keep Liat off his back. And, underneath the being pissed, a small, raw part of him worried. Yes, Seliah had come after him when he left her, had found him against all odds, had vowed that she loved him and wanted only him, but he wasn't stupid. He knew what he had to offer Seliah—or, more precisely, what he *didn't* have to offer—and that she could do far better.

Like Chaim Refoel, for instance. That thought made the piss boil.

"When you've achieved a meditative state," Liat said, after reaching *'one'* and letting the hum of the word resonate into

44

silence, "focus your attention on the moth. Extend your wizardry like an antenna, delicately sensing for where the creature is injured."

When they began practicing healing, Seliah had worried about where the injured animals would come from. She needn't have, here in the land of the eternally soft-hearted. All the denizens of Refoel—and many beyond—brought in wounded animals for healing. The gardeners, in particular, set aside any injured insects they came across, for junior healers to practice on. This moth was missing part of a wing, a beak-shaped wedge cut away by some enterprising bird. Jadren didn't need healing antennae to discern that much about where the creature was injured.

Still, he tried to follow Liat's directions, even as his mind wandered back to what might lie at the heart of Seliah's discontent. When both he and Seliah had been broken, both fucked-up, wretched examples of magic-workers unable to work much in the way of magic, both strangers to polite Convocation society, their pairing had made a kind of sense. As much as anything made any sense. Still, they'd been two of a kind, paired in their inadequacy.

But Seliah had improved, leaving him behind. She had healed on every level, no longer struggling with the after-effects of insanity. Every day she grew stronger, more confident and polished. And daily she seemed less like a half-feral swamp creature and more the high-house lady she'd been born to be. Meanwhile he remained mired in the same old bog—a thrashing monster too twisted and malformed to ever be more than a groping, burbling mess. It rankled deeply that she'd said that about him becoming Lord El-Adrel. What if she *did* truly long to head a high house? Seems like she wouldn't have brought it up otherwise, and it was arguably her destiny, with her powerful magic, intelligence, and resourcefulness. She deserved that life and it lay within her reach.

Especially with the continued availability of the lovelorn Chaim Refoel, with no familiar, no partner to help him lead House Refoel. Seliah loved it there in Refoel and would be happy staying forever, that much was obvious. She could become a legitimate citizen of the Convocation, produce well-fed, robe-clad cherubic babies, and be kept in style. She could become something more than a wet-nurse to a corked-up wizard who didn't even understand his own magic and posed a constant threat to her very life. One she didn't trust enough to be honest with. What in the dark arts could she be keeping from him?

"Once you have a feel for the injury," Liat said, a bit more loudly, "draw magic from Seliah to feed toward the moth's natural self-healing."

Jadren stole a glance at Seliah where she sat calmly beneath his touch, her eyes closed and expression meditatively calm as she stilled her magic and concentrated on feeding it to him on demand. As always these days, her water and moon magic felt smooth and undisturbed as a mirror. Shining bright and deeply cool as a mountain lake, her magic called to him with the seductive powers of the sirens. He burned to immerse himself, to drink deeply of her, to quench the raging inside him. Of course, that was exactly the problem. Rather than being one small swimmer, easily cooled by her depths as he dipped in, he was a volcano. He could vaporize her with one careless burp of his magic, leaving an empty crater behind.

In order to love, admire, and protect that pristine lake, he could only lumber about her edges, some rough beast sullying her perfection by scuffing in a toe now and then. He didn't dare go deeper, which had the effect of putting her even further beyond him. Like that reflecting, glassy lake surface, she revealed nothing of what thoughts lurked beneath.

What secrets she withheld from him.

"Lord Jadren," Liat said, snapping him out of his reverie, "you are not concentrating." The healer-wizard never raised her voice above a soothing murmur, but even so somehow managed to relay a substantial level of annoyance. "You're wasting the time of all three of us if you're not willing to focus on these exercises."

He snatched his hand away from Seliah, refusing to meet her inquisitive, sympathetic, and frankly forlorn gaze. She'd been acting like a kicked kitten since the night before, slinking about the edges of rooms and jumping at his least movement, like she expected him to strike her. As if he'd ever do that. It set his teeth on edge. He was the offended party here; she had no business acting hurt.

"These are ridiculous exercises," he snarled. "The same thing, over and over. And I can't do them." The poor moth fluttered helplessly in its open box, unable to fly out. A metaphor so blatant it was practically an attack.

Liat folded her hands primly. "In repetition, we build habit; in habit, we construct a foundation for our intuition to reply upon, one that liberates our thinking. With an intuitive foundation, there is no need for remembering or reconstructing. This frees our faculties for spontaneity and innovation."

"Yes, yes, I know. You've repeated that ten-thousand times."

"Then why must I repeat it, yet again?" Liat queried calmly, raising her brows into winged incredulity. "Let me follow that with another question: why do you refuse to learn? This is elementary healing." She glanced at the moth, whose wing visibly filled in. It flexed its dusty silver wings, then fluttered away. So easy for her.

"If you'd let me use the widget, maybe I could—"

"The ability to heal lies within *you*, not in an enchanted artifact."

"Demonstrably untrue," he countered. "I sure as shit can't do any healing without it."

"I believe you can learn this," Liat insisted. "You're allowing preconceived limitations to cloud your thinking."

"Perhaps I'm just that thick-skulled," Jadren retorted.

"Or, perhaps, you're just that afraid." She bounced the words back at him in perfect mimicry, making his petulance wincingly clear.

"I'm not afraid," he spat back at her, not caring how he sounded. "I'm bored. I'm out of my skull with boredom. When will we stop messing around with insects and do something interesting?"

"You believe you're ready to do *something interesting*?" Liat queried, her wizard-black gaze going to Seliah also.

Seliah gave him a cagey look, measuring and assessing his mood. "I think it would be good for Wizard Jadren to vent some frustration," she answered. "Maybe mix it up a bit."

"Don't patronize me," he snarled at her. If Seliah cared about how he felt, she wouldn't hurt him by keeping secrets from him.

Seliah looked to Liat. Though he couldn't see her face, he could swear she rolled her eyes. "I would really love to discover my alternate form," she said to Liat. "Is that something we could begin working on? I understand that it requires an open connection between wizard and familiar, excellent control and technique on the wizard's part—all skills we're working on—and it would be different enough to give us a fresh take." She was very carefully not looking at him.

"For a wizard to put their familiar in alternate form and, more critical, bring them back to human form again, is advanced work," Liat explained, shaking her head minutely. "Not all wizards are capable of it. Most, in truth, never master the ability. Those who do have already mastered other skills."

Jadren would be annoyed by her lack of faith in him if she weren't precisely on the money. "Too advanced," he agreed, not at all excited to fail at yet something else, particularly a party trick so profoundly tied to Seliah's wellbeing. "But I wouldn't mind killing something. Let's see if I can do *that* without the widget. Isn't there a rodent infestation in your crops or something that you all would welcome having eradicated?"

"All life is valuable," Liat answered with earnest serenity. "None here would ever take joy in the death of another living creature."

Jadren refrained from pointing out that this wouldn't stop

them from doing it anyway. "It would be a public service," he persisted, the magic rising in him, hungry to destroy. The evil monster wanting its taste of blood. "Come on, let me go red-mist a few rats."

"Jadren!" Seliah gave him an astonished—and rather horri-fied—look. "Don't say things like that."

"Or what?" He rounded on her, the liar and traitor he'd held close to his breast. "Don't pretend you don't know what I am. You saw what I did to Ozana."

"Yes," she bit out, then pressed her lips into a white line. "And got the red mist you reduced her to all over me. You did what you had to do, but I can't believe you'd joke about it."

"I'm not joking," he countered. Spreading his hands wide, he laughed. "Isn't that what you all want me to learn? I'm here to reliably reproduce an act of devastating violence, with you—my darling, personal power source—fueling me to even greater heights. Why mince niceties now? Let's go blast some rodents! Or, better, maybe a terminal patient or two who'd appreciate the fast, easy out."

Seliah shot to her feet, face pale, amber eyes haunted. "I don't even recognize you anymore," she spat in a hushed voice, before hurling herself out of the room.

The thud of the slamming door echoed in the quiet work-space and Jadren told himself he was glad she was gone. Maybe she'd run all the way to House Phel and leave him to his downward spiral.

"Well," Liat said into the fraught silence, "that was an interesting display. Did you accomplish what you wished to?"

"What made you think I wanted to accomplish anything?"

he countered. "It's not my fault Seliah has a soft heart when it comes to the necessities of her job."

Liat said nothing and Jadren—realizing he still stared at the closed door as if it might reveal some fucking clue about what was wrong with him—wheeled on her. The healer wizard stood in the same place, hands folded inside the long, dolman sleeves of her robe, watching him with quiet compassion on her dark-skinned, beautifully boned face. "We both know you drove Seliah away, probably with the intent of ending an uncomfortable training session. Most likely because you anticipated another failure, which fills you with fear. I, however, will not be so easy to banish, nor will I let you off the hook so easily."

"I don't know why you bother," he growled, pretty sure she was wrong and he could drive her away, too. If he possessed a true talent, it lay there. "I'm not at all afraid of failure, as it's been my constant companion all these years. Failure is such an old bedfellow that I'm inured to being a hopeless case."

She cocked her head. "Why do you say that?"

"Surely even you must acknowledge that I've made zero progress," he answered with silky sarcasm.

"Not true. You've mastered all levels of warding and numerous basic spell techniques."

"Hooray, I can do what any freshman wizard can," he spat. "That's hardly the point. I remain singularly incapable of actively controlling my healing magic. We understand nothing more about why I have the ability to heal myself—which continues to be beyond my conscious control—nor how I was able to reverse the healing to vaporize poor, sweet Ozana. I'm barely adequate at accessing Seliah's magic, hardly better than an adolescent wizard at the skills beyond the ones I came here knowing. I can make a few magical widgets and that's where my usefulness ends. My tenure here in House Refoel has been an epic waste of my time and everyone else's."

Liat raised a placid brow. "Did you have something else to do with your time?"

She wanted him to admit that no, he had nothing at all better to do, a humiliating fact in its own right. "Yes," he snapped. "I could be getting an actual MP scorecard—something you continue to withhold from me—so I could become a legitimate Convocation citizen and obtain gainful employment to support myself and my familiar."

"You already have gainful employment," she replied, "at House Phel. You could both return there and be welcomed."

"Yeah, and go down with that sinking ship," he muttered ungraciously. "No, thank you. I'll try my luck elsewhere."

"You've been offered a place here at House Refoel," she continued placidly. "If you master your healing gifts, you would be a tremendous asset."

"And if wishes were ponies, we'd all have purple ones that sparkle."

Liat gave him one last simmeringly patient look. Jadren had the impression she restrained a heavy sigh and congratulated himself for managing to stretch her eternal serenity to the breaking point. Then Liat withdrew something from a pocket inside her sleeve. She held it up so the official seal showed on the back and he stared at it, afraid to hope, unable to stop himself. "Is that—" he asked and broke off, suddenly too numb to move.

"Your MP scorecard, yes."

"How…"

"One of our in-house Hanneil wizards had some free time in their schedule the other day, so they were able to use their oracle head to assess you while we were in a training session."

"And you didn't tell me."

Liat didn't so much as blink at his accusing tone. "We did not. With the way your unusual manifestation eludes conscious control, we thought we might obtain a more accurate reading when you were unaware of the testing."

Yes, his thinking always got in the way. That was fair. Still… "But you didn't tell me you have an MP scorecard for me." His fingers itched with the craving to grab the thing. *So close.*

"Correct. I'm telling you now." She didn't exactly pull it back as he reached for it, but she did raise her brows. "You might temper your expectations."

He snatched it from her, beyond annoyed with Liat and her sympathy, and scanned the card with what he had to acknowledge was excited anticipation. Then frowned, trying to make sense of the scores. His MP scorecard looked like any other he'd seen, all officially official, with its neat march of columns and rows. Along the top, the major categories of magic headed the columns, then the long rows indicated the subgroups. With an amused smirk, he noted that water and moon magic had been added to the major categories, where they'd been only occasionally listed as subgroups in the past.

All due to Phel's re-emergence on the magical scene.

In the cross-section, the numerical scores indicated his potential in that category and subgroup. As expected for an El-Adrel, he had decent scores under Kinetic Magic and the various subgroups that applied to his family ability to make enchanted artifacts. He also demonstrated a scattering of adequacy at the magics that allowed him to establish wards and other basics of wizardry. It would have been odd if he didn't, those were so common. Under the major category of Healing Magic, however, his scores were all below three— essentially nothing. Barely more than a non-magical common-er might have.

"This makes no sense," he said, squinting at the numbers as if they might come into focus and be more meaningful. "You all said you sensed healing magic in me, an extraordinary amount." *But it's perverted,* Chaim had added. *Twisted in upon itself.*

Liat let out that heavy sigh she'd been so heroically re-straining. She finally sat on the low couch with the angled head at one end to accommodate treating both physical injuries and craziness. Patting the flat space beside her, she regarded him gravely. "Sit with me, Jadren."

No "Lord Jadren" now. He didn't want to sit. He wanted to pace and rail and scream the injustice to the uncaring sky. But, apparently, if he also wanted her to explain this meaning-less morass of his magical potential, he would have to pretend to be calm. Plopping himself beside the healer, he held out the card. "I'm agog to hear your explanation."

She shook her head, looking almost weary. "I don't have

one. None of us do."

How delightful to contemplate the lot of them debating his worthlessness. He could just imagine Chaim's pithy observations.

"Is there a mistake? An error in the reading?" He realized how foolish that was as he asked it. Oracle heads didn't make mistakes. They were infallible.

Liat huffed out a humorless laugh. "We wondered the same, honestly. Which is why our Hanneil wizard took the reading on three separate occasions. They all came out like this." She flapped a hand at the scorecard.

"But this shows I have no magical potential in healing."

"Don't we know it." She gave him a half smile. "Whatever allows you to heal yourself, and to channel that magic through the device—to heal or destroy—it isn't healing magic."

"Then what *is* it?" He asked the question helplessly, knowing Liat had no more answer for him than he did.

She held up her hands, palms to the sky. "Who knows? You're likely something totally new and we'll be creating a column on the scorecard in your honor next."

Something totally new. A created monster, produced by his mother's wiles and malicious experiments. How pleased she would be by the accomplishment. She'd turned out to be a genius after all, however mad. He glumly turned the card in his fingers. The scores it displayed in the standard magics wouldn't get him a job as anything more than a minor minion in a third-tier house. That would be no life for Seliah. "Why did you keep pushing me to learn healing magic if you knew I didn't have any?" he asked dully.

"Because you demonstrably *can* heal!" Liat burst out. "Whatever your magic is, you are able to heal. You can bring yourself and others back from the dead."

"Not quite fully dead," he corrected automatically.

"Enough so as to make no never mind. Jadren, you can do what none of us can, not even the most powerful healer among us. How could you *not* want to harness that ability? It makes me want to… *urgh!*" Liat coiled her fingers in the air, emitting a sound he'd never heard from the composed healer. "I could just throttle you sometimes. And that is not an urge I'm accustomed to having. You push me past all reason, I swear!"

Jadren waited a beat. "I do have that effect on people."

Liat swiveled her head to glare at him, wizard-black eyes snapping, then huffed out a laugh despite herself. "You're incorrigible."

"It's true," he agreed, flashing a grin, then sobering. If he didn't have healing magic, then they truly were wasting their time at House Refoel. "I don't know what to do," he confessed, past caring about putting up a brave front for Liat. He wished Seliah was there and winced, rubbing a hand over his forehead, recalling what a beast he'd been to her. *I don't even recognize you anymore.*

"Well," Liat said philosophically, folding her hands inside her sleeves. "There's only so much you *can* do at this point. It's clear that we healers have no more to teach you than anyone else."

"All of this time, wasted," he said with considerable bitterness. He *had* been spinning his wheels here. Having that panicked suspicion confirmed didn't make him any happier.

"Not wasted. You needed time to heal."

"So this has all been make-work to keep me occupied?"

"Not at all. You learned core competencies in your other magics. You have learned to work better with Seliah. You need her in more ways than I think you realize. Also, I hoped that…" She trailed off with uncharacteristic uncertainty, then gave him a wry, rueful smile, patting him on the knee. "I blame personal hubris. I couldn't quite believe that we couldn't break through at all, that I couldn't find a way for you to grasp something I've taught to thousands of students. I'm a good healer, but I'm an excellent teacher. I didn't want to acknowledge that I can't teach you."

"Every irresistible force eventually meets up with an immovable object," he observed. "Apparently I'm the one in thousands that can't be taught."

"That's not it," she said, brightening with enthusiasm, turning at an angle to face him. "I can't teach you healing because you're not a healer. I can drill you in the basics until I'm blue in the face, but no one in House Refoel can teach you to master the magic that makes you what you are at your core."

"A monster," he offered with a tooth-baring grin.

"In a sense, maybe yes."

"Wow, thanks ever so."

She shrugged a little. "Have you ever heard of the term 'hopeful monsters'?"

"Is that supposed to be a chirpy version of me?"

She laughed, genuinely amused this time. "The chirpy

version of you is hard to imagine. No, the term comes from evolutionary theory. That, as species evolve, refining their ability to flourish in a given ecological niche—or a new and changing one—it isn't always a gradual process. There's a theory that some creatures are born that are so different from the norm that they're essentially monsters, and that they represent a great leap in the species. Like being born with webbing that allows them to glide through the air right as their ecological niche is flooded."

"So, *hope*fully, they can glide from tree to tree and not drown."

"In this example, yes."

"And you think I'm a magical hopeful monster." Liat, along with everyone else, including himself, had no idea what Jadren's mother had done to create him. But he was pretty confident it had nothing to do with anything natural.

"I think you represent something new. Perhaps a step in another direction. I'm really not qualified to speculate."

"Even though you are," he pointed out wryly.

"Even though I am," she acknowledged. "But my main point is, I think there is only one place where you can learn the truth. Only one person who can teach you."

If he possessed a heart, it would have sunk. "Don't say it."

"Not saying it aloud doesn't make the truth disappear," Liat chided gently.

"I'm not going back to El-Adrel. Ever. Nothing can make me." He sounded five years old and, in that moment, didn't care in the least.

"No one is making you. You and Seliah have a home here

in Refoel as long as you desire it. I will continue to teach you, at least the skills I'm able to. By the by, I *do* believe you have the ability to put Seliah in alternate form. Your magical potential is there. Your focus, when you muster it, is admirable. And Seliah absolutely has the power to fuel the transformation, along with a committed interest in discovering it. The only aspect lacking is your own discipline to refine the skill to the point you need to be."

"Comforting."

"It's not my job to be comforting. Go to Maya for that. I'll also point out that, in addition to Refoel, you have a home at House Phel, much as you disdain their prospects."

"I don't disdain their prospects. I'm simply a realist about their total lack of a viable future."

Liat withdrew her hands from her sleeves and slapped her palms lightly on her robe-clad knees before standing. "Well, I suppose you have some decisions to make. We can meet again tomorrow if you decide to continue drilling in technique."

"Is there any point?" he asked wearily, dropping his head into his hands.

"Not if you're going to continue to throw temper tantrums like today's distasteful display," Liat replied crisply. Relenting, she set a gentle hand on his shoulder, a wave of calming healing magic filtering in to settle his jangled nerves. "You're a mess, Jadren El-Adrel," she said with what sounded like affection, "but you're not a lost cause. Go find Seliah and settle whatever disagreement you're having that brought you both in here in such terrible moods today. Then decide what you want to do. Together."

Jadren lifted his head to her knowing smile, wincing in chagrin. "Was it that obvious?"

"To a wizard-healer who works with bonded pairs to turn them into well-oiled teams? Yes."

"Any advice?"

She chuckled and patted his shoulder before stepping back and tucking her hands in her sleeves again. "Try not to be an asshole. It's the best rule of thumb there is. By the way, we have an MP scorecard for Seliah, too." Liat fished around in her sleeve, then brought out another card. "No surprises on hers, though her scores are impressively high."

He took in Seliah's card, noting that it pretty much matched what his mother had determined, via her own unorthodox methods. "Thank you," he said, feeling that the words didn't adequately embrace what having this information meant for them. They were almost like real people now.

"You're welcome." Liat smiled. "Now go fix your shit. That's professional advice."

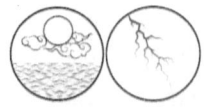

TRY NOT TO *be an asshole.* Jadren snorted to himself as he trudged back to the rooms he shared with Seliah. Easier said than done, as being an asshole came so naturally to him. But he could see Liat's point: if he wanted Seliah to confide whatever secret she was keeping from him, he'd make much more progress being patient and coaxing her to trust him than badgering and bullying her.

On that note, he abruptly turned at an open doorway leading into a sunny garden. With late summer finishing its reign before succumbing to autumn, the garden rioted with blossoms. Spotting one of the ubiquitous gardeners quietly weeding, he edged up and cleared his throat.

The robe-clad young person glanced up at him, squinting against the sun. "Yes, Lord Jadren?"

"Is it all right if I, uh, pick some flowers?"

"Of course. They're here for all to enjoy." They gestured to a set of shelves set under an overhang. "You'll find clippers and vases over there. For best results, fill the vase with water first, then immediately insert the cut blossoms."

"Thank you." There. He sounded not at all like an asshole. Picking out a pretty vase, he filled it with water from a rain collection barrel, then wandered about with his clippers, seeking out the blossoms he thought Seliah would like best. The big, fluffy-looking ones, he thought, along with a few of the wickedly dark ones. He was no artist, but the resulting bouquet looked pretty dammed good to his eye. Pleased with himself, he returned the clippers and resumed his journey to their rooms, hoping Seliah would be there.

If she wasn't, maybe he'd set up the vase in the middle of the room, turn down the bed, and scatter flower petals over the sheets. That would be romantic, which he owed her. The last time he'd set up a romantic and seductive scenario, he'd drugged and abandoned her. It should have occurred to him to make that up to her. "No time like the present," he assured himself, feeling more optimistic. Some romance, some lovemaking, then talking. They'd work it out. They always did.

"Seliah?" he called as he opened the door to their rooms.

No answer. Excellent. He could put his plan into motion. Whistling a jaunty tune, he bustled about the place, arranging the scene. Wine. They needed wine. And candles, though it was still afternoon. If he played it right, they could linger in bed until after dark. Which meant he should arrange for the evening meal. Finger foods they could feed to each other. Seliah would love this and forgive him.

He paused, frowning at the tug on the wizard–familiar bond, the sense of attenuation, as if Seliah were moving away from him at a rapid rate. Surely that couldn't be right. Seliah might be justifiably pissed at him, but she wouldn't leave him. Surely she wouldn't have run back to House Phel as he'd caustically predicted to himself.

Would she?

In a panic, he went to her closet. But all of her things were there, along with her favorite big-bladed knife. And the ever-replenishing moon-magic silver water flask Gabriel had given her, inscribed with the House Phel crest by his own hand. She wouldn't go anywhere without that. Relief flooded him.

And faded almost immediately as the sense of separation grew.

Then he found the note.

We told you to come home. Now you have to.

Seliah had been abducted.

He stood there, unmoving, wanting to howl, to rage, to make like the legendary Sylus and burn the world to the ground. But none of that would restore Seliah to him.

No, he could do only one thing, and it was the one thing he was terrified to do, had sworn never to do.

He must return to House El-Adrel.

Turns out they could make him, after all.

~ 6 ~

ALISE ELAL ROUNDED the bend in her elemental-powered chariot and took in the daunting and impressive sight of Convocation Academy.

The very last place in all the world that she wanted to be.

Especially returning this way, with her tail between her legs. After a daring escape in which she'd harbored dazzling visions of thumbing her nose at the academy and the entire Convocation, racing off to rescue her sister, and saving the love—and possibly lives—of her dear friends, this return felt more than a little anticlimactic. It turned out that thumbing your nose at society wasn't all that exciting. Nic hadn't needed rescuing at all, but was perfectly happy as Lady Phel and Gabriel's familiar. At least, Alise had managed to save Han and Iliana from being made into virtual slaves by Sabrina Sammael. The cooing-dove pair were cozily ensconced in the protection of House Phel, more in love than ever, and blissfully happy.

In truth, not having to daily witness Han and Ilian's true love was the one upside of returning to Convocation Academy to dutifully complete her education. Though the pair had been unfailingly generous about including Alise in their company, they couldn't change the fact that Alise was the third wheel on their merry chariot of love. Or, given the wizard–familiar dynamics hammered into them all since birth, a better metaphor was that Alise had been the awkward wizard-cart harnessing them to her like tandem pony-familiars. As much as Iliana and Han protested that they were happy to feed her their magic, she'd still felt like a parasite. A lonely one.

Did parasites feel lonely? Maybe they did, endlessly feeding off of others, taking their life energy, not truly wanted, only tolerated. A glum perspective that perfectly suited her mood.

The one other bright spot about leaving House Phel—a guilt-inducing one that lessened the sense of reprieve considerably—was no longer having to see Maman every day. Ever since Alise had severed the wizard–familiar bond between her mother and father, Maman had been unresponsive, lying in her bed and staring at the ceiling with her uncanny cat's eyes. Only Wizard Asa's healing magic kept the woman alive. And it was no kind of life.

Nic argued that none of them knew if the severing lay at the root of their mother's continued catatonic state or if it was the effect of Maman being kept in her alternate form for so long. Retaining the feline cast of her alternate form's eyes indicated that lingering issue might be to blame. And, true, Maman hadn't been responsive since they brought her back to House Phel. Still, Alise had spent every spare waking hour—and more than a few sleeping ones, when she couldn't withstand the pull of exhaustion any longer—at her mother's bedside. Alise had tried everything she could think of to reach her mother, to seek out the human woman slumbering inside her motionless body.

To no avail. Nothing Alise could think of or do had made any impact.

Nic had called Alise out on it, too, chastising her for tiring herself out and allowing her magic to get "brittle and thin enough to punch a fist through." Worse, Nic had enlisted a lower-level wizard to illustrate the point, a humiliating demonstration that led to the conversation where everyone convinced Alise—read: informed her in no uncertain terms that she didn't have a choice—to return to Convocation Academy. Ostensibly she was there to learn what she needed to know to be a proper wizard and not a brittle humbug unable to defend herself.

She was also there as a spy, which made her ignominious slinking back to the scene of the crime slightly shinier. Except that, naturally, she couldn't tell anyone about it. But at least she'd still be doing her part to help House Phel by sleuthing out the information they needed.

The carriage passed the warded boundary around the academy, a faint buzz of magic the only sign that she'd been recognized and admitted. Gabriel had corresponded via Ratsiel courier with the academy provost, establishing that Alise would be returned as required by the demand sent by the academy, as if she'd been accidentally shoplifted. He'd also set up House Phel as her guardian and the ones paying her tuition, room, and board, now that her furious Papa had disowned her. Not that she cared.

The land around the sprawling academy buildings rolled out lush with late summer, the velvet lawns spreading under the canopies of carefully groomed trees, all kept in prime condition by earth elementals and gardening sprites.

Groups of students gathered here and there, some of them in classes that had moved outdoors, others studying or at leisure, none of them paying any particular attention to the passing of her carriage. Through a gap between buildings, past the quad thronged with more students enjoying the lovely day, the lake showed silver-blue and mirror-still. When Alise had last seen it, the lake had been frozen over and she'd just won the sleigh race for her division. She'd been flushed with victory, proud of her wizarding skills at guiding the air elemental that powered the sleigh, with no idea that she would soon turn her entire life upside-down.

As the carriage swung into the circular drive to stop at the bottom of the grand, wide set of stairs that climbed up to the administration building, which looked like a castle out of a fairytale—a source of pride and simultaneously a point of ridicule among the students, past and present—Alise spotted a lone figure standing rigidly, clearly waiting to greet her.

Her brother, Nander. *Oh joy.* At least she wouldn't have to seek him out, as Nic had requested.

She had only one bag, having left most everything behind at school when they'd made their daring escape. Grabbing it from the seat beside her, she stepped out of the carriage. "Hallo, Nander. So sweet of you to greet me personally."

His already sulky lips turned down into a pout. "It's Wizard Ferdinand. I deserve proper respect."

Only fifteen and having manifested as a wizard over a year before, Nander embodied the worst of the adolescent wizard stereotype. Taller than Alise, he hadn't yet filled out, skinny and knobby-jointed. He'd proudly shorn his black hair to advertise his wizard status, as if anyone at the academy didn't know, and the buzzcut had the unfortunate effect of making his head look too big for his body. His eyes, once a green as brilliant as Nic's, had darkened with magic use, but had not yet reached true wizard-black. As a result, they looked a bit muddied, something that surprised her as her own eyes had gone full black within six months of her manifestation.

Nander possessed decently high MP scores, so he should be flowing plenty of magic. Unless he was slacking on his practicums, which was possible. He'd always been on the lazy side, something their papa had lectured him about any number of times. Still, most young wizards couldn't be restrained from practicing their newfound magic as often as possible.

Alise managed not to smirk at Nander's pompous attitude, but neither did she oblige him. "To what do I owe the honor, Nander—did you miss me?" She knew he couldn't have, as they'd seen each other more at home on school holidays than at Convocation Academy.

"Papa instructed me to meet you and pass along this message." He broke into a shit-eating grin, delighted with this particular errand. "You're to return to House Elal and face your punishment."

"Yes, I read the demand letters. As House Phel informed Lord Elal, I will not be returning to the house of my birth."

"Then you might as well turn around and go back to whatever bog you crawled out of. Our father has no intention of paying for your schooling, not after the disloyalty you've displayed. You are no longer an Elal. I'll be Papa's heir now."

With a shrug, she went around him to climb the stairs. "Tell me something I didn't know. House Phel is picking up the tab, so Lord Elal is free to do all the disinheriting he likes."

Nander caught her arm, his thin fingers pinching to the bone, a couple of guardian spirits manifesting to block her way. "You have disgraced House Elal," he hissed. "You and our wretched familiar of a sister. As the next Lord Elal, I intend to see that—"

She shook off his hand and, in the same moment, with scarcely a lick of magic—though she had plenty, as all the familiars at House Phel had insisted on filling up her magic stores as a farewell gift—she banished Nander's spirits. *Not so brittle now.*

"Don't fuck with me, Nander," Alise said in a pleasant voice she'd learned from Maman. She could tell someone to curl up and die and make it sound like a delightful option. "You're a long time, and a bucketful of magical skill, away from being Lord Elal. I wouldn't count your high houses before you inherit them. In the meanwhile, I'm twice the wizard you are, so I suggest you stay out of my face."

It was petty, but she was aggravated and taking a bit of spiteful action made her feel better, so she summoned a swarm of tiny fire elementals to waft under Nander's clothes and start pricking him with bitsy flames. They couldn't do much harm, but the sheer number of them made for vast itchiness. Nander jumped and began frantically scratching at himself. "What did you do?" he demanded.

"Oh." She widened her eyes in innocence. "Haven't you learned that one yet?" She tsked loudly, making a show of shaking her head in disappointment. "You really should attend to your practicums."

"Why should I?" he sneered. "Papa hates you now. More than he hates Nic, which is saying something. I'm his only choice for heir to House Elal and I don't intend to do anything to screw that up like you two did. *I* am a loyal son." He put a sanctimonious hand over his heart while still scratching madly with the other hand, but quickly dropped it. "Thanks for making it easy for me, sis."

Alise didn't bother to point out that their father had any number of choices from the many lateral branches of their enormous family. Sometimes it did more harm than good for a wizard to manifest young. On the flip side, someone like Han had suffered for years, waiting to discover if he'd be a wizard or familiar, manifesting so late that it had caused him all kinds of problems. But for Nander to gain such rank and power before he'd learned much about how the world worked would deform his already weak character. Guiltily, she remembered she was supposed to give him a message, too. She should've said so right away, rather than falling into the old pattern of bickering with her bratty little brother.

"Nic asked me to give you her love and good wishes," Alise said. "She also asked me to tell you that House Phel will cover your education, too, should you wish to separate yourself from our father."

"Oh, that's rich," he said on a sneer of contempt. "As if I'd give up being head of House Elal to go live in the swamps with the outcasts and losers."

"Be careful around our father," she advised, knowing

Nander wouldn't listen, but feeling she should say something anyway. That Nic would want her to. "He cares only about himself and maintaining his power in the Convocation. He's also been up to something nefarious with—"

Nander cut her off with a barked out laugh, that unfortunately broke with his recently changed voice, ending in an ignominious squeak that had him flushing angrily. "Listen, little alley cat, you are the one who should be careful. Papa blames you both for losing his eye, and for Maman's death, and he's going to make—"

"Wait," Alise interrupted, appalled that their father was telling people Maman was dead, "Maman isn't—"

"Alise Elal," a voice broke in with calm authority. Both Alise and Nander whirled in habitual guilt at the Hanneil proctor's sudden appearance. He eyed them sourly, no doubt using his magic to divine their thoughts. "I believe you're tardy for an appointment with Provost Uriel, Wizard Alise. And *you*, Wizard Ferdinand, I don't know where you're supposed to be, but I highly doubt it's here."

"No, Proctor," Nander muttered. "I—"

The proctor held up a hand to stop him, wizard-black eyes focusing, a buzz of Hanneil psychic magic in the air. "Ah, you are meant to be in your Remedial Wizardry practicum." The proctor glared owlishly at Nander. "I'm registering a demerit for you, Wizard Ferdinand. I suggest you get yourself to your practicum immediately and attempt to learn something. Now, and with haste," he added, when Nander hesitated, opening his mouth to say something to Alise.

Nander hastened away as instructed, glancing once over

his shoulder at Alise and mouthing something she couldn't make out and didn't care to. She would have to find him later and make him listen to the truth about Maman and what their father had done.

"As for you, Alise Elal," the proctor announced, "I shall escort you to the provost's office."

"I know the way, Proctor."

"That may be true, but you've also demonstrated that you cannot be trusted. If Provost Uriel agrees to reinstate you as a student, you'll find your liberties will be severely restricted. Come along." He gestured up the stairs, then fell into step beside her.

If Provost Uriel agrees... Alise had thought it was all settled. As little as Alise liked returning to Convocation Academy, she liked the idea of being turned away even less. It gave her a queasy sense of failure, thinking about letting down Nic and Gabriel and everyone else at House Phel. And before she'd even begun.

Despite the scolding over her tardiness, she had to wait outside the provost's office, literally kicking her heels in an antique chair too high for her to touch her feet to the ground. It made her feel like a little kid, which she suspected was deliberate. At last the provost's aide and familiar received a tiny Ratsiel courier for interoffice communication and nodded at Alise to go in. "You can leave your bag out here," he said, not unkindly. "I'll keep an eye on it."

Empty handed and wishing she'd had the opportunity to clean up a little from her journey, Alise entered the provost's office for the first time in her life. High in one of the building turrets, the office was ringed with a semi-circle of windows giving an expansive view of campus. Beautifully furnished, the room reeked of academia and storied tradition. The provost herself sat at a grand desk, her silver hair elaborately piled on her head, her skin dewy from the attention of grooming imps, though a spiderweb of lines fanned out from her wizard-black eyes. Those eyes observed Alise with keen insight, her House Uriel magic assessing and weighing Alise uncomfortably.

Uriel was another high house, like Hanneil, that bred and recruited wizards strongly gifted in psychic magic. Theirs, however, focused entirely on learning, academia, and interpretation of the law. Rumor had it that Hanneil and Uriel, once a single house, fought bitterly behind the scenes over more than young wizards with high MP scores in psychic magic. The original schism had reputedly occurred over the ethical application of their magic. In the current day, Uriel wizards ended up in many administration positions, or served on august bodies like the Convocation judicial council.

"Alise Elal," the Provost said in a strong voice that belied her ethereal appearance, "you and your sister, both, have managed to give me considerable headaches. What in the dark arts is going on with House Elal?"

A bit startled by the question, Alise allowed herself to take a breath and order her thoughts. "Begging your pardon, Provost Uriel, but my sister, Lady Phel, had already graduated from Convocation Academy before her...difficulties."

"Do you imply that her behavior is thus not my problem?" She sniffed delicately. "Quite the contrary. Convocation Academy prides itself on educating familiars as well as wizards.

For a Convocation Academy graduate, especially a familiar of Lady Phel's birth rank and MP scores to *run off*, in blatant disobedience to her house, her wizard, and Convocation proctor, violating all the ethics taught to her, reflects poorly on all of us. And, as amply demonstrated by ensuing events, in which another Elal, one of our outstanding wizard students, also runs off, this time abducting an additional two familiars, Lady Phel created a plague that must be disinfected decisively, lest utter chaos come down upon us all."

Had Nic and Gabriel realized what Alise would be facing in coming back here? She rather doubted it. She also had no idea what to say. She dearly wanted to argue that she'd hardly abducted Han and Iliana, but the Convocation wouldn't see it that way. Familiars weren't considered to have much autonomy. In Nic's case, she'd "run off" on her own, so there was no wizard to blame, but Alise had been the responsible party in the escape of Han and Iliana. They couldn't have done it without her. She supposed that was the best route to take: accept responsibility. Especially since Provost Uriel waited expectantly, clearly holding out for some sort of reply from Alise.

"I regret my role in casting a shadow on the reputation of Convocation Academy," she said, with perfect honesty. "I know there is no justification for my actions, but I am committed to mending my ways. I've returned to school to learn to be an upstanding citizen of the Convocation and to be the best wizard I can be."

The provost eyed her, no doubt mentally testing the truth of Alise's words, the depth of her commitment. Alise concentrated on her sincere desire to do just that. After all, if Alise had to be here, she might as well do her very best. And graduate as quickly as possible, so she could return to House Phel.

"Why should we take the risk?" Provost Uriel asked bluntly. "You've demonstrated that you're hardly a grateful or worthy recipient of the education here. Why should I believe you won't revert to your ill-considered behavior the moment some lovelorn familiar appeals to your soft heart and softer head?"

Insulted, irritated, Alise nearly pointed out that the provost's Uriel magic ought to tell her, but she managed to restrain herself. The wizard watched Alise cannily, awaiting an explanation, or a guarantee, which the provost would then assess for veracity. *Why indeed?* Alise wondered. She could hardly say because her clandestine mission to ferret out information for House Phel mattered to her more than helping out anyone else, nor would it be convincing to point out that the specific set of circumstances that had led to her assisting Han and Iliana in their escape was highly unlikely to recur.

"Because I've learned from this experience," she answered, knowing that much to be absolutely true. "Both my heart and head are harder now. I've witnessed the results of both Nic's actions and Han and Iliana's, how much they've suffered. And I have something that matters to me now more than any other considerations. I have a home at House Phel—if I graduate properly and do them honor with it. Lord Phel has agreed to pay my way, for which I'm immensely grateful. I'd die before I'd do anything to disappoint him and House Phel."

The provost studied Alise a long moment more, then let

out a soft sigh. "How is Nic doing?" Catching Alise's startled reaction, the provost chuckled. "I'm not a monster, young Elal. Nic was one of our best and brightest. I was among those truly startled when she manifested as a familiar, rather than a wizard. And her *difficulties*, as you so delicately phrase it, came as a sorrow to me. I do wish that... Well, water under the bridge. She's Lady Phel now and, while I understand there are a number of legal questions yet to be settled, she's not my problem anymore."

"She is doing well," Alise ventured, not at all sure of her footing in this wildly altered conversation. "Happy. She and Lord Phel are working hard to rebuild House Phel."

Provost Uriel dropped her gaze to the mirror-polished surface of her desk, tapping one finger idly. "They won't have an easy go of it, with the forces arrayed against them," she commented, as if noting the season. "You might remind her that House Uriel, at least, still falls on the side of ethics and the rule of law." Before Alise could reply to that rather astonishing statement, one that sounded like a warning, the provost pinned Alise with a sharp, obsidian stare. "You are re-admitted to Convocation Academy on a probationary basis. You will have a strict curfew, numerous social restrictions, and a heavy course load that should ensure you won't have time or inclination for any shenanigans."

The provost withdrew two sheets of paper from a drawer in the desk and passed them to Alise. One, a long list of the rules and restrictions, made Alise's heart sink. How could she sneak about and do research under these strictures? The other, her courseload, was intimidatingly long. She'd be lucky to find time to eat most days and, with the amount of studying she'd have to do to keep up with them all, sleep would become a luxury. And to think Nic had sent Alise back to school in part because she'd become exhausted at House Phel.

Then her gaze snagged on a class she'd never seen in the catalog before, an independent study on Convocation History. With Provost Uriel herself as her adviser on the project. She lifted her gaze to the provost, a question on her lips.

"Are the terms acceptable?" Provost Uriel asked in such a way that the question died before Alise could speak it. "I'm well aware this will be challenging on a number of levels. We needed to ensure that no one will be able to accuse you of being easily forgiven or rewarded for your behavior."

Alise could see that. Her re-enrollment itself would be her punishment. "The terms are acceptable, Provost Uriel," she replied.

"Good." She extracted something from a drawer, shimmering with quiet Uriel magic. "You'll need this pass. It will give you access to the archives for your independent study project."

"Thank you for giving me this opportunity to redeem myself. I won't let you or Convocation Academy down."

"Or House Phel, I imagine," the wizard replied drily.

Alise acknowledged that with a dip of her chin. "If I may make one request?"

The provost raised a single, silver brow. "You're hardly in any position to make requests, Wizard Elal."

"I'm aware." She allowed a respectful pause. "I have been disowned by House Elal and, as you note, House Phel is paying my way. May I be enrolled as Alise Phel?"

Provost Uriel didn't smile, but something in her air hinted of approval. "I'll have my aide submit the paperwork accordingly. Now be off with you. I believe you're late for class."

"Yes, Provost." Taking her ridiculously long list of restrictions and classwork, Alise obediently took her leave, feeling oddly optimistic for the first time since she left House Phel and everyone who loved her behind. She could do this.

~ 7 ~

VALE, AT LEAST, was as wholly committed as Jadren to leaving House Refoel in the dust. Not that dust dared encroach upon the verdant, idyllic valley. The gelding had grown sleek and ever so slightly overweight during their summer tenure in the land of healers. The horse pranced in high spirits as Jadren loaded up his saddle bags. Jadren was sure the noble-hearted horse had grown a little bored with lack of adventure.

Well, they would soon be on the move, going to the one place Jadren had sworn he'd never return to voluntarily. His dear maman always managed to find a way to yank his chain and reel him back, so he and Vale would be traveling to House El-Adrel with all possible haste. As soon as he extracted himself from the clinging tentacles of Refoel. Several of which tentacles were currently attempting to bar his way.

"Lord Jadren," Chaim said in a tone of strained patience, his healer's calm visibly cracking around the edges. "You can't possibly know where Seliah has gone."

"Incorrect. I know exactly where she is."

"She cannot have been abducted from Refoel lands," Chaim insisted. "We have safeguards and alarms. I would know if a hostile force had crossed our border, much less invaded the very building I dwell in."

"I suggest you rethink your assumptions," Jadren advised him, "as that's exactly what happened." *...we'll send transportation for you. It would arrive faster than you might think.* His father had tried to warn him, and Jadren had only realized that in retrospect. The "transportation" had already been nearby when he and Seliah read that letter. Lurking, waiting to spring the trap. And he'd failed her.

"If you would just give us time to—"

"No."

"One cryptic note isn't enough evidence to—"

"Yes, it is."

Chaim, unaccustomed to being rudely interrupted ever, much less several times in a row, huffed in exasperation. "There are official channels for handling this sort of thing! You know this. Let me employ our in-house Elal wizard to trace Seliah's—"

"No Elals," Jadren snapped, rounding on Chaim. "Lord Refoel, with all due respect, you seem to fail to realize that Seliah has been abducted in an illegal, malicious act—from within the bounds of your own house, whether you want to admit that or not—and you're maundering on about official channels."

"I don't agree that she's been abducted," Chaim argued. "We are all aware that Seliah was unhappy with you."

Jadren stilled, wondering if he imagined the hiss of Liat drawing breath through her teeth. "I fully admit to being an ass," he said in his friendliest tone. "I'm working on doing better. But Seliah? She is a class act, all the way. She would never be so cowardly as to run away instead of standing her ground. If you don't know that, you understand nothing about her at all."

"I apologize for any implied insult," Chaim said stiffly. "My point is that there is simply no way that hostile forces could—"

"Could and did, Chaim," Jadren ground out, his meager supply of patience exhausted, "whether you admit it or not. Somehow they did. This is war, whether you healers recognize it or not."

"The internecine affairs of House El-Adrel hardly counts as outright war," Chaim replied with a sniff.

That gave Jadren pause—just enough of one to make him think twice about punching Chaim in that sniffy nose. "Let's say you're right," Jadren conceded calmly, "and this is only a House El-Adrel affair. In that case, I'm leaving immediately for the house of my birth to resolve it."

"There is the matter," Chaim ground out, "of your potentially devastating ability to wreak havoc upon the world. I cannot in good conscience allow you to—"

"Try to stop me," Jadren invited with lethal intent. "I need the practice."

Liat quickly looked to the side, and Jadren was sure she'd suppressed a laugh. Chaim managed not to take a step back, but just barely. "At least take one of our elemental-powered carriages instead of that... horse."

He'd offered it as a concession, but only Chaim could make "horse" sound like an insult. "No way," Jadren replied, patting Vale's arched neck. He considered whether to wear Mr.

Machete—his trusty big blade of Phel's moon magic, which could melt the hunters—or not. He buckled the sheath to the saddle. He could draw it there easily and Vale would be helpful in a fight if it came to that. He doubted it would. They wanted him back at El-Adrel and would clear the way for him. "This horse is part of the team."

"I'll send a secured Ratsiel courier to House Phel for you," Liat volunteered, "to apprise them of the situation. Is there any particular information you'd like me to include?"

"Thank you, Liat." The offer moved him a surprising amount. "Just tell them…" He didn't know what. There was too much. "Tell them I'm handling it, that I'll ensure Seliah comes to no harm."

Liat's black eyes gleamed with emotion, and she nodded.

"Lord Jadren!" Pinny ran up, earnest face full of concern. "Here's the last of Seliah's things. Please tell her…" Pinny's face crumpled with anxiety.

Jadren put a hand on her shoulder. "She's going to be fine. They won't hurt her." *They'd better not.*

"I still think," Chaim began stiffly, "that we should—"

"Do you, Chaim?" Liat asked with deceptive mildness. "Think? Because it doesn't seem that way."

Chaim gaped at his sister, momentarily flabbergasted. Liat smiled at Jadren, unperturbed. "Good luck. Take care of our girl."

"I intend to." Better than he had been. He mounted Vale, ready to ride.

"Practice your drills!" Liat called after him, and he lifted a hand in acknowledgement, already losing the rest of her words in the pounding of Vale's hooves.

With relief, Jadren finally, finally chased the attenuated thread of his bond to Seliah. Too bad he wasn't a powerful wizard like the mythical Sylus, as he certainly possessed enough righteous rage to burn House El-Adrel to the ground. Nor could he pull off a Gabriel Phel and rip the roof off a tower from across the valley to rescue his beloved. What was with all the abducting of familiars lately, anyway? Exploiting that wizard–familiar bond to make everyone toe the line. If only there were a way to sever that bond. He shook the thought away.

He might not possess the ability to lay waste to his enemies—or his enemies' roofs—but he possessed buckets of wily contrariness. And the journey would give him time to plan. How to storm House El-Adrel and extract Seliah? Hmm...

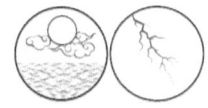

"GABRIEL!" NIC CALLED out, quick-trotting into the wizards' workroom at the far end of the north wing of House Phel. Several people, previously deep in concentration on various projects, glanced up in startled surprise. Not a common occurrence, to see Lady Phel in disarray, discomposed, and calling for her wizard. She ignored them all, along with their stares, rounded the deep pit of rippling water that was Nathi's home, and scanned the labyrinthine work space for Gabriel's tall, silver-haired form. He normally stood out in a crowd, and her bond with him indicated he was in this vicinity—and it had been his plan to work on the new product lines with the minions this afternoon—but she couldn't spot him.

The urgent missive from Refoel, annoyingly keyed only to Gabriel, burned against her sweating hand, and she groaned in frustration. Where *was* he? Tempted to yell for him again, louder, she restrained herself. It really didn't do for her to behave with so little decorum.

"Lord Phel is in the shielded room with the moon-magic apprentices," Iliana said helpfully, appearing at Nic's elbow, a concerned line between her brows. She'd woven her bright-red hair into two long braids that dangled forward over her shoulders and should have made her look like a little kid, but instead framed her pretty face, setting off her warm brown eyes. "I could ask one of the wizards to unlock it, but…"

"No," Nic said on a sigh. That work—teaching the younger wizards to extrude silver from moon magic—was conducted in a shielded room for a reason, as the results so far had proved to be unstable to the point of being explosive. Nic could wish that her wizard would stay *outside* of the blast zone, but she'd been the one to nag him to teach his skills to their minions. She looked longingly at the walled-off corner the wizards had installed, wondering if she imagined the muffled sounds of thumping from within. Determinedly, she turned her back on it. Gabriel's tendency to fling himself headlong into dangerous pursuits was of the many things she couldn't control and was attempting to get better about letting go of. "I'm sure they'll emerge soon," she added.

Iliana nodded encouragingly. "I'm certain of it. They've

been in there an hour and rarely stay longer than that. The poor apprentices practically collapse with exhaustion when they emerge." She dipped her pointed chin at the missive Nic clutched. "I see the Refoel crest—news on Jadren and Seliah?"

"Marked urgent and keyed to Gabriel," Nic replied, the itch of apprehension returning full force. Not that a few minutes would make that much difference.

"Oh." Iliana frowned in concern, her gaze drifted to the warded work area, then determinedly back to Nic's face. "Let me distract you then. Wedding plans?"

Nic groaned. "Dark arts, no. Actually—"

"Don't 'actually' me, Nic," Iliana broke in, her impatience with the countless delays making her forget protocol, never Iliana's strong suit to begin with. "We already lost the entire summer. Unless you want a winter wedding, which can be pretty, we'll have to wait until next year at this point."

"That's exactly what we have to do," Nic told her firmly. "Gabriel and I discussed and I've finally convinced him that this wedding nonsense has to be tabled." Maybe indefinitely for all she cared. Having a big party wouldn't change their relationship, but it sure would strain their already precarious financial position.

"It's not nonsense," Iliana protested.

"In the grand scheme, it doesn't make sense right now either," Nic explained, aware of other ears listening. She didn't like the minions knowing more than they needed to about House Phel's difficulties, but they could hardly be kept entirely secret either. The finances were her and Gabriel's business, but the legal matters facing them were public knowledge. "There's too much unsettled with our legal problems, plus we want Jadren and Seliah to attend and their status has been..." She waved the missive in her hand in lieu of trying to put words to the blank abyss of information regarding the wayward pair. Seliah's letters had been chatty, upbeat, and completely lacking in useful information. "Besides," she rubbed a hand over her swollen belly, "the baby will be born midwinter and I'd like to be able to dance at my own wedding, instead of sitting on the sidelines like a beached whale." Her Ophiel gowns—thanks to Wizard Dahlia's expertise—adjusted to her changing figure in as flattering a way as possible, but she still felt enormous, with months to go.

"I suppose that makes sense." Still, Iliana looked unhappy.

"Tell me how your work with Nathi is going," Nic said, hitting upon a surefire topic to distract Iliana.

Iliana brightened with enthusiasm. "Very well! We've found a fish diet she likes and she's thriving. And I'm getting better at communicating with her." Her smile dimmed. "Except I keep feeling like she's trying to tell me something and I can't figure out what she's getting at."

"I'm sure you'll figure it out," Nic reassured her. Iliana was so earnest, always wanting to do her best. As a familiar with Ariel magic, Iliana had been working on using her passive-magical abilities to sense Nathi's wants and needs. Nothing like having a giant, pink seahorse unhappy with their living situation and acting out. They had enough problems already. Nic's gaze went to the still firmly locked testing chamber.

"Would you like to say hello?" Iliana asked.

It took Nic a moment to recall the current conversation

and realize Iliana meant Nathi. Bemused, but grateful for something to occupy the waiting time, Nic nodded.

Leaning over the low wall that served more as a warning that a depthless pit of water lay beyond it than any other useful purpose—it certainly did nothing to contain Nathi or the water she displaced in her vigorous splashing—Iliana lightly slapped the calm surface. Almost immediately, a pair of widely spaced pink knobs broke the glossy surface, followed by the great, spiny head of the strangest creature Nic had ever seen. No matter how many times she took in the creature that looked like a seahorse the size of a sailing ship, the pink of spring rosebuds, with gloriously long eyelashes, Nic found herself marveling that Nathi existed. Judging by the sudden, arrested silence of the workroom, she wasn't alone in her continued astonishment.

They still hadn't determined how or when Nathi had been installed in the watery reservoir built into the manse, one that connected to the lake fronting the house. If Nathi knew, she wasn't saying. Of course, Nathi's communication with Iliana seemed to be limited to giving her name—a singularly clear moment—and otherwise generally positive or negative reactions to various kinds of fish.

Nathi lowered her long, reticulated snout and affectionately nudged Iliana, who'd climbed up on the low wall and stood on her tiptoes to embrace the creature, heedless of the water soaking her pretty gown. "You remember Lady Phel," Iliana said after a moment, turning to gesture to Nic.

Blinking her long lashes, Nathi inclined her head in an approximation of a bow, making fluting sounds like a musical instrument. "She understands you that well?" she asked with some surprise.

"More or less," Iliana answered. "She seems to get the intent of my words, or the images in my mind. I was imagining her being polite to you, and a lady's curtsy."

"Hmm." If a familiar with Ariel talents was able to do that much, Nic would love to see what an actual Ariel wizard could do. Though she'd hate to mitigate Iliana's excitement by bringing a wizard in. She supposed this wasn't a problem that needed solving, unlike twenty-seven other issues she could think of off the top of her head.

"I only wish I could understand *her* half so well," Iliana fretted. "I keep getting images of mist around the edges of the lake and—"

"Nic?" Gabriel seized her waist from behind, his big hands no longer close to spanning it as he once had. "What's wrong?" he demanded, spinning her to face him, his wizard-black gaze going suspiciously to Nathi, his magic intensifying.

That is, what there was of his magic. "You're running low on magic," she informed him. "Whatever have you been doing? Better have some of my mine."

"Something is wrong, Nic," Gabriel said with exaggerated patience, lowering his gaze to scrutinize her face, "or you wouldn't be here. I could feel you worrying from inside the testing chamber. The baby...?"

"The baby is *fine*," she told him, as she seemed to daily. The baby, safely ensconced in their cozy womb, was probably the one person out of everyone who was perfectly fine. "Have some magic and I'll tell you what's up."

He narrowed his eyes threateningly, his voice dropping to a warning growl. "Nic…"

"What if someone suddenly attacked?" she asked with wide eyes, figuring she probably looked like Nathi with her fluttering lashes. "You'd want to be at your best."

With an annoyed grunt, he pulled on her magic, the sensation so sweet, nearly erotic—more so now than ever, given all the playing they'd done around building and sharing magic—that she had to take a moment to maintain her Lady Phel composure. Gabriel felt it, too, making a low sound, deep in his chest, the tension sizzling through their connection. "Now start talking," he told her. Even though the command wasn't remotely sexual, she responded with vivid excitement. Too bad so many people were watching them, openly and covertly.

Not trusting her voice, she lifted the missive and showed it to him. If he hadn't been caught up with his concern for her, he'd have noticed it long since. Catching his breath at the sight of the Refoel seal, his alarmed gaze went to hers. "Seliah?"

"We won't know until you read it. It's keyed to you."

"Not here." Taking her by the wrist, not touching the missive she still held, he towed her out of the workroom, then out a side door that led to the lawn at the back of the house, gently sloping down to the lazily flowing Dubhglas River. Insects buzzed in the trees, making a heavy droning sound that somehow intensified the thickness of the humid air. As the house continued to restore itself, replicating how it had been centuries before the family lost its magic and fell from power—the untended manse eventually sinking entirely into the marshes—the gardens surrounding it also burgeoned in the late summer heat. Farther north, autumn would be making itself felt, perhaps the leaves starting to turn in Elal, workers harvesting the last of the grapes, but in Meresin, summer still reigned with a heavy hand.

A labyrinth of rose hedges had reconstructed itself at some point in the last weeks, growing with magical speed, the self-grooming bushes higher than even Gabriel's head, only the heavy, bloodred blossoms dripping from protruding stems breaking the otherwise crisp lines of the rows. Nic hadn't had time to explore the maze, though she'd heard tales from the others who'd gotten gleefully lost there, and followed along with interest as Gabriel led her into it. With unerring decisiveness, he brought them to the center, where a fountain rested in the middle of a rose-festooned clearing. A clever sculpture of a moon topped it, showing phases from fingernail to full, depending on where you stood, bright water shimmering in silvery sheets to the basin below.

"You didn't mention this fountain," Nic remarked, breathless with admiration—well, and from keeping up with Gabriel's long-legged stride. "So perfectly House Phel."

"I hadn't seen it before. This is the first time I've come here."

"How'd you find your way to the center so easily then?"

He gave her a bemused look. "I don't know. I just wanted to get to a private place and here we are."

His attunement to the manse then, a wizardly perk she could envy. She held out the missive and this time he took it. "Will my unsealing it notify the sender I've done so, like with the legal demands?" he asked.

She peered at the seal. "Not this kind, no."

With a grunt, he placed his finger on the Refoel sigil of a bee on a stylized blossom, the magic clicking almost audibly. He read swiftly, and Nic did her best to contain her impatience, very aware of Gabriel's magic sharpening and intensifying with his distress. "It appears that Seliah abruptly disappeared and Jadren believes she was abducted by House El-Adrel to force his return. He's left House Refoel on Vale, bound for El-Adrel and asked for us to be informed, but that he's handling it."

To Nic's relief, Gabriel remained relatively calm in the face of this dread news. "*Jadren believes,*" she repeated. "They don't know? How can they not *know*?"

He handed her the missive to read for herself, watching her face closely as she did. "I find it oddly phrased."

"I've met Liat Refoel," Nic murmured. "She has a way of couching information in ways that transmit more than the surface implies. See here that she says that Lord Refoel urged caution and investigation—along with certainty that no hostile forces could have trespassed on their lands. They want to be sure that we know that they weren't negligent with Seliah's safety. Or, if they were, that they're pursuing the cause and culprits. This looks particularly bad for them in light of their refusal to ally with us."

"Cowards," Gabriel observed.

"Maybe? They do share a border with House Hanneil and they are not ideal neighbors. Refoel could be maintaining neutrality out of self-protection. But this bit is interesting—did you read the postscript?"

"I didn't get that far," Gabriel admitted, peering over her shoulder.

"They're throwing us a bone," she observed wryly, "but it's one with some juicy meat on it. They won't contest our trademark on the water purification enchantments they use on their hot pools, the ones Seliah was canny enough to notice and notify us about. Refoel is agreeing to our terms for payment on continued use."

"*Our* terms?"

She gave him a winning smile. "You left it to me and I drove a hard bargain. It includes a contract for House Phel wizards to renew and maintain the enchantments."

"Well done," he said with an approving smile that warmed her to her toes.

"That income will be most welcome," she agreed. "Nice to have a spot of good news. On the flip side, House El-Adrel never replied to our missives about them unlawfully bonding Seliah to Jadren without our consent. I suppose I shouldn't be surprised by that, or that they apparently abducted her from Refoel, but they're a high house. They're not above the law."

Gabriel snorted. "The more I learn about so-called Convocation law and actual high-house behavior, the less I believe that any high houses abide by the rules."

Nic grimaced. "You may have a point. What my father and Convocation Academy painted as truth now seems like a pretty façade pasted over a rather nefarious reality."

Gabriel drew her into a comforting embrace, cupping her head and holding her close against his chest. "For all that you were educated in Convocation society and understand the etiquette, in many ways they kept you as ignorant as I was out here in the swamps of Meresin."

She laughed, a little, at his words, echoing one of the many insults hurled at House Phel. "Marshes," she corrected haughtily, drawing back and sharing a smile with him. "What do you want to do about Seliah?"

"What *can* we do?" he asked, very seriously. "You tell me. You know I want to extract her from their clutches, and bring them both safely back here."

"If they even want to be here."

"Yes." He sounded bleak. "It's still not clear to me why they remained at Refoel for so long. I don't understand how I failed them."

"Sometimes, my only love," Nic said gently, "people make decisions based entirely on their own difficulties, and those reasons have nothing to do with anyone else. It can be hard to bear in mind, but everyone out there is fighting an internal battle we know nothing about and likely couldn't understand, even if we did know the particulars. Jadren has more demons than we know."

"And they all lurk in House El-Adrel."

"Most of them, anyway." Nic suspected Jadren carried a fair number of them deep inside himself. "We certainly know his mother wants him in her possession, that she's always had a vested interest in controlling him, and it wouldn't be at all surprising if she wasn't using Seliah as leverage to compel his behavior."

"To get him to do what?"

"We don't know, do we?" Nic asked in return. "But I doubt

it's anything good for anyone but Katica El-Adrel."

"You asked me what I want to do," Gabriel said grimly. "I want to help Jadren recover Seliah. I don't want to sit here, waiting, exchanging legal missives with half the Convocation, cooling my heels while they're out there fighting for their lives and sanity."

Nic nodded, unsurprised. "I agree."

"I know you don't—wait, you agree?" Gabriel broke off the familiar rant, backpedaling with almost amusing alacrity.

"Yes," she answered drily. "I do agree. El-Adrel has committed a crime against us. They've separated a familiar from her wizard, both contracted to House Phel, regardless of their lodging at the time. We'll wait a few days, to give Jadren the opportunity to handle it, so we don't appear to be lacking faith in his ability, but then we should pay them a visit."

"*Pay them a visit?*" Gabriel echoed, visibly aghast. "I was thinking something more... aggressive."

"There, there, darling." She patted his muscled arm. "You can swing your sword about and throw condensed moonsilver spikes at people if they aren't cooperative. But yes, I say we visit House El-Adrel, in an official capacity. It's time for Lord Phel to beard Lady El-Adrel in her den."

"When we rescued you from House Sammael, Jadren wanted me to walk up and knock on the door."

"It's polite to knock."

"That's not what I meant."

"I know. I was lightening the mood. In point of fact, Jadren wasn't wrong. I know you thought at the time that he was setting you up for betrayal, but—regardless of the clandestine nefarious activities of the high houses—the Convocation does run on surface manners. Which means we need to take a couple of days before we can leave, to inform Convocation Center of our plans."

"In case, when bearding the lioness in her den, we are eaten by her?"

"They can write in our memorials that we were in the right and the law, not to mention etiquette, was on our side." She simpered at him, and he shook his head.

"Sometimes your dark sense of humor worries me."

"Take heart, my only love." She linked her arm through his. "This will be fun."

"That's not the word I'd have chosen."

"Better than staying home and teaching amateur moon-magic wizards?"

"That is absolutely true." He bent to kiss her. "Have I mentioned today how much I love you?"

"You have, but feel free to say so as often as you like."

"I love you, Nic. I'd be lost without you."

"I love you, too. And I am literally lost without you as I have no idea how to extract myself from this maze."

Chuckling, he patted her hand. "Allow me to rescue you, my lady."

With a dreamy sigh that wasn't at all pretense, Nic let him lead the way.

~ 8 ~

S ELIAH PACED AROUND the pretty apartments, the very same she'd been installed in on her first "visit" to House El-Adrel. While she understood the reasons for the lack of windows—because the house moved about and reshaped itself with enough frequency to disconcert the human occupants when the view outside abruptly changed—she still violently disliked the sense of being trapped indoors, with no way to get out. She felt much like a tasty tidbit packed into some interior compartment to preserve freshness, waiting to be consumed.

They'd prepared her for the part, too. As before, a cadre of servants had converged to dress her up, apply makeup, and style her hair, all very fancy. She looked fabulous, the quintessential high-house lady, but to say that she resented Katica El-Adrel's tactics was putting it mildly. It worried her that no one had spoken to her, not even to issue threats or the sort of taunting Katica seemed fond of. But, other than the groomers, who reminded her decidedly of stable hands not particularly interested in the horse they readied for show, she hadn't seen anyone at all.

Selly had been hoping for a visit from Fyrdo, as had happened before, and which was really the only reason she'd gone along with the program so far. Not that she'd had a choice when El-Adrel's automatons appeared from nothing, grabbed her and whisked her away from Refoel. They'd hit her with some sort of paralysis spell, too, that had prevented her from moving or speaking. She supposed it was a mark of how far she'd come, how much Liat's mental healing and Maya's gentle counseling had helped her, that she'd been able to take the immobility more or less in stride. But everything since they'd unfrozen her after depositing her in these rooms... well, she was doing her best to keep calm, knowing that—no matter what else happened—Jadren would soon arrive.

That was obviously the point of this whole enterprise. That letter hadn't worked to bring him hurrying home. Holding her hostage absolutely would. She hated that she was being used as leverage; she also knew that Jadren, even as badly as they'd left things, would come for her.

That was love in its truest form, she supposed. Not the spontaneous romantic love of novels, but real, enduring love, the kind that survived all the arguments and disappointments and thoughtlessly angry moments. She and Jadren would never be the epically romantic couple like Sylus and Lyndella, nor would they be like Nic and Gabriel, with their mutual adoration. No, she and Jadren were like two broken halves of a whole. They completed each other, but not seamlessly. Their jagged edges would always rub up against the other in uncomfortable ways, occasionally drawing blood, but never out of cruelty. They were able to be that for each other: the person who didn't mind a few bumps and bruises because they understood that neither of them was perfect.

She wouldn't trade him for anyone else in all the world. They'd get through this, just as they'd gotten through everything else together. She just needed to be patient and have faith in him. Patience had never been her strong suit, but her utter faith in Jadren more than made up for it.

"I just really wish I could at least see outside," she muttered aloud.

There wasn't a sound, exactly. But a sense of movement, of that distinctive, oiled-metal feel of El-Adrel magic, briefly furled and unfurled. The air of the room shifted, as if someone had opened a window in a distant room, and a cool breeze wafted in. Selly turned in a slow, suspicious circle, feeling as if she used her familiar's passive senses to sniff the air. At first, nothing seemed to have changed... Except that there was an odd sensation of movement, as if she rode in a carriage.

"House?" she asked aloud, not sure how else to address the structure. Jadren seemed to waffle on just how sentient the house was. He went from referring to her as an occasionally malicious and often interfering bitch, to denying that the odd and ancient manse was anything more than the product of generations of wizards specializing in creating enchanted artifacts tinkering endlessly with various parts of the house to the point that the layers of spells had somehow conglomerated into something larger and unpredictable.

Selly leaned toward the house being a thinking creature with her own agenda—one that favored Jadren and possibly also herself, by extension.

Nobody replied, but Selly could swear the house heard her. A soundless rumble vibrated through the room, and suddenly sunlight flooded in. Not only did a skylight appear above, but also floor-to-ceiling windows opened on three sides, with glass doors leading to a semi-circular balcony. Selly nearly ran out the doors in her delight, gripping the railing with fervor, and inhaling deeply of *outside*. Somehow her interior room had been elevated to the top of the house, giving her a splendid view of the shining rooftops made of many-colored metals, the glint of arching atriums, and cascading wings, all graceful with architectural splendor.

Here and there, too, the house was in motion. A copper fan unfurled in a seemingly endless cycle, disappearing into a roofline before appearing again. A long series of glass-roofed greenhouses snaked outward, opening into a beautiful garden Selly wouldn't have suspected of existing. In another direction—still below her—a series of turrets sported enormous bows mounted horizontally to some sort of cog and wheel device. Armed guards surrounding them pointed at Selly's new vantage, talking intensely and waving their arms.

The outer door to Selly's apartments banged wide, admitting Katica El-Adrel. Hooray, a visitor at last—and the last person Selly wanted to see. She edged just inside the open doors to the balcony. If it came to it, she'd jump over the railing and take her chances, rather than face the certainty of abuse and torture.

Tall, slim, and imposing, with a sheet of silver-threaded black hair that cascaded nearly to the floor, Lady El-Adrel carried herself with effortless grace and the unconscious poise of a woman who expects the instant obedience of everyone around her. Possibly in the entire known world. Fanning her hands on her hips, her long, gilded nails decorated with the El-Adrel lightning bolts that also zig-zagged from one shoulder of her form-fitting white pantsuit down her long thigh, she dragged a slow gaze around the transformed room, eying the balcony and altered view in particular, before settling her wizard-black eyes disdainfully on Selly. "What in the dark arts have you done?" she drawled, managing to make Selly sound like a naughty child in need of correction.

Stung, Selly nearly answered that *she* didn't do anything, then closed her mouth on the words, refusing to be thrust into the role of defensive miscreant.

"Do you realize this tower of yours is interfering with House El-Adrel defenses?" Katica prodded, narrowing her obsidian stare. "It's irresponsible of you to the point of catastrophic carelessness. Undo it."

Selly turned up her hands and shrugged. "I don't know how."

"You expect me to believe that?" Katica barked out a laugh. "The house has never produced anything like this before, in all my life, and in all the preceding history. What did my son teach you?"

"If the house has never done this before, then Jadren wouldn't know to teach me how to do it," Selly pointed out, very reasonably, she thought.

"Don't you dare think you can thwart me, Familiar," Lady El-Adrel snarled, advancing on her, magic booming silently through the air. Selly put her back to the railing, wondering if the house would save her if she jumped. Or was pushed. "Have you already forgotten how I can make you suffer?" the wizard demanded.

Selly lifted her chin. "You won't damage me. You need me to lure Jadren back—and to be his power source once he arrives."

Katica smiled, a thin, cruel slash of crimson in an alabaster face that would be lovely if it held any trace of humanity. "I can cause you considerable pain without damaging you beyond repair. I'd think you'd have learned that in my testing labs."

"Then why am I here and not there?" Selly gestured to the pretty rooms. Prettier now, as it appeared the house had continued the transformation, changing the floor to a mosaic tile showing blossoms native to the Meresin marshes. A painting hung on the wall of a graceful white manse, with a wide porch and tall columns, framed by old trees with spreading limbs. It looked like House Phel, but could it be? Selly shook away the thought as a distraction and focused on her current problem. "If you planned to torture me, why dress me up and set me up like a guest instead of the prisoner we both know I am?"

Katica rolled her eyes, shaking back her glossy hair, and struck a pose. Selly was abruptly reminded of Ozana—before Jadren red-misted her—and how like her mother Ozana had been. And yet, Katica didn't seem to be grieving her daughter. Of course, Katica never seemed to evince much emotion at all. "So dramatic," she said. "You belong to House El-Adrel, Familiar. You're not a prisoner any more than this chair is. "It was obnoxious of you to have House Phel make that pitiful legal bid, accusing us of stealing you." She made a gesture of incredulity, laughing derisively, then cutting it off with a snap. "None of you understand power. Convocation law is what *I* say it is."

"I'm sure the Convocation Judicial Council would be surprised to hear that, not to mention the other high houses."

"Believe me, you ignorant fool, they know who holds the power. Now, let us return to the subject at hand. Instruct the house to return your apartments to their previous shape and position."

As she issued the order, the wizard woman watched Selly with keen attention, enough to give Selly pause, tempting her to play stupid. If Katica wanted to compare her to a chair, then Selly would demonstrate all the cleverness and sentience of a chair. Except that Selly had a bit too much temper to playact effectively. "It's your house, Lady El-Adrel," she said instead. "And you hold all this power. *You* fix it."

Katica regarded her coolly, displaying all the regal reserve Selly lacked. "You will do as you're told."

"Demonstrably, I won't," Selly replied cheerfully, and plopped herself on the chair in question. Summoning a fragment of caution, she refrained from saying 'make me.' "Isn't that your job, anyway? Jadren told me that the head of House El-Adrel must be able to control the house itself. I'd expect you to have that ability. That, what was the word? Oh yes: the *power.*"

Some of Katica's composure frayed at the edges. But she still didn't take action to instruct the house to undo what it had done, which Selly found most telling. Clearly Lady El-Adrel didn't want to reveal how very little actual control she possessed over her own house. If she instructed the house and it didn't obey—or potentially, not even respond—she'd reveal weakness, a lack of power and control, which would be anathema to a woman like her. Worse, if Selly could do something Lady El-Adrel couldn't with her own house... well, *that* would not go over well.

"How about this," Lady El-Adrel said, putting on a charming smile in an about-face that raised the hairs on the back of Selly's neck, "you tell me what you said or did to result in these changes..." She waved a hand at the still-evolving décor, face going icily still as she caught sight of the painting that looked like House Phel. It had gained a reflecting lake in the foreground, with a mirror-perfect image of the manse, except for a pair of pink horns creating a ripple in the water. Curiouser and curiouser. Katica's wizard-black eyes returned to pin Selly like an unfortunate specimen destined to be dispatched. "In the interests of experimentation and greater knowledge. Repeat exactly what you did and said."

"I said that I wished I could see outside," Selly said, deciding it couldn't hurt to say so and Lady El-Adrel's reaction might give her some insight.

The wizard narrowed her black gaze on Selly, unconvinced. "It does you no good to lie to me. I can always torture the truth out of you."

"Didn't we cover this ground already?" Selly asked sweetly. "Besides, even if you do decide to end this boring, circular conversation and commence with this torture you keep threatening, you won't get a different answer. That is the simple truth."

Katica considered her for a long moment, seeming puzzled, not totally in control of the conversation for once. "Are
you truly afraid of nothing?"

"I'm afraid of plenty of things," Selly answered honestly,
"but not of pain or suffering. I've already endured the worst."

"I could make you regret those words."

Selly shrugged. "You could try."

Lady El-Adrel paused, scanning the room with her hard
gaze, which finally landed on the portrait of the white manse.
That was definitely Nathi swimming in the reflecting lake out
front. "If you only expressed a wish to see outside," Katica
asked, canny gaze sliding over to Selly, "why is the room
redecorating itself to reflect *you*? I assume that is House Phel."
She waved a hand dismissively. "Though prettified. The last
time I was there, it was looking considerably worse for the
wear from its long soak in the bogs."

"I don't know," Selly said, answering the only actual question. "Jadren says the house likes me," she added impulsively.
Somewhere in the near distance, a sound rippled out, like
wooden beams settling with soft crackles as a wind arose, like a
woman laughing softly in another room, or like an immense
feline purring. Selly couldn't help smiling in response.

Katica's wizard-black eyes narrowed to malicious slits.
"Don't be absurd. My son is a fool, but you don't have to be. I
can understand your ignorance, given your backwoods
upbringing and total lack of education, but really, it's embar-
rassing for us all when you spout such superstitious nonsense.
You may be only a familiar, but we expect better of our
people, regardless of rank. The house—even a house as old and

steeped in magic as House El-Adrel—doesn't have the ability or inclination to like or dislike anyone. I know you're ignorant of magic, but an enchanted artifact is simply that: an object infused with magic and tasked with a purpose, by a wizard, obviously. This house, *my* house, is a complex, many-layered enchanted artifact, created by generations of El-Adrel wizards, but it is no more able to form opinions than my automatons are."

Selly successfully suppressed a shudder at Katica's reference to the expressionless, inhumanly strong, metal humanoids who'd so ruthlessly captured her. She knew enough now to sense the animating spirits within the machines, courtesy of El-Adrel's collaboration with House Elal, Jadren theorized, but they were no more human than the hunters that had attacked her and Jadren after she'd rescued him from an early grave at the bottom of a cliff.

House El-Adrel—that was a different kind of alive. Not human, but also not a construct manipulated by another's will. Selly could swear that she sensed the house's interest and attention. Besides which, why had the house moved her apartments and decorated them to please Selly? She felt that she and the house shared a secret, a covert friendship. The house *did* like her, she knew it, and the house liked Jadren, no matter what he sourly claimed, and Selly could use that to her advantage. "I'm sure you are right," she replied to the expectant Lady El-Adrel, as meekly as she could.

Katica wasn't fooled by Selly's easy acquiescence, but she also had nothing to argue with there. She tapped the toe of one elegant heel, seeming to be at a bit of an impasse. "How did your hair come to be so long again?" she asked suddenly.

Startled by the abrupt change in subject, Selly put a hand to her now elaborately styled hair before she realized it and—almost guiltily—dropped it and tucked her hand under her thigh.

"I saw it cut short during the bonding ceremony with my own eyes." Lady El-Adrel paced toward her, face alight with excited interest. She reached out, narrowing her eyes in warning as Selly flinched, then took hold of a long lock of hair, extracting it from the coil it loosely dangled from, and tugged sharply. Running her fingers down the length of it, her magic buzzed around them, like cogs and gears flying into motion. "This is your own hair," she marveled. "How did you grow it so long in such a short time? Jadren did this, didn't he?"

Selly didn't want to answer, but she also didn't know how to escape this trap. No suitable lie sprang to mind. She certainly didn't want to throw Jadren into the maw of this particular wolf by admitting that he'd brought her back from near death and, in the doing, somehow restored her long hair also. Feeling more than a little like the cowering bunny cornered by that wolf, she stared up at Katica's keen, knowing gaze.

And shivered at the triumphant smile curving the wizard's cruel, crimson-painted mouth.

"I've done it," she whispered, mostly to herself, still rolling the coil of hair between her fingers. "Dark arts, but I've actually, finally gotten Jadren to do what I thought he could do. After all these years, I'd nearly despaired." She tipped her head back and laughed, a sound of pure, pealing joy. "I've done it! And success is so very sweet."

Returning her attention to Selly, she wrapped the hair around her finger and tugged sharply enough to make Selly gasp in pain. "Tell me what happened. Exactly. Leave out no detail no matter how small. And believe me, I will not hesitate to put you in stocks and cut little pieces off of you until I'm satisfied you've told me everything, as obviously Jadren can and will restore anything I destroy. Tell me how he did this."

"Why don't you ask me yourself?"

Jadren's jaunty voice had Selly wheeling around to the open balcony doors at her back. Dressed to kill in his black leathers, auburn hair and beard shining bright, Jadren stood poised on the other side of the balcony rail, clearly having just climbed up. He flashed her a conspiratorial grin, reminding her that she'd rescued him in nearly the exact same way back at the tribunal in Refoel, and she started to smile back—before Katica's steely grip on her hair yanked her attention away.

Selly at least got to enjoy the privilege of seeing Lady El-Adrel completely bamboozled by Jadren's unexpected appearance. He swung a leg over the balcony rail and landed with sinuous grace, wizard-black eyes caressing Selly with fiercely possessive concern. He drew his machete, the moonsilver gleaming with magic. "And take your hand off my familiar before I cut it off."

Jadren's mother recovered herself. "You think to harm me with a mundane weapon? Only you would be so pitiful as to—"

A bronze dart arrowed away from Jadren before Selly saw him move. It sliced over the back of her hand, making her yelp and snatch it back, releasing Selly's hair.

Jadren tsked, shaking his head. "Careless of you, Maman, to forget to extend your wards around Seliah, too. But then, you always were reliably selfish." He held out a hand to Selly and she ran to him, not at all too proud to let him gather her under one arm and shield her from his horrible mother with his body. "Are you all right?" he murmured, searching her face.

"Unharmed," she reassured him, her heart full to bursting. Though she'd never doubted that he'd come for her, she was overwhelmed that he had, that he'd climbed up the house to get to her. "How are you here already?"

"I hurried," he replied drily. "I was motivated," he amended. "Helpful of you to have the house create a way in for me."

Before she could reply that she hadn't done it on purpose—though it occurred to her that the house might have known exactly what it was doing—Jadren gave her a long, almost desperately rough kiss, drawing deeply of her magic, then broke it off abruptly, raising his head to focus on Lady El-Adrel with glittering intent. "Don't do it, Maman," he said in a lethal voice. "Or the next dart goes in your throat."

"You can't harm me."

"Oh, but I *can*," he said with easy confidence, "or shall I demonstrate how I killed Ozana?"

"Ozana was careless," Katica retorted, but Selly caught cold fear momentarily flashing through the woman's haughty poise, the wariness of the scientist confronting their own invention and knowing they'd lost control of what they'd wrought.

"Are you *sure*?" Jadren purred, menace in every line of his body. "Maybe Ozana simply wasn't aware of what you'd created when you sent her after me. You're always so meticulous with keeping your secrets, particularly regarding me, playing your cards so close to the vest. I'll bet you sent Ozana after her little brother to drag him home by the ear without ever telling her that the puppy she remembered had grown into a rabid dog capable of savaging her without notice."

Katica looked, more than anything else, weirdly fascinated. She certainly showed no signs of grief or remorse over her deceased daughter. A monster incapable of love was how Jadren had once described his mother, and Selly believed it. "How did you kill her?" his mother asked in a tone of professional interest that didn't at all disguise her burning need to know.

"Just used what you gave me," Jadren replied lightly, "and no, I'm not giving you any free information. Didn't your Elal spies report on what they saw of our little altercation?"

Lady El-Adrel wavered, seeming torn. "Spies?"

"If it helps," Jadren said cheerfully, "you should know that we are well aware of your clandestine collaborations with House Elal. You're not giving anything away there by admitting it."

Making a moue, she dismissed that with a wave of her hand. "I admit nothing. Besides, you have no proof to take to the Convocation."

"Who said anything about bringing the Convocation into this?" Jadren shot back smoothly. "This is between you and me. You asked how I killed Ozana and I asked what you knew already."

"Then you admit murdering your sister."

"Self-defense."

Katica stared him down, but Jadren said nothing more. She tossed her hair back, raising her artfully groomed brows. "She appeared to have been vaporized. How did you accomplish that?"

"What is that knowledge worth to you, Lady El-Adrel?" Jadren returned smoothly.

"Worth to me?" Katica sounded so astounded, she nearly sputtered, and Selly was hard-pressed to keep a gloating smile from her face. She didn't know what had gotten into Jadren that he'd gained this new confidence in standing up to his domineering parent, but she wanted to applaud. And shower him with kisses. And more.

"If you want to know how I killed Ozana, how I restored Seliah's beautiful hair," Jadren continued, glancing at Selly and running a proprietary hand over the curls that dangled down her back, before looking back at his mother and shrugging, "well, it seems we have some negotiating to do. You might begin by deciding how much this knowledge is worth to you."

She stiffened, nose wrinkling into a snarl. "I am *Lady El-Adrel*," she informed him, serene face creasing into harsh lines, her magic boiling in the air like molten metal. "You belong to me, both of you, and you will do as I tell you to do. There will be no *negotiating*." She spat the word with distaste.

Jadren wagged a finger at her, still holding Selly close under his other arm. "Ah ah ah, Maman. This isn't information you can extort from me. No amount of torture—even if I were to allow you to imprison either of us again, which I won't—

will extract the knowledge you crave. And isn't that what you want more than anything in all the world? Don't you long to know what you created when you made me?"

~ 9 ~

His mother clearly wanted to know, every line of her body vibrating with barely restrained, conflicting desires. Jadren apparently did know his mother as well as she knew him—perhaps even better. All those years of being her experimental animal, that perversely intimate sharing of pain and suffering, had given him key insights into his tormenter's mind. Perhaps it was no brilliant insight to know that Katica El-Adrel would give almost anything—maybe even anything at all—to realize her lifelong ambitions, but it was enough to give him what he needed to manipulate her.

A fucking epiphany, right there. No one would write books of philosophy on the profundity of his discovery, but epiphanies could be personal and this one would change his life. More important, it would change Seliah's.

"Fine," his dear maman finally ground out. "What do you want?"

"What are you offering?"

"I can't imagine what I have to offer that you could want," she answered haughtily, the game well and truly afoot.

"Can't you?" He tsked at her again, mostly because it was so fun to see it enrage her. "Imagine harder." He stroked a hand down Seliah's back. "I'm thirsty. Are you thirsty? Let's pour some wine. It's looking like this will take a while."

"I'd be happy to ring for that," Seliah said brightly, taking his cue with her usual alert wit. "Unfortunately, I don't have any refreshments here. I hope that the relocated apartments won't give the staff trouble in finding the way."

He tamped down on the instant anger, sliding his maman a black look. "You didn't see fit to feed Seliah?"

She glared back defiantly, which was good. Defiance meant Katica was on the defensive. "I'm Lady El-Adrel," she snapped. "It's beneath my notice to track when familiars are fed and watered."

"Then let's put that at the top of my list of what I want," he replied in the same tone. "Go arrange for food and drink. Then we'll negotiate."

"In exchange for what?" she asked cannily. "I need something, offered in good faith, to agree to continue."

"In exchange for us not climbing out of this window right now and leaving," he answered. He looked Seliah over. She looked gorgeous in the pretty, sapphire blue gown embroidered with glittering black lightning bolts, but it was hardly practical. And those House Blahnik heels were great as a come-fuck-me invitation—a summons he burned to accept, feeling as if she'd been torn from him for days—but not for shimmying down the ever-changing landscape of the house.

"I can manage," she told him, reading his thoughts as usual and bending to unbuckle the straps of the fancy heels, kicking them off. "I like going barefoot, as you know."

"I know." Overwhelmed with affection for his half-feral

love, he pulled her close, giving her a lingering kiss, delighting in her passionate yielding. All along the frantic ride from Refoel to El-Adrel, he'd fretted over how Seliah would greet him. He hadn't worried about his awful mother harming her, nor about any of his gut-deep terrors of returning to the house of his birth. No, all that had mattered was whether he'd pissed Seliah off finally and forever. Instead, it seemed that, as always, she forgave him his transgressions. He deepened the kiss, drinking in her quiet sounds of ardent response, considering telling her to put those shoes back on—and take off everything else.

"Oh, dark arts save me!" his maman exclaimed. "Shall I leave you two alone?"

"That would be grand, thanks," he answered without bothering to look at her. "And send up those refreshments." He bent to renew the kiss, but Seliah put a hand on his chest, gently stopping him, her amber eyes warm with desire and amusement.

"Later," she cautioned him. "I haven't seen Fyrdo yet."

That was enough to yank his attention back to the matter at hand, a metaphorical dousing with cold water. He threw his mother an equally chilly glare. "Where is my father?"

Katica pasted on a vague smile, fluttering her fingers in the air. "Around here somewhere..." She pretended to ponder, tapping one pointed nail against her lower lip. "Though, now that you mention it, I haven't seen him flitting about for some time." Her mien hardened to a sharp edge, all playacting dropped. "The traitor."

Seliah's distress tumbled through her magic, clouding the

bright moonlight and ruffling the deep waters. He felt the same.

"Let's start there then," Jadren said. "I want to see my father, and have a conversation with him," he added, thinking of Lord Elal's evil revenge on his familiar for a similar betrayal, keeping her in her alternate form until her identity dissolved, and hoping that his dear maman hadn't taken a page from that book.

Katica smiled in truth, thinking she possessed the upper hand again. She'd be wrong, but he let her think that for the moment. "I agree to your request, in exchange for information. How did you kill Ozana?"

"I used my healing magic," he replied, keeping it concise and knowing that tidbit would only incite her curiosity further.

"How? Explain," she demanded, and he rolled his eyes.

"That's all you get until I talk with Fyrdo." Seliah stirred under his arm. "Until we both do," he clarified.

Oh, his maman hated this, clearly longing to pitch them both off the balcony at their backs. He'd have to be very careful in how he strung her along. Once she figured she'd extracted every bit of data from him, Lady El-Adrel would have her vengeance for his temerity and it would be terrible, indeed. He'd have to make sure Seliah was well out of her reach by then. Perhaps himself, too, if he could manage it.

"Fine," his mother ground out, dragging the word over broken glass. "Come with me."

"I find I'm tired after that climb, not to mention riding all night to chase after my familiar." Jadren faked a yawn. "Bring my father here. We can all have a nice family lunch, after I have a nap."

Katica visibly fumed, her magic so jagged in the air that Jadren half-expected to be fried by lightning bolts. "There are limits to what I will tolerate from you," she warned him.

"No doubt," he agreed, very aware of the risk he ran. "But it seems we haven't found them yet. Now run along. Fetch."

She glared at him a moment longer, white-hot with fury, then spun on her heel and stalked out.

Seliah sagged against him. "Was that wise?" she asked, tipping up her face. "If you taunt her too far, she'll do anything to get her piece of flesh back."

"I'm sorry," he told her, feeling as if his chest might crack open with the sheer relief at embracing his beloved again. He pulled Seliah close, holding her far too tightly and unable to make himself let go, or even relax the tiniest amount.

"You don't have to be sorry," she said, breathless. "It was entertaining to witness, I just worry that your mother will—"

"Not that." At least interrupting Seliah's absurd misapprehension broke through his paralysis and he took her by the shoulders, staring into her peculiarly beautiful face. "I'm sorry I was an ass. I'm sorry I lost my temper and goaded you and Liat, that I said that shitty stuff about red-misting rodents. Even though I pretty much hate all rodents, they don't deserve that, and you definitely didn't deserve me behaving so badly and—"

"Jadren," she broke in gently, framing his face in her palms, lightly stroking his cheekbones with her fingertips in a soothing caress that went right through him, her water and moon magic cooling his ashen edges. "It's all right. You had a bad day is all."

"That's not all." He lifted his hands to grip her wrists, though he didn't pry her hands away. Couldn't make himself step away any more than he'd ever been able to leave her alone. "If I hadn't been so self-indulgent, having a temper tantrum instead of working to learn, you wouldn't have been alone to be captured like this and—"

"*Jadren*," she broke in again, with more emphasis, smiling a little through her obvious exasperation. "They'd been watching me, watching us, and simply waited for the opportunity. It was sheer coincidence that I was alone because of that terrible session. They could have grabbed me at any point. Fyrdo even warned us in that letter, with that line about transportation being closer than we realized."

"I thought of that, too," he told her ruefully. "Too late to do any good. If I had realized, I wouldn't have left you so vulnerable."

"Need I remind you that *I* am the one who stormed out of our session? I lost my temper—do you hold me to blame?"

"Yes," he told her, trying to look angry.

She blinked, taken aback, then sharpened her gaze. "You do not."

"I do blame you," he insisted. Dark arts how he loved this woman. "More, I think you need to be punished. A spanking should do the trick."

"Jadren!" she shrieked as he swept her up and carried her into the bedroom, struggling, but not fighting him with her wildcat strength as he knew she could if she wanted to. "You said you're tired from riding all night."

"An excuse to get rid of my mother. I'm feeling quite frisky."

"Well, she'll be back any moment."

"Not even close," he assured her, sitting on the bed and draping her over his lap. "Besides, the house likes you. Tell it to delay her until I'm done with you." He pinned her with a firm hand on her lower back, dragging up the frothy skirts to reveal the pretty Ophiel lingerie barely covering Seliah's perfect ass, made all the more enticing by her delightful squirming and kicking.

"I can't do that," she protested. "I—" Whatever she'd been about to say cut off with a yelp of shock as he smacked that lovely behind, leaving a satisfying handprint behind on her creamy skin. "Jadren," she breathed raggedly as he ran a caressing hand over that hot mark, unbearably stirred by the sight of his imprint on her. "Please." She wriggled against his caressing hand, her sex burning against his thigh.

"Please what?" he asked, his voice hoarse. She was right—they didn't have time for this, but he wanted her too much to stop.

"Ward the door," she said, going lax and languid over his lap, even lifting her bottom in wordless entreaty.

"Excellent idea." Later they would discuss how she'd gotten the house to modify itself for her. Replete with her water and moonlight, their magic burgeoning together with the erotic play—the perfect rationalization for indulging himself this way—he threw up wards on the door and the windows to the wrap-around balcony, belatedly realizing why his maman had been so shocked by his arrival over the balcony rail. The house had been thoroughly warded against ingress, layers and layers of enchantments over the years preventing anyone from entering without the current head of the house knowing and giving permission. Somehow, in accommodating Seliah's wishes, the house had also willfully shed those barriers to allow him in.

The realization filled him with exhilaration. Things were looking up. In celebration, he smacked Seliah's vulnerable bottom several times in succession, thrilling to her excited moans of encouragement. "I should have punished you like this sooner," he said, dragging the lacy panties down her thighs to expose all of her to his gaze. "You're mine to do with as I please, aren't you?"

She made an incoherent sound of agreement, fingers digging into the coverlet as she pressed her face into the bed. He spanked her several more times, loving how each stinging slap made her melt against him. Unable to deny himself any longer, he slipped his fingers into the crevice between her thighs, finding her hot and slick to the touch, and she cried out, clenching against him. With a consuming shudder, she orgasmed, her paler bottom flexing in the frame of the deep blue ruffles of the skirt. He knew her body now, knew how to prolong the pleasure, milking the climax so that she cried out several more times, her movements increasingly frenzied.

As the last climax wracked her, he stood, carrying her with him and dropping her on her back, bare legs dangling over the edge of the bed, the dress rucked up around her waist, the lacy panties still trapped around her long thighs. She held up her arms to draw him in.

He pointed at her. "Don't move."

She gazed up at him in heated, bleary confusion, amber eyes dark with passion. "What—where are you going?"

He retrieved those sexy heels from the other room, picking up Seliah's feet and propping one foot against his thigh as he buckled the straps onto her other foot. She watched him in bemusement. "I like these shoes," he told her. "Only good thing Maman has ever done." He licked the insole of her foot, arched and exposed by the multiple straps, rewarded by her gasp of erotic response.

Fastening the other shoe on her, he drank in the spectacle before him, Seliah's dark hair in disarray, tumbling over the bed, her eyes nearly gold as she lay splayed in the gown, naked from the waist down, her knees drawn up, endless legs finishing in those shoes that had been whispering for him to come fuck her the moment he saw them. Considering, he bent one of her knees, drawing the panties down over the shoe, freeing her legs, letting the lacy garment dangle around her other ankle.

"You might as well take them off entirely," she whispered, shivering under his hands.

"Don't argue with the artist," he told her. "This is how I want you."

She nodded, even though he hadn't asked a question, trembling as he slowly and deliberately parted her thighs, her swollen sex opening to his avid gaze. Groaning, he released her one leg, allowing her to find a comfortable position for it, and freed his cock. Still gripping her other ankle, the one decorated by her sensual, soaked lingerie, he gradually bent her leg until the panty-decorated shoe and foot were near her head. "Is this all right?" he asked, though she was a flexible thing.

She licked her lips and nodded again. "I feel very exposed."

"Good. I'm going to penetrate to the depths of you. You'll be hiding nothing from me."

Guilt flickered dark across her face. "Jadren, I—"

He stopped her with a kiss. "Later. Right now, there is only this. I missed you."

She gazed up at him, amber eyes misty with emotion. "I missed you."

"Good," he breathed. Positioning his achingly hard cock, he slid into her, hiking her knee even higher. She gasped as he buried himself deep inside her sheath, her muscles gripping him like the hands she vised onto his hips. "Too much?" He was panting from restraint, but uncertain if she meant to stop him or urge him on. "I know it's deep."

"So deep," she answered on a released breath. "So good. More."

She whimpered a little as he pulled back, making him smile and press a kiss to the arch of her foot, then pushed in, using his other hand to lift her hips, positioning her to take him even deeper. She made a guttural sound, breathing ragged, so he gave her a moment, sucking her big toe into his mouth—as far as the shoe allowed—while he waited.

"I didn't know you were so into shoes," she said, whiskey-voice, shuddering beneath him.

"Oh, Seliah," he replied, nipping her toe so she squeaked and undulated around him, her inner muscles spasming, "you have no idea."

She started to laugh, then gasped as he withdrew slightly and slammed home, her cries becoming screams of pleasure. From then it was all frenzy, the two of them tearing at each other, all finesse lost. He screamed, also, when she sank her teeth into his shoulder, her nails raking his ass as she dragged the leathers off his hips. He drove into her, deep and desperate, savoring her orgasms until he could restrain himself no longer, emptying himself into her with a strangled cry of completion, collapsing there, his face in her hair, their hearts thundering against each other, cradled in the embrace of her sinuous body and bright, quenching magic.

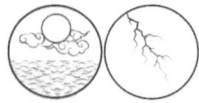

"IT'S GOOD TO see you again, too," she said, a while later, her voice throaty, her breathing no longer so frantic.

Laughing softly, he turned his face, finding the soft hollow under jaw first, thus kissing her there. "I love you, Seliah. With everything in me, I love you. You should know that."

She caught her breath. "Is this a prelude to another good-bye?"

He lifted his head, managing to lever himself up onto his elbows, so he could look into her eyes. "No. Why would you ask that?"

"It's a pattern with you," she answered drily, though with raw vulnerability beneath. "You only say nice things to me before you leave."

"You left me this time," he pointed out, still bleeding a bit inside from that moment of finding her gone.

"Not on purpose!" she protested, bucking beneath him.

Interlacing his fingers with hers, he pinned her to the bed. "Never leave me again, Seliah. Voluntarily or otherwise. I can't bear to be without you."

Stilling, she gazed up at him. "You mean that."

"With all my heart, if I had one that wasn't a shriveled husk."

"I guess you really *do* like these shoes," she said gravely, her eyes sparkling with amusement.

"Well, yes." He traced the elegant length of her thigh. "But you should know this is more than sex. I don't know how to love anyone, but I'm willing to learn if you'll teach me. I'll learn anything you want me to, putting you in alternate form, whatever. Just promise to be mine, always."

"I promise," she said, a secret smile curving her lips. "If you promise to be mine, always."

"I already am," he told her, shivering internally from the raw intimacy of it all, "but I promise anyway."

"Good." Her smile widened. "Because I love you Jadren El-Adrel. And I think you do a fine job of loving me already. High scores for your potential in love."

Breathing a laugh, relieved more than he could have anticipated, he kissed her, savoring her sweet yielding, the cool magic such a silvery counterpoint to her heated, sensual mouth. "Maman has been banging on the wards a while now," he told Seliah ruefully. "I suppose we should let her in."

Seliah's amber eyes went wide. "Jadren, why didn't you say

so?"

She began wiggling in earnest, stopping when he kissed her again. "This was more important. I want you to understand that—that this, you, is more important than anything else. I know I'm not the wizard you would have chosen, but you will always be first for me."

"You're wrong," she said, making his heart stutter. "You *are* the wizard I chose. The one I'll choose again and again and again."

"Thank you," he said, unbearably moved, unable to think of a better reply.

She laughed. "Now, let me up. I have to put myself to rights or she'll know what we've been doing."

Levering himself to his feet he offered her a hand up, helping her arrange the folds of her gown. "I think they'll know anyway. Here, let me." Turning her around, he picked at the fastenings holding her hair in the elaborate style, triggering them so they fell to the floor, her cascading locks tumbling free. Surveying her critically as she turned back around, combing her fingers through the coiling mass, he nodded in satisfaction. "You look like a feral creature in a fancy dress and smoking hot heels. Perfect."

Rolling her eyes, she seized his face in her hands and kissed him hard, nipping his lower lip enough to sting. "Dark arts only know why I love you saying such things to me."

"Questionable judgement, no doubt." He watched her ruck up the hem of the dress again as she looked about. "What are you doing now?"

She gave him the side-eye. "I'm dripping under here. I need

a cloth."

He stopped her with a hand on her arm. "You could leave it."

"Under other, sexier circumstances, I might. But if you're going to battle your mother, I'd like my concentration on that, thank you very much."

Freezing at that daunting suggestion, he gave Seliah a thorough perusal as she found a cloth and cleaned herself. A fetching sight, if he hadn't been rigid with terror. "Poppet," he said slowly, "I told you: I can't fight my mother."

"Jadren, darling." She came to him and kissed him, giving him a radiant smile. "You already are."

~ IO ~

SELLY WAS ABSURDLY happy, all things considered. She wasn't sure to what to ascribe Jadren's sudden willingness to talk about his feelings for her—to actually tell *her* he loved her, as opposed to telling everyone *but* her—since this wasn't the first time they'd faced the possibility of losing one another, but she wasn't going to look this gift horse in the mouth. She already knew the relative health of this steed, to extend the analogy, and she knew his worth.

More important, she finally saw a scenario where she could be honest with him about the bond-severing. She no longer worried—as much—that he'd jump on the knowledge that their bond could be severed in order to escape her. Or to do right by her. He didn't want to be parted from her and she could depend on Jadren's selfishness to win out over his occasional and absurd noble impulses. *Never leave me again. I can't bear to be without you.*

She hugged the words to her, tucking them inside a special pocket of her memory to keep with her always. She would have to tell him the truth of the bond-severing, eventually. As soon as they were clear of the current situation, she would. And it would all be fine. Now simply wasn't the right time.

He'd be annoyed with her, and they'd have to fight about it, no doubt, but it would work out. She wasn't putting it off so much as choosing the right timing.

That's what she told herself.

Holding Jadren's hand, she smiled at him and he smiled back, an echo of that erotic intimacy in his expression still. Yes, this was good and who could blame her for wanting to enjoy the relative happiness of the moment?

"Ready for the next battle?" he asked.

"Ready, general." She saluted smartly with her free hand, making him chuckle. "And you," she tendered, "are you ready to face your mother again?"

His entire demeanor hardened. "I'm tired of being afraid of her. Tired of her controlling all of us. I finally have some leverage over her, so I'm levering for all I'm worth. Wish me luck."

"What do you plan to do?" Trepidation filtered through her happiness, like cold rain turning a golden autumn day to chill gray.

"Whatever I have to do." He turned toward the outer door, raising his free hand to cancel the warding on it with a decisive gesture. As soon as he dropped his hand, the door flung open, revealing Katica El-Adrel, glowering in temper and seeming taller than ever. A bearded goat on a gold leash trotted beside her.

"Fyrdo," Selly breathed.

"Stop fucking around, Maman." Jadren's voice cracked out like a whip. "Bring him back to human form so we can have a conversation, as agreed, or I will doubt your commitment to further negotiations."

She simpered. "Whatever do you mean? I never agreed to putting Fyrdo back into human form."

Selly gaped, an odd sense of dislocation making her feel as if the ground shifted under her feet. Unless that was the house? No, she didn't think so. She just hadn't ever seen someone lie so baldly. She wanted to point it out, to declaim Lady El-Adrel for a liar, but Jadren—no doubt sensing Selly's outrage— squeezed her hand.

"Then it appears we're done here," Jadren said flatly.

"Not at all, Jaddy boy." Katica scratched between the goat's little horns and the pretty creature leaned against her thigh with all evidence of real affection. "I'm happy to return your father to human form, so you can talk about whatever you wish, though I'm sure you must know that being a brilliant conversationalist is not his forte. As soon as you tell me what I want to know." Her disdainful gaze raked Selly, her nose wrinkled as if she could smell the sex on her. "After all, you had your fun, making me wait. Now you pay the price."

"Come on, Seliah," Jadren said, ignoring his mother. "We're leaving."

Playing along, Selly nodded, and bent to unbuckle the shoes again.

"Allow me," Jadren said, crouching to do it himself, wrapping caressing fingers around her calf and ankle, looking up at her with an intimate and knowing smile.

"So much for your supposed desire to speak with your father," Katica sneered, clearly casting about for a hook to plant in Jadren that would stay put long enough for her to reel him in. "Your loyalty to and affection for him are weak, indeed." She snorted. "Of course, you always were a randy thing, unable to control where your dick led you."

Selly felt her face heating at the injustice of that insult. Even though she knew full well Katica was baiting Jadren, for her to say that about the effects of Jadren's self-healing, which his mother had used to manipulate him in ways that still gave him nightmares, was an exceptionally low blow.

Jadren didn't so much as glance at his mother, didn't even twitch. "I cannot control what you do with your familiar. Since you are refusing to cooperate, to negotiate in good faith so I can talk with my father, I have no other choice but to walk away. Forever."

"I forbid you to leave," Lady El-Adrel declared.

"Sorry to inform you: your orders mean nothing to me." He finished unbuckling the other heel and uncoiled gracefully to offer a hand to Selly, steadying her as she stepped out of the shoes. Finally, he looked at his mother. "We're leaving."

"I can stop you."

"You're welcome to try," he replied with silky menace. "Permit me to remind you how easily I dispatched Ozana. Do you truly want to risk me doing the same to you?"

Her fingers whitened, gripping the goat's leash. The goat danced with uneasy concern. "I'm your *mother*."

"Believe me, I'm well aware."

"You would never harm me."

"That's where you're wrong, *dear* Maman." Jadren's words sliced out, sharp and ruthless. "Have you forgotten how much pain you've given me? Anything I did to you would be a drop in the ocean compared to the cruelty you've rained down upon me my entire life."

Katica drew herself up, more rattled than Selly had ever imagined she could be. "You know very well that everything I did was to make you better, to refine and hone your magic. Sacrifices are often necessary for great breakthroughs."

Jadren shook his head, expression flat. "Even if I could forgive what you did to me, I can never forgive what you did to Fyrdo, to Seliah."

"They were simply incidental to what I hoped to accomplish with you," she replied almost desperately. "What I *did* accomplish! You can wreak destruction like no other wizard in the Convocation. Perhaps in all of Convocation history. You are unprecedented. Because of *me*. You should be on your knees thanking me for what I've done for you."

"I never wanted this, Maman," Jadren said, his voice hushed, shaking with emotion. "I don't want to be a killing machine, a monster."

"You are not a monster," she spat back. "You are the next stage of evolution, of something greater and better. You're a bleeding fool if you can't recognize that."

"I'm done with this conversation. Goodbye, Lady El-Adrel." He turned to the open balcony doors, guiding Selly with a hand on her back. It trembled, and she wanted more than anything to comfort him, knowing she couldn't because he wouldn't want to display any sign of weakness.

"I'll just bring you back," his mother warned. "And the next time, I'll simply lock you both in the testing cages rather than wasting my breath giving you the courtesy of treating you like family. It hurts me, wounds me to the quick, that my own child would be so ungrateful."

Jadren paused, his back to her. "Think very carefully about putting this viper to your breast. If you come after us again, I will decimate your house. Understand that this is within my power. I will lay waste to everyone in it, including you."

"Including your father?" she taunted. "Because I'll make sure he dies before I do."

Jadren glanced over his shoulder. "Better dead than stuck as a goat for the rest of his life."

"Oh, for the sake of the dark arts!" Katica huffed. "Fine. So much fuss over nothing. You always were stubborn about the wrong things. Talk to him, if it's so important to you." Her magic flashed, an immaterial lightning bolt momentarily eclipsing the daylight, and Fyrdo appeared, fully clothed in a suit that matched his wizard's, his auburn hair as bright as his son's, though somewhat disarrayed, his expression flustered.

"What..." He looked around, spotted Jadren and Selly. "Jadren! Seliah... It's so good to see you both, but... how?" Starting toward them with open arms, he halted at Katica's hiss of warning. Visibly pulling himself together, he turned his attention to Lady El-Adrel, who eyed him with a decidedly jaundiced look. "My love, my wizard," he gushed, "how may I serve you?"

The change in Fyrdo from concerned—and overjoyed—father to obsequious servant set Selly's teeth on edge, but she held her tongue. Jadren had a plan to play out this little scene and she wouldn't disrupt it.

"Our son wishes to have a conversation with you," Katica

said, making it sound as if Jadren wanted to confer with worms, as if he hadn't just won a significant contest of wills with her for the privilege. She seemed intent on behaving as if nothing of note had occurred. "So: converse." She waved a hand in noblesse oblige. "Shall I call for tea?"

"The terms were that I talk with him alone," Jadren specified. "You can wait outside."

"I'll do no such thing. I never agreed to that."

"Maman," Jadren said with withering patience, "you seem to be unclear on your tenuous position in this negotiation. I have what I want; I have the power to keep it. There is nothing you can give me, nothing you can promise to entice me to give you further information. You are standing here on my sufferance, which is waning rapidly."

"You can't speak to me this way." Katica El-Adrel's face had gone ashen, pinched with strain, all pretense vanished, her magic so fierce in the air around them that Selly felt like her eyes would start watering, and she had to suppress the urge to cover her ears. "I won't stand for it," Katica continued, wizard-black eyes like pits in her sharp, white face. "I'm tempted to call you on your bluff, wizardling."

"It's no bluff." Jadren faced his mother fully, placing Selly behind him, guiding her hand to his waist. Right, she needed to be the one keeping contact with him, ready to provide him with magic. Good thing she was full to bursting from their erotic play. "I'm willing to go to extremes to free myself of you, Maman," he said without inflection, "but can you say the same—are you willing to risk losing your most successful experiment?

"I made you. I can make another like you."

Jadren made a show of wincing. "Ooh, thank you for playing, but that's not an option."

"You don't tell me, little boy," Katica sneered. "I make the rules. I have others like you, very promising. Better, in fact, not such a disappointment in every way."

Others? Did Jadren have younger siblings he didn't know about? Fyrdo fixed his gaze on the floor, giving no sign he'd heard or understood.

"Upon my life," Jadren replied steadily, "I vow you'll never have the opportunity to warp anyone else's life like you did mine." Beside her, Jadren had slipped his hand beneath his leather vest, apparently in a gesture of putting his hand over his heart in solemn promise—or threat—but Selly knew he had the widget poised, inverted to channel death rather than healing. Through their physical connection and the bond, he drew on her magic. Not heavily, more to widen the channel between them, preparing to pull the power necessary for a devastating blow. Though she dreaded what might happen next, Selly obligingly opened her end, giving him whatever he needed.

If he needed to kill his mother, then so be it.

Katica, no fool, didn't miss Jadren's movement. "You think to use your new tricks on *me*? Something the Refoel healers taught you, no doubt. I have news for you, baby boy: you can't heal someone to death."

"What do you think I did to Ozana?"

That penetrated her cool confidence, giving her a moment's pause. "You had to have used some sort of enchanted artifact. Your healing magic works only on yourself—and it can't be weaponized."

"Try me," Jadren replied flatly. "Or are you afraid to?"

Fyrdo, still confused from being in alternate form, looked back and forth between the squared off wizards. "What is going on?" he asked, plaintive, not at all like his formerly robust and jolly self.

"Oh, you are going to regret challenging me," Katica cooed to Jadren, ignoring Fyrdo. She raised her hands and her magic. Small darts peeled themselves out of the beaded lightning bolts of Lady El-Adrel's glamourous pantsuit, swarming around her, transformed and elevated by her wizardry, pivoting midair to point directly at Selly, a glittering golden arrow of death by pain. Selly knew those darts well. Once they contacted flesh— her flesh—they burrowed in, spiraling to organs and bones, shredding everything in their path, killing her by agonizing increments. Katica met Selly's gaze and smiled. "You remember these, don't you, pet? They hurt. Then they kill you. And I won't summon a healer for you this time. It's in my best interests to let you die. Jadren has only gotten uppity since I gifted you to him." Her lip curled. "I should have known he'd be ungrateful."

"Stay behind me," Jadren told her quietly. He didn't need to tell her twice. Selly was happy to put the bulk of him between her and those awful darts.

Katica tracked the movement, naturally. "Don't imagine he cares about you. He's only using you. He'll sacrifice you to get to me, drain you dry and discard you without a backward look. Hasn't he proved that to you? Abandoned you, as no wizard ever does with their familiar. Failed to protect you. You might imagine you care about him, but that's only the bond. Save yourself and step away from him. Remove yourself from the line of fire."

"So you can kill me anyway?" Selly replied, her voice surprisingly steady.

"Kill you?" Katica shook that off, giving Selly a very serious look. "Not if I don't have to. With my son dead, you'll be unbonded. You're a valuable familiar, a precious asset to House El-Adrel. Come with me and I'll find you a better wizard. Someone whole, not crippled with self-doubt. Someone with *real* magic. Someone educated, who knows how to give you what you crave as a familiar. You need discipline, a firm hand, and I can see to it that you have it. Now is your opportunity to show your loyalty to the house of your bonding."

"Loyalty?" Selly repeated incredulously. She moved closer against Jadren's back, putting them into more physical contact, trying to show him without words that she didn't believe any of it. "Such a dry word. But then, you don't understand love, do you? Well, I do, because I come from a normal, healthy family. People who actually know the meaning of the word. Even before we were bonded, I loved Jadren. I would die for him." This close to Jadren, she felt his intake of breath, the brightening of his magic. She didn't understand his surprise at her declaration, however. He'd known how she felt.

Katica sniffed in disdain. "Oh, dear. You really aren't terribly bright. I hadn't realized until this moment the true depths of your idiocy. You've backed a losing horse. You're ignorant of the Convocation, so you don't understand how powerful a high-house wizard truly is. Jadren is barely capable of the basics. He can't protect you from me, even if he manages to pull his head out of his ass long enough to even try. He's never been able to stand up to me."

"You forget, Maman," Jadren put in quietly, "that I've made no promise this time to allow you to use your wizardry on us. I have us both warded."

"Your pitiful wards can't hold up against me," she replied, shaking her head in mock sorrow. "But it's precious that you're trying." Without warning, the golden darts shot forward, a blur of motion, fast as lightning. Selly flinched, unable to prevent the reflexive need to duck. She managed to hold firm, however, just as Nic and then Liat had taught her. That repetitive training worked, it turned out, force of habit overriding her instinctive terror.

Jadren hadn't bluffed, though Selly hadn't sensed his wards going up. The darts collided with the invisible, curved surface in a flurry of eye-blinding gold sparks before glancing off. She wanted to jump in triumph, perhaps throw a rude gesture at the wizard woman, but Jadren's intensity didn't lessen an iota. By this, she understood this duel was far from over. Confirming it, the darts assembled again in a lethal aura around Katica, nearly vibrating in the wedge formation as they adjusted slightly mid-air, all pointing at Selly. With the open balcony at her back, she had nowhere to go, and Jadren's lanky body could shield her only so much.

"So, you've learned a few tricks, after all," Katica breathed on a disdainful laugh. "But it will take more than a midlevel wizard's wards to withstand *me*. Or have you forgotten who I am?"

Jadren laughed in the same way, humorless, shimmering with similar power. "Oh, dear Maman, I've forgotten nothing. Do your worst. Nothing can eclipse what you've already done. I have literally nothing to lose." Though Jadren came by his coloring from Fyrdo, for the first time Selly clearly saw his mother's stamp on him. The same clean-boned intensity, the bow of their finely carved lips and their wizard-black eyes, alike in shape and magic. The way Jadren always said a monster lurked inside him; the monster so obviously inside Katica. Maybe it had nothing to do with magic and everything to do with ruthless use of power.

"My worst it is. Fyrdo, to me," Katica snapped out.

Fyrdo wavered, looking back and forth between his wizard and son. He rubbed his forehead, in the spots where those little horns had been. "Jadren? Are you really here? I told you to run, to never come back, when I—"

"Father," Jadren interrupted, preventing Fyrdo from confessing his role in their previous escape, just in case Katica didn't already know everything. "Are you all right? We're here to help you."

Katica hissed like a snake. "You don't have permission to speak to my familiar!" The darts flew at them again, drilling into the wards, visibly slowing as if meeting molten glass, sparks flying. Jadren pulled on Selly's moon magic only, separating it from the water magic—which Selly hadn't realized he'd found a way to do—chilling and thickening the wards, the darts slowing nearly to a halt, embedded in the shield like beads on a gown, the "fabric" of the wards undulating under the onslaught of Lady El-Adrel's magic. "Fyrdo!" Her voice resonated with command, making the man startle, then shiver all over as if he still had fur, an uncanny sight. "I gave you an order."

And yet, Fyrdo still managed to resist, gazing around the room and blinking as if trying to focus his eyes. Nic's maman had been like that, too, after being too long in alternate form. Her eyes never changed back to normal. Selly didn't know what a goat's vision was like, but certainly different than human. "I like the new windows," Fyrdo said, drifting in that direction. "So pretty."

"Familiar Fyrdo." Katica's voice dropped in dire warning. *"To me."* One of the darts undrilled itself from the shield, zipping out to bury itself in Fyrdo's shoulder.

He yipped and jumped, whirling to give his wizard a wounded look, like a puppy unfairly punished. "Why?" he asked, no longer sounding quite so plaintive, a hint of demand in it.

"You're better trained than this," Katica informed him coolly. "To me, Familiar. I have need of you."

Even though the command wasn't directed at Selly, the ritual words impacted her on a deep level, both erotic and emotional, making her want to kneel and offer everything, and gladly. Keyed into the bonding then, a connection forged by magic and that could be severed by magic. Was this what she meant about familiars craving a firm hand and discipline? Because this felt good, on a deep and foreign level. Fyrdo shuddered, taking a step toward Katica, longing in every line of him, grief in his eyes.

"That's it," she purred. "Good boy. Come to me and I'll reward you."

Encouraged by Fyrdo's acquiescence, Lady El-Adrel increased her magic, the darts sending up a high-pitched whine as she used her power more lavishly to drill through Jadren's wards.

He pulled more magic from Selly, still judiciously, but a stronger draw than before. She understood without him telling her, just how precarious their situation was. Jadren would need her magic to deal the killing blow—a great deal of it, but neither of them knew precisely how much—and if he bled off too much maintaining the wards, they might fail in this ultimate confrontation. At which point they'd be defenseless, at the mercy of an enraged Katica El-Adrel. If Fyrdo touched his wizard, she would have access to all of his magic. As Jadren had dourly predicted, he likely couldn't win against his mother with the full power of her familiar at hand.

"Dad," Jadren said, an edge of desperation to his voice that Selly hoped only she could hear. He'd come to the same realization. More likely, he was way ahead of her. "Don't go to her. Come to me. I'll protect you."

Katica let out a hoot of laughter. "He can't protect you. He can't even protect his own familiar. Besides," she added, her voice cajoling, a smile caressing Fyrdo with such intimacy that Selly felt intrusive to have witnessed it, "you're mine, Fyrdo. You know it in your bones. You belong by *my* side. You love me, most and best."

Fyrdo gave Jadren an agonized look, even as Katica's

strumming of the bond to her familiar vibrated into Selly's bones. How Fyrdo withstood that enchanted summons, she didn't know. This was entirely new to her, this deliberate pulling on the bond to elicit a familiar's obedience. Gabriel would never do that to Nic, if he even knew how. She wanted to ask Jadren if he knew how to do this—though she doubted he would either—but she didn't dare risk breaking his concentration.

"Don't harm our son," Fyrdo pleaded with Katica. "I'll come to you, if you agree not to injure him."

Katica put on an expression so aghast, so utterly shocked and crushingly disappointed, that even though Selly knew it to be theatrics, she cringed internally along with Fyrdo. Sparks flew dense as fog as the darts drilled deeper into the shield, coming ever closer to their faces, and Selly fancied she smelled smoke. "Fyrdo," Katica growled, "you forget your place. You do not make bargains with me. You have one job: obey. *Now do it!*"

The wizard loaded so much power of command into those final three words that Fyrdo fell to his knees, clasping his hands to his bowed head, as if battling a sudden, agonizing headache. Even Selly took an involuntary step forward before catching herself. Through her bond to Jadren, she felt his stab of surprise, the slight faltering of his magic. A dart made it through the wards, gaining speed as it emerged with an audible pop and Selly couldn't help trying to duck.

She couldn't have evaded the thing, especially as it unerringly changed trajectory to drill straight for her eye, but Jadren's hand shot out, taking the full force of the dart into his own flesh. Clenching it in his fist, he opened his hand again to drop the shattered pieces—and drops of blood it had drawn—to the floor. He smiled, a cruel slice of mirthlessness, another echo of his mother. "You'll have to do better than that."

"Fyrdo, this is your final warning," Katica ground out, moving close enough to her familiar to deliver a swift and painful-looking sharp kick to his ribs. Fyrdo barely flinched. "Stand up and serve me or I will make you suffer like you never imagined."

Selly hadn't been sure why Katica didn't simply seize Fyrdo and use his magic whether he complied or not, but now she saw how the wizard kept her gaze and attention on Jadren. Moving closer to him than the distance of a kick wasn't something she wanted to risk.

Fyrdo looked up at her, still clutching his head, then scrabbled away, putting himself behind the flank of Jadren's wards. "No more," he said. "I can't take any more."

"Oops," Jadren crooned. "Looks like you'll have to fight me without your familiar's magic, Maman. Ready to concede?"

Katica clenched her own fists, emitting a wordless shriek of fury, before clawing back her composure. "You have sadly miscalculated. I'm embarrassed that you came from my loins. When I say you forget who I am, I mean you've forgotten what it means that I am Lady El-Adrel. You battle not only me, but my entire House."

Selly only had a moment to process what that meant before utter chaos ensued.

~ II ~

E L-ADREL WIZARD MINIONS, accompanied by their familiars, stormed through the outer doors—and the open balcony doors on the other three sides—like an unstoppable flood. Along with them came clockwork creations of all sorts, from small crablike crawlies with vicious pincers to the human-sized automatons infused with an elemental-level of intelligence from Elal-bonded spirits. Other enchanted weapons buzzed and whistled, adding to the cacophony and bristling with intimidating weaponry.

Jadren hadn't forgotten that his mother could command an army of wizards to battle him, but he *had* counted on her stubborn pride keeping her from stooping to calling for reinforcements. The one time her hubris would work in his favor... But then, Jadren always had shit for luck.

Clearly, she was even more desperate than he'd hoped. Fyrdo's defection had dealt her a severe blow, one he viscerally understood now in a way he hadn't been capable of before, with Seliah's stalwart, loving presence at his back. She gave him the strength for this confrontation—something he'd once thought impossible—and not only via her brilliant, cooling magic. Seliah believed in him, wanted him to win, and not just to save her own skin. Wizards always made out like they controlled their familiars to the nth degree, but Jadren had just witnessed how the human side of any person could prove stronger than the wizard–familiar bond.

Fyrdo might love Katica as his life-partner and lover, but he also loved his children. That love had led him to risk his life and sanity to help Jadren and Seliah escape—and now to defy her, refusing to help her destroy their son. That had been a stroke of good fortune Jadren had dared to hope for, but had cynically refused to allow himself to expect. Fortunately, he'd had the foresight to set the wards around Seliah and him in a full circle, wary of those open windows at their backs.

But he couldn't extend the wards to protect Fyrdo, and he couldn't hold the shield forever. Particularly if he hoped to have any firepower left to blast his mother into the black depths she'd crawled out of. He hadn't come here planning to kill her. He hadn't thought he could. Now he had no choice. He couldn't leave without doing so. She'd been right about that much: she'd always come after them and if he wanted any kind of life with Seliah—which, amazingly enough, it turned out he did—then this had to end today.

Only, he had no idea how to fend off this army of wizards, any number of whom could easily kill him on their own, much less en masse. And he didn't dare unleash the death-strike via his widget, with his wards up. He had too little experience with that power, and the only other time he'd used it, he'd had no wards up. No telling what might happen. It could very well bounce back on him and Seliah, with unhappy results.

His mother drew herself up, smiling in joyous triumph.

"You're a fool, ten times over. Surrender now and remand yourself into my custody, and I'll let your familiar live."

"We'd rather go down fighting, you infernal bitch!" Seliah spat over his shoulder.

No wonder he loved her to distraction. He cocked an eyebrow, pretending that the combined attacks of a hundred wizards from all directions wasn't draining them both to the point of system failure. "Let's reverse that offer," he said, as nonchalantly as he could, even as his wards grew opaque from all the enchanted objects flying at them, his brain fogging from the effort of maintaining the rapidly thinning shield around them. "*You* surrender and we'll leave, promising to never return."

Predicably, his dear maman laughed. "You are outwitted and outmagicked. There's no way you can stand against this kind of force. You have no allies to help you—" She broke off at the surge of magic all around them, the floor flexing with an undulating ripple beneath their feet, the walls seeming to billow like lungs taking a deep breath. "What...?" Katica gasped.

The wizards and familiars all vanished, leaving only the four of them and sudden quiet, the various artifacts and automatons leeched of power and collapsed to the floor, a few whirring sadly before they stilled. Lady El-Adrel looked about her at the junkyard of lifeless metal, Fyrdo huddled behind the curve of Jadren's wards. She fastened her gaze on Jadren. Her wizard-black eyes held a rime of fear that he would find most satisfying if he weren't also confused. He tried to cover it, to look confident and triumphant, but he had no idea who had intervened either. Had some wizard—

"The house," Seliah whispered reverently. "She's helping us."

"Don't be absurd," Katica spat at Seliah. "The house is an enchanted artifact. Infused with centuries of magic, yes. Able to make decisions and act of its own volition? No."

A flutter of sound rippled through the structure around them, a symphony of old-house noises: the creaking of wood as the temperature changed, the soft pinging of glass as leaves tapped against it, the chorus of rain on a tiled roof, the musical flexing of metal. All of it combined to make not exactly a voice, but the rumble of disagreement and an echo of derisive laughter. With prickling awareness, Jadren fully believed all of Seliah's wild suppositions about the house. House El-Adrel was sentient. And just maybe on their side.

The big question was *why*? What did the house want? It might have apparently worked in their favor for the moment, but...

His mother had narrowed her gaze, the darts that had been relentlessly still boring through his wards going still as she extended her wizard's senses to the structure around them. "I am your lady," she informed the house, casting her gaze about, a hint of uncertainty in it, "which means you obey me."

"I don't think the house is interested in being commanded by someone who thinks she's only another enchanted object," Seliah said.

"Nobody has the slightest interest in what you *think*," Katica spat.

"The house does," Seliah replied pertly. "More, I think

she's on our side."

"I wouldn't be so sure," Jadren said to her under his breath, admiring her bold impudence and wary of how the words further inflamed his mother. Katica might have lost her reinforcements, but she remained a formidable foe. "If the house is helping us, why did it leave her here to continue to attack us?"

"Because this part is up to you," Seliah answered, promptly and with confidence he didn't deserve. "Isn't that how this works? The house wants you as Lord El-Adrel, but first you must defeat the previous head of the house."

He felt as if a lead ball dropped through his gut. "That's only how it works in novels," he muttered back, trying to master the queasy terror. He couldn't be Lord El-Adrel. He didn't want it and he wasn't powerful enough.

"Him?" His mother squawked out a caw of disbelief, her amusement genuine. "He's a mediocre wizard at best, with no spine, no ambition, no ability to govern. He can't even control himself, or his familiar, apparently." His sweet maman listed off his flaws and failings, echoing his own self-doubts. Or…maybe she'd been the source of them all along, and he'd dutifully learned to echo her. "I have news for you, Familiar," she continued. "Your brother might have ascended to the lordship of a house, but that's only because nobody cared about the Phels of Meresin. He got the job nobody wanted and he won't be able to hold onto it. He's only playing at being what real Convocation wizards and houses have honed for centuries. And Jadren, he's inept, uneducated, bumbling, not even a citizen of the Convocation. He's a coward. Remember how you wept and pleaded with me over that harmless little eye-socket device, Jadren?"

That lead ball in his gut rolled around queasily, threatening to erupt through his throat. *"Don't,"* he managed to say.

His mother smiled, pleased to have gotten to him. In a display of control and an indication of just how much reserved magic she still possessed, she pressed her open hands toward him and—even as the darts resumed drilling through his wards—golden chains extruded themselves from her palms. Hooks dangled from the links. Large and small, all were excessively sharp to ease burying themselves in flesh and barbed to hamper their extraction. Animated by his dear maman's magic, the hooks lifted, seeming to reach for him. "Remember these?" his mother purred, eyes alight with malice as he cringed. "You always did hate them the most. Look at how you cower. You can't even—"

"Duck," Jadren whispered to Seliah, even as he pulled on the flood of her reservoir of pristine water magic, infused with the argent moon magic, shining bright. Dropping the wards, he threw them around Seliah and Fyrdo, a blanket of protection, and took the onslaught of his mother's darts—verbal and physical. They riddled into his flesh, the pain an old and familiar friend.

At the same time, he threw every bit of magic in him through the brass tube, willing the widget to work.

Katica El-Adrel squeaked, her wards collapsing all at once, and she exploded into a red mist.

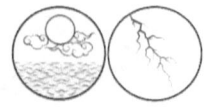

JADREN AWOKE ON his back, staring up at a cloudless blue sky. His skull pounded and every pore ached, his very bones gasping for water.

"Drink this," a warm voice said, a shape moving in to block his view, which he realized was of a skylight. Sunlight silhouetted the person's dark hair, picking out red highlights around the edges.

"Seliah," he said, only it came out as a croak, barely there.

"Drink," she urged, a smile in her voice, and he became aware of her flask pressed against his lips, the water issuing from it preternaturally delicious, purified with Gabriel's magic.

He drank gratefully, some of the parched feeling easing, and wondered what he'd done to himself this time. Surely not another cliff...

"Now magic," she said, laying her hands on his skin.

"No," he protested, earning a fierce growl from her. She seemed fine—though her face remained in shadow—so whatever had tried to kill him this time hadn't harmed her.

"Yes," she replied firmly. "You agreed never to argue with me again about using my magic. You need it, so drink up of that, too."

His memory had big, shredded holes in it, but he was fairly certain he'd agreed to no such thing. But he was entirely depleted, barely able to breathe, much less argue, so he sipped of her magic.

"More," she urged, though she hardly needed to. One taste and this endless hunger that lived inside him roared into avid life, demanding all the magic she could give. Which wasn't much, he quickly realized. Seliah always burgeoned with so much magic that he'd only rarely encountered her reserves this low. Making himself stop before her well went dry, he closed his eyes and lay there, letting her water magic fill his cells with life-giving moisture again, the moonlight flickering through his nervous system, zinging and shimmering with welcome vitality.

He became aware of his surroundings, El-Adrel magic ticking all around, the presence of hordes of other wizards and familiars, someone sobbing with heartbroken and wrecked abandon. "What happened?" he asked Seliah, the urgency of not-knowing a new panic.

"You don't remember anything?" she asked with uncharacteristic caginess.

He considered what he remembered, memories knitting themselves together as he healed, and realized that, as Seliah shifted and the light glanced over her shadowed face, she was covered in a patina of crimson. Those weren't red highlights in her hair. Seliah had the kind of black hair with blue undertones, not red. No, that was a fine scarlet mist of...

His mother.

"Dark arts curse me," he whispered. He'd killed his own mother. And that sound, that was his father, sobbing out his grief. His emotions tumbled in a turmoil of relief, horror, joy, and a deep, grinding, formless regret.

"Dark arts *saved* you," Seliah corrected sternly. "Saved all of us. Your magic, whatever it is, no matter how dark, how monstrous it seems to you, saved my life and Fyrdo's. Never forget that."

"She's dead, truly dead?" He couldn't quite grasp it. At the same time, he recoiled from the surge of exaltation. His mother. His tormenter. His killer. Gone forever. No longer able to harm anyone.

"Ring the bells," Seliah responded solemnly. "Lady Katica El-Adrel is dead. Long live Lord Jadren El-Adrel."

What? Those words worked to galvanize him, pricking him to lever into a sitting position. Dizziness swamped him with instant regret, but he made himself stay upright. "No no no," he practically stammered. "I can't be Lord El-Adrel." *Uneducated. Inept. Bumbling. Coward.* "I can barely work magic. I can't do anything."

"Not true," Seliah replied with impatience. "That's your late-mother talking."

"It is true," he insisted, rather desperately. "Think about it. When I tried to make something of myself, what happened? I immediately ran afoul of those Hanneil wizards and got myself killed. I get myself killed all the time."

"Fortunate that you can heal yourself and come back from the dead then," Seliah said agreeably.

"This isn't funny, Seliah!"

"I never said it was, but you need to get a grip on yourself. Your father needs you to be strong. All of House El-Adrel needs you to buck up and deal, including the house itself. Including me," she added.

"You don't seem particularly needy at the moment," he

griped, resenting her disregard for what had been a fine pity party.

"That's because I'm giving you the tough-love portion of care and feeding of wizards," she said. "*Think* for a moment, Jadren. There is a vacancy at the head of this very powerful high house. Your mother died without naming an heir. What will happen? Will all the wizards of El-Adrel happily come together to have logical debates and amicably vote for the best person to govern this house?"

He snorted at the ridiculous suggestion. "You clearly don't know wizards if you think that..." He trailed off, subjected to that knowing glare again. His brain wasn't quite clicking on all cogs yet. Of course she knew that. He dropped his muzzy head in his hands. "You're right," he admitted. "They'll battle for the position. It will get ugly."

"And the worst of them, the most willing to go to extremes, to employ ruthless power to attain their goal, will win," she finished for him.

"The way of the Convocation," he agreed ruefully.

"Not any longer," Seliah replied firmly. "Not on my watch. House Phel needs all the allies we can get. House El-Adrel deserves a real leader, someone who cares about the house, its tradition, and its denizens."

"That rules me out," he retorted. "You know I don't care about anyone but myself."

"That's no longer true, if it ever was. You're a good man, Jadren. You'll be a great high-house head."

"With you at my side, I suppose." He meant it to sound sarcastic, but a lilt of uncertainty made the words into a question.

"Always and forever," she answered solemnly. "Consider this. If you are Lord El-Adrel, you can free all the captives in your late-mother's laboratories. You can have the house collapse everything on the other side of that tunnel into horror. End that nightmare permanently."

She did know how to get to him. "Tempting," he allowed. More than tempting. The prospect of dismantling the torture chamber that had warped his early life, whose terrors haunted the twisted depths of his heart and mind still... Well, it wouldn't change the past, but he could cleanse the future of its taint.

"Another El-Adrel wizard might elect to continue your late-mother's work," Seliah continued relentlessly.

He eyed her. "You just love saying 'late-mother,' don't you?"

Her gaze flicked uneasily to the sobbing coming from Fyrdo's direction, the sounds quieter now, but still soul-grating. "Fyrdo mourns her death, but I do not."

No. No, Jadren couldn't grieve either. Though he was sorry to have made Fyrdo witness her ghoulish demise. He'd have to find a way to help his father through this. Maybe a jaunt to House Refoel and time in that ridiculously peaceful valley under Maya's healing care.

"When you are Lord El-Adrel," Seliah continued thoughtfully, "you can investigate and dissolve the conspiracy between Elal, Sammael, and El-Adrel. You could expose their treachery. The Convocation would celebrate you as a hero!"

"You're laying it on a bit thick now," he informed her

wryly. Though Seliah was right. He'd have a much easier time doing everything if he headed up El-Adrel. Power could be handy. For so many reasons. And he wouldn't be a minion of anyone else's, which held definite appeal. "It's going to suck," he confided. "Being in charge, especially since neither of us is a power-mad megalomaniac interested only in furthering our insane schemes."

"We could always take up a few schemes as a hobby. Dabble in megalomania on a small scale. A creative outlet, if you will."

"I always knew you were more than half crazy." Absurdly, he nearly laughed at her sally.

"And yet you love me anyway." Her full lips quirked in a half smile.

"I suspect I love you because of it, which says something about me."

"Birds of a crazy feather."

"Well, my crazy birdie lover, your plumage is covered in blood, so I suspect mine is also. We'd better get cleaned up before we go confront whoever the house didn't eat and convince them to accept me as Lord El-Adrel."

"I doubt the house ate them," Seliah replied. "I think she redeposited them elsewhere."

Jadren regarded her in considerable bemusement. "Did the house tell you that?"

"You laugh, but you have yet to acknowledge that I was right about the house all along."

"True," he conceded. "You were right and you told me so. Sufficient?"

She nodded. "Sweet words, indeed, though I could wish for happier circumstances. Let's go brave the minions of El-Adrel."

"This won't be easy," he warned her.

"Nothing fun ever is."

A laugh escaped him. "Help me stand?"

"Asking for help? You must be crazed, indeed." But she shouldered herself under his arm, levering them both to their feet.

He braced for the sight of the gore-splattered room but, to his vast surprise, the pretty, airy, and sunlit rooms shone pristine. No signs of the duel remained, not even the magic-dead artifacts remained. Only his mother's—his late-mother's—lethal darts lay scattered across the polished wood floor. The chains must have dissolved along with her. Good riddance.

"Those darts extruded themselves from you as you healed," Seliah said, following his gaze to the inert things. "You took them all into yourself. Not a one touched me or Fyrdo. It was stupidly fucking noble of you."

"My new middle name." He surveyed the room, still not sure of his own perceptions. "Where is all the blood—why is it only on us?"

"The house absorbed it all," Fyrdo answered in a broken, wounded voice. "Katica is now a part of the house she loved. The house that birthed her. The house that betrayed her in the end."

Jadren made himself go to his father, to look him in the eye, both of them smeared with the blood of the woman who'd been so many things to them both, a figure of tortured love, the queen who'd ruled them utterly. Who knew how they'd emerge from this utter collapse of her power over them?

"I'm sorry," he said, meaning it, tepid and weak as those words sounded.

"Sorry?" Fyrdo repeated, bewildered, scornful. "You murdered her. Your own mother. In cold blood."

There had been nothing cold about it. His fury had blazed hot, an immolation to cleanse them all from the insistent taint of corruption.

"I had no choice," he told his father, softly, with all the remorse he felt for this one person who'd ever loved him, who'd been the sole reason he'd survived to see this day. "She would have killed Seliah, and probably you, too, for refusing to help her against us. I couldn't allow her to keep doing these things. I couldn't let her dig her hooks into me again." Literally and metaphorically.

Fyrdo nodded, tears falling freely. He lifted a hand, let it fall. "You won't understand this but, despite everything, I loved her."

"Oh, Father." Jadren had to swallow to loosen his throat against his own very real tears of grief. No, he wouldn't ever mourn Katica El-Adrel, but he could and would grieve for the mother she'd never been. The woman he'd loved as a child, with all the fierce and innocent attachment that somehow managed to endure even over years of abuse. If he hadn't loved her, maybe he'd have found a way to separate himself from her before this. "I do understand," he said quietly. "Sometimes we love despite our better judgment. All we can do is try to live by that good judgment and let our hearts do as they will."

"I don't know what I'm going to do now," Fyrdo said, eyes unfocused. "I can't live in this house that killed her."

Jadren hesitated, feeling he should correct that statement, wondering at how his father had already rewritten history to make House El-Adrel the villain and not his beloved son. And yet, he couldn't refuse that favor. He couldn't bear for his father to hate him. So he only nodded. "There's time to decide. Let's get cleaned up and you can rest."

Seliah stopped Jadren as he guided his father toward the bathing chamber and the grooming imps. The earth elementals would make quick work of the gore. "I think you shouldn't clean up," she said, seriously enough that he thought she'd deadpanned the joke. But she meant it.

"You want me to go to the great hall and confront my late-mother's minions covered in her discorporated body?"

"Yes. With the holes riddling your leathers from her attack. A lot of this blood is yours, you should know, from those darts. When they see you like this, it will remove all doubt."

"Of my sanity?"

"That you are weak or incompetent in some way," she replied seriously, not taking the bait. "Your very appearance proves you cannot be killed. What better way to forestall challenges and more duels? You defeated Lady El-Adrel in a pitched battle. No one will want to take you on, if they're smart."

"You're assuming a great deal about the relative intelligence of the House El-Adrel minions," he retorted drily. Still,

Seliah had a point. "I wouldn't have succeeded if Fyrdo had gone to her. She would have outpowered me."

"Don't you see?" she asked gently. "That's part of you, also, that your father loves you and wouldn't act against you, despite enormous pressure. And the house. She chose you and acted to protect you."

He still wasn't sure about that part. "I think the house chose *you*," he said, pointing a finger at the large and detailed painting of House Phel on the wall, its frame an ornate silver design of waves and the moon moving through its various phases.

"And I chose you and you chose me." She shrugged and smiled, as if it all made sense. "Now, what do you think— should I go as is, refugee of a great wizard's duel? Or I can clean up and be full, glamorous lady."

"I vote clean up. I love you, but seeing you covered in the remains of my late-mother is a bit off-putting."

~ 12 ~

MONTHS BEFORE, SELLY wouldn't have credited it, but she had to admit that Nic's training on how to present herself as Convocation royalty came in handy at last. Bathed in the hottest water she could coax the fire elementals into heating for her—though the earth elementals removed the blood and gore, she still hadn't felt truly clean—and with her hair and makeup done, she felt like a new person.

Well, if not a new person, then a considerably more polished one. The servants Jadren summoned, all of them wide-eyed and giving the blood-soaked wizard a skittishly large berth, took away a still-weeping Fyrdo to be sedated by the in-house Refoel healer, and also brought Selly a selection of Ophiel gowns. She selected the richest-looking one, made of shimmering gold cloth, worked in lightning bolts in the same thread, so they showed only subtly.

"Look what showed up for you," Jadren said, gesturing at an open jewelry box on the table.

She peered at the glowing jewels within, a necklace and dangling earrings. "They're beautiful."

"They're moonstones. They simply appeared, so I assume they're a gift of the house," he added drily.

Giving him a questioning look, she hesitated, hovering a finger over the stones. "Do you think they're safe?"

He snorted. "In this house? Nothing is safe. But you're the one all fired up to be Lady El-Adrel with your buddy the enchanted artifact the size of a house." His wizard-black gaze roved over the apartment, which continued to expand and decorate itself. A few potted plants had appeared, including what looked to be a citrus tree in a nook with bay windows.

She studied Jadren during his moment of distraction, trying to determine how he was truly coping. He felt brittle, in much the same way Alise had felt brittle, his magic worn thin from that epic strike that destroyed his mother once and for all, and Selly questioned whether she'd been right to push him to take the seat as head of the house at this moment. If anyone truly challenged him, he might be too weak to fight them off. She had plenty of magic still, and it was rebuilding swiftly. They'd agreed to wait until right before they left the relative safety of their rooms for him to replenish from her. Jadren had some idea that the more he replenished on his own, the less he'd weaken her, which she doubted. But she'd let it go.

On the other hand, he looked truly terrifying, caked in drying blood, his pale and unblemished skin showing through the rents in his leathers. His auburn hair, not at all bright, stood up in spikes, bloodred and menacing. The brass widget on the chain around his neck showed incongruously clean, somehow more threatening just for that. His wizard-black eyes glittered with feverish light, deep pits in the blood-smeared, white skull that was his pinched and hollow face.

She stood by her evaluation that seeing would be believing, for any House El-Adrel denizens who hadn't been summoned to the duel and relocated forthwith. She also worried that she might be pushing her wizard too far. What Jadren had just endured, the extreme action he'd been forced to take—for she knew full well he'd only launched that final, devastating attack because his late-mother had pushed him over the edge of sanity, threatening him with those hated chains—well, that experience would have the sanest person gibbering in a corner.

"Stop looking at me like you're worried I'm going to fall apart," Jadren snapped, turning that too-sharp gaze on her.

"I'm not," she assured him, just a small lie. Picking up the earrings, she fastened them onto her ears. Enchanted artifacts, they attached themselves upon contact, little screws twirling to gently pinch her earlobes. A bit unsettling, but also convenient.

"I'd offer to help with the necklace," Jadren commented, in far too neutral a tone, "but..." He held up his blood-smeared hands, the dried stuff flaking off the knuckles and other creases. "You look so lovely," he added, almost wistfully. "We'll appear as the beauty and the murderous monster she's taken to her breast."

"Whatever intimidates them enough to make them think twice about challenging you," she replied with enough conviction for them both. "Once you're Lord El-Adrel, you can appeal to their good sense and better natures."

"We'll need that support for the Convocation to confirm the appointment."

She should have realized there'd be legal hurdles to leap. A thought struck her. "Will the Convocation be able to confirm you in the role if you're not a citizen?"

"They wouldn't be, no, but..." He grimaced and waved a hand at one of the bags the servants had brought up. They'd retrieved Vale from where Jadren had hidden the horse in the woods nearby, bringing up the saddle packs at Jadren's direction. "Look in that outer pocket there. You'll find something for you, too."

Curious—and particularly intrigued by his expectant attitude—Selly rummaged in the pocket he indicated and withdrew the two cards, peering at the numbers in the rows and columns stamped on the expensive paper. Belatedly, she caught on. "MP scorecards," she breathed. "How did you get these?"

"Liat." He raised his brows expressively. "They had a Hanneil wizard clandestinely evaluate us while we worked. Yours is quite what you'd expect."

She nodded, mostly out of agreeable habit, not really seeing the march of numbers at the nexus points where moon and water magic showed her highest scores. Bending most of her attention to Jadren's scorecard, she tried to make sense of it. "Isn't this column healing magic?" she asked with a frown.

"Yup."

He continued to watch her, tension riding him, saying nothing more.

"Unless I'm reading it wrong, it looks like you have almost no healing magic."

"You're reading it right."

She looked up. "Then you *don't* have healing magic."

"Nope."

"Then how…" She wrestled with putting her confusion into words.

"A question for the sages," Jadren replied. "Or for my sainted late-mother, who won't be answering any questions now."

"That's why you tried so hard to negotiate with her," Selly realized aloud. "You hoped for answers."

"No hope of that now," he said bleakly.

"We'll find a way," she assured him, with optimism she didn't feel. "Maybe her co-conspirators will be able to shed some light."

"If I brutalize them enough?" Jadren asked sarcastically, but stared at the blood on his hands.

"Maybe you should wash." After all, she had been nearly desperate to get clean, to wash the evidence away, and Katica hadn't been her parent. She'd had the luxury of hating the woman with unadulterated loathing, not a conflicted emotion in her. Selly couldn't imagine murdering her own mother or father—or really anyone at all. She only provided the power for Jadren to do it, which she knew didn't excuse her or protect her from equal guilt. But she also didn't have to make that terrible decision.

Jadren threw her an irritated glance. "Don't back off your convictions now, poppet. Blood-spattered monster striding into the great hall is what you envisioned and that's what you shall get."

"That's what *they* will get," she corrected, with satisfaction.

"Let's get this over with." He buckled Mr. Machete to his hip, just in case it came to that, and crooked an elbow for her to take his arm, then winced. "Never mind."

Though she had to compose herself to look nonchalant, she slipped a hand through the opening, his sleeve damp and sticky with the gore, not dried as on his skin. "There is nothing you could be or do that would keep me from touching you, Wizard," she said, meeting and holding his stark gaze.

"I hope you never have cause to retract that sweeping statement," he retorted, but he laid a hand over hers on his arm, squeezing her fingers.

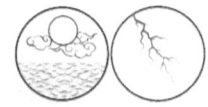

As if they'd been called to assembly, the wizards and familiars of House El-Adrel awaited them in the great hall where Selly had eaten dinner seated at a table on the elevated dais on her first visit to the house. She'd sat there stewing in anxiety and confusion, uncertain of whether Jadren cared for her and was trying to protect her or if he'd been bent on betrayal all along and she'd been a fool to trust him.

Sliding him a surreptitious glance, she marveled at how far they'd come since that day—and how fortunate she was that this man loved her. His skin, pale as white marble, made his handsome face look hard and sculpted like some mythical being. The dried blood darkened his beard, clinging there where it flaked off his cheekbones. His beautiful mouth sat in stern lines, wizard-black eyes glittering like obsidian as he swept the room with his contemptuous gaze, playing the murderous conqueror to the hilt.

He also drew lightly but steadily on her magic—one reason she'd have made sure to touch him no matter how grisly he looked—maintaining the wards he'd erected around them.

But nothing flew at them, no surprise attacks as he'd dourly predicted. Instead, the crowd parted for them, creating an aisle up the center, leading to a grand chair Selly recognized as being Katica's from that dinner. The table, however, had vanished or been pushed off to the side, along with the other chairs from that night, leaving only the one on the dais, like a throne from a fairytale. The same banner hung vertically behind, glowing white, diagonally bifurcated by a lighting bolt worked in metals of all shades, seeming to repeatedly strike the ground, a dazzling work of art created by some magic Selly didn't know. It seemed to be suspended from nothing, well below the high-arched glass ceiling, showing glorious sky above.

As Jadren proceeded through the crowd, his gaze fixed straight ahead, the wizards and familiars bowed deeply, then continued to sink to one knee, remaining there in a posture of humble fealty.

"Maybe this will be easier than we thought," she murmured under her breath, just loud enough for Jadren to hear.

"Or they plan to trap us up against that wall and, once we're cornered, attack *en masse*," he replied, just as quietly, far more cynically.

"I'm sure the house won't let that happen."

"I wish I shared your certainty." On the heels of his words, a shifting sound clicked through the mostly silent hall, like scales sliding against each other, growing gradually louder. A few murmurs of surprise and dismay ran through the crowd. The sensation of movement beneath her feet, now familiar, had Selly smiling. Sure enough, behind the throne and banner, the wall peeled itself apart, curling like old paint—or dried blood—and revealed a set of doors three times as tall as a person. In stately splendor, they swung outwards, revealing a verdant garden with meticulously trimmed trees and roses trained to climb in intricate patterns on stone walls that looked as old as anything in the house.

"The queen's garden!" someone exclaimed.

"I've never heard of a queen's garden and, even if I had, it's not supposed to be there," Jadren confided to Selly. "Is there nothing the house won't do for you?"

"She answered *you* this time," Selly pointed out. "You no longer have your back against the wall."

"At least not literally. The metaphorical situation hasn't changed much."

"Aww, is that any way for my blood-spattered monster to talk? How about a violent roar of malevolent rage to clear your system?"

"You're really not funny," he growled, and she smiled secretly, pleased with herself.

They turned to face the assembly, all of them down on one knee, faces turned upward, a sea of skin, hair, and eye color, punctuated by impenetrable wizard-black gazes. Jadren let them stew, the seething magics of all varieties spiking with emotion, various expressions of horror, fear, and titillation running like waves through the crowd. Many of them eyed

Selly with curiosity-piqued interest.

Jadren raised one hand high, as if commanding silence, though no one had dared speak above a murmur. "Behold," he said in a carrying voice. "I bear on my hands the blood of Katica El-Adrel, the one who birthed me. In the wake of her death, as she passed without naming an heir, I claim her place as head of this house."

Beautifully done. Selly was hard pressed not to wiggle with glee, but she managed to preserve a serious mien.

"Are there any who would challenge me on this?" Jadren continued, flipping her glee to annoyance. It was one thing if he had to fight off challengers, but no need to issue an invitation. Still, no one moved or spoke. In fact, many of those glittering black gazes lowered nervously. It seemed they might get away with it being easy.

Silly her.

A man stood, bringing a woman with him, and stepped into the aisle, posing there a moment. Selly would've known him for one of Katica's get from the dramatic presentation alone, even without the physical resemblance. Unlike Jadren and the late, unlamented Ozana, this man didn't have Fyrdo's coloring. Instead, he took after their mother, with long, shining black hair, golden-brown skin, and a wizard's glittering dark gaze. He didn't wear the house colors, nor any lightning bolt emblems that Selly could make out. Instead he'd dressed in a rich-looking burgundy silk suit, so meticulously tailored to his form that Selly knew it must be of Ophiel make.

"Your brother?" she asked, very quietly.

"Bogdan, yes."

"How many siblings do you have, anyway?"

"Fewer every day."

He wasn't wrong, but that was hardly an informative answer. But Selly let it go. Bogdan and his companion had drawn too close for even *sotto voce* conversation.

The woman following after Bogdan wore a gown that matched his, also gorgeous, clearly cut from the same cloth. Her bronze hair flowed well past her shoulders in well-groomed waves, matching her skin. Obviously his familiar, she must have bonded to him some years ago, for her hair to have grown in so much since the ceremony. She carried herself with pride of place, still a submissive step behind the tall, graceful man, keeping physical contact with a hand on his arm, which meant they were prepared to use magic.

Selly braced herself, readying her own magic, hoping that they had enough juice for a confrontation. Maybe they *should* have waited. Jadren, sensing her unease, patted her hand soothingly. Right. Worrying helped nothing.

The pair stopped a respectful distance below the dais where Jadren and Selly stood before the lone chair. "Jadren," Bogdan said, no more inflection in his voice than if he'd correctly identified a type of apple.

"Bogdan," Jadren replied in the same tone. "Helen. I present my familiar, Seliah."

Bogdan didn't acknowledge Selly in any way, not even by a flick of his black gaze, which remained trained on Jadren. Helen, however, met and held Selly's gaze, a sense of mutual recognition in her eyes. "It's apparently incumbent upon me," Bogdan continued, "to point out the obvious. El-Adrel is a high house of the Convocation, not a medieval fortress. We do not determine right to govern here via feudalistic violence. The rule of law is the mark of a civilized society. Are we become animals here in House El-Adrel? I think not."

A murmur of agreement ran through the assembly, though no one rose from their humble stance. They seemed inclined to let Bogdan take the brunt of Jadren's ire. Though Jadren didn't feel angry to her. His magic hadn't intensified, instead clicking evenly along, perhaps even a hint of amusement in it.

"Indeed, Bogdan," Jadren answered coolly, "we claim to abide by rule of law in House El-Adrel, but I defy anyone here to argue that Katica El-Adrel followed any law but her own. Had she followed Convocation law, even simple courtesy, she'd have named an heir. Instead she toyed with us, encouraging her progeny to battle amongst ourselves, not unlike those animals you name us, aggravated, abused, and stoked into a frenzy to be placed in a ring at each other's throats for her amusement."

"Is that why you murdered Ozana?" Bogdan inquired in a polite tone that masked nothing of his intent to lay Jadren open. Selly wanted to hiss at the wizard. It would be one thing if she believed Bogdan asked out of genuine grief or concern, but nothing about him made her think he cared about anything but this verbal fencing match.

"I killed Ozana in self-defense," Jadren answered, creating a stir with the admission. "I have witnesses to attest to that fact and the Convocation has elected not to prosecute."

Bogdan raised his brows. "And I suppose your current claim is that you also murdered our mother in self-defense."

"Yes," Jadren answered tersely. "As a great many of you can attest, having been summoned to help put me down."

A shuffling amongst the assembly, many of them casting their gazes askance.

"I don't hold that attack against any of you," Jadren added, raising his voice for all to hear. "You did your duty to your house and your lady wizard, as required by your contracts. I offer you all amnesty. You may continue in your current role here at El-Adrel, subject to future performance and contract reviews, naturally, without reprisal. Likewise, should you wish to depart, I will release you from your current contract without penalty." That declaration caused a susurrus of surprise, like a sudden breeze stirring the leaves of a tree.

Bogdan aped an astonished face, making an O of his mouth, while Helen behind him narrowed her eyes in speculation, studying Selly, for some reason. "You have been too long in the company of those idiots at House Phel," Bogdan declared. "Wearing a mundane weapon because your wizardry is too weak to fight like a proper wizard. Is this what we can expect then? The corruption of a fallen house, tainting El-Adrel's noble tradition, with posturing over *change* and *equality*." He sneered the words, making them empty husks.

Selly wasn't at all bothered by the smears on the house of her birth. She was too busy assimilating Jadren's about face. After all of his complaints about Gabriel's idealism, comparing it to an infectious disease and proclaiming the certain dire results of it, now Jadren was offering to renegotiate contracts.

Jadren flicked her a sideways glance. "Told you that shit is infectious," he whispered, and she had to choke back a laugh.

Loud enough for everyone to hear, Jadren replied, "I have traveled and seen more of the world. I've spent time at other high houses and observed both the good and the bad of other customs. I propose we learn from the good examples and shun the unproductive. It's only civilized," he added, pinning Bogdan with a surly smile.

"You think to curry favor with our people," Bogdan decided, sweeping a hand at the room. "But this idea is soft-headed. It's ill-advised of you to risk the safety and security of House El-Adrel by emptying it of magical defenses. What if all the wizards leave—what then?" Bogdan countered.

"Then I'll hire new ones," Jadren answered softly, "though I rather doubt many will choose to leave, given the freedom to decide for themselves, along with the opportunity to labor under someone uninterested in exercising cruelty in the name of power."

"And yet you appear before us covered in gore, admitting to more murders," Bogdan shot back scornfully. "You truly expect anyone here to believe you won't follow in our beloved late-maman's footsteps?"

"Which is it, brother?" Jadren inquired silkily. "Am a threat to El-Adrel or too soft to protect her?"

Selly might have been the only person to catch Jadren's double meaning, but the house heard, giving a happy sigh of settling wood.

"How many more will you murder in the pursuit of power?" Bogdan demanded.

"I will kill whoever I must, if they attack me or mine," Jadren answered, his words implacable. He caressed the assembly with his gaze. "And I can kill with a thought, so bear that in mind."

They believed him. Shock, horror, speculation—all these ran over people's faces. But none showed any sign of doubt. Jadren clearly meant what he said, and even Selly felt a frisson of fear.

~ 13 ~

BOGDAN LOOKED UNIMPRESSED. Of course, Jadren's older brother always had possessed the knack of seeming impervious to any and all drama raging around him. Quite the feat, given the high pitch of everything their family engaged in. Behind him, Helen studiously averted her gaze from Jadren's, but her magic sang with potent alert. Bogdan had come prepared to duel, and with more than words. Somehow Jadren suspected Mr. Machete wouldn't be any help, either.

"If you mean to be Lord El-Adrel," Bogdan said, tapping a finger on his chin to appear thoughtful, all an artful pose, "then you must prove your ability."

Jadren didn't like this at all. Why had he let Seliah talk him into this ridiculous move? Let Bogdan be Lord El-Adrel. He could have the job for all Jadren cared.

As if reading his mind or sensing that his commitment to this course faltered, Bogdan smiled in premature triumph. "Or perhaps you can't. With an untrained familiar on top of your own woefully inadequate education—facts of which everyone in this room is perfectly aware—perhaps you hesitate to engage me in a duel." He made a moue of disappointment borrowed directly from their late-mother. "Of course, that would imply you're not at all strong enough to protect this house. A one-trick pony, it seems."

Oh, Jadren would just love to red-mist his arrogant brother. But he was also feeling weary of death, of orphaning familiars. He had no affection for Helen, but he also bore her no ill will, and she was devoted to her wizard. He'd developed a soft spot for familiars, it seemed. "I'm not interested in killing you, Bogdan," he found himself saying.

"Afraid you can't?" Bogdan asked, pouncing with glee.

"Oh, I know I can. I will, if you force me to. But you're an excellent wizard. You and Helen are a skilled team and House El-Adrel is fortunate to count you both as assets. Why would I want to lose you over nothing?"

"I hardly count this contest as nothing, brother," Bogdan grumbled, though he didn't quite conceal his startled pleasure at the unexpected compliment. "I won't meekly step aside to allow you to claim the rank and position that should be mine by right of birth."

He wasn't wrong. In any normal family or house, Bogdan would have been their mother's heir. He was nearly her equal in MP scores, a practiced and skillful wizard, a decent politician, and not obsessed with controlling others. He'd likely make a decent house head. Except that Bogdan would want to continue the experimentation in the name of honoring their late-mother's legacy and adding to the El-Adrel product line. Bogdan was greedy, loving wealth a bit too much, which wouldn't serve their house or people as they deserved.

"My lord wizard," Seliah said, loudly enough for her voice to carry. She was trying to sound meek, which she did not do well. "I understand the El-Adrel tradition is that the head of the house must also head the house itself." She swept a hand at their environs. "Perhaps a test of control between you and Wizard Bogdan could decide the matter."

Jadren risked taking his eyes off Bogdan and turned to give her an incredulous look. Seliah beamed back at him, full of confidence, her close-lipped smile smug. The bitch. He narrowed his eyes at her and she fluttered her lashes. Rubbing a hand over his forehead, which had begun to throb, only to have dried blood flake away, he wondered what he'd done that he'd ended up in this position.

"Done," Bogdan declared, seizing the opportunity with a bit too much alacrity, especially considering that a mere familiar with no rank (yet) had suggested the idea. "How shall we—"

"We'll do it now," Jadren interrupted, still giving Seliah the stink-eye, which seemed to bounce off her sincere and shining faith in him. While he'd always been fortunate that the house didn't attack him as she did others, and arguably had protected him more than once, saliently against Ozana when they were children, he didn't kid himself that he knew how to *make* the house do anything. As he'd often told Seliah, the house did as it liked. Even including trying to squeeze him to death not all that long ago. "What do you propose?" he asked Bogdan, giving him the courtesy of choosing his weapon, so to speak.

"Three modifications to the house," Bogdan replied, his tone easy, but his mind clearly **racing** to set terms most advantageous to himself. "Increasing level of difficulty, wizard must detail the intended result before manifesting it. No claiming of accidental results. Two out of three wins."

"And in the event of a tie?"

Bogdan bared his teeth in an anticipatory grin. "Sudden death."

"It might be more sudden than he realizes," Seliah muttered.

Jadren managed to keep a straight face. That was his girl. "With or without familiar assistance?"

Bogdan's assessing gaze went to Seliah. He nodded to himself. "With." Looking pleased, Bogdan seemed to think Seliah would be a hindrance to Jadren. He had no idea.

The assembly cleared a space under the center of the atrium, people seeming relieved both to rise from their kneeling positions and to get out of the line of fire. Though Jadren spotted at least two other of their siblings in the crowd, neither stepped up to make a bid for heading the house. Knowing them for the vultures they were, Jadren suspected they were biding their time, waiting to see what pieces of carcasses might be left over for them to gobble up.

"I hope you know what you're doing," he muttered to Seliah as they took up a position on one side of the cleared area.

"Me?" She was going for innocent, apparently, nearly cooing the word. "You're the wizard. I'm just the fire beneath your kettle."

"This is not a good time to needle me."

"Just keeping you at a nice boil," she replied. "Bogdan is a poser. You've got this. Remember that the house likes *you* and wants you for Lord El-Adrel."

"Remember that the house is fickle and follows her own agenda." But he took Seliah's hand, interlacing their fingers, grateful for her presence beyond the magic she shared so generously. "And you're the one she's put herself out for, so do try to be helpful, if it's in you."

"I'll consider it," she replied loftily, but squeezed his hand in solidarity.

"As challenger, I'll go first," Bogdan announced, neatly snagging that advantage. "The first modification shall be cosmetic."

Now Jadren would have to go second and Bogdan would enjoy the additional benefit of naming the third challenge. Oh joy.

"I shall change the color of the tile floor." Bogdan, with Helen behind him, hands on his shoulders, made a grand gesture. He was an excellent artificer, and his magic *tinked* out like clockwork, rippling through the polished metal of the floor, changing it to shimmering gold with embossed lighting bolts in a deeper shade. The assembly politely applauded.

"Does that count?" Seliah hissed. "All he did was change the floor color himself. The house didn't have to help at all."

"Semantics," Jadren answered quietly. "Nobody besides you believes the house is anything but a very large and complex enchanted artifact to be adjusted at will."

"You do," she retorted. "And you might consider *asking* her, instead of enforcing your wizardly will."

"Are we talking about the house or you?" he retorted.

"Same and same. Now, do something she'll like."

Something the house would like? He had no idea what a

house did or didn't like. Considering, he thought back to the changes he'd seen the house make spontaneously over his lifetime. Besides decorating Seliah's apartments to please her, he couldn't think of a... *Aha.* Forming the image in his mind, giving it the clarity Liat had taught, he suggested the modification to the house, offering his and Seliah's combined magic to fuel the change.

It felt very odd, not unlike having Vale pluck a proffered bit of apple from his palm, the touch both delicate and hinting at a strength that could chomp off his fingers if it chose. He was so focused on keeping his intention clear, on wooing the house the same way he'd pet Seliah into purring pleasure, that he didn't note the alteration until the assembly made a sound of surprise, followed by a scattering of less enthusiastic applause. Jadren saw that the house had taken his idea and run with it, changing every other tile to be silver, embossed with moons at successive phases, surrounded by stylized water waves. Alternating with Bogdan's glittering lightning bolts, the effect created an illusion of motion, the moons seeming to rise and set across the room with stately grace, spinning through their phases.

"Amazing," Seliah breathed.

"Are you making a point, brother?" Bogdan demanded, in quite a different tone. "Is House El-Adrel to be diluted by association with House *Fell?* This is what we may anticipate if you are Lord. Our ancestors weep."

"My turn to propose the next challenge," Jadren said, rather than deigning to stoop to an exchange of insults and retorts. His mind raced, grasping for something he could do that Bogdan couldn't. What would be the next level from cosmetic, that wouldn't escalate too much?

"Substantive extrusion of furnishings," he declared. After all, he'd had the house help him with disposing of fouled bedding before, providing him with fresh after one of his battered reprieves from his late-mother's depraved experiments. Oh, and after the time Seliah *shot him with an arrow.* "There should be two chairs—one for Lady El-Adrel as well as myself, and something more our style."

Forming the image in his mind, he practically beseeched the house to behave, gratified when a rumbling sound alerted him to the change behind them. Drawing Seliah to the side to see, he watched as the raised dais slowly sucked down the former Lady El-Adrel's thronelike chair. For a long moment, nothing more happened. It stretched out long enough for Bogdan to snicker.

"Oops," he called. "Did you run out of magic already? Because—"

He broke off as the dais stirred, swirling like a whirlpool before extruding two chairs. They were black, as Jadren had envisioned, and stylized—quite a bit more than he'd wanted—with pink upholstery, which was decidedly *not* what he'd asked for.

"Very funny," he muttered to the house, receiving a sense of scintillating laughter. At least he hadn't declared his exact intentions, so couldn't be held accountable for failing to miss his mark.

"Pink pillows for your delicate ass?" Bogdan inquired on a sneer.

Jadren lifted their joined hands, kissing Seliah's fingertips. "The new Lady El-Adrel's favorite color."

"It isn't though," Seliah said, very quietly.

"It is now," he returned. "Because your house-friend has a sense of humor as twisted and inappropriate as yours, which I lay entirely at your feet."

"Are you serious about making me Lady El-Adrel?" she asked. Bogdan was scowling, apparently considering his next move.

Jadren regarded her with some surprise. "Isn't that what you want?"

"Rank doesn't matter to me, you know that," she said, hesitating over something more.

"I know, but I also don't intend to treat you as my late-mother treated Fyrdo. You will lead this house with me the same as Nic and Gabriel do. If you're willing," he added, suddenly uncertain.

The smile she gave him was radiant enough to light a windowless room. "I would like that. I'm just surprised you want to follow the example of naïve idealists."

"Apparently love empties out the brain," he observed as cynically as possible. "Besides, if you're making me do this, you don't get to slack off on the responsibility."

"I shall remove those abominations," Bogdan announced.

Jadren waggled a finger at him. "Extrusion of furnishings. Not elimination. Or do you forfeit?"

Bogdan fumed. "Fine. Since you seem so cozy with your little familiar..." His magic surged, the metal design in the center of the floor bursting into pieces and reassembling itself.

Seliah made a murmur of dismay. "I liked your design," she explained when he glanced at her.

"We'll have the house put it back," he promised. Despite his playful exchange with Seliah, Jadren watched with a narrowed gaze and growing trepidation as the object took shape. A bed, with four posts equipped with chains. Cute.

The bedding, he noticed, was pink, confirming that the house continued to play her games, but he could hardly challenge Bogdan on the point. In point of fact, Bogdan swept a hand at the invitingly turned back blankets and bowed toward Seliah. "Your favorite color, Familiar El-Adrel, on which to be mastered. If your wizard is even capable of it."

"Asshole," Seliah said through her teeth, and Jadren had to cover his laugh with a cough.

"For the final challenge," Bogdan continued, "a substantive alteration to the house. One directed by the wizard, undoing something the house has done without direction." He smiled thinly. "After all, isn't that the point here? The head of House El-Adrel must be able to protect and rescue its denizens from unexpected changes in the house that threaten their lives."

Jadren waved a languid hand. "A feat arguably accomplished only sporadically by previous heads. As I recall, the former lady lost a number of people over the years to disappearing doorways, etcetera."

Bogdan shook his head. "Regrettable, truly. But as Lord El-Adrel, I promise no one will be neglected or abandoned."

"I'm curious," Jadren inserted. "Where were you and Helen when our late-mother called her minions to support her in attacking us? I don't recall seeing you in the room, before the house conveniently moved everyone elsewhere."

"She didn't summon me," Bogdan answered, defiantly looking around the room. "She wanted me to remain behind, to take over leading the house, in case of the unthinkable, which is what occurred."

"Ah." Jadren kept it short, knowing his disbelief would read clearly to the assembly. Bogdan had refused the summons, hoping to save his own skin, probably for just this moment. "So, are you going to do anything?" he inquired, looking about. "I'm not seeing any great, potentially life-saving alterations to the house."

"Observe, little brother," Bogdan replied. Settling himself, he drew on Helen's magic, his own burgeoning and the familiar growing pale, weaving on her feet to the point that only holding onto her wizard's shoulders appeared to be keeping her upright. Whatever Bogdan planned, it would take a great deal of power.

"I don't think we'll be able to match them for sheer output," Seliah said quietly. "Not after the magic you expended red-misting your late-mother."

No, they really couldn't. Jadren was no expert on measuring wizardly tricks, but even he could sense that Bogdan had amassed far more magic than he and Seliah possessed combined, at the moment. "Then we'll have to hope the house meets us at least halfway," he replied. "Because whatever Bogdan is doing will be massive."

As if on cue, Bogdan raised his hands, glittering with jewels. "Those open doors to the outside are a grave security risk," he declared, "as is being on the ground floor. I command this room to be securely sealed and to rise, rise, rise!"

It was a dramatic and effective bit of theater, the assembly gasping as the floor shuddered beneath their feet. Magic poured out of Bogdan like golden oil released from a vast reservoir, seeping into the floor and walls, easing and accelerating the movement. The great doors to the garden slammed shut, erasing the view of it falling below as the hall rose in the air, accompanied by Bogdan's chanted urging. Metal bars snaked over the doors, weaving in, then sealing over, taking on the surface covering of the other walls, soon no hint remaining that there had been any egress.

Beside him, Seliah stifled a sigh, her gaze turning upward toward the glass-paned ceiling, the last indication of a world outside this house.

"Last chance to escape this fun house forever," he murmured to her. "I could concede to Bogdan. Or throw the match." A large part of him hoped she'd agree, which was to be expected, but the part of him that urged her to say no, that they were sticking it out came as a surprise. Since when had this become something he actually wanted?

"No," Seliah replied, that sigh still in her voice. "We are going to win and we are going to make this place better, a home worth living in."

"That's my girl." He said it in equal parts ruefulness and satisfaction.

"Behold," Bogdan declared, well pleased with himself. "Not only have I demonstrated my ability to modify the house as I choose, to force it to undo changes it made on its own and to follow my will instead, but I have permanently altered the security of this hall so that it is unassailable. I'm sure everyone will understand if you're unable to top this, little brother—or even come close to matching it."

The assembly seemed to agree, quietly talking amongst themselves, speculative gazes on Bogdan. A familiar sent running to confirm returned with the news that all was as Bogdan had declared it to be.

Jadren experienced a sinking feeling of despair, his magic and enthusiasm ebbing low. "We don't have the kind of power available to work a change of that magnitude," he said to Seliah. "Even with you at full power, I'm not the wizard Bogdan is. His ability to manipulate physical objects is unparalleled."

"Then be the wizard *you* are." She turned to face him, amber eyes earnest. "Work to your strengths."

"I thought the moment for me to red-mist Bogdan had passed," he commented wryly.

Seliah was already shaking her head. "Not that. Use your magic for good."

"It's only good for keeping myself alive."

"Not true. If your magic isn't healing, then what is it?"

"This is an unanswerable question, now that Maman is dead."

"Wrong. She didn't know either, or she wouldn't have experimented on you. It's in you to know." She poked him in the chest with a pointy finger. "It's inherited magic, right? All of you have it to some extent, manifesting as a resistance to being damaged."

"Hmm." She had a point. And the answer seemed to be

there dangling elusively just out of reach.

"Do you need more time, Jadren?" Bogdan called mockingly. "Or—"

"Yes, thanks," Jadren said back. "Appreciate the offer." Turning his shoulder to the fuming wizard, he focused on Seliah. "Keep going. What else?"

"Why did you restore my hair when you healed me? That's not healing either."

He frowned, trying to remember. "I like it long and I missed it. I wanted to put it back. Restore it so that..." He trailed off, not quite able to put words to his ability, but feeling closer to it than ever.

"Yes." Seliah nodded eagerly. "Your magic is strong in kinetics and time manipulation, your MP scorecard showed. In penetrating to the realm beyond what most of us understand. Maybe your magic is more a kind of repair and restoration that you do to yourself, but also apply to anything."

His mind and heart raced, excited by this possibility as he hadn't been by anything he'd attempted in all his life. Then he deflated. "We still don't have enough magic to match—"

"Tik tok," Bogdan called out in irritation. "I'd have insisted on a time limit, had I known you'd be dragging your feet like this."

"Poor planning on your part," Jadren shot back. Still, if he was going to do anything, he needed to do it soon, as the assembly grew restless, many shooting him concerned looks. He was losing their confidence.

"We don't need a ton of magic," Seliah said in a rush. "Consider this: the house knows this about you and wants you to restore her to the way she wants to be. Maybe this shifting and changing and trapping people isn't malicious but more like... well, like the kind of insanity you and I both experienced. Magic stagnation and other weirdnesses." She waved her free hand vaguely.

"Other weirdnesses," he repeated, utterly charmed by her, and also fiercely intrigued.

"I don't know how to explain it in magical terms," she snapped in frustration. "It's just a working theory."

"No, I think you're on to something." He and Seliah had both had their magic go awry, turning back on themselves, expressing in ways not under their control. If House El-Adrel had developed a kind of consciousness, perhaps she had suffered, from inattention and inability to fully exercise her magic, or some such. Could be that the shifting around of the rooms were the house's version of nightmares, of calling out in her sleep, kicking and fighting against unseen foes. He could sympathize. "I wonder if the painting of House Phel was a clue," he mused.

Seliah caught her breath. "Nic and Gabriel raised the manse from the marshes and restored it to its former state. You and I always use that metaphor of losing ourselves to the trauma states as being like going underwater, sinking into the bog. When you helped free me of madness, you said my magic tasted foul. Stagnant, poisonous stuff that had to be drained away. Which you did."

He nodded along, that thrill of epiphany zinging along his nerves with a feeling of correctness, of hitting upon the right answer. Even better, if they were right about this—and he felt sure they were—then it shouldn't require much magic at all. "But how do I declare what I'm going to do if all I'm doing is freeing the house?"

"I'm sure you'll think of something." She grinned cheekily, and he simply had to kiss her.

"You could always just use the bed," Bogdan observed cattily.

"Does sarcasm run in your family?" Seliah asked with a grimace. But she was excited, too, a shimmer of anticipation in her that they were on the correct track.

"Apparently it goes with the resistance to death."

"Spitting in the face of danger? That tracks."

"Jadren!" Bogdan shouted. "Enough stalling already. Act or concede."

"Here goes nothing," Jadren told Seliah, giving her one more quick kiss.

"Exactly," she replied. "Stand back and allow the wave to break."

Jadren raised a hand for silence, needing to this time, as the assembly had fallen into gradually rising conversation during the lull. "Denizens of House El-Adrel," he said, waiting for the last of urgent talkers to self-consciously wind up. "Like me, many of you were born in this house and have spent your lives here. We have always had a conflicted relationship with her—proudly telling tales of her whimsical changes and gleefully speculating on how many bodies lie trapped within her walls. We are also wary of becoming one of those bodies. I believe every one of us has some story of being trapped by disappearing doors or stairways, minor aggravations and major, even life-threatening dangers. This is a fundamental legacy of House El-Adrel."

Bogdan faked a yawn. "Is this relevant?"

But the crowd of people—wizards, familiars, mundanes—all listened with interest, many nodding with wry smiles. Yes, everyone had a story about the house they all loved and feared in equal measure.

"We live without windows," Jadren continued, ignoring Bogdan, "so as not to be alarmed by the changing scenery as the house contorts herself. We enter and leave only with the assistance of the head of the house, which is hardly a workable solution."

People exchanged affirmations over that. Functionally it meant they'd had to wait for ages for a group large enough for Katica El-Adrel to deign sufficient for her attention.

"I propose that we no longer have to live like this." Jadren allowed that startling statement to settle. "We know from old tales, from drawings and other artwork, that the house wasn't always this way. This isn't normal. These are symptoms of a house in distress. The sleeping contortions of an intelligent being unable to metaphorically breathe."

Some looked skeptical, but other faces showed dawning understanding like his. It made so much sense.

"This is absurd," Bogdan sneered. "First of all, this is building, nothing more, and it's the centuries of layered and conflicting spells that create the effects we currently wrestle. Second, even if this fairytale is true, what in the dark arts do you propose to do about it, Jaddy boy?"

"I'm going put her back the way she was."

Grasping the brass widget around his neck, in the direction he'd used to heal Seliah, he glanced at her and squeezed her hand. She nodded solemnly, amber eyes on fire with anticipation, her magic flowing into him sweetly, moonlight illuminating a dark night, water refreshing a desert landscape. Not a huge amount, but it should be enough. Wrapping his hand around the widget, mentally aiming it at the house in general, he formed the idea for her. Not an instruction or command, but an invitation. To wake, to be free of the chains of time and controlling wizards. In some ways, the house had been as much a prisoner as he had been. No wonder they got along.

At first, nothing happened, and Jadren focused on the same ideas he'd used to heal Seliah. *Bring her back whole and functioning. Put things to rights. Let her heal and live.*

The crowd murmured, a rising tide of speculation, a few people yipping in surprise, as the house *rippled.* That was the closest he could come to describing the sensation. No groaning of wood or clacking of metal this time. Instead, the house seemed to physically shimmer, a sensation of startled joy singing through the very foundation. Then she woke and unwound.

Yes, the floor moved beneath them, but with a smooth gliding, the walls unfurling like a flower blooming. Open archways appeared, leading into other hallways, and rooms beyond. Some glimpses revealed rooms and entire wings Jadren knew he'd never seen before, that perhaps hadn't been seen in generations.

Windows opened into the autumn afternoon, showing a

stable landscape and hints of towers still growing, a pool with flowing fountains out another, and the blooming courtyard someone had referred to as the queen's garden returned, to Seliah's laughing delight.

The transformation seemed to take hours and no time at all, the house settling into her new—or perhaps ancient—conformation, with a hum of satisfaction. Everyone, including Jadren, seemed to be holding their breath, but nothing happened. Birds sang outside the windows. A warm, flower-scented breeze wafted in, and fountains played a musical song.

"I remember those fountains," an elderly wizard called out. "They vanished when I was a small boy and no one could bring them back, not even then Lady Brantly El-Adrel. At night, they shine with colored lights, if they're the same."

Bogdan had an expression of terrible realization on his face, the knowledge that he'd been defeated. Except that he refused to accept it. "It appears we have a tie," he declared. "Three for three. We agreed: sudden death."

~ 14 ~

THE CRUSHING COURSELOAD perversely served to settle Alise back into her former life, far more quickly than she expected. Rushing from class to class, snagging every spare moment to study—sometimes completing required reading even as she walked to that class—left her with little time or mental energy to reflect on her changed circumstances.

On the rare occasions she had a moment alone with her thoughts, it rankled deeply that she'd gone from being a contracted House Phel wizard, the lone worker of Elal spirit magic in Meresin, valued wizard and member of the family, to simply being a student again. And not exactly a celebrated one. Her professors treated her with suspicion, wariness, or sometimes outright disdain. More than one even commented on the pointlessness of starting Alise on a module that would take weeks to complete if she was just going to run off in the middle of it.

Her classmates weren't unkind, but neither were they convivial. Wizards and familiars didn't much mix—not like the cheerful mass of uncategorized students, days she missed sorely—so she was confined to the manifested wizards, most of whom gave her the side-eye for her shenanigans and association with House Phel.

Once manifesting as a wizard, those students concentrated on completing their advanced studies and otherwise devoted themselves to political maneuvering. Some would return to the houses of their birth, to take up the family business, but the majority needed to find good positions at established houses, preferably high houses or at least tier two houses. Naturally, many of them would end up at tier three or lower houses, but nobody aimed for that.

With House Phel on probation, a status made even more precarious by the several pending legal matters, no one had any interest in cultivating that connection. Besides that, everyone recalled that it was Alise's own sister who had started the alarming new trend of familiars attempting to run away from their rightful wizards, and that Alise had been involved in the most recent bad behavior. Being associated with her conveyed zero advantages and arguably numerous disadvantages.

On top of all of that, Sabrina Sammael had not returned to Convocation Academy, and the blonde wizard who'd ruled the social hierarchy at the school had not been shy about Alise's offenses against her before Sabrina stormed off home to get daddy—not incidentally head of high-House Sammael—to fix her problem. Sabrina had been obsessed with Han as long as anyone could remember. The moment he'd manifested as a familiar, she'd pulled strings to have him bonded to her. That he'd evaded her power move and, adding insult to injury, defied the rules and ran off with Iliana, a "mealymouthed, milksop *familiar*," of all people, had driven Sabrina into a rage that the school still dissected with relish. Sabrina hadn't hesitated to catalog Alise's many faults in the process, which dealt the final blow to her reputation, with little regard for the truth.

As a result, no one bothered with her much. The few who did ask for her tale, usually in titillated whispers, were promptly discouraged by the thought-seekers. Those proctors kept a close eye on Alise, as the provost had promised. She supposed she should appreciate that they ensured she had plenty of quiet time to concentrate on work. The sooner she completed her studies, the sooner she could go home to House Phel.

But she was lonely. Even Nic's cheerful letters delivered daily by Ratsiel courier—Alise had no idea where Nic found the time to write daily, with all her responsibilities—didn't do much to make her feel better. Life at House Phel went on without her and sometimes reading about everyone's doings only reminded her sharply that she wasn't a part of it.

If not for her clandestine quest to unearth documents regarding House Phel from the Convocation archives, she might have despaired. As it was, the challenge kept her going when she began to wonder about the point of completing her education. And the independent study assigned by the provost provided her with the perfect excuse to raid the shadowy depths of the library. Of course, with her wall-to-wall course schedule leaving no time during the day for searching the archives, that meant she mainly spent time there after dinner, when the place was at its shadowy maximum.

Alise would finish her meal alone in the crowded dining

hall, reading one of her assigned texts under the watchful eye of a proctor, then proceed to the library. The pass the provost had given her turned out to give her an alarming amount of access to the archives. All Alise had to do was wave the magically sealed pass indicating she was engaged in a secret, top-priority research project for Provost Uriel and the librarians, all high-caliber House Harahel wizards, would unlock gates and rare-document display cases for her, then leave her be with nothing but admonitions to be careful.

Being able to summon her own fire elemental and use her Elal wizardry to compel the elemental to use all of its energy to produce light and no heat both endeared her to the meticulous librarians who feared fire more than anything and allowed her to penetrate the darkest corners on her quest.

A quest that so far had utterly failed to yield any House Phel records. It was so perplexing she'd nearly gotten to the point of asking where those archives had gone. All the other existing high houses had huge archives, well lit and clearly labeled. Entire rooms were devoted to the oldest houses, but even tier three houses had at least a shelf or two of records. They were organized more or less in terms of founding date of the house, something she suspected had happened organically, with the oldest houses near the back of the library, in the original sections that now held only shelves and no study tables, and the newest in rooms and on shelves that had clearly been more recently added to the front of the library. As she had no idea when House Phel had been originally founded—that information was no doubt, frustratingly, in those archives she couldn't find—she didn't know where to look for even a telltale gap in the stored records.

Thanks to her Convocation History course, she did have a list of all the houses recognized at any point in Convocation history, along with their current status. It was a bit out of date as she'd taken the class fairly early on, as did most Convocation Academy students, so it didn't list House Phel at all, not even on probationary status. That was due to timing, however, as Gabriel had only petitioned to have the house restored a couple of years before. She'd ask for an updated list, but that wouldn't serve the clandestine aspect of her project very well.

The list did prove one important point, however: several houses were listed as defunct, the house name having been retired by the Convocation when the associated family failed to produce wizards of sufficient MP scores, the people essentially returning to the ranks of the mundane. Alise found the archives for *those* houses, by dint of slow searching. Most only occupied a shelf, or part of one, and most had never risen higher than an ambitious tier three before subsiding again into obscurity. Most interesting, each of these sets of documents was capped by a final notebook with the official Convocation seal. It effectively ended the archive of the retired house, and it summarized the essential house data: date of founding, date of retirement, and all of the wizards certified by the Convocation as belonging to the family line of the house. Those were particularly helpful as many of the other archives were magically sealed so she couldn't open them. Probably keyed to only members of those houses.

The glimpses of history these summaries provided fasci- nated Alise, and she had to exert self-control not to follow her curiosity down a rabbit hole of Convocation history, far more interesting than anything she'd ever studied in class. Some of the archives were centuries old and contained intriguing allusions to magic systems and products she had no idea had ever existed. In fact, they likely didn't exist now and she smiled absently at how the ambitious Nic might react to knowing about some of these. Not that many could be fit into the House Phel product aegis, but if anyone could find a way, she could.

But that wasn't Alise's assignment, so she put those books aside, continuing in her quest. With no luck at all. She couldn't seem to find anything at all on House Phel. Night after night, week after week, she searched until she began to feel sure that she'd explored every dark and gritty bit of the library.

She even resorted to summoning a higher level spirit to help her search, as a last resort. The summoning itself had gone fine. Her strengths lay in Elal magic, after all, and she was pleased with her improvement in those skills, substantially better than she'd been before she'd come back to school. The spirit had taken to the task with obedient fervor, which gave Alise a little burst of pride, as she'd accomplished what few wizards, even high-level wizards in House Elal's employ, could do. The more complex a spirit, the less inclined they were to be enlisted for human tasks.

She'd hoped she could teach a higher-level spirit to recognize the simple pattern of characters that spelled out "Phel." After all, House Elal was known for using spirits of all types to spy on everyone in the Convocation. Alise had been disinherited before her father taught her those proprietary tricks, but there had to be a way to instruct the spies in *what* to seek out and report. They couldn't be reporting everything—that would be an unworkable onslaught of information. She should be able to do it, too. But no.

After several more weeks of wasted effort—and a considerable amount of magic drain that advanced her quest not at all and gained her only several scoldings from her professors—she gave up on it and released the spirit, to its gleeful delight. So much for her pride in her amazing wizardry.

Alise blamed mental overload, because it took her way too long to hit upon the other obvious explanation: the spirit hadn't found anything because there was nothing to find.

But how could she be sure? It was difficult to prove that something *wasn't* there. Not unless she'd exhausted every resource and there was a major one she hadn't yet touched: the librarians.

Some nights, after she'd canvassed the same obscure corners she'd examined before, Alis felt like she'd come to know everything in the archives better than the librarians themselves. But that wasn't true. Alise lacked the Harahel magic that allowed them to mentally catalog everything they'd ever seen, touched, or read. Some Harahel wizards could even retain entire texts, so she'd heard, or hundreds or thousands of them, making House Harahel the ultimate repository for the institutional knowledge of the Convocation. They were one of the original twelve high houses. House Calliope—tier two— might do the actual printing, but Harahel controlled the information that went into everything published. Which meant that they could very well be culpable for seeing to it that no House Phel records remained.

It also meant that only they could confirm whether or not those records existed. Solution: she needed to forsake total secrecy, come up with a cover story, and simply ask one of the Harahel wizards for the Phel archives. She didn't like exposing her interest, but she'd exhausted every other avenue.

Decided upon the course of action, Alise figured she'd wasted enough time, and sought out the night librarian. The archives had pretty much emptied out, giving her the most privacy she was likely to get. A few students lingered at the study tables at the better-lighted front of the library, solo or finishing work in quiet groups. Alise spotted one of the dark arts professors, an academy fixture, who always said she did her best work at night. The students were never sure if she was making a joke on her expertise, but Alise could confirm that the elderly professor spent hours every night at the table unofficially reserved for her, the green shaded elemental light focused on her rune-covered pages casting an eerie pool of emerald around her.

The night librarian gave Alise a half-smile of question as she approached, setting aside the book he was reading, marking his place carefully with a thin bookmark. With a circling of his finger, to show her he had it handled, he created a bubble-of-silence ward around them, so as not to disturb the other patrons. The faint sounds of rustling pages faded away.

"It's past midnight, Wizard Alise," he observed mildly. He was one of the younger ones, no doubt assigned to night duty because of that youth. Unless he was nocturnally inclined, like the dark arts professor.

"I like the nighttime," she answered, surprising herself, as she hadn't really been in the habit lately of responding to anyone with anything but the required answer. This was part of her plan, she decided. Be pleasant. Have innocuous conversation so as not to transmit the urgency of her inquiry. "It's... soothing." She surreptitiously glanced at the nameplate on the desk, realizing she didn't know his name, though he somehow knew hers. "Wizard Cillian."

"Soothing," he repeated, cocking his head. He wore his chestnut curls short, as most wizards did, but not close-cropped, so they tumbled around his intelligent face almost boyishly. Alise suspected the unruly length came from him failing to pay attention and enlist grooming imps regularly, rather than as a style choice. In point of fact, one of those curls fell across his forehead just then and into his eyes, causing him to brush it back with what seemed to be a habitual gesture. "And it's Cillian, with a hard C."

Embarrassed by her error, and by exposing her rudeness in having no idea who he was, she flushed. Mentally, she nudged the fire elemental tailing her to move farther back, hopefully casting her face in shadow.

"Did you need something, Wizard Alise?" Cillian prompted, his gaze wandering to the book he'd set aside with a hint of wistfulness for whatever had absorbed him. "You usually tell us you don't need assistance," he added with raised brows, making her think she had spoken with him before and had brushed him off in her single-minded focus.

"Yes. Please," she answered, summoning a smile that felt creaky on her face, hoping it would evoke some vestige of politeness from her empty social well. "My sister, who is Lady Phel now—"

"I know who your sister is," he interrupted, not unkindly, but with a bit of reproof. Of course, a Harahel wizard wouldn't like any suggestion that they don't know information of note. "Nic hasn't been gone so long from the academy that we've forgotten her."

"Right," she replied, certain her cheeks had grown even warmer. When had she become so awkward, even shy? *Too much time alone.* She couldn't think of the last time she'd had a conversation with someone who wasn't a professor or fellow student, and then only about schoolwork. "Lady Phel—Nic—asked me to look up some information in the House Phel archives, but I haven't been able to locate that section." There, reasonable, plausible, and not untrue.

"Naturally, I can help with that," he said briskly, steepling his fingers together. "And I can teach you how to locate that section for yourself. The archives are organized by founding date—have you got that?"

"Er, no." She said it apologetically, feeling as if she'd let him down.

"I see. That makes it more difficult, but not impossible. There have been many houses over the centuries, but Phel was a high house, if I recall correctly, so the information should be readily available. Give me a moment."

Something about the way Cillian said "if I recall correctly" made Alise think he only said so out of an attempt at humility, as the opposite was unthinkable. That level of self-confidence should've been offputtingly but she found it oddly endearing.

Of course, it was nice to talk to a skilled wizard who was sure of their abilities, but who wasn't interested in ruling the world. Most Harahel wizards didn't have familiars, as they rarely needed to draw heavily on magic. Was there ever a library emergency? Alise suppressed a chuckle at the thought.

Cillian frowned at her and Alise opened her mouth with an excuse, thinking he heard the laugh and suspected her of mocking him. "I'm not finding this via the usual indexing. Can you ask your Phel family for the founding date?"

Her Phel family. No one else had used that phrase with her and it gave her a surprising surge of sentimental nostalgia. "That's actually one of the things she asked me to look up." She hurried on as Cillian's brows climbed. "There's some debate among the family of the exact date and the house records are... in less than ideal condition."

He leaned forward, instantly intrigued. "Is it true that the entire manse sank into the swamps?"

"All but the center section and even that part flooded," she answered, bemused to find herself happy to do so. "Everything on the lower shelves of the library was destroyed," she added, knowing that would be of interest to him and oddly wanting to tell him interesting things.

Gratifyingly, he blanched. "Had they been properly recorded?"

She knew he meant recorded in the House Harahel collective memory and she hated to disappoint him in his earnest concern. Maybe she shouldn't have mentioned the drowned books. "I don't know. But it seems likely that they complied with Convocation customs."

"That's not necessarily true," he chided, fretting over these books he'd never known existed until this moment. "Not all houses want the expense of an in-house Harahel wizard. We're often at the bottom of the list of priorities. And, ironically enough, high houses are the worst! They have all the resources in the world but will they pay for a librarian? No. In their arrogance they think they have everything handled, that they can do as they please and no one can criticize them." He finished, color high, and clamped his lips shut on further ranting. "I apologize, Wizard Alise," he said stiffly, recollecting his company. "No offense intended toward High House Elal, or to the legacy House Phel."

Amused with him, and with the ongoing revelation that not everyone mentally genuflected to the high houses and Convocation law—apparently being a bit of a rebel opened one up to confessions from other free thinkers—Alise smiled at him. "It's really fine. The high houses *are* arrogant and many think only of their own aggrandizement and not the good of the whole."

He appeared bemused himself. "You have a lovely smile, when you smile for real."

For real? Alise felt that smile fade, sinking off her lips like blood draining away. When had she developed fake smiles, ones so obvious that this random librarian recognized them without even knowing her?

"So," she prompted him, being as businesslike as possible, "there's no way to locate the House Phel archives without knowing the founding date?"

"I wouldn't say that," he answered, a bit offended by the

implied slight to his abilities, as she'd hoped. Pretending to friendliness as a cover was one thing; giving him ideas was another. "There's always a way," he continued. "Let's go look. Sometimes there's no substitute for the evidence of your own eyes." He pulled out a sign saying he was temporarily away from his desk, along with a tiny Ratsiel courier stationed beside it so that patrons could summon him if they needed immediate assistance, and then came around the desk. "Let's begin with the oldest archives and work our way forward."

Alise walked along with him, deciding not to explain she'd already tried that method. In the first place, one always felt silly insisting you'd looked everywhere, only to have someone else find the thing immediately, as if it had somehow only been invisible to you. Also, she'd asked for help, so she'd bide her time and see if his Harahel wizardry and librarian status allowed him to find something she couldn't. If he couldn't, then she could conclude the records simply weren't there. Though what the next step would be—other than messaging Nic to admit defeat—she wasn't sure. She hated to think she'd failed House Phel, but pretending otherwise served no one.

"I apologize, Wizard Alise," Cillian said, hesitating over the words, and after they'd passed through several rooms in silence. "I was overly familiar, commenting on your smile like that. Also, I shouldn't have said anything about it being past midnight. Or about high houses. I didn't mean to offend. Sometimes my mouth runs away with me. A most regrettable flaw."

She started to smile, then stopped, self-conscious about whether it looked like a real one or not. "It's all right," she reassured him, pouring sincerity into her tone. "I wasn't offended and I don't think that's a flaw, regrettable or otherwise. I'd much rather listen to someone who speaks their true mind than all the ones who mouth platitudes and Convocation-accepted opinions."

He slid her a sideways look. "You mean that."

"Why wouldn't I?"

"I don't know," he mused. "You're not what I expected, I suppose. All the nights I've watched you come and go from the library, speaking to no one, keeping to yourself, so aloof and poised, lovely as a candle flame and just as untouchable, I—" He broke off, shaking his head. "And there I go again. Dark arts take it. I don't know what's wrong with me, more than usual anyway. Please forgive me."

"There's nothing to forgive," she replied lightly, though she was shaken—and terribly curious despite herself to know what else he'd been about to say. How did one politely ask someone to continue saying alarmingly interesting, flattering, and totally inappropriate things about yourself? *One doesn't*, an inner voice answered, one she recognized as her maman, the eternal arbiter of etiquette. Though Alise hoped Cillian would continue in the same vein, he remained obdurately silent now. So, he'd known who she was for some time, and had been paying attention to her coming and going. And she'd been so absorbed in her own thoughts that she'd never once noticed him noticing. *Which is just as well*, she reminded herself. *You can't afford to have friends. Look what happened to you last time, with Han and Iliana.*

"We really need more lights back here," Cillian said on a

sigh as they reached the oldest archives in the darkest corner.

"Allow me." Alise brightened the fire elemental still tailing her shoulder and summoned several more to position themselves at intervals along the shelves. "I've instructed them to light only," she said as Cillian opened his mouth in obvious alarm. "No heat or burning."

"Handy that," he commented, relaxing. "Though these back rooms are chilly enough that a little heat wouldn't be unwelcome. That's not a suggestion, though," he added hastily.

"I didn't take it as such. I know how you librarians are about fire," she said teasingly.

A joke that clearly fell short, since he shuddered in horror. "It's bad luck to even say the word," he replied, very seriously, beginning his search at the far end. "I'd love it if House Salis would develop a way of fireproofing books."

"Does it matter, if Harahel has them all memorized?"

"People meet with unexpected accidents," he answered vaguely, absorbed in his task. "We try to build in redundancy, but even the most powerful Harahel wizards have finite capacity. We also have fewer dedicated house members all the time, as wizards with the correct combination of MP scores often find better paying work elsewhere. House Harahel doesn't have much in the way of income. Without the Convocation contracts, we'd be destitute." He paused, glancing over his shoulder, gentle black eyes wide. "That's something else I shouldn't have said. You have a knack for making me even more garrulous than usual."

"Everybody tells me that," she replied drily.

"Truly?"

"No." She laughed. "Nobody has *ever* told me that. I was being sarcastic."

"You have a pretty laugh, too." He turned back to the shelves, saying something scathing to himself under his breath. "Anyway, House Harahel still births plenty of wizards each generation, so please don't think we're in any danger of having our status revoked. Lady Harahel would have my head if *that* rumor began making the rounds."

"Your secrets are safe with me."

"You know, I think they are." He tossed a grateful smile over his shoulder. "Which is good, because you're easy to spill secrets to."

"It's the bubble of silence," she told him somberly. "It does that to people."

"Ha." He whirled and pointed a finger at her. "*That* was sarcasm. I'm getting better at recognizing it."

Alise watched him work, feeling a bit useless and therefor restless. She could be using this time to better effect, like parking herself at one of the nearby study carrels and memorizing the incantations for the next day's advanced practicum in potions, not anywhere close to her best skill. Still, she found herself curiously reluctant to walk away. Cillian talked to himself all the time, too, maintaining a running conversation with himself about the houses, their archives, the state of the documents, the library system overall, and occasionally, a comment about that house and some bit of gossip from their ancient history. He seemed to have forgotten Alise's presence entirely, and she listened, oddly charmed by him and also entertained. So, she stayed within his warded bubble of silence, her wizard senses showing her the boundaries of it, following along as he moved.

He worked faster than she had, checking off houses against the list in his mind, moving through the stacks from room to room, their environs grower brighter and newer, until he came to an abrupt halt. "That can't be right," he declared, jamming fists to hips and glaring around at the shelves.

"They're missing?" Alise tendered with mixed feelings. Disappointing not to find them, but also something of a relief to be vindicated in her own search results.

Cillian jumped at her question and turned on her in considerable surprise. "I forgot you were here."

So much for the flattering fantasy that the eccentric librarian wizard was fascinated by her. Of course, having people forget her existence was pretty much standard for her, so she could hardly hold it against him.

"Still here," she replied mildly. "No House Phel archives?"

"No." He sounded personally offended, stabbing a finger toward the shelves. "These are House Xerograf archives and they were founded only 150 years ago and I *know* House Phel came and went before that. I've been wondering for a while now, thinking some of these houses had to be founded after Phel, but I wasn't *sure* until now. Still, this is impossible."

~ 15 ~

"CLEARLY NOT ACTUALLY impossible," Alise pointed out, not above enjoying turning a bit of pedantry back on Cillian, though he seemed oblivious. "I was willing to accept that I couldn't find the House Phel archives, but if *you* can't, then they must be missing. Simple logic."

"There's nothing logical about this. There must be some other explanation." He sounded as if he were asking a question, but not of her. Instead, his accusing glare roved over the library at large, as if it had somehow failed him.

"Are any other house archives missing?" she asked.

Now he fastened his offended gaze on her. "Archives don't go missing," he answered crossly. "That's the whole point of archives, to preserve and keep them."

"But would you *know* if others were missing?" she persisted. "You didn't know the House Phel archives were missing."

He spread his hands wide in frustration. "How are you supposed to notice something that isn't there? It's not as if they left empty shelves behind, a big, glaring gap shouting 'hey, look, stuff used to be here and it's gone now...'" He trailed off, awful understanding dawning on his face.

"Who would 'they' be?" Alise asked, pouncing on the opportunity. When Cillian stared at her blankly, she waved a hand. "Who could do that? Who could remove the archives of an entire house and rearrange the shelves so no evidence remained that a significant number of documents had disappeared?"

"Nobody," he answered, stricken. "I mean a librarian theoretically could have the access, but no one would. Certainly not anyone from Harahel. That goes against everything we stand for."

Somehow, she absolutely believed him. That didn't mean there weren't wizards in his house who would act otherwise, but Cillian was totally earnest. "Would someone in Harahel have the knowledge in their heads? You know, memorized."

He considered that, then shook his head. "Unlikely. The houses, especially high houses, tend to be proprietary about their records and don't like anyone looking at them who isn't properly authorized. Most of these are keyed to house members only," he added sadly.

"I'd noticed that. Why store the records here at Convocation Center here if no one can read them?"

"Not *no one*," he corrected in his pedantic way, but she found the trait charming enough that it didn't bother her. "There are channels for authorization. When Lord Gabriel Phel registered to reinstate the house, he'd have received authorization, along with the ability to authorize others, which he could then convey as he saw fit. So we know the archives had to have been here when he received the Convocation blessing and..." Cillian trailed off, arrested by whatever he saw in Alise's face. "The archives were *not* here then," he said on a breath of realization.

Curse her transparent expressions. This would be tricky to navigate, but it was already too late. It wasn't a question so much of trusting the librarian wizard as enlisting him to her cause at this point. Better to have his help than reporting back on her. "No, they weren't. Almost certainly not," she amended. "Gabriel—Lord Phel, I mean—wasn't given access to the archives when he received the probationary reinstatement. He wasn't raised in the Convocation so..."

"So he didn't know to ask for them and it apparently didn't occur to anyone to mention their existence—or lack thereof. How could that have happened?" He gazed around at the quiet shelves as if expecting an answer, before pinning Alise with a knowing stare. "You're not surprised."

"I've been searching for weeks now," she replied, sounding defensive to her own ears.

"No, it's more than that. You suspected the records had been taken and only asked me to help to corroborate your suspicions. Ohh," he breathed, face lighting with understanding. "Nic Elal, erm, Lady Phel, that is—she told her wizard that he should've been given access to the Phel archives. They already suspect that he was deliberately diverted from them and asked you to ferret out the truth. You're a *spy!*"

His voice rose so high with elated discovery that Alise wanted to shush him, even knowing that they remained inside the bubble of silence. "No, that's not it," she protested. "I was looking for my own curiosity and—"

"Oh, come now, Wizard Alise," he chided in that schoolmarmish way that she found ridiculously engaging. "Let's not play stupid among friends. You've been in here night after night, combing these archives, which have nothing to do with your rather crushing courseload, even with the flimsy excuse of that independent study. You haven't been losing sleep for idle entertainment. You're doing this for House Phel, to attempt to save them from their enemies."

"Their enemies?" she echoed, feeling caught quite flatfooted. And she thought she'd been so subtle and discreet.

"Yes, yes, of course." He waved away the prevarication like a stink in the air. "Everyone knows House Phel is teetering on the brink of collapse. They faced an uphill climb to begin with and, well, to extend the analogy, there's a substantial legal avalanche poised just above. It doesn't look good."

Dread curled in Alise's stomach, making her feel ill. "I don't think it looks that bad," she said weakly. She swayed on her feet, the edges of her vision darkening.

"Here now." Cillian caught her by the arm, frowning. "You're running on fumes. When was the last time you ate?"

"At dinner," she answered indignantly, wanting to tear away from his supporting hand—she had her pride, after all—finding herself unable to muster the strength. It would be more humiliating if she fainted, so she didn't dare try too hard.

"Which was easily twelve hours ago, and I doubt you ate much then," he retorted, sounding most annoyed. "You never do."

"Have you been watching me?" she asked, wishing she could take back the words when he blanched.

"No! No, not like that. You're just about the only person who doesn't try to smuggle snacks into the library," he added, sounding pleased to have hit on what had to be an excuse. "Besides which, your magic is very thin. When was the last time you replenished from a familiar?"

"I don't know." She really didn't remember, which bothered her more than she wanted Cillian to know. Like she needed someone else in her life beating her up about wearing her magic thin. "One of the practicums," she said, as that sounded likely.

"At which point you used up everything you got to perform whatever dog and pony trick the professor required, no doubt."

"You don't know." Her annoyance gave her fuel to yank her arm away, finally.

"I do know." he sounded equally aggravated. "I graduated from Convocation Academy, too. Just because I can't do combat magic and hurl fireballs or summon ninety-seven non-burning fire elementals to light my way doesn't mean I don't know exactly how much the coursework, especially the practicums, of which you have three, as I recall, exhaust everything you've got and then some. Speaking of which," he added as she gaped at him, "you should release some of those elementals. They're only draining you more and we hardly need them to show us what's *not* here. Come with me."

He took off at a brisk stride, Alise hurrying to catch up and belatedly releasing the fire elementals. Not that Cillian was correct and not that she felt immediately better to have done so. He'd taken down the silence bubble, too, so she held her tongue on the several barbed remarks she'd like to offer on his unsolicited opinion.

"Where are we going?" she hissed as she caught up with him at his desk, where he gathered up his book and a few other supplies—including what looked to be an empty bag of snacks—and traded good mornings with a Harahel wizard librarian who now sat behind the desk.

It was morning already? Her admittedly tired brain finally registered what he'd said about dinner being twelve hours before. They'd apparently worked all night.

"I'm feeding you breakfast," he answered, as she caught up with him at the library doors, which he held open for her. "And finding you a general-use familiar."

She didn't bother to explain that she didn't like bothering the familiars who were bonded to no one and worked for the Convocation. Too much time in Meresin with their different ways of thinking, and with Han and Iliana, and Quinn, all familiars and her closest friends. Not to mention Nic, her own sister. She'd become squeamish about using a familiar's magic when it didn't feel freely given. Something nigh impossible to explain to anyone solidly part of Convocation society.

"I can feed myself," she confined herself to saying, then wondered why she was following him so obediently and slowed at the juncture to the dining hall.

"That's in question," he replied acerbically. "Not that way; this way."

Streams of students and faculty flowed in increasing volume, unusual for this early in the morning, their morning chatter subdued. "The dining hall is the other direction," she objected. Of course, he knew that.

"I know that. I have better food in my chambers."

They passed an El-Adrel clock on the wall, ticking away the relentless truth. Shit. It was even later than she thought. "I have class," she said, the sleepless night abruptly slamming into her as if the giant clock had fallen on her head. It would be a really long day.

"I'll send a note to the Provost excusing you."

"You can't do that."

He glanced at her, surprised. "I *can*. I'm technically faculty."

"I mean," she corrected, "you don't have to do that." Why would he do that?

Shrugging one shoulder, he pointed the turn in the labyrinth of hallways, heading toward the faculty quarters where students weren't allowed without invitation. "I want to. Besides, how can we pursue this fascinating mystery if you're stuck in class?"

Grateful for his discretion in not saying aloud what the mystery involved, she grappled with his question. "We?" she finally repeated, aware that her tired brain wasn't at its sharpest.

"Of course. You asked for my assistance. I have not yet fulfilled your very reasonable request for help as a library patron."

"You don't have to help me further," she said, coming to a halt as he did, outside one of a row of ornate doors facing an open arcade on the other side, the second floor archways overlooking the central quad. The sun poured in, golden with autumn light, sweet with a chorus of birdsong.

"What we miss being inside the library, huh?" he asked,

pausing to look and listen, also. "Come on in."

He pushed the door open for her and held it. "Don't mind the mess. The housekeeping elementals handle the dirt, but I'm afraid I'm not terribly tidy."

That was an understatement. Alise peered around the modest quarters: a small sitting room with glassed-in windows giving onto one of the back courtyards, an open door leading to a bedroom, a compact nook near the front door with a food preparation area. And every possible surface piled high with books, scrolls, papers, small figurines of various monsters—mythical and real—and absolutely nowhere to sit.

"Just move anything," Cillian said. "Wait, not that." He darted in front of her as she went to move a pile of books smugly occupying a large armchair. Taking the topmost with reverent care, he moved it to a high shelf, then scrutinized the pile, extracted several and stacked them on the desk already piled teeteringly high with more books. "It looks like there's no system," he said apologetically, "but I know where everything is."

"That makes sense."

"It does?" He set a kettle on the burner with a tiny fire elemental bonded to it, ticking it to heat with a lick of magic. Then he began extracting items from a House Frigere cooler.

"Yes." Fearing she'd fall asleep the moment she stopped moving, Alise elected not to sit after all and instead wandered around the cozy room. A fireplace, currently unlit, was neatly laid, and the glimpse of his bedchamber showed more piles of books on the table next to the bed, but the bed itself had been made, the counterpane unwrinkled. "No doubt your Harahel wizardry and training are at work there, allowing you to catalog everything. I bet you always know exactly where everything is. Enviable, really."

"True. I'm good at keeping order for other people in the library, but for myself—why bother? I could spend my time in such more interesting ways. Cinnamon roll?"

"Excuse me?"

He held out a plate. "Cinnamon roll. I made them myself."

She took the plate, set it on a rare, clear corner of the counter, perched on a stool there, and peeled off the outer coil. The sweet yeasty smell made her want to gobble the whole thing, but she restrained herself to a polite nibble. Sugary and warmly spicy, she nearly moaned aloud at the deliciousness, chewing thoroughly before indulging in another, bigger bite. Realizing she'd closed her eyes, she opened them to find Cillian watching her with a grin.

"Good?" he asked, though he clearly knew that wasn't in question.

"Amazingly good." She peeled off another layer of outer coil. "Is baking an interesting way to spend your time?"

"It lets me think about interesting things. And it's soothing. And I get to have cinnamon rolls, so it's a win all around." Something sizzled on another elemental-heated surface and he turned to deal with it. The scent of frying meat hit the air, a savory counterpoint to the sweet roll. "How do you like your eggs?"

"As long as they're not hard as old gum, I don't care."

"I know what you mean. How a person eats a cinnamon roll tells you a lot about them," he continued conversationally, his back still to her.

"Oh?" Alise studied her half-eaten roll, which looked more like a tower than a circle now, with the gooey center exposed and upright. She hated to think what that said about her.

"Yes. Some people just bite in and eat it like any bun. Others, like you, uncoil it. Unlike you, however, most uncoilers eat the soft center first." He set a mug of steaming tea before her, fragrant as midsummer blossoms.

"All right, I'll bite, so to speak—what does this tell you about me?" She sipped gingerly, suppressing a sigh at the zinging heat of spices.

Turning, he set a plate in front of her with several strips of bacon, softly scrambled eggs with bits of chive in them, and pile of fresh blueberries. "Meticulous, careful, controlled."

That wasn't wrong, but it also sounded dreadfully boring.

"And you either save the best for last or deny yourself the best part altogether," he added with a nod at the cinnamon roll center still perched on her plate. "We've established you prefer your food soft, not hard, so…"

She popped the final piece of roll into her mouth, where it practically melted in a blaze of sweet goo. "Maybe that's just eggs," she said after swallowing, then dug into said eggs.

"Maybe." He had a way of saying the word like he utterly disagreed but didn't want to say so.

"Besides," she added, stung by his noncommittal reply, "life is difficult. There's no sense avoiding the hard parts and pretending the sweet is there without suffering through the rest."

"Why, Wizard Alise, how astonishingly cynical you are at

such a tender age."

"I just turned eighteen. Hardly a tender age."

"A matter of perspective." Digging into his own food, he said nothing more.

She noticed he ate the center of his cinnamon roll first, and before anything else, leaving the discarded outer coils in an untidy heap. Attempting to think of a neutral bit of conversation to fill the void, she startled at the knock on the door.

"Ah, that's Marah, no doubt." He went to the door cheerfully greeting the woman who entered.

She was middle-aged, with brown hair and matching eyes, a veiled weariness to her, though her smile for Cillian seemed sincere. She was also a familiar. "Need a topping off, Wizard Cillian?" she was asking. "You must be working hard as it's only been a few—" She stopped short at the sight of Alise. "No, I don't do students. Them academy folks don't like me interfering with their programs."

"As a personal favor, Marah," Cillian coaxed. "This is Alise and she's wrung out. I need her help with a project and I can't do that if she's out of juice."

Marah studied her, not in a friendly way either. "Alise Elal, is it? You're the one that done run off."

"It's Alise Phel now," Alise answered with all the composure she could muster. "And you need not give me your magic. Cillian made an assumption."

"She's a cool one, ain't she?" Marah asked Cillian. "Breakfast smells good."

"Let me make you a plate," Cillian said as if nothing could please him more.

"Hmph." Marah eyed Alise then held out her hand. "All right then. Open up a vein. Lucky for you I haven't serviced anyone yet today, so I'm full to the brim."

"Thank you," Alise said, not allowing herself to recoil from the indecent-feeling suggestion, "but really I'm fine."

"She's not fine," Cillian said from the cooking station.

Marah raised her brows at Alise. "He's a stubborn one, but I have a fondness for him. Might as well drink up, wizardling. If you don't, someone else will."

Cillian glanced over his shoulder, giving her what passed for a fierce look from him. "If you don't, I'll report you to the healers."

"All right, already," Alise snarled in exasperation. Not that she disliked the healers, but the treatment would go on her record, and cost House Phel. They didn't need to be paying out more for her upkeep out of their lean coffers than they already were. She clasped Marah around the wrist, as taking her hand felt too intimate, and sipped lightly of the magic she offered. It wasn't bright and sweet, like Han and Iliana's magic, but it pulsed strong, steady, even hearty.

"Take more than that, little wizard," Marah said, not un-kindly, her expression stoic. "Sounds like you'll be needing it."

Because Cillian added his stern glare, Alise took more—just enough to feel not so transparent. Not brittle, as Nic had put it. Taking her hand away, she nodded to Marah. "Thank you for the gift. I appreciate it."

Marah cocked her head, looking quizzical. "Odd one you are. It's no gift. That's why they pay me."

"And a bit extra for the trouble," Cillian said, giving her a coin and a plate. "Your breakfast, madame."

"Madame he calls me," Marah said to Alise with a jovial wink, pocketing the coin. She plucked up her cinnamon roll with a coo of pleasure, uncoiled it entirely, tipped her head back, and fed the long strip into her mouth, chewing as she lowered it—soft end first. Cillian gave Alise a knowing smile and she rolled her eyes at him.

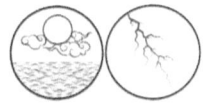

"SO," HE SAID, after Marah left and he piled their dishes with the cooking implements, turning an earth elemental loose to clean them, "what's your theory?"

"Theory?" She felt sharper, replenished with food, tea, and magic, but the warm weight in her belly allowed a drugging drowsiness to creep in around the edges.

Cillian tapped his temple. "I'm sure you have one. You're working through the evidence, keeping an objective perspective to analyze your findings, but you have a theory about where the missing Phel archives went to."

"I really don't." She shook her head to emphasize the fact. "I don't even know where to begin on locating them, except..."

"Aha. Here we go."

She wrinkled her nose at him. "Well, if I can figure out who had the motive to move the archives, along with the access to do so, then I might have a shot at discovering where they went to. Of course, answering that question loops back to why we want to see what's in those archives to begin with."

"Hmm." Cillian gazed at her with solemn interest. "So this is more than Lady Phel wondering who designed the historic flatware."

"While I can see Nic being interested in that under certain circumstances—mostly so she could most cost-effectively replace missing items—she has more pressing questions at the moment."

"Such as?"

Alise contemplated him. This was treacherous territory. "I think I've said enough."

Cillian leaned his elbows on the counter, knocked over a mug full of House Calliope styluses, which he quickly rescued, then put his chin on loose fists, regarding her closely. "You need help, Alise," he said quietly. "More important, I think you need a friend."

"I have friends," she replied, a little too fast.

"Are any of them here?"

She opened her mouth and closed it, not willing to outright lie about it, especially when Cillian clearly knew the truth. "It's House Phel business," she said instead. "I'm not at liberty to share certain information."

"How about I take an educated guess?" Cillian continued, not waiting for permission. "As previously noted, House Phel has a number of enemies. At last count, they—you—faced legal attacks from Elal, El-Adrel, Sammael, and—for some odd reason—Iblis. Some of these enmities are fairly well established and go back a considerable amount of time. Others—"

"Wait," Alise interrupted, forcing her sagging spine straight. The cushy armchair was looking better and better all the time, which meant she'd likely pass out the moment she dared sit in it. "How do you know all of that?"

He gestured expansively at the room. "I read a lot."

"Yes, but if the Phel archives are gone…"

"Ah, but the other house records remain."

"Do you have authorization to access those?" she asked with excited curiosity.

"Some." He shrugged, more of a wriggle with his chin still propped on his hands. "There's also plenty written about the houses and their many and varied conflicts over the centuries that's not exclusive to the individual house archives. You should know that from your Introduction to Convocation History courses."

Those had never been her favorite—dry lists of names and dates, but she regretted now not having paid better attention. She considered her options. Cillian could be helpful. He also owed his primary loyalty to House Harahel.

He watched her keenly, understanding dawning in his expression. "You think Harahel magic could be involved."

"I didn't say that," she protested hastily. Great—all House Phel needed was another outright enemy.

"You didn't have to," he replied grimly. "I asked who had access and opportunity to remove the House Phel archives and the obvious answer is Harahel librarians would. But you lack motive. House Harahel has no reason to conspire against Phel." He held up a hand to stop her as she opened her mouth. "If we did, or do, I'd want to know. As I said, it goes against everything we believe in. Like House Refoel, alone among the Convocation houses, Harahel remains neutral because we have a higher allegiance—to preserving knowledge. You have no reason to trust me, but you can trust in that."

He held her gaze for a long moment, and Alise realized she did trust him. For no reason and probably unwisely, but she did.

"If it's not Harahel," she said, deciding to take the leap and take advantage of this walking encyclopedia, "then I look at other possibilities for access and motive."

"Logical," he agreed, an intrigued sparkle in his soft black gaze and a pleased smile ghosting on his lips. "You have a suspect."

"I might. Riddle me this. How many houses have gone from high house status with a full complement of powerful wizards to no status at all?"

He opened his mouth, then closed it thoughtfully. "Over how much time?" he countered, but she sensed he was giving himself time to think.

"That's something we don't know for sure—more that's been lost—but no more than a few generations. At most."

Cillian frowned. "Some houses disappear entirely. They don't have a family wizard so everyone disperses to other houses, for protection and income. High houses though—they're too big to fail like that. Even if Harahel declined sufficiently—and don't you dare say I suggested even the remotest possibility of that aloud—we'd go to tier two and hang on to our proprietary interests."

"Has that happened often?"

"I can think of five—no, six—incidences. In all cases, however, the house in question neglected to take the basic measures to infuse magical potential back into the main breeding lines. That's why the Betrothal Trials were instituted to begin with, you know, to provide a more civilized method for testing compatible fertility between high potential wizard–familiar couplings, to ensure high MP-scoring baby wizards to keep the house going."

"So, is it fair to say that House Phel going from high house to non-existence, to the point of the house itself sinking from sight and the entire area of Meresin basically going wild and falling out of Convocation society is a singular example?"

She had his riveted attention. "Yes," he breathed. "It should be a case study, if nothing else. Everyone would want to know how Phel crashed and burned so quickly, if only as a cautionary tale."

"But no."

"But no..." He drew out the words thoughtfully, black eyes keen on her face, a thousand thoughts racing behind them. His magic, quiet as it was, hummed palpably, sorting through reams of information. "You suspect House Hanneil."

She didn't bother to dissemble. "Who else might collude with the houses you mentioned—save Iblis, which is a special case—and who else has the power to make so many people forget such a salient event?" she asked softly.

He was quiet a long moment. "Now I'm wondering what else might have been disappeared from Convocation archives."

"Seems entirely possible that more would be missing. Is there a catalog outside of Harahel memory?"

"None to speak of. Harahel memory is magically infallible, so we rarely bother, unless someone requests a list for them to use without our assistance."

"Is Harahel memory proof against Hanneil magic?" she asked, knowing he wouldn't like the question but having to ask anyway.

"Hanneil is prohibited from using psychic magic against other Convocation wizards without express consent," Cillian told her, saying what they both knew and neither believed to be true anymore.

"This is what I'm thinking," Alise said, "and I'm trusting you to keep *my* secrets here: Hanneil colluded with Elal, Sammael, and El-Adrel to bring down House Phel in the past and are acting against them now."

He whistled soundlessly. "A formidable array of opponents. Why would they have it in for House Phel?"

"An excellent question. Also, why did Gabriel and Seliah pop up again with massive magical potentials, after generations of basically nothing?"

"Seliah?" he asked with a frown, and Alise realized that almost no one outside of a tight circle knew about Seliah's very existence. All this time of barely talking to anyone had apparently loosened her lips as much as Cillian complained of in himself. Still, Seliah wasn't a secret, so there was nothing to worry about, except her odd reaction to this quirky wizard.

"Gabriel's sister, a powerful familiar. With probably as much magical potential as he does."

"She didn't attend Convocation Academy either?"

"No, for the same reasons." Alise stopped short of explaining how no one had known to recognize Seliah as a familiar and how severely that had impacted her sanity, nearly costing her life. That was Seliah's business.

"Ah, then she must be the unnamed Phel familiar listed in the lawsuit involving illegal bonding to an unnamed El-Adrel wizard."

"How do you know so many details?"

He raised his brows. "All documents come through the library to be indexed, cross-referenced, and filed in the archives. It's part of my job."

"Yes, well, Seliah is bonded to Jadren El-Adrel." Alise knew that much was true still, as she hadn't severed the bond between them and she doubted anyone else could. Or, if someone else had discovered the trick, wouldn't dare defy the Convocation that way. At Cillian's continued puzzlement, she remembered no one knew about Jadren either. "My brain is tired," she said on a sigh. "Jadren is the son of Lady El-Adrel, but he never attended Convocation Academy either."

"Before this," Cillian said, bemused, "I'd have sworn that every high scoring, magically gifted person in the entire Convocation had been at least recorded in the archives and thus Harahel memory."

"Harahel memory might not be as infallible as we'd want to believe," she said gently, expecting an indignant retort.

Cillian only considered that thoughtfully. "If House Hanneil is back to their old ways... or never ceased with their psychic warfare, only took it down to a more invisible level." He pursed his lips, then nodded at her. "Nothing to it but a trip home. You'll like House Harahel."

All right, her brain was tired. All of her was tired, but she surely wasn't understanding. "I'm not going to House Harahel."

"Of course you are. You have to come with me." He began sorting through books, stacking up a few, as if deciding what to leave or take. "This is your quest, your assignment. I can get you an audience with Lady Harahel and the senior wizards, but you have to be the one to do the petitioning."

"Petitioning?"

"For a full records reveal of what Harahel knows about anything related to Phel. Don't worry, they'll want to know about this evidence of Hanneil's interference, but the petition has to come from a representative of your house."

"I'm not exactly—"

He gave her an owlish look. "Didn't you say your sister asked you to be their spy?"

"That's a little dramatic."

"Unless you want to send a Ratsiel courier to House Phel to have them send someone else—not incidentally risking someone else finding out you're looking into this—then you need to come with me. It's an opportunity you can't afford to miss. I have to work tonight, but I'll spend the time looking for other gaps in the archives. More evidence is always better. Then we can leave tomorrow morning. I'll arrange transportation."

"I can't leave Convocation Academy." *Again.* "I'll be permanently expelled. This is my second and final chance," she continued with considerable agitation. Although, a small part of her danced with excitement at the prospect of escaping the oppressive atmosphere of the academy.

"I'll provide you a note. Extracurricular research for your 'independent study.'" He actually put air quotes around the phrase.

"Wizard Cillian Harahel," she ground out, curling her fingers in frustration, "you can't just rearrange my life on a whim."

"Why Wizard Alise Phel," he returned mildly, holding an open book and looking at her over it, his soft gaze sharper, "I thought your spying mission, and a matter of grave import to the foundation of Convocation society, would be of utmost importance to you. Isn't that why you're here?"

"I'm also supposed to graduate," she pointed out. "Provost Uriel—"

"Has never assigned anyone an independent study before. Clearly House Uriel is invested in what you'll discover and is subtly aiding you."

She stared at him in consternation. "But..."

He waited, then repeated gently, "a matter of grave import to the foundation of Convocation society. Besides, you can study in the carriage. I'll take over guiding your independent study," he added with a surprisingly wicked smile for his otherwise haplessly cheerful self.

"Wonderful."

He pointed at the miniature El-Adrel clock on the wall. "Time is fleeting. Best make that appointment with Uriel. And take a nap. No library tonight for you."

She stood there a moment, not at all sure what to say to this wizard she'd met only hours before and who seemed comfortable running her life. "Why am I even contemplating doing as he tells me?" she asked herself aloud. Herself had no answer, but Cillian did.

"Because what I'm telling you is only logical." He sounded slightly perplexed that she didn't already know that. "Meet me at the front steps at first bell."

With chagrin, Alise realized she would be there.

~ 16 ~

"**I** REALLY DON'T like the sound of sudden death," Selly muttered to Jadren.

"The death part is metaphorical," he muttered back. "At least, I hope it is."

Selly wasn't so hopeful. She didn't like the look on Bogdan's face. He knew he'd lost the match in spirit, even if they'd technically tied according to the letter of the deal. Jadren should've specified terms more clearly, but then they'd have needed some kind of arbitration for the subjective qualification of who'd done better wizardry. Still, she'd think that the vastly rearranged—and happily humming—House El-Adrel should be evidence enough for anyone that Jadren should head up both the tangible and intangible aspects of the house.

"Besides," Jadren continued, squeezing her hand reassuringly, "Helen is clearly tapped out while you, my magnificent moonflower, still have deep reserves of magic."

True, but Bogdan had to know that, too.

"I propose this," Bogdan said, with a thin, triumphant smile that raised the hairs on the back of Selly's neck. Oh, this was not good. "As we have demonstrated we are equal in making modifications to the house, as long as we have magic from our familiars, let us have a test of pure wizardry, to determine the better wizard. A contest without access to our familiars."

He was clever, Selly had to give him that. "You should just red-mist him now," she told Jadren unhappily.

"You have so little faith in me?" Jadren gave her a mock surprised look. They both knew he was close to tapped out himself, drawing on her magic more heavily in preparation. That, however, did nothing to address his physical exhaustion. He needed food and rest more than anything.

"I agree to your terms," he told Bogdan, in a carrying voice, and Selly would've winced if that wouldn't have been a giveaway of her trepidation. "However," Jadren continued, sliding her his 'oh ye of little faith' look, "for a fair and just test of our true abilities, I propose we hold the duel tomorrow. After all," he said sharply, as Bogdan opened his mouth to protest, "I already defeated one wizard in a duel today, Lady El-Adrel, herself. Can you say the same, Wizard Bogdan?"

Of course, he could not, and the assembly murmured in agreement. Taking in the mood of the room, Bogdan finally nodded, looking none too happy. Unfortunately, he wasn't done being crafty. Selly saw it before he opened his mouth, his wizard-black gaze resting on her. "I agree to those terms and propose another. In the interests of ensuring that neither wizard can bend the rules by resorting to accessing their familiar's magic once the duel begins, we agree that we each arrive at the duel with our familiars in alternate form."

Selly nearly groaned aloud. They were doomed.

"Oh," Bogdan said, making a show of chagrin. "Unless

you're not able to put your familiar in alternate form? Not all wizards possess the skill and everyone here knows you lack education in the more advanced techniques of wizardry."

Jadren had gone still beside her. They both knew he couldn't admit to lacking that ability, not and head a high house. The assembly watched them expectantly, the mood of the room clear. At last, Jadren nodded slowly. "Agreed. Now, let us adjourn to discover where our apartments have gone with all of this shifting about."

Before Bogdan could reply, the assembly sent up a grateful cheer of approval, dispersing without further instruction.

"Well," Selly said, "at least they're already following your direction. They have accepted you as Lord El-Adrel."

"They were just tired of standing around," he replied drily. "And they missed lunch. Make no mistake that, if we turned up tomorrow with you still as human as ever, they'd turn their backs on us. They'd probably put me to death—or do their level best—and start squabbling over who gets you next."

It took Selly a moment to process the import of his words. "If we turn up tomorrow?" She had enough presence of mind to keep her voice hushed, although the din of conversation, people exclaiming over alterations to the house, and general noise of a crowd all jostling to leave an enclosed space at once meant they were unlikely to be overheard. Despite Jadren's suggestion, it seemed many of the El-Adrel denizens headed, not deeper into the house, but toward the various gardens and courtyards now available to them. Maybe Selly wasn't the only one who'd tired of looking at walls all the time.

"Obviously, we have to leave," Jadren replied with exasperation. "Everyone will be distracted with the changes to the house, so it's the perfect time to escape."

"Escape!"

"Shh. Not so loud. Let's discuss in our apartments. We need to get our stuff anyway."

Keeping her mouth shut, and assembling her quiver of arguments for when they were in private, Selly went along with Jadren. For the time being, at least. He also held her hand—not hard, but firmly enough that she knew he intended to keep ahold of her—so she had little choice but to stroll by his side, pretending to be a sweetly obedient familiar. Had Jadren brought her bow and arrows? She could still shoot him. Again.

It took a while to make their way out of the great hall, as many people stopped him for a word or two. Some only offered greetings, but most seemed to have agendas, thinly cloaked or otherwise, with suggestions, complaints, and vague offers of support in exchange for unnamed future dispensations.

Finally they broke free into a wide, graceful hallway that hadn't been there before. Jadren looked up and down it, judging the best direction, and Selly pointed. A glittering trail of dancing moons streamed over the tiles going off to the left. Jadren snorted in disgust. "Why does she always pick you? Clearly *you* are the one she likes." And he set off in that direction.

"I'm sure it's just that lightning bolts would be confusing," Selly replied lightly. "Look—she's using other ways to direct people."

"How helpful of her," Jadren grumbled cynically. "Probably this is all some elaborate plan to devour us all."

A window shutter beside them flapped in annoyance and a life-sized painting of a woman—apparently some El-Adrel ancestor with elaborate robes and wizard-black eyes—briefly scowled at them and stuck out her tongue.

"Yeah," Jadren shot back, scowling at the painting and making a rude gesture, though a laugh threaded through his voice. "Back at you, sweetheart."

They made it back to their apartments, still apparently high atop a tower, overlooking a much-changed view. Selly didn't have time to take it in, as Jadren let go of her hand as soon as the doors closed behind them, saying, "Quick. Get your things together. The sooner we go, the better."

She sat down and folded her arms. "I think we should stay."

"Have you lost what's left of your half-feral, crazygirl mind?" he demanded incredulously. "Didn't you hear the terms of the deal? I'd have to figure out how to put you in alternate form, preferably also with the ability to get you back *out* of whatever benighted, beastly form you take on, in less than a day and a night."

She shrugged. "So, we figure it out."

Arrested, he stared at her, a picture of utter astonishment. "You *have* lost your mind," he said in a wondering tone. "How sad. Don't worry, darling. I'll always take care of you."

"Very funny," she retorted. "I'm perfectly serious. You're meant to be Lord El-Adrel so we'll figure out a way to meet this challenge."

"Have you forgotten the lesson of Refoel?" he demanded. "I can't do any wizardry at that level."

"I remember you didn't try."

"Besides which," he continued, "I'm not meant for anything of the sort. I gave it a shot. Bogdan called my bluff. We're done here."

"Well, *I* am not done here."

"Is it so important to you to be Lady El-Adrel?" he demanded, throwing up his hands. "Is it the power you want? The wealth, the status? You saw your role model. I wouldn't say my late, unlamented mother lived an enviable life."

"No," she answered, holding onto her patience. "You know me better than that and I refuse to be distracted by you picking a fight with me over nonsense. An argument we've had before, I might mention. I want this for *you*."

"Well, I don't want it," he hissed, crouching as if hunted.

"*And* I want it for House Phel," she continued, talking over him. "I want it for all the people whose lives you can make better. The house wants it for you, and for them, and you owe her for helping you today."

"Is the house going to teach me how to put you in alternate form without killing you?" he asked, the question positively dripping with sarcasm. "Because, just in case that hasn't penetrated your addled brain, that's what's at stake here. And please recall that I have no idea what I'm doing." He finished on a near shout, waving his hands.

"Maybe the house *will* help? I don't really know. What I *do* know is that countless wizards and familiars have accomplished this feat before us, so it's clearly doable. Gabriel and

Nic managed without knowing how."

"Gabriel is hugely more powerful than I am," Jadren pointed out acerbically. "I harbor no delusions there and neither should you."

"And yet you've accomplished feats my brother couldn't imagine. Aren't you always telling me that magical types and talents and skills are all so varied that there's no truly comparing them? That the Convocation uses magical *potential* scores for that reason, rather than some magical actuality score."

"I'm pretty sure that was Liat, not me," he replied drily, but also a bit more calmly, so she thought she might be getting through his instinctive panic. Then he visibly changed tactics, coming to her and going down on one knee before her chair, prying her hands off her arms and enfolding them in his. Gazing earnestly up at her, he seemed to have forgotten his gore-smeared state. His handsomeness shone through regardless, that sterling core of his character that hadn't been warped by all that had been done to him, no matter how scarred and dinged. "I love you, Seliah." He said it like an explanation.

"I love you, Jadren." She waited.

"Don't you see?" He rubbed his thumbs over the backs of her hands, though he was the one who needed soothing, not her. "It's not worth it to me. Nothing that jeopardizes your life is worth it. I can't believe you think I'd risk harming you just for some stupid ambition."

"But it's *not* stupid," she said, turning over her hands to grip his. "And it's not ambition. This is something you need to face, to get through, to overcome. Your mother is dead, but some of your demons still live. You're not done with this battle."

He narrowed his gaze at her. "What are you dressing up in philosophical language instead of saying to me directly?"

She took a breath. "I think you always run away."

Paling, then flushing, he started to tug his hands away, but she held on. "I'm not saying you haven't had reason, but you've gotten into a habit of running instead of fighting. If you run from this, there is something you'll never get back."

"What?" he snarled. "The opportunity to be Lord El-Adrel? Because that's easy to walk away from. Some things aren't worth fighting for, poppet."

She nearly smiled at the way she'd accurately hit that nerve, but remained serious, because this was important. "No, my love: you stand to lose your self-respect."

He stared at her a long moment, skin drawn tight over his cheekbones, before he recovered and drew on his cloak of bitter cynicism. "Ah, that's where you've gone wrong. You see I can't lose my self-respect because I've never had any. I have only self-loathing, so being a coward and running away like a scalded dog, yipping piteously with my tail tucked around my balls, is exactly in character. If you can't accept that about me, then there's no point in us going on."

Her stomach went cold as congealed porridge at the implicit threat and she couldn't help but be glad that she still hadn't told him about the bond-severing option. In Jadren's black moments like this, he was likely to seize on that possibility, if only to punish himself in his relentless self-flagellation. "I don't accept it," she told him crisply.

His betrayed expression, before he covered it over, told her everything. She held onto him. "I accept *you*," she said firmly, "and you never let me take the easy way out. You never cut me slack for being a crazy girl and losing my shit to the point of getting me captured and you nearly killed."

"That's because—"

"Because you expected better of me. And I expect better of you. Sometimes love means pushing each other when we need it."

"Seliah... You see things in me that simply aren't there."

Losing her patience, releasing him, shoving him away, she stood and paced to the open windows. A vast, lovely estate had pushed back the woods with rolling gardens and countless fountains. More people than she'd ever seen at El-Adrel roamed the winding pathways or gathered on arched, picturesque bridges. "Look at what you wrought," she said, mostly to herself. "This is something beautiful and important."

He came up beside her. "The house did it. You did it. I never did anything like this before."

She turned to face him, leaning her hip against the curli-cued railing. "You're not the same person you were, Jadren. You've changed, and grown. So have I. Stronger together, remember?"

"Can't we be stronger together somewhere else, where I'm not risking your life?" he asked plaintively.

She nearly laughed, he sounded so put out. "How about we agree to this? If we can't get alternate form to work, fine. If we do manage to do it and you lose the contest tomorrow, fair and square, also fine. But if we give up without even trying—

Jadren, how can we look ourselves in the mirror if we do that?"

"Ah." He wagged a finger at her. "See, that's where you've gone wrong. The trick is to avoid mirrors. Denial requires relentless vigilance to evade anything smacking of truth."

"Jadren." She let her tone say everything.

"I know, I know." He scrubbed his fingers through his hair, coming up short as he hit the snarls of dried blood. "I'm disgusting."

"In a temporary, superficial way that can be immediately remedied." She smiled at him, letting all her love show. "Go clean up already. And then we'll start looking. Hopefully the house will help there."

Jadren regarded her blankly. "Looking for what?"

She grinned. "The El-Adrel arcanium."

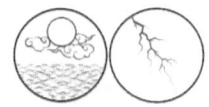

JADREN FOUGHT HER on it, of course, up to and including flat denial of even knowing what an arcanium was, until she told him that House Phel had one and that she knew Nic and Gabriel used it. He had rather a fit about that, saying she could know no such thing because—even if it was true and she wasn't utterly deluded—it would be a secret and she therefore couldn't possibly know about it.

She countered with the clear and painfully obvious fact that she *did* know about it, therefore it must exist, as he absolutely knew what she was talking about and so she hadn't made it up.

"Do you even know what an arcanium is?" he demanded scathingly.

Well, not exactly. She knew about Nic and Gabriel's because she'd eavesdropped on them when she was more than a little insane. Skulking around outside of windows, listening to conversations had been all in the course of a day for her. But even then she'd understood that they kept it a secret, as best they could, along with its location.

Then, after Lord Elal tried to take over the House Phel arcanium, when he and the Sammaels attacked, where and what the arcanium was had become pretty much an open secret. The denizens of House Phel didn't discuss it, but that was out of loyalty and respect for Nic and Gabriel's privacy, not ignorance.

"It's for building and working a lot of magic," she informed Jadren loftily. And for sex, she didn't say. That was largely guessing from hints Nic had dropped, and the secret, sensual smile she got when making oblique references to it.

Jadren made a rude noise. "You're guessing."

"All right, yes, I'm guessing at some of it, but I know they used the arcanium to discover how to put Nic into alternate form in order to prove they were bonded to the Convocation proctor so she wouldn't take Nic away." Selly avoided adding *so there*, but just barely. "You were present for that," she pointed out to him.

"Yes, but you were not," he retorted immediately. "The last anyone saw of you between the proctor's edict and Nic dramatically pulling a silver phoenix form out of her ass, was you escaping over the side of the house and disappearing again."

"Yes, well…" She mostly remembered that part. She had been well and truly out of her head then. "I didn't go far, and I spied on the goings on. And why are we arguing about these particulars? Every house worth their status, especially and including the high houses, has an arcanium. El-Adrel must also and you're just trying to duck looking for it, even though it's your right as Lord El-Adrel."

"Except I'm not Lord El-Adrel!"

"This again? You are unless Bogdan proves otherwise. Quit being a marsh slug. Go clean up and let's go find the thing. Or take a hot bath and a nap, if it will make you less cranky, and *then* we'll go. Come on. It will be fun."

He glared at her in impotent mutiny, clearly beyond annoyed to be called "cranky" and just as clearly unable to think of a retort that wouldn't sound cranky. Looking down at himself, he muttered something about being filthy and feeling it, then stalked off into the bathing chamber.

Selly left him alone, figuring some quiet time with his thoughts could only help. She tested out her own power as, if not Lady El-Adrel, then familiar to the lord *pro-tem*, and summoned servants to bring food. It worked like a charm and by the time Jadren emerged in the clean clothes she'd had them bring from his old apartments, freshly groomed and looking wickedly handsome, she had a feast laid out for them.

"Am I being fattened up for sacrifice?" he asked sardonically, but much more in his usual vein and not the strained, sharp-edged sarcasm of his worst self.

"You're welcome," she replied smoothly. "It was no trouble to arrange for all of your favorite foods. Your happiness is my happiness."

He snorted and sat, piling his plate with food and eyeing her half-empty one. "Glad you didn't feel compelled to wait for me."

"And clearly my happiness is your happiness, too!" she chirped, earning a grudging half-smile before he wiped it away with a mock frown.

"You know," he said, after downing half of what was on his plate, practically inhaling the food, "even if there is an El-Adrel arcanium, the location likely died with my mother."

"Fyrdo would know where it is. Or where it was, anyway," she amended.

Jadren gazed at her a long moment, a world of turbulent emotion in his gaze. "I don't think I can ask my father to give me that information," he finally said. "Even if I could bring myself to do it, it's entirely possible he won't answer—and that he'll never speak to me again."

"He will," Selly said with firm compassion. "Fyrdo just needs time to heal from the blow."

"Seliah, I murdered the love of his life, his wizard, in cold blood. Time can't mend a gulf like that."

"It wasn't cold blood. She was doing her level best to murder you, after abusing you your entire life. Fyrdo is aware of all of that. Once he gets over the shock of grief, not to mention the severing of a bond that's been integral to his being for decades, he'll want to be part of your life."

Jadren shoved food around his plate, then let out a hollow

laugh. "Not everybody thinks like you do. You're one of a kind." He reached across the table, lifting his pained gaze to hers, offering his hand palm up. She put her hand in his, gripping it. "I know I'm impossible," he said softly. "I lash out at you when I shouldn't. I'm a coward who's fucked in the head and will never be the partner you deserve, but I'm so grateful that you've stuck with me, Seliah. You are the one person I can always count on to tell me the truth, to be always loyal. Losing you would destroy me."

Selly ignored the stab of guilt at the reminder that she still hadn't told him the full truth. Now wasn't the time, not with the task ahead of them requiring their full attention, not to mention the sudden-death duel the next day. There would be time enough after, once Jadren was securely in his new role at House El-Adrel, to discuss the fact of the bond-severing and its implications for Convocation society. They might even laugh about her worrying so much about telling him.

She squeezed his hand. "Then you'd better not lose me," she told him, hoping to make him smile.

He managed a smile, but there was no joy in it.

~ 17 ~

DESPITE JADREN'S GLOOM and palpable dread, Selly couldn't contain her excitement. She had complete faith in Jadren's ability to put her in alternate form—she wasn't at all worried about some dreadful accident, regardless of his dire mutterings—and she couldn't wait to find out what sort of animal she'd be. For all the times people teased her about being feral, mostly wild, practically a creature of the marshes herself, they likely didn't understand how much she'd longed for real claws and teeth, for the ability to pass like a silent shadow, a true denizen of the wilderness and not a human intruder.

Besides which, from all Nic had taught her about erotic play being part of building magic, she anticipated excellent sex in her immediate future. How could a girl worry with that on the brain?

They wandered through the transformed house, hand in hand, searching for clues to the location of arcanium. Selly had wanted to simply ask the house to lead them there, but Jadren still didn't trust the house not to trap them in some doorless room just to torment him. Nor had they asked Fyrdo, which Selly understood. So, instead, they drifted more or less aimlessly, passing myriad other people, most of whom greeted them cheerfully, nearly all addressing Jadren as Lord El-Adrel.

"They just know where their bread is buttered," Jadren replied sourly when Selly commented that everyone already considered him head of the house was a good sign. "No doubt they're paying similar court to Bogdan, hedging their bets."

Selly refrained from commenting. "Most houses have their arcaniums in a tower," she said instead, keeping them mentally on task.

"How would you even know that?" He slid her a sideways look.

"People gossip. And that's where wizards always are in the novels. Sylus had a workshop in a tower."

"Are you positioning yourself as Lyndella to my Sylus? Because things didn't go so great for her."

"Have you read that book?"

"The winters here are long and dull, especially when no one could leave the house and Maman—my late mother, I mean—was absorbed in her studies and the rare experiments that weren't on me. I've read everything in the library. More to the point," he continued, "and focusing on reality, not romantic fiction, you may have noticed that, with the massive reconformation of the house, places that weren't towers before are now, so it goes to figure that former towers likely aren't anymore."

"The house wouldn't mess with the arcanium though."

He sighed, long and dramatically. "I feel like a broken wheel spinning in a rut I can't escape, but how could you possibly know that?"

"I just… sense it." She shrugged, unable to put it into words. "It's like the house is a wizard, too, right? She would respect the arcanium. It's part of her but also kind of… sacred to the head of the house."

"The house is *not* a wizard," he said decisively.

"She's capable of working magic."

"Only on herself," he countered. "She can transform or restore herself only, and…"

He trailed off, the realization occurring to him at the same time as it did to Selly. "Just like *you* do," she filled in with excitement. "You *are* using El-Adrel magic, on yourself just like the house does!"

"Except that the house is basically one gigantic enchanted artifact, or an assembly of them, and I'm an organic, living creature. At least," he amended, "so I've always believed."

"But your mother's research—she also worked on creating those automatons, embedding them with Elal spirits to give them more life. What if she was trying to figure out how to—" She broke off in horror, only realizing her steps had slowed when Jadren tugged her hand, pulling her along into a new corridor.

"Create living beings, like a race of enchanted people, owned and operated by her?" He sounded remarkably blasé about the possibility.

"That's horrible," she said softly.

Jadren slid her an ironic grimace. "I don't know whether to be surprised, appalled, or amused at discovering where your line in the sand is regarding my late-mother's house of horrors. After everything you've witnessed and experienced, *this* is what bothers you?"

"Apparently so. It's just so very wrong to try to make people."

He shrugged, nodding back to a group who hailed him. "Is it any more wrong than making the automatons?"

"Those aren't people. They're spirits inside metal bodies."

"Some would argue we're spirits inside flesh bodies. How is it different?"

She gave him an unhappy look. "It just is. People are more complex than those Elal-bound spirits."

"Are you sure?"

No, she wasn't, which only made everything worse. Jadren let go of her hand and slipped an arm around her waist. "Don't think about it anymore right now, sweetling. She's dead and her horrifying agenda with her, and we have an insight into my magic that we didn't have before."

"True," she agreed glumly, unable to quite shake the pall of that discovery, imagining an army of soulless people, all belonging to Katica El-Adrel, mindlessly following her whims. Another reason to stop Bogdan, who she could see continuing the legacy.

"Why do you think wizards traditionally keep their arcaniums on top of towers?" he asked.

"I don't know. Why?"

"I'm asking you."

She slid him a suspicious look. "You're just trying to distract me."

He kissed her cheek, gave her a last squeeze, and let her go, taking her hand again. "You're always doing it to me. I thought

I'd try it. But I do have a point. I'm trying to establish some logic here. Why towers? Because they're isolated with very little around them. So you're less likely to be bothered and, should some major working go dramatically awry, fewer people around to be incidental casualties."

"Makes sense," she agreed.

"House Phel has no towers."

"Maybe they sank."

"Aha!" he stabbed a triumphant finger in the air. "We know that's not the case because the house has been restoring itself, just like House El-Adrel did. If there had been towers, they would've sprouted by now."

"An unsettling way to describe it, but all right, I see your point."

"So where is the House Phel arcanium?"

She glanced around, as if someone might be eavesdropping. "Almost certainly under the lake."

"Dark arts, of course it is. Wily Phel wizards. And with water all around, the water magic would be stronger."

She was following his line of logic now. "What would be the heart of El-Adrel magic?"

"The center of big piece of clockwork? I don't know."

"And where would be most shielded from bystanders and kept secret?"

"The house could really keep anything secret that it was tasked to," he answered thoughtfully. "More than any other Convocation house, I'd think, House El-Adrel would be able to prevent anyone who shouldn't find the arcanium from finding it."

"Say, I know," she said as if just hitting upon a new and exciting idea. "Let's ask the house to help us find it."

He shook his head wearily. "You think you're funny, but you're not."

"You think I'm funny," she replied winningly, dancing a little alongside him, enjoying how he tried not to smile. "You try all the time not to laugh at my jokes, but it's a struggle and—" She broke off on a gasp.

"What?" Instantly, he'd thrust her behind him and mustered his magic, a blank metal implement in his hand, ready to make it into a weapon to kill whoever threatened her.

"That courtyard." She pointed to the doors that had opened to an enclosed space, surrounded by sheer walls of a dense black substance, with no roof. "It wasn't there before."

"Most of this house wasn't there before," he observed wryly, but he studied the smallish area. "Interesting that those doors just happened to open as we came by and while no one else is around."

"This is it." She nearly squealed in anticipation, all other concerns forgotten. "Let's go in."

"I'm pretty sure those were the famous last words of many a now-dead person," he observed, allowing her to tug him reluctantly along. "Along with, 'hey, watch this.'"

"Hey," she said with a grin, "watch this." And she stepped into the courtyard.

To her disappointment, nothing happened.

Until Jadren set foot inside.

The moment he did, the doors closed with silent and seamless finality, sealing them inside what seemed to be a lidless box lined entirely with light-absorbing material.

Jadren went to one wall bending close to study it, then tentatively touching it, then with more assurance running his fingertips over it. "I think it's made entirely of lead," he commented thoughtfully.

Selly went to peer over his shoulder, touching the wall also. It felt like sueded leather, only hard, an almost fuzzy texture to the curiously dense-looking stuff. "What's the significance of that?"

"It's a kind of mineral that blocks all kinds of metallic and magical properties," he answered absently, mind clearly racing in another direction. "We use it to store enchanted artifacts that give off debilitating energy or are likely to be dangerous in some way. Also, if you want to hide an artifact from a finder, they won't be able to sense it through lead."

"So this is basically a shielded room," Selly said. "Except for the sky."

"Maybe." He turned in a slow circle, scrutinizing the blank walls rising several stories high. "I expected an arcanium to have more to it, however. Tools, supplies, works in progress."

"How would you know?" she couldn't help teasing. "Have you ever been in an arcanium?"

He slid her an unamused look. "Funny girl."

"Told you."

"I think," he continued in that same thoughtful vein, obviously intrigued despite his misgivings, "that there is more, if we trigger the mechanism correctly."

Right. El-Adrel and their endless fascination with toys. "You're the El-Adrel wizard," she acknowledged, "so you would know. How do we turn it on?"

"Arcaniums are for a wizard and familiar pair, so I understand," he added hastily, before she could poke at him again, "so come here."

She went happily enough, taking his hand and moving with him to the center of the room. Nothing happened. "Did you try turning it off and then on again?" she whispered.

He ignored that one, saying, "The lead won't respond to magic, so there must be a trigger here that does, but where would it be?"

"I have an idea," she said. "Kiss me." She nearly giggled at the jaundiced look he gave her at that suggestion.

"I know you're insatiable," he commented drily, "but we do have an agenda here. Unless you want to run away with me to some hideout where we can forget this nonsense and I promise to service you as often as you like."

"Tempting," she replied in all sincerity, "but not yet. Nic says that sex and magic are rolled up together and that erotic play increases magic buildup."

"Oh, well," he drawled, "if the all-wise Nic Elal says so, it must be true."

She poked him in the ribs. "You know it's true, also. You've used it yourself."

"I don't know that," he protested, far too innocently—and also drawing her into his arms, a wicked gleam in his eye. "Still, a beautiful, sensual, half-feral woman offers you sex and what can you do?"

"No sane man would say no," she murmured, the heat billowing up in her belly, shimmering with anticipation.

"I'm far from sane and I still can't say no," he purred in reply, running his hands over her body, one dropping to cup her bottom and the other sliding up under her hair to press her against him. She closed her eyes as he came in for the kiss, then sighed half in disappointment, half in sheer pleasure as he dropped the kiss on her eyelids, first one side, then the other, his breath feathering warm and sensuous over the delicate skin. "I love you, Seliah," he said softly. "In the end, that's all that matters."

"Yes," she agreed on a sigh. "This is the most important thing in all the world."

And when his lips met hers, it was true. Everything else fell away and only he existed. Jadren. His heat, his scent, the lean lines of his body pressed into every curve of hers, his silky beard against her face and the even softer, satin feel of his lips and the scorching interior of his mouth. His magic, delving into hers and unspooling it, inviting her into him with the same erotic skill as he coaxed her tongue to tangle with his. Like perfectly oiled clockwork, his magic ticked all over her skin, pinpoints of passion, tingling and teasing, caressing and stoking.

She'd expected mischief from him, an edge of violence and danger that he often brought to their play, but this was different. This was love. Languid, needy, and needing. And she sank into it, sank into him, submerging herself, opening and offering everything.

Vaguely, in the background, she was aware of movement, of the near-silent assembly of perfectly matched pieces, smoothly fitting together just as she and Jadren did.

"Seliah," he breathed against her mouth, not letting her go, not lifting his head. "Look."

Mimicking him, she didn't pull away, but watched from the edges of her peripheral vision, dazzled by the gleam of metal pieces spiraling in a slow-motion whirlwind of construction. The room built itself around them, forming a ceiling and cylindrical walls, the floor slipping beneath their feet and furniture assembling itself from nothing. As they both watched in wonder, slowly pulling a distance apart as they became more confident they wouldn't break the spell, the arcanium manifested itself in gleaming colors of hundreds of different metals and other materials. Cabinet doors appeared on the walls, and various workspaces extruded themselves.

"The El-Adrel arcanium," she said, feeling it needed to be spoken aloud, fully expecting Jadren to chide her for making an observation on the blisteringly obvious.

"Yes," he said, in the same hushed tone. He shifted, catching and holding her gaze. She became aware that a fine trembling ran through him. "Thank you, Seliah. Without you, I would never have known this."

"Are you getting soft on me?" she teased.

Narrowing his gaze, he nudged her hip with his groin, demonstrating his impressively hard erection. "Obviously not," he replied, capturing her mouth in a bruising kiss. "I think that, however, we won't want to use *that*."

His tone held such a scathing quality of disgust that she glanced over her shoulder at what his glittering black gaze fixed on. It was a chair, very like the one she'd seen and experienced in Katica's torture chamber of a "laboratory," with articulated extensions to bind a person's arms and legs into whatever position their captor desired, the main section cradling their torso and a headrest with an additional strap to go across the forehead. She cringed, remembering the pain inflicted on her in that other chair, then moved between it and Jadren to block his sight of it, knowing his memories eclipsed hers by hundreds of thousands of times.

"We won't," she promised him. "She's dead. She can't hurt you anymore."

The hard, haunted edge to his face softened and he smiled at her, almost gently, and stroked her hair back from her forehead. "My darling, girl," he murmured. "You are so fierce I sometimes forget what an innocent you are. The chair is intended for the wizard's familiar, to maximize extraction of magic through pleasure or pain, ideally both."

"Oh." Her throat struck, drying immediately. Then she firmed her will. "If that's what's needed in order to—"

"If that's what's needed to put you in alternate form," he interrupted, "then we're not doing it. I draw the line there, Seliah. I know how you feel about being restrained and I'm not doing that to you, ever, so forget that right now."

She dropped her forehead to his chest in overwhelming relief, realizing she'd begun to tremble. She'd overcome a great deal, but she didn't know if she'd ever get over that core-deep dread of being trapped and unable to move. Maya had counseled her that some fears become part of you and never fade or disappear, that she might just have to learn to live her life around that, like finding solid ground through a landscape riddled with bogs.

"I hate to think of Fyrdo in that thing," she said.

"Then don't," he said wryly. "I certainly intend to scrub the image from my brain and disinfect thoroughly afterwards."

Selly winced. No one wanted to picture their parents having sex, much less something like this. She noticed his erection had wilted and could hardly blame him. He noticed her noticing, lifting her chin with one finger and giving her a thorough kiss. "Don't worry. I'll get it back. We don't want the chair," he said to the room in general.

A feeling of listening, different than before, and general expectation hummed in the walls around them, the metal scintillating as if moving. The chair melted into the floor, becoming one with it.

Jadren raised an auburn brow. "Fascinating."

"How much of that is you and how much the house?" she ventured.

"I'm not entirely certain," he admitted. "It's different in here. *I* am different. The power... magic is flowing into me and not from you. It's El-Adrel magic, purified and intense. I've never felt anything like it."

She'd been aware that he wasn't drawing from her and tried not to feel a little bereft that he didn't need her magic. Especially as he left her side to prowl about the room, investigating the contents of the cabinets and the jumbles on the benches of works in progress. One cabinet held several heads, reminiscent of Katica's automatons, but with variations that turned Selly's stomach. As much as the laboratory had been a house of horrors, this place might be worse.

"We have a lot of purging to do," Jadren commented in

disgust, then glanced at her when she only grunted a reply. Taking her in, he strode to her and cupped her face in his hands. "You've gone pale," he noted with concern. "It's too closed in here. This isn't good for you, we should—"

She stopped him with a sharp shake of her head, wrapping her fingers around his wrists—not to pull his hands away, but for stability. She gazed into his beloved face, knowing she trusted him beyond anyone else in all the world. "We're doing this," she said, as firmly as she could, ignoring the quaver in her voice. "Together," she added with a twist of a smile. "I lectured you about running away. Well, I'm not going to run from this either. This place isn't evil in itself, just because it was used for horrible things. Yes, we'll purge it and make this arcanium our own, but in the meanwhile, we need to use the magic here to practice putting me in alternate form."

He smiled, a rueful half-smile. "I was hoping there would be instruction manuals. There aren't. Seliah... I don't know how."

"Well, what did your late-mother do when she transformed Fyrdo from a goat back into human form? I know you were watching. And you saw Gabriel do it with Nic, too."

He pursed his lips, thinking. "The two wizards did it very differently. I don't know if that's because Gabriel wasn't taught and made it up himself or if it's the difference in magics."

"Any kind of wizard can do it, right?"

"Given that they're sufficiently powerful, that's what I understand."

"So it would make sense that each wizard would use whatever type of magic they're most powerful in. With yours..."

"You think it's this restoration thing, putting things back the way they should be," he replied, following her line of thought."

"Exactly."

"Except your alternate form isn't the way you should be."

"Except that it *is*," she argued, happy to be feeling more excited now than full of dread. "No one knows what a familiar's alternate form will be until they first manifest it, right? The form doesn't run in families, doesn't follow any pattern that anyone has been able to discern, even after centuries of study. It seems to be a combination of the familiar and the wizard they're bonded to—unique to their blend of magic. So, in a way, you would be extracting my alternate form from within me and combining our magics to restore my alternate form to me, one that I wouldn't otherwise be able to access."

"Given how fucked up we both are," he commented drily, "I think we should expect you to become something truly monstrous, in that case."

"Will you still love me when I'm a swamp creature oozing green slime?" she asked, deadpan.

"Funny girl. And yes." He kissed her lavishly. "Because you'll be *my* green-slime-oozing swamp creature."

She giggled, surprised at how light she felt, almost giddy. "Forever and always," she agreed. "So, how do you want to do this?"

"No," he countered, his smile taking on a wickedly sexy curve, "how do *you* want to do this?"

"What do you mean?" And why was she suddenly breathless with desire?

"The little I've heard implies that putting a familiar into alternate form, at least the first time, requires a transportation beyond the confines of normal fleshly experience, which is why sexual pain and pleasure work so well."

"Maybe you shouldn't have disappeared the chair of torment," she muttered.

"Don't even suggest it," he retorted sharply, then ran his hands up and down her arms, though she hadn't thought she needed soothing. Maybe it was for his own sake. "You want us to be stronger together. You say this alternate form would combine our magics? Then we create this magic ritual and we do what you crave. So," he dropped his voice to a sensual purr, "tell me, Seliah—what are your fantasies?"

~ 18 ~

IF SELLY THOUGHT her mouth had gone dry and her breath came hard before, it was nothing to how she felt in the face of Jadren's bald question. It was all she could do not to look away, though her face grew hot. Jadren waited for her answer patiently, not without keen interest, however. Even contemplating how to answer the question felt like foreplay, and the desire bloomed and billowed between them. It seemed to echo off the shining metal walls on some subliminal level, urging her on to some wild, reckless behavior. Still…

"My fantasies?" she squeaked.

"Yes." He inclined his head gravely, wizard-black eyes alight with mischief and arousal, his expression intent. "You have to tell me what you want, Seliah. It's important that this be your fantasy. Your deepest, darkest fantasy. Preferably something taboo."

"Why does it have to be a taboo, deep, dark fantasy?" she asked, fascinated despite herself, her nerves sizzling with anticipation, her nipples taut peaks and her sex already swollen and aching.

Jadren saw it in her, too. Or felt it, or both. He stroked the bare skin of her arms, just brushing the side-curves of her breasts, tantalizing and teasing. "Because our deepest fantasies hold power," he answered on a near whisper. "Breaking taboos releases that power."

"How do you know?"

"I've read a lot of books. Long winters. Ancient library with many books on everything you could imagine."

"I like that image of you, dreaming the snowy days away in the library." He had so few good things to say about his growing up.

"You're stalling." He lifted a hand to cup her breast, passing a thumb over her hard nipple, making her gasp and lean into him. "Tell me, Seliah."

"I don't know that I can," she confessed, breathless, utterly self-conscious.

"You can," he coaxed. "You trust me, as I trust you. And it's only the two of us. No one else will ever know."

She refrained from pointing out that the house would. The house, however, as invested as she seemed to be in the politics of her denizens, whatever level of self-determination she possessed, likely didn't have much prurient interest in human sexuality. If she did, she wouldn't tell. Still…

"You won't think less of me?" she asked, tentative and—all right, she could admit it to herself—embarrassed. Jadren delivered contempt so easily. She didn't think he would make fun of her for something this important.

To his credit, Jadren regarded her somberly, no sarcasm, no taunting. He leaned in to kiss her, lingeringly, opening the bond between them so she'd feel his love and intense regard, his hand cupping her breast almost reverently. "I love you,

Seliah," he murmured to her. "I admire you more than any person I've ever known. I love your ardent sexuality, how abandoned you are, how passionate. I want to break every taboo there is with you."

Now there was an offer. She wanted that, too. Dropping her gaze, unable to look him in the eye for this, she whispered, "I liked it when you spanked me."

She didn't imagine the quiver that ran through him. "I liked it, too," he answered, dropping a hand to run it over her bottom. "And?"

"I want that but more. Harder. I want…"

"Yes?" His whisper vibrated with intensity.

"I want you to keep going. Until I cry." She looked up at him, hesitant, unable to bear not knowing how he received this. He watched her with no judgment, black gaze fixed on her. Only the two of them. "And I liked when you made me kneel, for the bonding ceremony, even though I said I didn't then."

"That was different," he replied, sounding as if he completely understood.

"Yes." She nodded unnecessarily. "It was. But I want that. Make me cry, and kneel, and… like that."

"I can work with that," he answered quietly. "You can tell me to stop any time, you know that, right?"

She nodded again, then shook her head and blew out a breath. Never had she been so aroused. And tense as a fraying rope. Both longing for what would happen and a bit afraid of it. Breaking taboos. "I want to be able to tell you to stop and for you to ignore me. I want to fight you and have you laugh, the way you do when you're being cruel, and… do things to me anyway."

He nodded along, reflecting her gesture. "Are you sure?"

Was she? "Yes."

"Then I need a way to know if you stop being sure. A code word. Or phrase."

She considered. "How about 'green slime'?"

Cracking a smile, he shook his head. "Funny."

"Told you."

"Then green slime it is." He sobered. "Are you ready?"

Eep. All right, here they went, stepping off the cliff. "Yes."

"Then let's proceed with your punishment," he told her, his tone altering, going hard and demanding. Turning his back on her, he strode to a stool perched by a workbench and sat on it, one heel on a rung and the other on the floor. He patted his upraised knee. "It's time for your spanking, Seliah. Come here."

Shivering with arousal and trepidation, she slowly went to him. She hadn't expected to be so complicit in this happening, that he would make her willingly go to him. Reaching him, she bent over that upraised knee, uncertain how he wanted her.

"You can do better than that," he instructed coldly, with that exact edge of cruelty that had always excited her in him. "All the way over, ass high in the air."

She had to go up on tiptoe to do it, and drop her head toward the floor. It wasn't like on the bed, not at all comfortable. Instead, she felt precarious, out of control, unsure what to do with her hands. "I don't think—"

"*Don't* think," he ordered crisply, a heavy hand settling on her upper back, pressing her down more to drape her weight more fully over her lap. She reached for the floor with her toes, barely able to scrabble for purchase. "You do as you're told. Now, pull up your skirts."

It took a moment for his instruction to penetrate, the blood already going to her head, the vulnerable position making her feel already frantic. And now he wanted her to pull up her dress? It didn't matter that he'd seen her naked bottom any number of times. This was different and she shuddered, wondering at herself that she'd asked for this.

"Seliah..." he drawled warningly, delivering a sharp smack to her upraised bottom, making her gasp and already tears spring to her eyes. She hadn't cried at all before, it had been too stirringly sexy, but this... This was too much.

And yet, with shaking hands, she obeyed, scrunching up the layers of skirts until they bunched around her waist, the air cool on her bare legs and bottom.

"Pull down the panties. I want to see your naked ass." He waited while she fumbled, face burning, and tugged down the barely there lingerie, having to lift her hips and kick a little to get them off and down her thighs a bit. "That's enough," he told her, caressing the curve of her bottom, sliding his fingers down the crack of it and into her dripping sex, making her squirm. "Oh," he breathed. "Such a naughty, randy little thing you are. Enjoying this so very much, aren't you? Well, you won't be so frisky in a moment."

Withdrawing his fingers—she couldn't help moaning in protest—he brought his hand down hard. Much harder than ever before. And it hurt far worse than she'd anticipated, stealing her breath. Before she could recover, he spanked her again. And again. And again. The stinging slaps rained down on her upraised bottom in a relentless rain of pain. She flailed, kicking her feet, her fingertips reaching for the floor, but he held her in place over the fulcrum of his knee with easy strength. She sobbed for breath. Increasingly frantic, clenching and writhing to escape the blows, her skin growing hot and sensitive, so each slap burned more.

A knot grew hard and tight inside her and she fought against that, too, against all that had gone wrong in her life, the unfairness, injustice, pain, and horror she'd witnessed. And all the times she'd held on, that she'd battled to keep her head above water—the insanity, the changes in her that made no sense, the changes in Gabriel and their lives turned upside-down, her parents' confusion and despair, so much of it her fault, though she didn't understand how or why, Jadren leaving her, her being torn from him—she'd powered through, refusing to yield to fail, to crumble under the pressure. Until now... when she could let go.

All at once, that tightness, that death grip she'd maintained on her self-control convulsed.

And cracked wide open.

She burst into tears, weeping and crying piteously. The tears flowed hot and without reserve, all temptation to withhold any scrap of poise or consciousness gone. She was shredded, without will, emptied and aching. The spanking continued, pain and arousal intertwined, her mind floating somewhere in an endless sea of it. Time ceased to have meaning. The boundaries of self blurred. She was only that which yielded.

She became aware of being lifted and lowered to the floor, where she collapsed, panties still partway down her thighs and binding them together, making her ever more aware of how slick they were, her sex throbbing in time with her burning bottom. Jadren moved her like a limp doll, arranging her onto her knees, then came around to stand before her, nudging his glossy boot tips into her field of vision. "Kiss them," he ordered softly.

Still weeping copiously, with a wrench of her heart, she did, pressing reverent kisses to his boots. She loved him without reserve, with boundless trust and a depthless need she could reveal only in this way. Fervently, she kissed his boots, willing him to understand how he'd flayed her open.

"Good girl," he murmured, and a fresh spate of tears escaped her. "Kneel up and look at me."

She did her best, given that her entire body felt like lettuce left in the sun to wilt. Gazing up at him, she found him looking on her with a kind of terrible compassion. "How does it feel," he asked her softly, "to weep that way?"

"Exhausting," she answered tremulously. "Exhilarating. Liberating."

He caressed her cheek, wiping the tears away with his thumb. "Then you should thank me."

"Thank you, Jadren," she whispered, turning her face to kiss his wet fingers, excruciatingly aware of her bottom, hot and aching on her heels. "I love you."

"Even now?" he asked, a hint of raw vulnerability in the question.

"More than ever," she told him, willing him to believe it.

He smiled, then grasped her jaw, lifting her chin and stretching her neck so she rose a bit off her heels. "Was it enough, do you think?" he asked with that same lethal compassion.

Tears leaked from the corners of her eyes, salt in her mouth. "Yes."

"Are you sure?" he asked, but she had no answer. "I think I need to see. Stand up."

He helped her to stand, wobbly as she was. "Bend over the stool," he told her, "and grasp the rungs nearest the floor."

She started weeping again, or was still weeping, thinking to tell him no, but she obeyed, helpless to resist. Fabric rustled as he lifted the dress, draping the long, lavish skirts over her upper body, enshrouding her in the dim light, exposing the rest of her. The panties bit into her thigh as he pulled them tight. They gave with a hiss, ripped apart, as flimsy as her thoughts of resistance.

Because, she realized on some vague level, she didn't *want* to resist. Being putty in his hands allowed her to melt into a state of pure being, of utter relaxation. *Jadren,* she purred in her mind. So, when he told her to spread her legs wide apart, she did, opening her most intimate, vulnerable, and sensitive part of herself to him, along with her heart and soul, all of her utterly excavated and offered to him.

He caressed her, delivered more stinging slaps, the pleasure and pain intertwining to become the same sensation, and she whimpered, writhing in encouragement and escape that were somehow also the same. The gown shivered around her, loosening as he triggered the magical fastenings. Briskly, he stripped it from her, leaving her naked and returned to her splayed position over the stool, exposed, his to toy with.

And toy with her, he did. Running his hands over her possessively, indulging himself and exploring every crevice, bringing her close to orgasm but never quite there, offering that pleasure-pain in ceaseless rounds until she knew her body to belong fully to him, an instrument for him to play.

His magic clicked into her, oiled clockwork penetrating her, sipping along the inside of her skin, delivering small shocks that wound her tighter. Climax hovered, inevitably drawing near and impossibly distant. Her wizard, marking her with his magic, taking her magic as he extracted and wrung responses from her quivering body.

She barely discerned the trigger, so like the rest of the endless torment, the ceaseless teasing, exploding without warning into pure moonlight, silver white hurled into a starless night. Contorting, convulsing, climaxing with wild abandon, she folded and unfurled, blossoming into a dark flower, birthed by all that had nearly drowned her before.

A long pause.

Stretching, she purred at the elasticity of her body, the languid, lightning-fast feel of it. Sitting on her haunches, she wrapped her tail around her forepaws and looked around the room. The colors had changed, still vivid, but all in shades of reds and greens. The minute differences between small changes in texture stood out like shadowy chasms. The world exploded with scent, varied and full of depth as the colors. Oh, and…

Jadren.

He sat, sprawled on the floor, knees akimbo and hands dangling between, his hair and beard fiery, black eyes wide pools, as he regarded her with astonishment, delight, and a whiff of faint alarm. The emotions colored his scent, rich and masculine, delicious, all of him. Prowling to him, she rubbed her whiskers along his jaw on either side. Marking him. *Hers.* Satisfied, she licked him, one long swipe up the side of his throat and face. He tasted good, too, quivering under her raspy tongue, emitting a low laugh.

"Is this how I'll die then?" he asked her, unmoving. "Eaten by an enormous black, wildcat, more fearsome than ever seen by any swamp creature." Tentatively, he lifted a hand to rub behind her ears. That was lovely, so she butted against his hand for more. "If you did, Seliah," he breathed in wonder, "if you chose to rip out my throat and feast on me until nothing remained, I'd die happy. Look at what we accomplished."

She decided curling up in his lap would be even lovelier, so she did, ignoring his yelps of pain and reminders not to use her claws, as he collapsed backward under her weight, laughing hysterically. This was fun! Sprawling over him, she pinned his slighter form with her heavy, feline one, holding him down with big paws on his shoulders—and just a tiny bit of claw, only enough to make him yip—she washed his face while he flailed at her.

"Enough, Seliah," he begged through gasps of laughter. "You're rasping my face raw, you great beast. Let me up."

She decided not to. Flexing her claws, she informed him of her decision, playfully biting the join of his neck and shoulder.

"All right, swamp creature," he yelped. "I was kidding about letting you eat me alive." Clockwork magic ticked along the underside of her skin, bones folding, spinning, flesh moving through invisible cogs, and she was back in human skin, naked and folded in Jadren's arms, draped over him on the floor. "Hello, beautiful," he murmured, pulling her into a deep kiss.

Never had she felt so alive, so fluid, so very much in love. Winding her hands behind Jadren's neck, she sank into the kiss, pressing every part against her. Already liquid and open to him, she received him as he sank into her, joining their physical bodies with such keen pleasure, such immediate erotic lightning, that she began to climax and kept going, each thrust propelling her higher, their magic as intertwined as their bodies. And when he shouted his completion, hands vising into her human flesh as if he'd never let her go, she sank her teeth into his shoulder, scenting her feline mark on him, setting her human one atop it like a seal. *Mine.*

She hadn't been aware of saying it aloud, but Jadren nodded against her, body melting into hers so they had one skin, one mind, one magic. "Yours," he said. "Forever and always."

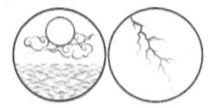

A LONG TIME later, they stirred, swimming up from the depths of the—literally—transformative experience. Jadren buried his face against her throat, pressing a kiss to the sensitive hollow there, echoing her groan of protest as he rolled away, bringing her with him so they lay on their sides facing each other. He studied her with somnolent, satiated black eyes, lovingly brushing a strand of hair out of her eyes. Gazing at her with tender affection, he whispered, "This floor is really hard."

She burst out laughing. "So much for sweet nothings."

"I'll tell you all the sweet words you like—though they won't be nothing—in the comfort of a cozy bed."

"I'm holding you to that," she replied, sitting up and registering stiffness in her body, no longer so boneless and languid. Jadren might have a point.

He grinned back, easily, no bitterness or cynicism in it, as he sat up also, casting a measuring look around the quiet room. "Well, that was fun," he said. "I like having an arcanium."

"Then you better aim to win tomorrow, so we can keep it."

"Today," he corrected. "And I plan to."

"It's already today?"

"Very early today, but yes. We were at it a while."

"I lost track of time," she admitted.

"Understandable." He smiled at her fondly, trailing a finger down her cheek and giving her a sweet, lingering kiss. "That was a remarkable experience. Life-changing."

"I've never heard you laugh like that," she told him. "When I had you pinned, licking your face."

"I don't think I *have* ever laughed like that," he replied, a hint of wonder in his voice. "I certainly never felt like that before. You are a miracle, Seliah."

"You're the one who worked the miracle, all-powerful

wizard of mine."

"It was remarkably easy," he said, almost musing aloud. "Once I found the key, it was practically automatic. You're right about how my magic works. I felt like I simply shifted you to the correct form, like repairing an artifact, a simple realignment of its inner workings."

"Alas," she said on a dramatic sigh. "In the end, I'm only an object to you. Just another enchanted artifact to employ in your rise to glory."

"My *favorite* enchanted artifact to employ in my rise to glory," he corrected with a jaunty grin, patting her bottom as she rose to stand. "Best get dressed, poppet. I'd like to get some sleep in a real bed before we clean the floor with Bogdan the blustering bully."

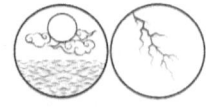

THEY SLEPT LATE into the morning, having made their way through the early, dark, and mostly silent hours back to their new apartments atop the house. Seliah awoke a few times, feeling that she should be up and about, always lulled back into drowsy slumber by Jadren's soft caresses, soothing and luxurious, feeling as if she purred in human form under his stroking hands and murmured reassurances of love.

As he'd promised. And, as he'd also promised, the sweet words meant far from nothing.

When she awoke for the final time, Jadren was gone, leaving her alone in the bed.

With a stab of terror, she sat bolt upright, staring wildly around the quiet room, late morning sunlight streaming in. No sign of Jadren anywhere. He'd left her again, this time without even a note on her pillow and—

He appeared in the doorway, bare-chested, wearing half undone, close-fitting trousers in his signature black, a shiny leather that caught the light, with gold lightning bolts forking down his lean thighs on either side. "Did you think I left?" he asked quietly, no mockery in it.

Watery with relief, Selly nodded, shoving back the tangled mass of her hair, which seemed to have gained a level of sentience of its own overnight, the way it persistently coiled about her. "I should have known better," she offered weakly, a bit embarrassed now by the extent of her panic.

He shrugged a little, coming toward her and sitting on the bed, taking her hand. "I did teach you otherwise," he said, with a lift of his brows, "leaving you as I did. But I promise you, Seliah: never again. You were right about everything. We *are* stronger together and nothing will part me from you, not even death. Which is easy to promise since I can't die."

A horrible thought struck her, surprising her with its force. "But I can. I'll grow old and eventually die, while you—"

He laid a finger over her lips to stop her, his somber expression revealing that he *had* thought of this before. "I'll keep you healthy and in prime condition. We have many, many years ahead of us together. Yes?"

Moved, she nodded, giving him a kiss.

He returned it with relish, then broke off, placing a last kiss

JEFFE KENNEDY

on her forehead. "You get the easy prep this morning, not needing to dress, but I have to finish getting groomed. There's food for you, if you want to eat before I transform you."

"No transforming me first and tossing me a bloody, raw steak?"

"I was thinking tuna, but no. It's not good for you to eat in animal form, especially this new in the process. I know that much."

She filed that information away, enjoying the view of his narrow hips and tight ass in the snug black leather pants. "Nice outfit."

"The house provided it." He spun and struck a pose. "Are the lightning bolts too much?"

"They could be pointed at your groin," she offered in a helpful tone, giggling when he scowled at her. "Not too much," she answered seriously. "Today is for show, Lord El-Adrel."

"Hopefully more than show," he replied, a bleak undertone to his light riposte.

She slipped out of bed and stretched, naked and taking her time, shaking her hair back to leave her body exposed to his gaze. To her everlasting satisfaction, his wizard-black gaze fixed on her with glittering intensity. *Many, many years ahead of us together.* That sounded awfully good. Prowling toward him, feeling the cat in her blood—she couldn't wait to try out the form in the marshes—she patted his cheek, then trailed light fingertips down the fiery hair arrowing to his groin, finishing by toying with the half-open placket and the denser growth of silky hair there.

"I believe," she told him in all sincerity. "You wouldn't dare fail me."

His mouth quirked in a half-smile. "Feral creature."

"And don't forget it."

~ 19 ~

JADREN WAS HAPPY. It took him awhile, to identify the unfamiliar, burbling emotion. It felt a bit like having a bleeding wound in his gut, except in reverse, with wellbeing flooding into him like pure water from a fresh spring. Once he realized what it was, he began to worry.

Surely being happy couldn't be good. Something was certain to go wrong.

Like whatever Bogdan had up his sleeve. His brother wouldn't go down without a fight, and a dirty, ugly fight at that. Fortunately Jadren wasn't only bubbling with ill-advised happiness, he also brimmed over with magic—from Seliah plus the El-Adrel arcanium. He should be fine without her reservoir of magic. Never had he been so replete, nor felt so confident in his skills as a wizard.

It must just be habit, worrying like this, expecting disaster. Or it was long and bitter experience. Kind of a toss-up, really.

"Ready?" he asked Seliah.

Despite his grumbling that it was unnecessary, she'd used the grooming imp, declaring she couldn't bear having snarled hair a moment longer. She'd also donned a figure-hugging gown of black, with artfully placed gold lightning bolts enhancing her curves with subtle suggestion, which told him that she wanted to look the part when he brought her back to human form. Just in case.

"Meow," she replied, playfully curling her fingers at him like claws.

He shook his head. "This whole being a powerful wildcat thing is making you very difficult to live with."

"You have no idea," she purred batting her lashes, and he was hard-pressed not to laugh.

"Now I understand why wizards like to put their familiars in alternate form," he observed wryly. "It's the only way to shut them up."

"It's not the *only* way," she replied, pursing her full lips sensuously. "You could always put your—"

He snicked his wizardry into her being, very much like fitting a key into a lock, and flipping her into alternate form before she could finish that very enticing suggestion and seduce him into making them late for the duel. Probably Bogdan would find a way to have that be a forfeit and wouldn't that be a fitting end to this effort? Hoisted by his own insatiable cock.

Seliah sat before him in wildcat form, gazing at him with knowing amber eyes. She was a beautiful creature—glossy black fur, broad head crowned by high, tufted ears. Her impossibly long tail, also tipped with a black tuft, curled in front of her, tapping with a hint of impatience her immobile form didn't otherwise reveal. Lavish black whiskers fanned from her soft, almost smiling muzzle, the bare hint of impressive white fangs protruding. Her massive paws, so soft and fluffy looking at the moment, could extend curved claws the size of his hand.

He hadn't been kidding that she could kill and eat him. And that he'd die a happy wizard.

"Let's go win this thing, beautiful," he said and she uncoiled, coming to stroll beside him. She stood so high at the shoulder that she was at hip-level to him, allowing him to rest a hand casually on her back as they walked through the halls. People started at the size of her, instinctively flinching back, especially when she let those fangs show. They made an impressive sight, he realized, catching a glimpse of the pair of them in a row of tall mirrors as they passed. He was no longer the cringing, whimpering whipping-boy under his mother's thumb, but a wizard who'd come into his full power, with a familiar unlike any the convocation had ever known.

"Maybe we should make you a jeweled collar," he said conversationally. "With a dangling medallion—a crescent moon would be pretty—so you can sit beside me and look all feral and impressive."

She slid him an amber glare, so very like her expression in human form that he nearly choked on a laugh.

"No? Well, we can discuss." He scratched her behind the ears where she liked it best. "You could have a matching one for human form," he suggested in a lower voice, for her keen ears only. "To wear on special occasions."

She turned her head and caught his hand between her teeth, faster than he could yank it away, not biting down, however. This was how cats played, he knew, and recalled how she'd treated him like a giant scratch- and chew-toy in the arcanium.

"With your consent of course," he added. "Please don't eat my hand before the duel. I'd like to show our people I'm capable of appearing *not* covered in blood, mine or anyone else's."

With a rumble that could pass for a laugh, she let him go.

Most of the population of the house had already assembled in the great hall, making it an even larger crowd than the day before, everyone wanting to witness the historic event. Today would see a new head of House El-Adrel, one way or another.

The excited murmurs rose in volume as people spotted Seliah. He'd fretted a little whether anyone would challenge who she was and whether he'd been the one to put her in alternate form, until Seliah very reasonably pointed out the improbability of any other explanation. Where else would he get a huge, black wildcat that wasn't engaged in trying to eviscerate him?

She was right. Besides which, familiars in animal form looked decidedly magical to anyone with any level of sensitivity to wizardry, and she would be the only familiar in alternate form in the entire house that people hadn't seen before. Still, he worried, looking for the pitfall here. Surely this couldn't be that easy. Nothing ever was.

When he'd suggested as much to Seliah, however, she'd responded that he was scarred and traumatized, lacking in self-confidence, that he expected disaster because he was afraid to dare to be hopeful. He'd retorted that she'd spent *far* too much time in Maya's company and that maybe she should've become a Refoel familiar, if she liked that kind of soul-searching talk so much. Instead of growing annoyed, Seliah had kissed him and told him everything would be fine, which somehow grated even more than if she'd taken him up on the fight he was trying to pick. She'd seen right through that, too, and told him to save it for Bogdan.

Bogdan. How he hated that guy. True, he hated all of his siblings, but fucking Bogdan might be his least favorite. After Ozana, of course. With her demise, he supposed Bogdan had gotten a promotion. *Oh joy.*

The insufferably smug son of a bitch—an epithet that worked quite nicely as literally true in the worst sense, in this case—waited for him in the center of the great hall. The exact center, where the pattern of lightning bolts converged into what appeared to be a fulminating sun radiant around a crescent moon. Jadren caught Bogdan giving the pattern a glare of scowling promise, as if he already planned how to replace the design should he emerge the victor. Jadren dug his fingers into Seliah's plush fur. Too late to run, so he had no choice but to win.

On Bogdan's shoulder, Helen sat in falcon form. She appeared composed and alert, as raptors did, and rather oblivious to the import of the coming duel. Of course, it had surprised Jadren that Seliah remembered so much of her experience in alternate form, something he put down to a bigger, more complex brain in that great, feline head of hers. She bumped his thigh with it, as if objecting to the thought, then ran her whiskered cheek from hip to knee. Marking him with her scent, the possessive creature. Oddly, it gave him a boost of confidence.

"Bogdan," he said by way of greeting, squaring off with his elder brother. The sun shone at high noon, streaming in hot through the glass far above.

"Prepared to die?" Bogdan inquired, as if asking after his health or how well he'd slept.

Jadren managed to cover the flash of dread, producing an insouciant smile. This was a duel to the death? That hadn't been in the original terms. Or had it? *I really don't like the sound of sudden death,* Seliah had said. Fool that he was, he'd assured her it was metaphorical. Apparently not.

"I'm not so easy to kill," he answered easily, projecting his utter lack of concern.

"A family talent," Bogdan agreed with an arrogant tilt of his head, reminding Jadren that he wasn't alone in the ability to self-heal. Jadren was, however, the most extreme example, which was why his late-mother had singled him out for the dubious honor of being the subject of her most diligent experiments. Which meant he'd learned a great deal about recovering from more extensive physical damage that he doubted Bogdan had ever suffered.

"Nothing like family," Jadren replied amiably. "Are there any rules at all?"

"Kill or be killed." Bogdan delivered the ultimatum with flat decisiveness.

Jadren became aware of the hush of the surrounding crowd, hanging on every word. "No collateral casualties," he specified. "Our people should not be harmed over our quarrel."

"Oh dear, how soft you've grown, baby brother, contaminated with the weak morals of those House Phel phools," Bogdan said on a sneer. "No wait. You always were like this: spoiled rotten, no spine, just a sniveling little mama's boy, forever hanging off her skirts."

Seliah rumbled out a growl at this gross mischaracterization of Jadren's warped childhood, and he petted her soothingly, which served to soothe himself. "Familiars should be out of the line of fire," he added. "I insist on those two rules."

"We can't access their magic while they're in animal form," Bogdan explained, as if Jadren might be just that ignorant.

"Exactly," he agreed cheerfully, "so there's no need for them to be anywhere near us."

Bogdan narrowed his eyes, gaze lingering on Seliah. Jadren didn't think he imagined the glint of admiration and the hint of jealousy in those eyes. *Yes, my familiar is bigger and scarier than yours.* He scratched Seliah behind the ears and she cast him an adoring look. *Plus, she loves me and is by my side out of free will and loyalty.* A thought following on that one niggled at him a bit—that the bonding enchantment mitigated some of that free will. Seliah possessed such ferocious self-determination that he more and more often forgot that she'd had no choice in bonding him, no matter how much she might love him. Still, nothing to be done about it.

"Fine," Bogdan said, waving a hand negligently, sending Helen winging off to perch at the top of the El-Adrel banner. "My rule one is no devices." He circled a finger at the widget hanging from the chain around Jadren's neck, then expanded the gesture to indicate the various bits of useful, mutable metal he'd embedded in the fancy outfit, and Mr. Machete on Jadren's belt. "Or silly weapons. Second, familiars may not intervene physically. Keep your kitty away from me at risk of forfeit."

"Fine," Jadren replied in the same tone, watching with half an eye as they both divested themselves of supplies into bowls hastily brought up by pages to hold the pile of implements. He wasn't worried about Bogdan withholding anything. If he used a device after this, he'd forfeit. He wouldn't cheat. Not that way, anyhow. He wished he could shake the unsettling sensation that he was missing something.

Jadren crouched, putting himself at eye level with Seliah's fierce amber gaze, using looping the widget on its chain around her neck as an excuse. "I know you won't leave the room, but—" He breathed a laugh at her low growl of denial. "Just get as far away to the side as you can. If the worst happens—" He continued to talk over her rising rumble and didn't flinch at her bared teeth. "I want you to run," he told her. "You should revert to human form if I die—stop with the denial and *listen*—but if you don't, go to Refoel. Chaim will help you and he..." Jadren found himself suddenly and ridiculously choked up. Oh, sure—every wizard got weepy before a duel to the death. "He would be a good wizard to you. You know he cares for you and you... you love Refoel. I know you do."

Seliah lifted a big paw, claws carefully sheathed, and set it on his shoulder, then licked his face with her raspy tongue that abraded his skin stingingly.

"Are we done with this rather nauseating demonstration of sentimentality?" Bogdan inquired. "I swear, Jaddy boy, if it weren't for the family resemblance, I'd wonder if you carried any El-Adrel blood at all."

Unabashed—actually pleased that he wasn't recognizably an El-Adrel anymore, as that could only be an improvement— Jadren kissed Seliah on her soft black nose and stood, watching her stroll off and enjoying how the crowd hastily parted for her. She picked a spot on the raised dais, leaping up to sit on her haunches on the thronelike chair that was hers, looking for all the world like a queen surveying her territory. At least she was close to the doors leading outside. He didn't doubt she could climb and clear the high walls if it came to that, regardless of the traps atop them. Probably the house would help her.

"Let's finish this," he said to Bogdan. "I haven't had lunch yet."

"You always did talk a big game," Bogdan replied, "but you never learned to walk the walk."

Following on that tediously cliched declaration, Bogdan hit Jadren with raw power.

Jadren had himself warded, naturally, but a generalized ward as he hadn't been sure what form the duel would take. Setting a ward to be thick and resist his late-mother's horrible darts, to slow their relentless drilling, was different from a ward to resist the overwhelming heat and focused energy of a lightning bolt made of pure magic. For that was how it felt, the magic leaking through his wards to scour and scorch his skin, like lightning embodied in a sandstorm.

He adjusted, able to strengthen his defense against the

incendiary blast, but that put him on the defensive. Bogdan smiled, knowing it, adjusting his outpour of magic to erode Jadren's wards, forcing Jadren to scramble to alter his defense again, eyebrows, lashes, and beard singed from the inferno, the unpleasant smell of burning hair reminding him of all that was at stake. Meanwhile, Bogdan's wards shone pristine and untouched. Jadren hadn't even gotten off an attack yet.

Well, that was going to change. Ignoring the magical fire penetrating his inadequate warding for the moment, Jadren hurled his own lightning bolt at Bogdan's head. Just enough to disrupt his brother's concentration from funneling the seemingly endless streak of sand-fire drilling through Jadren's shields. It worked—only for a blink—but that was enough time for Jadren to pull on his store of Seliah's moon-iced water magic. Making his wards double-walled, he filled the interior with the cooling substance, mentally thanking Liat for her endless tutorials on wards and repetition, mentally apologizing to her that he'd ever questioned the usefulness of those drills.

Bogdan recovered fast, sneering at Jadren's attack, though his exact words were drowned by the roar of his fire-blast. No big loss. Bogdan's attack continued at unremitting full power, cycling through variations that tested Jadren's new wards, to no avail.

Trusting the wards to hold for a while, feeling his burns tingle as they healed, Jadren took a moment to think. Bogdan was using power at a tremendous rate, clearly hoping to take Jadren out in the first few minutes of the duel with over-whelming force. It was already too late for that strategy to work, though Bogdan had yet to realize it, his face contorted in a rictus of determined aggression.

Maybe if Jadren had suffered less in his life, he might've been blown away in the first few moments of Bogdan's attack, succumbing to the pain and shock—but if Jadren was good at nothing else, he could certainly endure suffering. He wouldn't fail Seliah so easily.

And, unlike Bogdan, he could string two thoughts together and have them make sense.

Jadren changed his own bolt of lightning into a grappling hook, splayed claws of wizardry digging into his brother's wards and tunneling through. As he'd hoped, Bogdan assumed Jadren was trying to drill his way through and thickened the wards. Jadren clawed a bit deeper... then yanked, simultaneously applying corrosive magic to the edges of the shield, where Bogdan had neglected to make it as strong, focusing primarily on protecting himself from attack from head on. Bogdan's ward flexed, bowed, then broke apart all along the edges. Dropping the detached ward to shatter uselessly to the floor, Jadren hurled a lightning bolt at Bogdan's face.

As Jadren had hoped, Bogdan poured magic into deflecting the attack and erecting a new ward. It happened fast, as Bogdan might be an ass, but he was also a proficient wizard. Jadren had counted on Bogdan concentrating on that effort, and on enjoying his moment of recovered triumph, grinning widely until his face went blank with shock as Jadren's magic slapped him on the back of the head.

Bogdan reeled, dizzied from the blow, his hair briefly on fire and blood pouring down his face from the cracked skull. Jadren poured more metal-melting magic into reaching around, hopefully to deal a more devastating blow—Bogdan was already recovering, curse their family healing ability—but his attack bounced off. Bogdan had already wised up to that trick and encased himself in a full bubble of glassy ward. So much like glass, in truth, that Jadren's lightning now flowed into it, fusing it into greater strength.

Cursing himself for being a fool and underestimating his opponent, Jadren extracted the claws of his now useless probe, having to work fast to get it away from the magic-sucking field of Bogdan's ward. Nice trick, and one he wouldn't mind learning if he had an option *not* to kill his brother.

While Jadren fought to get clear of the sticky stuff, Bogdan turned tables on him, funneling a surprise attack from below. Tiles burst up in a fountain beneath Jadren's feet, peppering him with sharp-edged, ceramic shrapnel, temporarily blinding him and slicing him to ribbons. Worse, the pit hollowed out by the whirlwind of magic opened up beneath him and dropped him with painful jarring nearly to his chest. The tiles whirled down as fast as they'd exploded up, piling around him and melting with the heat of Bogdan's magic, sealing Jadren into place and compressing his torso painfully. If he needed to breathe to stay alive, Jadren would be a goner soon. Unfortunately, he *did* need to breathe to stay conscious. As soon as he passed out from lack of air, his wards would collapse and Bogdan could waltz over and leisurely kick his head off. Bogdan always had been a kicker, not liking to bruise his pretty hands.

Jadren hadn't yet had to survive decapitation. Maybe he'd grow a new head—or a new body from the old head—but he doubted Bogdan would give him the opportunity. He'd be a headless pile of ash very soon if he didn't get his shit together. Stupid not to have warded beneath his feet.

Frantically, he hurled bolts at Bogdan, who indeed strolled nearer, smiling in anticipation, enjoying himself now that he stood poised to defeat Jadren. Already the edges of Jadren's vision faded to gray, black curling over like smoke to take him under to final oblivion. Seliah roared in the distance, a protest and a spur for him to fight back. But he couldn't break through Bogdan's wards, couldn't penetrate the fused-glass bubble of his brother's shielding. Including under Bogdan's feet. Jadren checked.

In a last ditch attempt to escape his fate, Jadren did possibly the stupidest thing he'd ever done in a long life of making exceptionally stupid decisions. He let his head fall limply to the side, as if he'd lost consciousness, and collapsed his wards.

Silence reigned, punctuated by Seliah's mournful roaring. With his eyes closed, he couldn't see Bogdan's approach, but he used his passive wizard's senses to track as his brother's magic drew near. Bogdan would have to drop his own wards to deal the killing blow, if he indeed decided on a physical attack rather than magical. It would be wiser of him to go with magical attack to at least disable Jadren for the necessary total dismemberment, but Bogdan had never demonstrated much wisdom. Must run in the family.

"You always were weak," Bogdan hissed as he drew near. "But thanks for clearing the way for me by disposing of Maman. In gratitude, I'll make this quick." Drawing his foot back, Bogdan loosened his wards.

Thank you, Mr. Predictable. Jadren took the first blow, letting it snap his head back. Painful, but worth it as Bogdan chuckled and, in his renewed confidence, dropped his wards entirely.

Unable to resist witnessing the moment, Jadren opened his eyes and hit Bogdan with almost everything he had left. No widget to point, alas, but he knew how the inversion of the restoration magic felt now. Shaping it in his mind, he willed Bogdan's flesh to come apart, to return to an earlier state of being, when it was all separate cells. Bogdan staggered, blood blooming all over his body, immediately soaking his clothing, as his skin dissolved.

The crowd gasped and, in some cases, shrieked. Some cheered. But, though Bogdan fell to hands and knees, shaking his head like a dog desperate to rid himself of something foul, he didn't discorporate. While he was distracted, Jadren used his little remaining reserved magic to extract himself from the tile trap, looking to Seliah—still on her chair, but standing up and coiled to leap to him. He shook his head at her in warning, hoping she'd see and take heed.

Meanwhile, he climbed out of the pit, every bone aching as his body struggled to restore itself and Jadren prevented it, glad to have that much skill. If he survived this, he could access Seliah's magic to heal himself. Saving what little he had kept in reserve was more important. He thought wildly about how to end this. Bogdan was visibly recovering, and Jadren had just enough magic to deal a killing blow, but only barely, and it would have to be perfectly targeted. Fortunately, Bogan was out of magic, too, his potency diminishing as he healed himself. He was weak, defenseless, and Jadren was so tired of killing.

"Do you yield?" he asked, standing over Bogdan, surprising them both.

"Never," Bogdan ground out, sending a lick of lightning toward Jadren that flickered out and died before even reaching him.

Jadren refrained from mocking him, not wanting to goad the wizard further, and extended a hand. "Come on, Brother," he said quietly. "Let's end the El-Adrel family infighting. Enough already."

"Maman should never have sent you to Phel." Bogdan groaned, bit down on it. "Finish this."

"It's stupid and wasteful," Jadren argued. "We're stronger together, curse it." If Seliah could hear them, he hoped she was enjoying the told-you-so moment.

Bogdan raised his head. "Correction: I'm stronger than you. And smarter. Helen!"

It took Jadren far too long to catch on, staring stupidly at Helen—in human form—bursting from an envelope of concealment, Elal magic like his mother had used having cloaked her presence. She wrapped arms around Bogdan's waist, and he practically glowed with the magic he pulled from her. Feeling as dense as the lead lining of the arcanium, Jadren looked to the falcon still roosting on the banner.

"Anita leant me her familiar," Bogdan explained, getting to his feet, dried blood flaking away as his skin regenerated. "Careless of you not to verify."

"I should have known you'd cheat," Jadren said through gritted teeth.

"You really should have," Bogdan said with false sympathy, then chuckling, unable to contain his glee. *"Honor* and *ethics* and *integrity* are for losers, Jaddy." He sneered every word. "Offering me a chance to yield, to work with you." He snort-cackled. "I'd say you should have killed me while you had the chance, but you never had the chance. You don't have enough magic in you to change your familiar back."

"She can still kill you," Jadren replied, seeing Seliah was poised to do so.

"No, she can't." With a flick of his fingers, Bogdan sent a bolt of lightning at Seliah, knocking her off the chair, and sending her rolling bonelessly down the dais steps to lie in a crumpled heap. Jadren howled in rage and despair. Through the bond he knew she lived, though barely. He took a step toward her, but Bogdan threw chains around Jadren's ankles. "Too weak even to ward. This will be fun, taking you apart, piece by piece. Let this be a lesson to all of you," Bogdan declared to the silently aghast assembly. "I will rule this house with all the ruthlessness of a true El-Adrel. Any who crosses me can expect to meet this fate. No one can stand against me."

"Not even your father?" Fyrdo stepped out of the crowd. He looked worn, lines of grief and exhaustion creasing his normally cheerful face, but he held himself straight and proud as he moved to Jadren's side. "I'm disappointed in you, Bogdoodle. I've told you over and over not to bully your brother."

"Father..." Bogdan seemed unable to come up with more. "What are you doing here?"

"I live here," Fyrdo replied gently, putting his hand on Jadren's shoulder. "And I'm lending my magic to the cause.

Take it, Jadren," he said, tapping his fingers three times. *I. Love. You.* "Disable, don't kill, for my sake."

And there it was, he realized—the reason Jadren had hesitated to kill Bogdan, when he'd already killed his mother and his sister. Fyrdo loved them all, whether or not they deserved his regard. It was his gift, that unconditional love, and something deep inside Jadren wrenched as he realized his father loved him still, even after all he'd done.

That nothing he'd done or would ever do, could dim that love an iota.

It was a staggering realization and, in that flash, that moment of epiphany, he resolved to be that kind of father, himself. As he'd told Seliah, his mother hadn't known how to love, was perhaps incapable of it, but his father did. He had two parents, and he could choose.

Bogdan seemed to have a bit of an epiphany also, realization and awful knowledge contorting his face. He summoned his magic, the air crackling with ozone and the static of a devastating strike that would kill both Jadren and Fyrdo, but Jadren had already filled himself with his father's magic, warm and infused with love just as Seliah's was. He funneled a strike at Bogdan's head, ripping away his consciousness. He should recover. For Fyrdo's sake, Jadren hoped so, but that was the best he could do.

Even as Bogdan crumpled to the scatter of broken tiles at their feet, Helen struggling to soften the fall with her slighter build, Fyrdo dashed over to his other son.

Jadren ran to Seliah.

The in-house Refoel healer beat him to her, but barely.

"Apologies, Lord El-Adrel," she panted as she set hands on Seliah's glossy black flank. "I didn't dare interfere."

"Understood," he told her. "It was an untenable position. Can you heal her?"

"It would be easier if she were in human form..." The healer wizard trailed off in question.

Yes, what magic could the misbegotten youngest El-Adrel child, who'd never shown signs of being much of a wizard, actually perform? But he realized that she wasn't questioning his ability, simply being humble in the request. He wasn't used to people respecting him.

You'd better get used to it, he thought he heard Seliah say in his mind, even as she returned to human form, her amber gaze seeking and finding him immediately.

"Are you all right?" she asked, trying to sit.

The Refoel healer held her down firmly. "Lord El-Adrel is better off than you are, my lady, so please lie still a moment longer."

Seliah mostly obeyed, though she reached a hand for him. Taking it, he pressed a fervent kiss to the back of it. "Did we win?" she asked. It would have been a demand, had her voice been a little stronger.

"Yes, Lady El-Adrel," he answered. "We won. Everything is going to be all right now."

A smile trembled over her lips. "A happy ending, just like in the novels."

"The happy novels anyway."

"Those are the best kind," the Refoel healer inserted. "Hate those tragic endings. Won't read them. There you go, Lady El-

Adrel. Good as new."

Jadren helped Seliah to her feet, steadying her on the heels she'd insisted on wearing, and helping her straighten the fancy gown.

"How's my hair?" she asked him, gaze sweeping nervously over the crowd attentively waiting for them.

"You look beautiful," he told her.

She slid him a dubious glance. "You don't. You look like you went through a hay thrasher."

"I don't even want to know what that is," he teased. "Sounds like a stupid farmer thing."

Narrowing her gaze, she lifted her chin. "Keep it up and you'll find yourself going through one for real." Dipping that chin at the assembly, she lowered her voice. "They're waiting for you to say something wise and inspirational."

"They'll be waiting a long time, in that case," he commented wryly, but he considered what to say. This was a turning point for House El-Adrel. It deserved commemoration. He opened his mouth, hoping the right words would come to him—and stopped as a Ratsiel courier flew in through an open window at such a high speed that it could only be an emergency communication. The flash of silver instantly told him it came from House Phel.

"Gabriel," Seliah gasped. The courier went straight to her, dropping a small envelope in her hands.

Jadren's gut tightened. This would not be good. "What does it say?" he asked gently.

She lifted swimming amber eyes to his. "House Phel is under siege."

~ 20 ~

"**B**UT *WHERE* DID they come from?" someone in the panicked throng crowding the study hall demanded querulously.

Gabriel ignored the question, which wasn't really directed at him anyway, making his way through the mad scramble of House Phel denizens. They'd accumulated more minions than he could name anymore, and they all—from the youngest student apprentices to the most senior wizards—seemed to be dashing around in fruitless alarm.

"First Sammael and Elal attack, and now this!" someone else cried stridently.

Han was doing his best to direct the evacuation from the most open and vulnerable parts of the house through to the wizards' workshop, the only room in the manse without windows to the outside, except the arcanium. Still, Han wasn't a military commander and these weren't soldiers. No one was listening.

"You'd better take control," Nic advised, rushing up to him, breathless, dark curls plastered to her temples with sweat, smears of blood on her gown. None of the blood looked to be hers, just broad stripes on her skirt where she'd wiped her hands. "They're afraid, but they'll listen to you."

"Not when I tell them we're outnumbered and outpow-ered," he grumbled, wincing when she shot him a severe look. "How is Asa holding up?"

"Don't give up the battle before you've even fought," she chided, proffering one of her lists. "The infirmary is full, but Asa is his usual inimitable self. Narlis is with him, plus a few other familiars assisting and volunteering their magic."

He glanced at the list she'd handed him, noting the infor-mation she'd gathered from various reports, spirits sinking as he realized it was even worse than he'd dreaded.

"Gabriel, my only love," Nic said sternly, slipping her hand into his. "One thing at a time. Get the vulnerable to safety."

He nodded, gathering himself. If Han was no general, neither was he. To think Gabriel had once believed he'd live a simple life as a farmer, battling nothing more terrifying than worms in his orchards and locusts in his crops. Drawing on Nic's magic, he used that to amplify his voice. "Everyone, quiet!" he thundered.

And everyone cringed, clapping hands to their ears, some yelping in physical pain.

"Maybe a little much," Nic muttered, emerald eyes alight with amusement despite the grim circumstances.

"Sorry," he muttered back, and ratcheted down the vol-ume, not needed anymore anyway since they'd all fallen silent, faces turned toward him. The trust in their expressions nearly did him in. How could he fail them all so thoroughly?

"Steady," Nic murmured, flowing warm, wine-rich magic into him.

"Yes, we were attacked, suddenly, brutally, and with numerous casualties," Gabriel told them, going for utter honesty. No sense denying the obvious. "At this point, the enemy forces appear to have entrenched behind their camouflage to lay siege so there is no longer any immediate danger. But there is no doubt they are still out there and will attack again. Wizards and familiars with combat experience or capability of any kind, remain here. Those of you without that skill set, or if you simply prefer, proceed to the wizards' workshop, where you'll be safest."

"What if we want to surrender?" someone shouted from the back, an edge of panic in their voice.

"Yeah," another called out. "I didn't sign up for this. You're supposed to protect us!"

"Oh, nonsense," Nic snapped out, her carrying voice and Elal pride needing no amplification. "Every single one of you knew House Phel was in a precarious position, which is why many of you got hired on or were given exclusive apprenticeships with the most powerful water- and moon-wizard in the entire Convocation."

"The *only* one..." one of the instigators muttered unhappily.

Nic picked him out and pinned him with a disgusted glare. "That's right, Wizard. The only wizard who could teach you to use the magic everyone else told you was useless. You took the risk to sign on with House Phel in order to enjoy the benefits of what Lord Phel could teach you. And now you're whining about us being under siege, something a child could have predicted? Your behavior has been noted for future performance reviews. Meanwhile, you—all of you—have been given the choice of two options: assemble here to assist with defense or take safety in the workshop. Pick your path. Now."

"Lady Phel?" Quinn Byssan put up her hand.

"Yes, Quinn," Nic said, losing the harsh burr of disapproval.

"Could I suggest a third option?" Quinn asked. "Some of us have no combat ability or compatibility—my glass magic won't help much and dark arts know Han hasn't gotten anywhere teaching me self-defense—but we would be useful taking inventory of food supplies and so forth, and developing a rationing plan, in case we're looking at a siege of some duration."

Nic glanced at Gabriel questioningly, unwilling to countermand his orders, no matter how much sense the suggestion made. He was already nodding at Quinn. "Good thinking. You're in charge. Report directly to Nic. Those of you helping with defense, report to Han."

"Now we're taking orders from familiars?" a new voice grumbled.

Gabriel wasn't sure if they referred to Nic, Quinn, or Han, but he had no patience for the absurdity of the protest, regardless. He produced a thin smile. "The next person to complain about anything at all gets to be the first test subject on assessing the location of the enemy."

That worked like a charm, everyone immediately dispersing. Still holding Nic's hand, he tugged her into the temporary peace of the library. The tall windows shimmered with the ward he'd hastily erected around the entirety of the manse.

"Where do we stand?" he asked her, glancing at the list she'd given him, the words and numbers on it making little sense to his numbed brain. Easier to hear her summary.

"About two-thirds of the house denizens were inside the boundary of your wards when the horde manifested," she replied crisply. "As you would expect for the middle of the day approaching harvest season, most everyone else was in the fields and orchards, along with a generous helping of wizards, familiars, and others enjoying the beautiful autumn weather." She grimaced for that unfortunate timing.

"Confirmed deaths and injuries?" he made himself ask, then sat on the arm of a chair. He couldn't relax, but he also needed a moment.

"Ten deaths confirmed. The hunters killed anyone nearby when they decloaked, before establishing their perimeter. We know that because they left the bodies in plain sight." She swallowed, rubbing her rounded belly. The stretching skin itched her and he'd been rubbing oil on it for her in the evenings. "Injuries... we just have no way of knowing."

"My parents?" he asked, not really wanting to hear the answer, but needing to.

"They were out of the house," Nic answered with quiet compassion. "They're not among the dead, but more than that, we can't be sure."

"And the dead?" Much as he worried for his parents, and all the people outside his wards, he couldn't squelch the utter relief that Nic had been inside the house when the horde appeared and attacked without warning.

"There's a list of names on the back of that sheet," she

answered quietly. "Mostly non-magical folks, but we lost Wizard Faith and Familiar Michael who were walking on the far side of the lake."

Gabriel scrubbed a hand over his face, knowing he'd have to set aside grief and regret for later. Knowing also that the list of names would grow. "And the assessment of how they managed to surround us without us knowing?"

She sat in the chair he perched on, losing verve like a puppet with cut strings. "Elal magic is our best guess. I kept thinking I sensed it, but dismissed that as wishful thinking because I miss Alise. Now I'm so glad she wasn't here and is safely at Convocation Academy."

"The downside of that is we could use her wizardry to send out spirit scouts."

"Don't remind me. If *I* could do it, I would," Nic replied with bitterness.

He feathered fingers over her hair. "I didn't mean it that way."

"I know." She reached up and linked her fingers with his. "I just feel so cursed helpless."

"We all do." He let out a breath. "Elal magic how?"

"Some kind of cloaking, as you surmised," she answered, shaking her head. "Not anything I was aware of, but it seems Elal spirits were employed to hide the approach of the horde until it was too late. Iliana is a mass of guilt. Remember how she said Nephi was trying to tell her something but she couldn't understand what? Apparently it was this. They've been massing for more than a week."

"There's no way Iliana could have extrapolated this turn of

events from Nephi's emotion-images."

"I could have. I should have because Seliah wrote about it in her initial missive from Refoel. Remember how she told us that the El-Adrel wizard and automatons who attacked them were cloaked in the same way? The clues were right there, but I didn't give them as much attention as I should have."

"You can't second-guess these things," he told her. "I didn't give it much thought either."

"But *I* should have." She shook her head impatiently, curls bouncing. "All I could think about was my father colluding with El-Adrel. I didn't follow her warning to the logical conclusion."

"*This* is the logical conclusion?" he asked incredulously. "An army of hunters and spirit-driven automatons surrounding House Phel is something you think you could have predicted?"

"Yes." Dropping his hand, she propelled herself from the chair, restlessly pacing to the window, skirts swirling in a rustle of color, hissing like her impatience. "We knew they were coming for us, that they were plotting and scheming. All this time that we've been going back and forth with those legal actions and counteractions and motions to do jack shit, only gave them the time to plan this battle. They'll crush us, Gabriel," she said bleakly, turning back to him. "We should talk about evacuation, if that's even possible."

"The countryside outside the wards is likely even more dangerous," he pointed out, though they both knew that. "We can fight. This isn't insurmountable."

"We're facing virtually indestructible automatons," she shot back. "Not to mention thousands of hunters."

"We'll use moonsilver to melt—"

"No," she interrupted. "We won't. I haven't told you the worst parts yet. Wizard Faith and Familiar Michael had moonsilver weapons on them. They didn't work."

Real fear trailed cold down his spine and coiled into his gut, wrapping itself around his entrails and beginning a slow strangulation. "What do you mean?"

"Exactly that!" Nic spat, throwing up her hands. "We have eye-witnesses. They used moon-magic silver weapons on the hunters and it did *nothing* to them. Something else Seliah warned us about, remember? She encountered that hunter that was resistant to moonsilver and it knew it would be. It was smarter, too, she said. More adaptable. I've got that letter here somewhere. I need to reread it, though it's too late now." With that bitter declaration, she paced to her desk and began rummaging through the neat stacks of papers, scattering them with sharp gestures, with no regard for her usual orderliness.

Gabriel went to her, going behind his beloved and pressing his body against hers, reaching around to set his hands on hers, to still her frantic searching. "Take a moment," he said. "Deep breaths."

"We don't have time to take moments," she bit out, her voice watery now. "And breathing won't save us."

"We *do* have time," he corrected, taking deep breaths himself, in the hopes that she'd match them. "Being under siege is entirely about time, and fortitude."

"That's when you're waiting for allies to arrive. We have none." She turned in his arms, facing him. As he'd suspected, she'd been weeping, her face wet with tears. "There's more."

Yes, he'd heard the plural when she mentioned the worst parts. "Tell me."

"They're digging a trench to drain the lake."

"They aim to expose the arcanium."

"It seems so. My father knows where the arcanium is, so that would be his strategy. Expose the arcanium and cut off our access to it. I should have let you kill him when we had the chance."

He touched her damp cheek. "It's not our fault that we made a choice to spare his life. It wasn't only you. I decided, too."

"And that's our weakness," she replied grimly. "My father always taught me to be ruthless in victory, or it doesn't stick. Now you and I are paying the price for that moment of sentimentality."

Gabriel didn't think not wanting to kill her own father—a man she'd once loved, admired, and emulated—qualified as sentimentality. But he also knew Nic well enough by now not to try to argue with her in this rare black moment.

"I'll expand the wards," he told her. "With our current access to the arcanium, I can build enough power to move the bubble of the ward past the lake."

"It won't work." Her mouth, like her mind, was fixed. "You'll just trap those creatures inside with us."

"It will work," he insisted. "I can move it outward incrementally, pushing them away."

"That will mean pushing everyone currently outside the wards away, also," she pointed out with dogged fatalism. "Are you prepared to watch your people, perhaps your parents, hammer on the outside of your wards, screaming to be let in while the hunters dismember them?"

Horrified, he stepped back, putting distance between them before he realized he'd done so. "How can you suggest that?" he demanded.

"Because that's what would happen. I know you, my only love, and you would not be able to turn your back on them. You would let them through the wards."

"Of course I would!" That she could imagine otherwise sparked an insulted rage in him.

"And doom us all," she continued relentlessly. "Because you open your wards to our friends, our family, you open them to your enemies."

Despair settled over him with the realization of her correct assessment of the situation, on all counts.

"It doesn't matter," she said, stepping close enough to set her palm on his chest over his heart. "We could generate the power to extend the ward-bubble as you suggest, but you couldn't sustain it. Not even you, my powerful wizard. Even now the wards are a constant drain on you."

"A trickle," he corrected. "I barely notice. And I'm being conservative, doing as you've taught me—keeping my own reserves full and drawing from you as you replenish."

She gazed at him in sorrow. "A trickle over time is enough to carve a deep canyon. Eventually we'll both be losing more magic than we can replenish. Once we lose the arcanium— we'll have to collapse the tunnel to keep the enemy from using it to get inside—we'll lose magic even more rapidly. And that's not counting what we'll expend on magical counters to the attacks that will surely come."

It was so unlike Nic not to have a plan. His sunny, determined, and relentlessly optimistic wife was nowhere to be seen. "I thought I was the gloomy one in this relationship," he teased.

She didn't laugh, or even crack a smile. "I don't see a way out of this," she admitted. "We're trapped inside your wards, with finite supplies of everything. Anything we might do is only a delaying tactic to forestall our inevitable defeat."

"We can petition for help," he said, knowing he sounded desperate. "The Convocation won't allow this outright act of war."

"Won't they?" She pursed her generous lips, dropping her gaze. "For all we know, they support this action. They never wanted to reinstate House Phel. This will neatly get rid of the house, and us, forever."

"We need to tell Seliah to stay away," he realized. "Jadren, too, if they're even able to leave House El-Adrel..." He trailed off, realizing with a bitter grief that matched Nic's that he might never know if Seliah was all right.

"She'll be all right," Nic told him with firm conviction, reading him easily. "Jadren won't let anything happen to her. We'll send an emergency courier to them. Tell them what's happened and to stay far away. At least they'll be on the side of the winning team. Alise, too. We need to warn her and send her funds to allow her to stay and graduate."

"Key the courier to Seliah only," Gabriel said. Not that he thought Jadren couldn't be trusted, but just in case. Nic's knowing look showed she knew what he was thinking but wasn't going to call him on it.

"I'll send messages throughout the Convocation," she decided. "And I'll pay off all of our debts."

He felt himself pale. Nic knew the finances better than he did, but even he knew the balance of their debt versus their current accounts. "That will drain us utterly."

"Our money might as well go the route of our food and magic supplies," she agreed grimly. "It's too late for us to behave like a ruthless high house. We might as well stick with the noble, honorable, and self-sacrificing route." The smile that curved her lips had nothing to do with happiness. "I'll include a note explaining, that we face overwhelming attack by forces from Elal, El-Adrel, Sammael, and likely others, and that we don't wish them to suffer due to our unpaid bills. That should make them feel guilty."

"Will it make them feel guilty enough to come to our aid?" he asked, knowing the answer.

"Highly unlikely, but I'll enjoy poking them about it."

"*Should* you warn Alise?" He expected Nic's immediate indignation and held up a hand to ward her off. "Pay her remaining tuition, yes, but she'll want to come help, if she knows."

"Seliah will want to also."

"Yes, but Jadren will stop her. Who's to stop Alise?"

"We'll send the missive to Provost Uriel," Nic decided. "She'll make sure to keep Alise under lock and key." She grew thoughtful, tapping her lip.

"What are you plotting?" It encouraged him to see Nic moving into strategy mode, even if she was working off the assumption that theirs was a hopeless cause.

"House Uriel has always been an enigma," she answered musingly. "They rarely take overt sides in any Convocation squabbling, but unlike Refoel, it's not based on any kind of stated neutrality. They simply don't participate, which leads to speculation that they *do* take action, it's just surreptitious."

"Covertly pushing events in the direction they prefer?"

"Maybe?" She raised her elegant, black brows, a glimmer of hopefulness in her haunted gaze. "It would be serendipitous for us if they wanted events to go our way."

"Is that likely?"

She shrugged, fatalistic. "No, but it's not unlikely either. Uriel is no friend or ally of our enemies. They loathe House Hanneil, and were one of the primary forces in creating the sanctions after the wars, the ones that bound Hanneil into agreeing never to use psychic magic in warfare again. If Alise has managed to find out anything in the archives about Hanneil having a role in taking Phel down, that would help our cause immensely."

"Has she indicated any progress?"

Nic shook her head, puffing out an annoyed breath. "Just the opposite. She's using coded language, so I can't be sure, but reading between the lines indicates she hasn't found any House Phel records at all, which is telling right there."

"But doesn't help us."

"No." Leaning both hands against him, she rose on tiptoes to give him a kiss, full of love and resignation. "Nothing can help us now, my only love. All we're doing is attempting to control what they write on our tombstones."

The image of a grave marker with Nic's name on it gripped him in an agony of fear unlike anything that had gone before, bringing home the urgency and tragedy of what they faced. He was no longer happy she was inside the house, trapped within the wards. "We have to get you out."

"That's impossible," she snapped, dropping back to her heels. "Besides, I'm not abandoning you in your hour of greatest need. I'm your partner as you've so determinedly insisted upon. We're a team and I'm not leaving you without a familiar."

"But to save the baby…" he said without thinking.

"Gabriel Phel." She drew out his name with cold ire. "You have never treated me like nothing more than a vessel for this baby. Don't you dare start now."

He raked a hand through his hair, gutted that he'd hurt her, wondering if he could find some way to convince her to go, if he hurt her more. With a sigh, he realized that not only couldn't he do it, she would never fall for it. "I didn't mean it that way," he told her softly. "I was trying to manipulate you with it. I apologize."

"As well you should." Her green eyes glinted with fire, and he braced himself for her wrathful takedown of his character. Instead, she sagged. "If I could pull some trick to save you from this, I would try it, too." Wrapping her arms around his waist, she leaned her cheek against his chest.

He held her in turn, rubbing her lower back where it often ached, cupping her head in his other hand. She felt so small, so fragile a container for such ferocious intelligence and spirit.

"Dying together in a last stand against our enemies isn't

nearly so romantic in real life as it is in books," she commented.

Amazingly enough, he laughed, the feeling raw against his
ribs, so constricted with grief. "Well, we're in early stages,
yet," he replied. "Maybe it will feel more romantic later."

"When we're half-starved and out of magic," she agreed.
"Anything will sound good then." They were silent a long
moment, just holding each other. With a sigh, she withdrew
from his embrace, leaving a cool emptiness behind. "Besides, if
we were to get anyone out, we have the non-combatants to
consider, the full innocents in this. Like Maman. And Laryn."

Stunned by that comment, he thought she must have
misspoken. "Your mother, yes, has no choice in being here, but
Laryn is hardly an innocent."

Nic waved a hand in the air, equivocating. "That's the
wrong word. Laryn has no choice about being her, indeed
never wanted to come here and be part of our house. She's a
prisoner, condemned to die along with us."

"And you call me the idealistic one," he commented wryly.
"I don't mind Laryn going down with us."

"Along with her and Asa's unborn child?" Nic inquired
silkily with raised brows.

He set his teeth. "I don't like that I see your point."

"I suppose the point is that this is an invidious situation.
Mainly I wish I'd sent Maman somewhere safe." She sighed
again. "I'd better write these letters and send the couriers. We
need to get them out before they start an aerial bombardment
and you have to close the wards overhead." She turned to the
disarrayed piles of correspondence, frowning as if someone

who wasn't her had messed up the order, and began ordering them again.

"Are they likely to do that?"

"Hmm?" She glanced up from her work, mind already racing ahead to completing the task. "It's what I would do," she said, smiling humorlessly, "which means it's what my father will do."

~ 21 ~

I T FELT WRONG to be enjoying herself, but Alise found herself doing it despite her best efforts to be serious and to feel bad about leaving Convocation Academy yet again, as she'd *promised* not to do. Even with Provost Uriel's tacit approval—if that was the case—she was breaking her word. And here she'd thought she couldn't possibly encounter again some greater cause to tempt her away from her resolve.

This seemed to be a theme in her life.

So, she shouldn't be feeling this sense of freedom and excitement, the sheer pleasure of being out in the world. It hadn't helped that Cillian handed her a basket of fresh-baked, still warm cinnamon rolls when she met him at the bottom of the steps at the appointed time. The elemental carriage he'd borrowed from another faculty friend wasn't the newest model and showed signs of wear, but it was comfortably appointed. Naturally, it was also loaded with books.

"What is a road trip but an excuse to read nonstop and have snacks?" he said to her by way of greeting. He had the top down on the carriage, despite the edge of chill in the air. "If you're too cold, we can put the top up," he added, "but I also brought blankets for until it warms up. The House Ananiel forecast says it should be sunny and clear."

"I like the top down. Reading books and having snacks is an excellent excuse to snuggle under a blanket," she said, meaning to be funny, but realizing that the sally sounded kind of flirtatious, which she hadn't intended at all.

Fortunately, Cillian seemed to be as oblivious to flirtation as the air elemental powering the carriage. "I already programmed the elemental," he said, almost apologetically. "But if you want to check my work, I won't be offended."

"Why would I check your work?" she asked, slinging her overnight bag into the enclosed boot at the back of the carriage and climbing in beside him.

"Because you're the Elal-magic expert," he replied. "I'm basically a glorified walking card catalog."

She rolled her eyes. "Oh, please." And, because of that, she pointedly did *not* check the air elemental bonded to the carriage—and tamed to be easily programmable by even the lowest level wizard—as she would have normally done. Not because she was compulsive about that kind of thing; it just made sense to be thorough. Still, the "Elal-magic expert" comment stung a bit, so she restrained herself.

"We should be at House Harahel by nightfall," he told her as she settled in and the carriage glided smoothly into motion.

"Too bad Harahel is in the opposite direction from Meresin," she said wistfully. "It would be nice to stop in and say hi to the family." More than nice. She fretted that no one there would want to worry her if things weren't going well.

Cillian gave her a sympathetic smile. "It must be nice to be so close to your sister. Unusual for high-house families," he added, "at least the politically powerful ones."

"We weren't always," Alise told him, a bit surprised with herself for blurting out that unsavory truth. The Cillian effect of making her equally garrulous continued. "When Nic fled the Betrothal Trials, she didn't even tell me. She ran off to the lands beyond the Convocation and intended to never contact any of us ever again." It still hurt, she realized.

"She was protecting you," Cillian offered. "Eldest child syndrome. She wouldn't have wanted to involve you in her problems and potentially affect your reputation and future."

"Mostly she didn't trust me," Alise replied. "For all she knew, I'd turn around and betray her to our father."

"Would you have?"

She nearly spat at him for asking such a question, then realized he watched her with pure curiosity, and no judgment. "Maybe," she admitted. "Lord Elal might be the most powerful wizard in the Convocation—or was, no knowing what shape he's in these days—but he also ran our family like his own personal kingdom. We all worshipped him and feared him in equal measures. None of us wanted to cross him. He could be so generous when we pleased him. And so vindictive when we didn't."

Naturally, she thought of Maman then, victim of Piers Elal's vengeance, her cat's eyes staring blindly at nothing, her mind perhaps gone forever. Would Nic tell Alise if their maman passed away? Maybe. Maybe not, if Nic thought she was continuing to protect her baby sister.

"Sounds rough," Cillian said with sympathy, but left it there, which she appreciated. She really didn't want to dig into that morass of the past. "Here, this might take your mind off being homesick."

He handed her a book and she took it automatically, not really seeing the cover as that word ricocheted through her. *Homesick.* Was she? When she left House Elal for the academy, she'd never once felt this longing to be back, not like she dreamed of House Phel and the people there. Home. House Phel was home.

"I think you'll find what it *doesn't* mention very interesting," Cillian said, pointing to the bookmark he'd inserted.

She opened the tome—a history of the high houses of the Convocation—to the marked page and read. It was very dry, the sort of recitation of names and dates that made her eyes cross with instantaneous boredom. Going back to the founding of the Convocation, the historian demonstrated a fiendish love for details, particularly those that glorified the establishment of Convocation law and custom, delving with glee into the minutiae of which house set which precedent. None of it relevant to her interests.

"Why am I reading this?" she asked plaintively, after forcing herself to read several pages.

Cillian put down his own book and gave her an owlish look. "What do you notice?" he prompted in his schoolteacher manner.

"I notice a lot of dates and incredibly boring precedents for laws."

"What else?"

She closed the book with a thump—keeping his bookmark where it had been, since she wasn't a monster—and leveled a glare at him. "Enough with the game-playing. Just tell me, Wizard Cillian."

"Why Wizard Alise," he replied, sounding a little hurt, "I'm not playing games. I thought you'd like to experience the joy of discovering for yourself."

She rubbed the spot between and just above her eyebrows, which tended to ache when she was tired or frustrated. Right now, she was both. "I take joy from having information, not in the acquiring of it."

"Never thought to meet such a strange creature," he muttered to himself, narrowing his eyes at her. "How much did you sleep last night?"

"None of your business," she snapped.

"So... barely any?"

"I had several tasks to tie up before I could leave," she answered. "I don't have the same freedom you do." And didn't that rankle? She'd had a life for a while, before she'd given it up to pursue this fruitless task of looking for information that wasn't there.

"Eat a cinnamon roll," he suggested, pointing a finger at the basket she'd set at her feet.

"I'm pretty sure food doesn't substitute for sleep."

"Maybe not, but it helps. Besides they're getting cold, which shows a distressing lack of regard for the unique delight that is a cinnamon roll still warm from baking."

"When did you bake them anyway?" she asked sourly, snagging a roll from the basket, if only to shut him up about it. Deliberately messing with his observational data on personality and eating habits, she bit into the side of the roll, disregarding the pattern of coils, telling herself it didn't matter if it felt out of order. The sweet warmth penetrated right through her exhaustion, wrapping her up like a hug. She kept any sign of the pure bliss off her face, however, lest Cillian get more ideas about running her life.

"Earlier this morning," he answered absently, his gaze and mind back on the book open on his lap.

She nearly choked on her cinnamon roll. "How *much* earlier this morning—or did you have magical assistance?" Alise wasn't any kind of expert on baking, but she'd helped Nic with the running of House Phel—and the feeding of its growing population—enough to know that bread needed lots of time to rise. Hours. And that was before the actual cooking part.

"Please." He looked physically pained. "Baking requires enough magic inherently without mucking up the process with other entities. Remember I work at night? I slept yesterday, worked a half-shift at the archives, then went back to my apartment for baking and packing." He slid her a knowing look as she devoured her second roll. "I figured you'd need feeding."

She didn't stick her tongue out at him, because that would be immature and disgusting, covered as it was in half-masticated cinnamon roll, but it was a near thing. "Will you, pretty please with cinnamon on top, just tell me what you found in this book?"

"Fine, fine." He heaved an exasperated sigh that was clearly for show. As she'd expected, he was more than pleased to reveal the fruits of his research. "The author—Wizard Dolores Harahel, you'll note—was scrupulous about chronicling the history of the Convocation in precise order. She was known for it."

"I did notice," Alise commented drily. Then, relenting, she added, "I'm sure the trait is admirable in a historian."

Cillian chuckled, more amused by that than she'd expect. "She has her detractors, as it's a rather stultifying approach. But it's useful to compare this text—obviously a recent re-issue by House Calliope—with the original. Or one of them." He caught her peering around for this original he spoke of. "Not here," he specified. "Books that old are in the rare book archives, but I did take a look at the oldest copy in the Convocation library last night, and I memorized these pages. I'm very interested to compare them to what's in the Harahel archives, as I know we have a first edition there."

"Are we getting to the part where you tell me what the differences are?"

"You're a sassy one. Remember how I mentioned that House Xerograf was absolutely founded after House Phel? And yet Wizard Dolores Harahel mentions House Xerograf before any mention of House Phel."

"Maybe House Phel didn't contribute to these legal decisions." Knowing the current members of the Phel family, she could believe that being a scofflaw and iconoclast was a family trait. No wonder they pissed off the other houses enough for the most powerful to conspire to have done with House Phel once and for all.

"Aha! Excellent logic. I thought of that, too."

"Of course you did," she muttered, not quietly enough, because he threw her a grin, undaunted by her sarcasm.

"That's why I consulted the original in the archives. House Phel *is* mentioned in that version."

Alise stared at the book in her hands. "That *version*," she repeated. "Is that common practice, to change the contents when they reprint books?"

"No!" Cillian shot a finger into the air. "It is not common, my excellent student, nor is it ethical. If they do make any changes, they are supposed to include a note to that effect. It's acceptable to correct errata in later versions, but not to eliminate blocks of text. Essentially these newer texts have rewritten history. Wizard Dolores Harahel must be spinning in her grave."

"So, what was in the original that got eliminated?"

"I'd need to do a sentence-by-sentence comparison, so I'm not certain yet."

"You could've done that instead of baking cinnamon rolls," she felt compelled to point out.

"I could have, if I'd had days instead of hours. I researched enough to identify the major lacunae in the historical information, confirming that House Phel did participate in developing Convocation law. The house was very involved in a great deal of legislation, especially involving familiars, their rights as citizens, and protecting them from experimentation."

Alise believed that, too. "Gabriel Phel must be the reincarnation of one of his ancestors," she remarked.

Cillian looked interested. "Do you believe in that sort of thing?"

Did she? No. But...

"No," she answered decisively. Convocation teaching was

clear on the subject. There was no life after death. If there was, wizards would have found a way to penetrate that veil and contact souls on the other side. House Elal had been—speaking of historical research—very involved in that research. Even the most powerful Elal wizards had been unable to summon the dead. Spirits existed in the world, from simple elementals all the way to the highest echelon spirits such as those used in combat or for more complex tasks, but none of them had ever existed as living, corporeal beings. That had been conclusively established, which Cillian should know, and she told him as much.

"There's a 'however' in your tone, however," he said, very seriously, but she suspected him of teasing her.

"Magic is something else entirely and there is evidence that it replicates from the past," she informed him loftily, quite sure he knew this, too. "For example, House Phel itself—once Nic and Gabriel elevated it from its watery grave—has continued to restore itself according to patterns no one living remembers. Nic says it's because Gabriel's wizardry connects to his wizard ancestors and thus informs the house on a level that isn't conscious."

Cillian looked fascinated. "I've read theories on the subject, but never witnessed it. There are vanishingly few opportunities to observe real-life scenarios of that kind. I'd love to visit and see for myself."

Alise nearly said they should go right then, but naturally they could not. They had a mission at House Harahel and were expected. Just imagine if she'd taken the permission to go on this field trip with Cillian, and then diverted off to House

Phel instead. She'd not only never graduate, they'd likely make her a pariah in the Convocation. "If you already know what's missing from the Wizard Dolores Harahel's history by comparing this recent edition with the ancient one, why do we need to go see your family?"

"Aha." Cillian held up a finger. "Because our text is original, to the point of containing margin notes in Dolores's own hand. We also have—or should have—every edition printed since. I want to see when the alterations first occurred. Besides which, there's the matter of you bringing this petition to the attention of Lady Harahel and her senior staff."

"Right." The petition, in which she wasn't at all sure what she could and couldn't say. "I was going to ask you, what—" She broke off as a Ratsiel courier bearing the Convocation Academy conformation zoomed up to the carriage, flashing urgently. Shit. This was it. Her worst fears come true. She'd be humiliated. Scorned. She'd let down the people who mattered to her the most. Would they have sent hunters, too, to drag her back in a collar and chains like they'd done to Nic and Seliah? "Didn't you tell Provost Uriel that you were commandeering my presence?" she demanded, panic fluttering in her breast.

But Cillian was frowning in confusion, tapping the air elemental to stop the carriage. "I did, of course, and Provost Uriel sent approval." He accepted the message the courier carried and the creature departed immediately, clearly not programmed to await a reply. Reading, his frown deepened. Alise's fear sharpened.

"What is it?" she asked, the whispered question all she

could manage. When Cillian leveled a sympathetic look on her, she nearly burst into tears. "Just tell me."

"Provost Uriel simply passed along a message sent to her," he replied, handing her the letter.

It was from Nic.

In that moment, Alise discovered what her worst fears truly were.

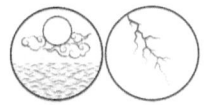

"BUT YOUR PHEL family sent the letter to make sure you stayed away," Cillian argued. "Your sister—Lady Phel, who has the authority to command your obedience—explicitly instructed you to stay at Convocation Academy. For your *safety*," he added, unnecessarily stressing the word. "I'm not taking you to House Phel."

"You don't have to." She pointed at the dome housing the air elemental waiting to be told to restart the carriage, and where to go. "I can reprogram the elemental with a thought from here."

"You would just leave me by the side of the road?" He sounded more curious, as if she were some sort of fascinating specimen, than upset.

"I don't *want* to." She really didn't, she realized, and not only because it would be an incredibly callous thing to do, especially after his many kindnesses to her, all of them undeserved. "*We* have to go back near Convocation Academy, anyway. I could drop you off."

He studied her with interest. "But not if I fight you on this?"

She shook her head. "I'm going. I'll do whatever I need to do to get to House Phel, even if that means using harsh tactics."

"You'd summon warrior spirits to evict me from the carriage?" His voice rose, less with incredulity than a thrill of excitement. She so did not understand this guy.

"Don't make me go to those lengths." But she would if she had to. She was an Elal, through and through, apparently. The resolve burned steady in her. No remorse, no guilt. She would leave him his food and books though.

"Alise," he said, gentling his tone and manner. "Please don't do this."

She understood he meant going to House Phel, not strongarming him. "I have to. They're my family. They mean more to me than anything else."

"Even your own future? At best you'll destroy your prospects in the Convocation with this disobedience. At worst…" He trailed off, his quiet black gaze bleak. "Alise, you could be killed."

"I know that." She did know. They could all be killed. But she'd rather that than live her life alone, with everyone she loved dead. What kind of life would that be?

"Nic doesn't want that for you," he persisted. "Lord Phel doesn't either. They paid your tuition and board, plus extra to set you up until you find a position you like if you don't want to go back to House Elal."

"I'm never going back to Elal," she snarled. "They're behind this. Don't you see?" Done with waiting, she used her magic to reset the air elemental, giving it instructions to proceed with all haste to loop near enough to Convocation Academy for Cillian to get a ride, but not near enough for anyone to interfere with her plan. The carriage smoothly turned in a circle and sped back the way they'd come, the sun higher and more golden-warm, but the day no longer lovely and full of freedom. "They have no allies," she continued in the face of Cillian's accusing silence. "No one else will come to help them. It's a hopeless situation."

"Exactly." He waved his hands in the air. "What can you, one wizard, no matter how exceptional, do to save them?"

"I'll figure out something," she replied grimly.

"You're not thinking straight," he said, frustrated. "I could recite any number of tales to you about supposed heroes doing exactly what you're contemplating and dying anyway."

"Aha, but they wrote stories about them." She slanted him a crooked grin, but he only glared at her.

"At least come to Convocation Academy with me," he pleaded. "Talk to Provost Uriel. Maybe she'll have ideas. Maybe she can rally the Convocation to assist Phel."

More likely they'd lock her up and keep her from leaving. "Cillian," she said, abandoning his title since he'd done so with her. She supposed they'd become friends now, of a sort. "If anyone in the Convocation was going to help House Phel, they'd have offered alliances by now. They'd be rallying to support House Phel against their attackers, including sanctioning Sammael and Elal for their previous attack. Has anyone even discussed those possibilities? You read everything, so tell me if there's something I missed."

"You didn't miss anything," he replied unhappily. "The rest of the Convocation seems to be turning a blind eye."

"Waiting for the strongest to survive," she said. "As they always do."

He pursed his lips, not liking that, possibly searching for an argument. "It's also possible that Hanneil is interfering there, inhibiting any movement toward helping Phel. If they're truly involved. But we have no proof of that."

"I think the time for proof is past," she pointed out. "It's too late to do anything but fight back to the best of our ability."

"And if you lose?"

"Then we'll have lost either way," she answered impatiently. "All I know is, I'm not sitting cozy at Convocation Academy pretending I care about studying when the only good part of my world goes down in flames."

"Oh, Alise." He looked so sorrowful she nearly wanted to comfort him. "There are so many good parts of the world. There are... all the books. And cinnamon rolls!" He snatched up the basket and thrust it at her. "Have another one."

"All the cinnamon rolls in the world can't sweeten the bitterness of this defeat," she replied, and he lowered the basket.

"Fine then," he said, but he extracted a cinnamon roll and handed it to her anyway, dropping it in her lap when she didn't take it, and taking one for himself. "We'd better eat up so we're ready. Too bad we don't have a familiar with us."

"With *us?*" She began to unwind the coil, realizing he was right.

"Yes. I'm going with you."

~ 22 ~

To Selly's surprise, Jadren didn't argue at all about going to the rescue of House Phel. What did surprise her was that he insisted on taking time to send a number of messages first, arguing that sieges take time and no one at House Phel on either side of the battle line was going anywhere very soon. Fortunately, Katica El-Adrel had employed veritable army of secretaries who even now scrambled to do Jadren's bidding.

"You wanted us to head up House El-Adrel," he pointed out with asperity. "I warned you that it would involve tedious administration, but no—you were all 'I love paperwork, Jadren. Let's do all the boring paperwork!'"

She assumed that silly, high-pitched voice was supposed to be her. "I never said any such thing and I do not sound like that."

"Close enough." He was remarkably cheerful, given the circumstances, frequently petting Mr. Machete, once more hanging off his belt. "I can't wait to see Gabriel Phel's face when I dramatically rescue him and all he holds dear. Ha! That will show him."

"Show him what?" she demanded. "Gabriel always believed in you."

"I know it." He shook his head in disgust. "With no good reason, too. So this will show him he wasn't wrong."

"You make no sense at all," she informed him, awash with love.

"I'm certain I warned you about that," he replied with a half-grin, lifting her hand to kiss the back of it. "All right. I've officially closed the labs, put everyone working there on probation until they can be properly interviewed, and liberated the... inhabitants." He stumbled only slightly over the word, a bare tremor in his magic. "Where's my letter to Refoel?" he asked in a raised voice.

"Here, Lord Jadren." A young man hastened over, flapping the paper to dry the ink, then bowing as he handed it over.

Selly read the finished missive over Jadren's shoulder, still with some misgivings. Jadren was taking a sterner tone with Lord Chaim Refoel than she'd thought wise, but she'd also acceded to Jadren's wishes. They were equals now, both lords of high houses and—Jadren had pointed out with a touch of arrogance that was frankly hot—in the informal social hierarchy of the Convocation high houses, El-Adrel outranked Refoel. The letter reflected it.

"Perfect," Jadren said to the secretary, who flushed at the praise. "Send this via Ratsiel courier, followed by a copy to go with the group we're sending via carriage to House Refoel, just in case he needs reminding. Receiving payment in advance should sweeten his temper."

"Are you sure you should require that they ally with us and House Phel?" Selly asked, fretting. She absolutely agreed that the former occupants of the labs would do best at Refoel. She and Jadren had asked if Liat and Maya would personally handle those cases, given their familiarity with the trauma experienced by Jadren and herself. If anyone could rehabilitate Katica's victims, those two could. She just worried about Chaim's reaction to being told that Refoel would break their traditional neutrality and come to House Phel's aid, or pay the price of earning House El-Adrel's enmity.

"It will be good for Chaim to make an actual decision," Jadren remarked sardonically. "Besides, he owes both Phel and El-Adrel for his attempts to suborn *you*."

"Jadren, he never did more than make a case for me being his familiar."

"You were and are *mine*," Jadren replied with a hint of a growl under his otherwise pleasant tone. "It was a serious breach of etiquette for him to approach you when you were already bonded to me and do so without speaking to Phel first."

"I'm a person, not a shipment of oranges whose price needs to be negotiated," she replied, a little irritated.

Jadren snagged her about the waist, pulled her close, and kissed her. Then, holding her gaze, he murmured, "You are much better than oranges. Infinitely more precious."

Unable to help herself, she laughed, pushing him away and wriggling out of the embrace. "My *point* stands."

"Yes, well, I'm speaking the language Refoel will understand. Are my letters to Elal or Sammael done yet?"

"Here's the draft for House Elal, Lord Jadren." A young woman hastened up, brandishing the multi-page document. "It includes all the contract renegotiations between El-Adrel and

Elal."

Jadren flipped through them, making a few notes, occasionally chuckling to himself. "That will burn Piers Elal's ass good and proper."

This business-tycoon aspect of Jadren had come as a bit of a shock to Selly, in truth. But again: hot. He'd gone through the El-Adrel alliances with Elal, Sammael, Tadkiel, and several other houses with amazing rapidity, demonstrating a surprising flair for and understanding of the various agreements. Selly found it all especially amusing given how much he'd griped about Nic and Elals being wily in their business dealings.

"What about House Hanneil?" she asked when the secretary took away the notes on Elal for the final version.

"We'll see what remains of them when all is said and done," he answered thoughtfully. "With any luck, they'll expose their role in this—including their egregious violation of the sanctions that allowed them to remain a high house after the wars—and the Convocation will take them apart piece by piece and redistribute the spoils."

"And if they don't?"

"We'll cross that bridge." He reviewed the drafts of the other letters and contract renegotiations. "All right, that only leaves naming my heir." He glanced at her with a grimace. "I won't leave House El-Adrel to be battled over by the scavengers, should the worst happen to us. The problem is a serious dearth of palatable candidates. Do I leave it to Bogdan in the hopes that a near-death experience will have transformed him into something less than an asshole?"

"You could name Fyrdo heir," she suggested. The whole

room stilled, it seemed.

"My father?" Jadren asked.

"Is there someone else named Fyrdo around here?" she countered sweetly.

"Funny. Fyrdo is a familiar." Jadren's gaze swept the cadre of secretaries, who all resumed their writing with poses of great intensity.

"Why, Jadren, you bigot," Selly said. "Your father probably knows more about running House El-Adrel than you do, after all these years. He's smart, insightful, kind, and he loves El-Adrel. He'd be a fine lord and it will give him something to do, to absorb his grief. In fact, you should make him regent in your absence."

"But he's not a wizard," Jadren protested, sweeping a hand in a grand gesture to encompass everything. "What if the house acts up?"

"Then he can instruct wizards what to do," she answered with impatience. "Just because wizards are the only ones who can use magic doesn't mean that they're the only people capable of taking action."

Jadren stared at her a moment longer. "The Convocation will have convulsions over this."

"Good. They need to break up their stony traditions."

Shaking his head at her, he dragged over the implements to write the decision himself. "Dark arts save me from Phel iconoclasts." He pointed the stylus at her. "I'm naming Fyrdo regent, as you suggest, but you will succeed me in governing House El-Adrel in the event of my death, with Fyrdo after."

"Me?" she squeaked. "I can't run El-Adrel."

"See, that's what I said and you didn't listen to me. What goes around, comes around. It will give you something to do, to absorb your grief. And prevent you from running into Chaim's arms," he added under his breath.

"So much for your heartfelt speech about me going to Refoel upon your demise."

"I was out of my mind then. Woozy from blood loss. I don't know what I was thinking."

"Jadren," she said softly, waiting for him to look up at her. "Nothing would absorb my grief. I would run El-Adrel for you, but I would never bond another wizard."

His lips twisted in a rueful smile. "Never is a long time."

"Nevertheless," she replied, meaning it.

"The Widow Wizard Lady El-Adrel," he mused. "Has a nice ring to it. You should commission a poet to immortalize our tragic tale."

"I'd rather commission one to immortalize our triumphant victory."

He grinned, a malicious edge to it. "That's my girl. We're going to hit those attackers from behind so hard and fast they'll never know what happened."

"I know your magic, and that of the El-Adrel minions we'll bring, can take out the automatons. But what about the hunters?"

"We'll cross that bridge."

"They're immune to moon-magic silver, remember. Nic said as much. Just like the one that went after me."

"The one you killed, on your own, without backup, re-member."

"Only by chopping it into pieces too small to do me any harm," she replied bleakly, not caring to remember that nightmarish fight. Maya had helped her to resolve the underlying causes of the frenzy she'd gone into then, when threatened, but those memories were akin to the swamping insanity that had enveloped her mind so much of her life. She was better, but she'd never be completely free of any of it, and she didn't care to revisit that mental abyss worse than the most cloying bog. Still, she had to face this. "And we don't know that I killed it. It might have spawned into a myriad of hunters resistant to moon-magic silver." Who might even now be surrounding House Phel. Wonderful.

"Hey." Jadren's arms were around her, snuggling her close against his lean, hard body. "You did what you had to do," he said against her ear.

"I know."

"It's not your fault that awful people created awful creatures. But we are going to destroy them. We found a way before and we'll find a way again."

She nodded against him. "Because we have to."

"Has been done. Can be done. Must be done." He kissed her cheek lingering there. "There's always the option to run away with me to that theoretical hideout where we'll forget this nonsense and I'll devote my considerable energies and talents to sexually servicing you as often as you like."

She giggled. "Tempting." Then, drawing back enough to frame his face in her hands, stroking his silky beard, she smiled at him. "How about once this is done, we go away somewhere and do just that? You and me, alone together somewhere pretty, with no expectations."

"Deal." His lips brushed hers, opening and deepening, and she sighed with all her body, sinking into the sheer pleasure of him, despite their audience. Something clattered onto the desk beside them. They jumped, like kids caught out, then both stared at the silver dagger that had suddenly appeared. Jadren swept the assembly of scribes with an accusing black glare.

"It dropped out of thin air, Lord Jadren," one explained with wide eyes, holding up empty palms as if in surrender. It would take time to get the denizens of House El-Adrel to shed some of their fear of their lord.

"I see." He turned that stare upon the dagger. "That's Phel's magic."

"Gabriel's old dagger," Selly confirmed, picking it up. "I remember this from when we were younger. He's had it forever. Or used to."

Jadren took it from her, handling it judiciously, studying it with his El-Adrel artifact magic. "He didn't extrude this one from moonsilver," he noted.

"You can tell?"

He flicked her a wry glance. "I'm surprised you can't. I should send you back to study with Liat."

"Ha ha."

"No, this is a standard steel dagger inlaid with moon magic, the way Gabriel made things in the beginning—which, not incidentally, violated El-Adrel's trademark. In fact, I know exactly which dagger this is and how it got here. It's the one he and Nic lost on the barge when he brought her back from Wartson. The one my late, unlamented mother used to blackmail Phel into accepting me as a spy in their midst. The house apparently knew what it was and is giving it back."

"Oh, well then," she said brightly, taking it back from him. "This is my favorite dagger!"

"You are my favorite familiar," he replied, running a hand down her hair. "Shall we go ride to the rescue of our friends and family?"

"Yes, let's get that taken care of."

She only hoped they would be in time to save House Phel from sinking into ignominy a second, and final, time.

~ 23 ~

N IC HADN'T REALIZED how monotonous a siege would be. It was an odd kind of tedium, too, born of long periods of nothing happening, underlaid by the singing tension of dread of what might happen, interspersed with moments of utter terror when something did happen.

It was a very strange way to live: becoming so bored you began to wish for something to happen, until you remembered that the only thing that *could* happen would be terrible. She occupied herself with what she could, trying to keep busy so she wouldn't worry about those things she couldn't control. Which was pretty much everything at that point.

The aerial bombardments had begun not long after she predicted they would—possibly in response to the flock of Ratsiel couriers she'd sent—and Gabriel had been forced to close the wards overhead. They'd had a time of it chasing down the tiny machines that had whirred their way through the manse, seeking flesh and burrowing in with terrifying speed. Elal spirits of various kinds had made their way in, too. To Nic's immense frustration, and despite her sensitivity to Elal magic, she could detect only some of them.

The one bright side was that the higher-echelon, warrior

spirits could be dealt with directly using mundane weapons. There had been bloody skirmishes throughout the lovely manse, Han's cadres of fighters grimly battling the semi-corporeal beings. Dispersing the entities entirely had taken wizards, but—although they had no one fully skilled in Elal wizardry—enough of their minions possessed MP scores in spirit magic that they'd been able to team up to eventually disperse the things. It had taken more magic than they could afford, but the moral victory had been worth it.

The remaining spirits created further problems, however, primarily the poltergeists that had burrowed their way into the framework of the manse, causing mischief resulting in minor injuries and major frustrations. The wicked creatures had a knack for chaos, interrupting at critical moments and driving everyone crazy. Worst of all, they seemed to be immune to all efforts to expunge them. Alise could have done it, Nic was sure, and she caught herself regretting not having her sister with them.

Until she reminded herself how glad she was.

She was in the infirmary, up on a ladder with a crowbar attempting to pry off the window molding to uncover a poltergeist burrow, when Gabriel found her. This particular gremlin had been harassing Asa and his assistants by stealing bandages and ointments off trays just as someone was reaching for them and also contriving to drop cold water onto sleeping patients. Asa was strained to the breaking point. As their only healing wizard with a steady supply of wounded to deal with, he needed all of his wits about him. It didn't help that he, in particular, was also wearing thin on his critically needed healing magic.

The poltergeist lurked at the end of a thin tunnel, probably created by one of those wood-eating worms that had infested the place before they hired the House Pestis exterminator wizard to come and work their magic. It had squeezed itself into the very back and Nic was offering it emotional tidbits, luring it to stick its snout out long enough for her to snag it with the canned enchantment one of the minions had fabricated. "Come here, sweet baby polty," she crooned. "Have some nummy emotions. Just for you."

It crept forward, wanting the turbulent emotions poltergeists thrived on, but suspicious of her.

"Polty polty," she sing-songed. "Come on, sweetie muffin ba—ack!" She screeched as someone seized her by the waist and lifted her into the air, and she flailed before realizing it was Gabriel.

He set her on her feet and spun her around to receive the full force of his glare. With his fulminating frustration at being unable to do more to counter their enemies, his glare packed considerable force, indeed. His moon magic had gone to the dark face, flaring about him in a palpable wake like black wings. "No. Ladders." He punctuated the words forcibly, fists on his hips.

"I wasn't going to fall," she protested. "And I almost had—"

"Everyone says they're not going to fall. Nobody thinks they will until they do." He gave her rounded belly a pointed stare. "We're trapped in here with no access to a House Gaia wizard should you go into labor prematurely."

"Listen to you," she griped, "talking like only House Gaia

can help with this pregnancy. I feel quite certain that Meresin women have been giving birth quite successfully without Convocation wizardry to assist. Laryn had her baby without Gaia's assistance."

"She had Asa's help."

"As would I."

"Not if the baby comes early and Asa is buried in dealing with the wounded."

"You're borrowing trouble."

"All of this is beside the point," he countered swiftly. "You shouldn't be taking foolish risks."

"Don't you call me a fool, Gabriel Phel."

"Lord Phel. Lady Phel," Asa interrupted the increasingly heated argument in his calming healer's voice. "Tempers are short throughout the manse, but you set the example and there are witnesses."

Flushed at the chastisement, Nic rounded on Asa, lowering her voice because he held the sleeping infant in his arms. That had been another bright spot, the birth of little Cornelis. "I was *attempting* to satisfy your request, healer, by nabbing the poltergeist everyone else has failed to." They all winced as a tray of implements hurtled through the air and crashed against a wall, showering broken glass and pungent oil. Cornelis woke with a wail. "We'll never catch that fucker," she muttered unhappily.

"I won't apologize," Gabriel retorted, as if she'd been speaking to him. "I refuse to prioritize a nuisance over your health."

Someone shrieked, then cursed angrily, an assistant running with towels to mop up the water—and the person who'd gotten doused. "I never imagined being aggravated to death," Asa said on a weary sigh, handing Cornelis to Narlis, who'd come hurrying over.

Her creased face lit with joy and Cornelis quickly quieted, waving his hands at Narlis. "You're a good boy," she told him, carrying him off with promises of a nice bottle. Laryn, still listless ever since the bond-severing, hadn't shown any inclination to nurse Cornelis and indeed seemed indifferent to the child. Nic was glad they'd kept Laryn in House Phel until the birth, instead of sending her back to Refoel, or the house of her birth, but more than once Nic had considered using the woman for hunter bait.

Asa watched Narlis and his son go with a wistful smile before turning back to them. "Lord Phel is correct, Lady Phel—we can cope with this spirit, annoying as it is. At least you gave us a reprieve while it hid from you."

"I almost had it," Nic repeated, giving Gabriel some of his glare back. But he wasn't looking at her, studying Asa instead.

"Your magic is looking thin," Gabriel noted. "I'll send a familiar to you."

"There's no one available right now," Asa replied, "but thank you. All the familiars are tapped out after answering that call for magic to build that weapon they hoped would wipe out the hunters."

"No one asked me," Nic said with surprise. She hadn't even known about it. "What weapon?"

"It doesn't matter since it didn't work," Gabriel said wearily. "And I gave orders that you're not to be tapped for magic as you insist on keeping me refilled."

Wary of repeating her earlier error in arguing in front of the rows of patient-filled beds, Nic sunk mental jaws into her temper. "I have more than enough magic to keep you going and also—"

Gabriel took her by the arm, gently but implacably, and drew her into an empty examination room. "We lost the arcanium," he said quietly.

"Oh no." All anger fled, she sagged at the news. "I knew they were getting close, but..."

"Despite Nathi's best efforts to run off the crews, they reached the arcanium at dawn. I collapsed the tunnel myself." Emotion swam in his wizard-black gaze, a grief Nic shared. Losing that private, intimate retreat felt like an enormous blow.

"You had to do it," she told him, willing herself to mean it. "We knew that was coming–and that we couldn't let them inside the manse."

"I know." He leaned against the exam table, exhaustion in every line of him. "But I'm wondering—what are we holding out for?"

She nearly snapped a reply, but realized she had no good answer. "Because the alternative is giving up?"

"I mean, what is it they want from us? Are there no terms for surrender?" he asked, expression bleak.

"Surrender?" she echoed. "They don't want our *surrender*, Gabriel." She had to tamp back a bit of impatience with him, aware that Asa had been spot on that her temper had frayed to nearly nothing. Still, how could he not realize the uncaring wall of the Convocation they'd fetched up against? She'd known from the beginning that he was the sort to beat his head brainless against that wall, but not that he'd continue to ignore the fact of it.

"Then what *do* they want?" he demanded, half angry, half plaintive.

"Annihilation." She let the word hang there. "They tried to destroy House Phel before and very nearly succeeded. If not for your re-emergence as a Phel wizard, that would be a done deal."

"And Seliah's," he reminded her.

Nic shook her head. "Seliah would have foundered in her untapped magic, succumbing to insanity. *"You* were the trigger. It's you they want to destroy. They won't settle for anything less."

Gabriel studied her for a long moment, desperation creeping into his gaze. Though she'd wanted him to face reality, she found she deeply regretted seeing him lose the last of his innocence. Naturally, she'd been the one to do it. Perhaps if Gabriel had found someone else, a different familiar, things would have gone differently for him.

"I accept that that's the case," Gabriel was saying, "but we should be able to negotiate for safe passage, at least for noncombatants. Your mother. Cornelis."

"Negotiate with whom?" she asked in turn. "We face a mindless mob out there, magically tasked to be single-minded in their intent to overrun us completely. They kill anyone they encounter, taking no prisoners. Even if we appealed directly to Elal, El-Adrel, and Sammael, offering surrender, we have no way to get a courier out to them. Also, we have nothing to offer them that they want."

"Your father wants you," Gabriel pointed out remorselessly.

"Well, he can't have me," she snapped.

"Isn't being alive worth it?" he persisted.

"No." She was firm on this one. "Not if you are dead. And before you suggest that Sammael might take Han and Iliana, they'll give you the same answer. Not every life is worth living."

"I know." He rubbed his forehead. "I do understand, truly. I just feel like we're only delaying the inevitable. If their goal is our utter destruction, as it seems to be, and our ability to withstand them weakens every day, every hour—what are we hoping will happen? Unless you think someone might come to our aid…"

No. No one was coming. They'd never had any hope of that. "I don't know," she told him. "I only know that I refuse to roll over. They will win—I harbor no illusions there—but I don't want to go down in history as someone who turned belly up and willingly offered her throat to the enemy."

He stared at her in horror. "Don't even say that."

Raising a brow at him, she nearly smiled. It settled and reassured something in her that, despite her best efforts to instill her own cynicism in him, he retained at least a bit of that naivety she so loved in him. Rubbing a hand thoughtfully over her belly, she contemplated that another woman might be less selfish than she was and try to live for their child, but she didn't want to survive Gabriel, couldn't live in a world without him.

He'd brought color to her life and, when he died, he'd take it with him, leaving only endless gray behind.

Reading something of it in her, Gabriel drew her into an embrace, their child snugged between them. "I'm sorry," he said, face pressed to her hair.

"For what?" Though she'd kept her voice steady, tears made it watery, much as she tried to hold them back.

"For not being able to save us." He sounded so resigned, so despairing, that it broke her heart. "I should never have started all of this, shouldn't have given into my hubris and determination to reinstate House Phel. I look back at who I was then, so foolish and naïve, as everyone recognized but me, going through the mouldering books in the library of a rotten manse, dreaming of reclaiming something I never fully understood. I don't understand now why I wanted that when this is all I ever wanted." He held her tighter then drew back enough to kiss her. "I wish I could work an enchantment to wipe all of it away except this: you and our child. I love you so much, Nic, and it's all that matters."

No point in trying to be strong, she wept freely now. "We have this," she told him. "This moment, this time that we've had, they can't take it away. Our story will be eternal."

His lips quirked. "Like Sylus and Lyndella?"

"Yes, exactly like..." She trailed off as a thought hit her.

"What?" Hope lit his face, apparently too strong for even her rationality to fully quench. "You've thought of something."

"Sylus devastated his enemies," she said slowly, "in the wake of Lyndella's death. He exhausted his magic and died himself, but he killed them all and scoured the landscape bare."

Gabriel regarded her with a frown. "That doesn't sound like a promising solution."

"No, but that's what's held us back, right? That we've been trying to find a way to win, to fight our way out, keeping everything we've built intact."

"Well… yes." He lifted a brow. "If we annihilate ourselves, I think we're still just giving them what they want.

"Not if we take them with us." The idea hung there, just out of her grasp.

"I don't understand, Nic."

"I don't either, but there's something there. They have us surrounded, but if we can draw them to concentrate their forces enough to thin or abandon enough of an avenue…"

"Then we can at least get our people out," he finished, brightening.

"Yes. And then, while they're escaping, you unleash your full abilities and we take them down with us."

"It could work," he agreed slowly, "though, if we're going down in a self-destructive blaze, I'd prefer to take Igino Sammael, Piers Elal, and Katica El-Adrel down with us. And the entirety of House Hanneil," he added wryly, "while I'm making a wish list."

She smiled in sympathy. "We might not get that. But, it's possible that we could sow the seeds of their demise. Let me give it some thought. After all, I come from a legacy of conniving and traitorous people."

"I love the diabolical workings of your Elal mind," he told her.

"Such is our romance," she said wrinkling her nose. "In the

meanwhile, I agree to conserve my magic for you only. We can still stoke my levels with games in the quiet of our bedroom, even if it isn't the arcanium."

"It seems a little wrong to devote ourselves to sex while the house burns down around us."

She patted his cheek. "We must take one for the team. Soldier bravely on and do what must be done." Turning thoughtful, she considered. "I do have a potential solution for one problem. Laryn can earn her keep by acting as Asa's familiar."

Gabriel regarded her with surprise. "Do you think she'll agree to it?"

"If we posit it as feed Asa or go be hunter bait, she will," Nic said grimly, rather relishing the prospect of delivering the ultimatum to the traitorous bitch.

"I don't like the idea of forcing a familiar to give up their magic, as you know..." Gabriel began, then grinned when she snarled at him. "Simmer down, marsh cat. In this case, I agree. Laryn can pull her weight or take her chances outside the wards."

"Well, that solves one problem." She winced as something large crashed on the other side of the door. "If I agree to let you hold the ladder, will you let me trap that fucking poltergeist, at least?"

Chuckling, he gave her a formal bow and offered his arm as if they proceeded to a ball. "It would be my pleasure, Lady Phel."

"So gracious, Lord Phel," she replied, taking his arm and lifting her nose in the air. "It's always a pleasure to plan mutually assured destruction with you."

She wasn't sure, but she thought she heard him release a sigh before he covered it with a brave smile.

~ 24 ~

J ADREN SURVEYED THE situation from the top of a tree, using
an El-Adrel device that magnified the view nicely. "Arrogant," he muttered to Seliah, who perched on a nearby branch
in feline form, impatiently lashing her long, black tail. "They're
not even bothering to cloak themselves anymore, or even to
mount a rear guard."

Seliah growled in what sounded like agreement, adding a
querulous note of inquiry to the end.

"You'll get your opportunity to disembowel some hunters,
oh bloodthirsty one," he assured her, pocketing the scope, so
he could swing down to the ground, where a considerable
force of El-Adrel wizards and familiars awaited, all armed for
battle. Seliah simply leapt from the tree with enviable ease,
landing soundlessly beside him. Good thing he wasn't the prey
she was after. He'd feel sorry for the hunters if they weren't
soulless abominations.

"All right," he told the assembly, still rather bemused to
have their rapt and respectful attention of a small army. Not
bad for the House El-Adrel whipping boy. If only his younger
self could see him now. He sketched out the map on a handy
screen made for the purpose, lines appearing where his finger

drew. "Here is the manse proper, with the drained lake in front, and the river behind."

It had given both him and Seliah a pang to see the silver and glass dome of the Phel arcanium exposed at the bottom of the dry crater that had once been a lovely, calm lake. Hunters formed a ring around it, facing outward in guard formation, while automatons crawled over it, using tools to attempt to penetrate the tough outer shell. The upside was they clearly hadn't found a way in yet. Also, Phel had been smart enough to collapse the silver tunnel that led back to the manse, a precaution that must have pained them but Jadren congratulated him for the foresight.

"Lord Phel is maintaining a ward here." Jadren drew in the perimeter. "It's closed overhead and likely below as well, as there are indications of attempts to tunnel beneath. We have to assume everyone is inside. We know Gabriel Phel, at least, is alive and well, as the wards are definitely his and standing strong." He added that last for Seliah, who kept gazing longingly toward the manse as if she'd love nothing better than to run for it directly. "The outer perimeter of the attackers, both hunters and automatons, forms a ring here." He drew in that circle as well.

"I propose this. We disperse all of you with the ability to deactivate the automatons in a wide circle. At my signal, we'll approach, tightening our noose around them, taking out all of the automatons at once. A small group will move forward to take care of the ones attempting to dismantle the dome."

"And the hunters?" someone asked.

"I have something up my sleeve there," he answered, hoping he sounded confident. He had an idea, sure. Whether it would work? Up for grabs.

"Lord El-Adrel?" another wizard asked, raising her hand. It still took him a moment to realize they meant *him* with that title. "I'm familiar with the, ah, former Lady El-Adrel's work on creating those automatons. They've been animated with Elal spirits, encased in protective armor. It won't be easy to deactivate them, particularly from any distance."

"It would be much more effective to detach the animating spirit first," her familiar agreed, exchanging a look with her wizard.

"I'm sure it would," Jadren returned caustically, "but unless an Elal wizard just happens to pop up out of the shrubbery, we're fresh out of—"

"An Elal wizard like me?"

Jadren whirled, blinking just in case his eyes deceived him, and testing with his wizard senses just in case illusion magic did, not quite believing the sight of Alise emerging from a copse of trees. A young wizard followed her, looking as bemused as Jadren felt. Seliah, with a ululation of delight, bounded toward Alise, who manifested a warrior spirit in reflexive shock between them.

"It's Seliah!" Jadren shouted to Alise, hoping he wouldn't have to take drastic measures to protect his familiar from a friend.

Fortunately, Alise had already realized that, her wizard-black eyes wide with surprise and pleasure. "Seliah?" She knelt to embrace the big cat with zero fear, Seliah's tail lashing with her own happiness. "You've found your alternate form—and such a gorgeously fierce one! Absolutely perfect for you. And I'm so happy to see you again." She lifted her gaze to Jadren. "I wish the circumstances were better."

"Nice of you to pop out of the shrubbery on cue, baby Elal," he drawled, walking over to give her a hand up.

"Sorry about the lurking. We were being circumspect as I wasn't entirely sure why you were here with an El-Adrel army." She raised her brows, her accusation implicit.

"Ah, yes." He stroked his beard, giving her his best evil villain impression, then swept a bow. "Allow me to introduce myself. I'm the new lord of House El-Adrel, and this is my familiar, Lady Seliah El-Adrel." Seliah managed a graceful bow also, extending a foreleg and inclining her large head. "It's a long story," Jadren added with a rueful grimace, "but my minions here can confirm."

"All hail Lord El-Adrel," his army chorused on cue, and he rolled his eyes for Alise, who laughed.

"I suppose stranger things have happened," she conceded. "Congratulations. This is my friend, Wizard Cillian Harahel, late of the Convocation Archives."

Jadren gave him a friendly dip of the chin, his curiosity more than piqued by the mild-mannered, scholarly looking guy. "And you, baby Elal? We understood you'd been packed off to the academy to resume your studies." He waved a hand at Seliah by way of explanation. "Have you run away yet again?" He clucked his tongue at her, enjoying her discomfiture. "Does daddy know?"

"Hey," Cillian said, showing some fire, "don't talk to her that way. Lord El-Adrel," he added belatedly. "And she's Alise

Phel now. She deserves your respect, not your mockery."

"That's right," Alise said to Jadren, giving him a superior smile Cillian wouldn't be able to see from his position behind her. "Show me some respect, Jadren. Especially if you want me to yank the animating spirits from those automatons so your people can deactivate them."

"Well, you have learned to be a good little spy," he allowed, grinning back. "I don't suppose you come bearing evidence of Hanneil's collusion in the fall of House Phel?" He kept his gaze on the Harahel wizard to catch his reaction to the accusation. Young Cillian showed no surprise, instead seeming grimly resolved.

"Not yet," Alise allowed. "But we're closer than before. We were on our way to House Harahel to petition them to intervene and review the records when I got the courier that House Phel was under siege."

"I imagine they told you to stay far away, as they did with Seliah," Jadren observed, "and, like her, you took that as an invitation instead."

Alise didn't look in the least chagrined, meeting his gaze steadily. "I could not hide in safety while they suffered, any more than either of you could."

"Noble idiots, the lot of us," Jadren agreed cheerfully. "Fully infected with Phel idealism."

Seliah yowled in agreement, butting her head under his hand.

"Did Houses Phel and El-Adrel just become allies?" Alise asked with a quirk of a smile.

Jadren held out a hand and she clasped it. "The beginning

of a beautiful coalition."

"If any of us survive," Cillian inserted, "this will be one for the history books."

"Will House Harahel stand with us?" Jadren asked with interest.

Cillian cocked his head, thinking. "Depends on what we find out about House Hanneil, is my guess, but Alise can tell you some interesting things about House Uriel's interest."

"Is that right?" This was sounding more promising all the time.

"I'll explain later," Alise said. "After we liberate House Phel."

Jadren swept a hand gallantly, inviting her to the battle-field. "Let us kick some ass."

"Did someone call for ass-kicking?" another voice called out.

Jadren turned to the new voice, wondering who was jumping out of the bushes now, bemused to find a phalanx of farmers brandishing everything from kitchen knives to scythes to wicked-looking sharp hooks at the ends of long poles. The couple standing at the forefront looked vaguely familiar, very like Gabriel and Seliah. Indeed, Seliah started bounding toward them, then stopped, lashing her tail in consternation as if just remembering the form she currently wore.

"Gabriel Senior," the man said. "But, since that gets confusing, you can call me GF. My wife, Daisy. If you're all looking at cutting down those monsters and liberating our kids, well we want a piece of that harvest."

The crowd behind them shouted in agreement. Jadren

took in the piecemeal army of common folk with their makeshift weapons, catching Seliah's eye. "You realize there's magic involved here," he told them. "Powerful magic."

"Of course we do," Daisy replied with a snort of disgust. "We're farmers, not idiots. We might not be wizards like our son and daughter, but we're not helpless either, nor are we cowards. We've been watching you all assemble here and we're ready to offer whatever support we can. I don't know where Seliah is—I can only hope that she's still all right as her letters say—but our son is in there, along with our daughter-in-law and unborn grandchild. We're not losing them without a fight."

"Get us through that guard perimeter," GF added, "and we'll get you into the house. We've learned a thing or two about killing those hunter critters."

"Chop'em up into fine enough pieces, they can't keep coming," someone else called out.

"Also," Daisy added, "we might not be powerful wizards or familiars, but we've been living with water all our lives, and we know ways of encouraging it to move from where it shouldn't be to where we want it."

Jadren considered that with interest and rising optimism. "Could you, say, *encourage* water back into the lake?"

Daisy glanced at several women in the crowd, who nodded in solemn agreement. "That water belongs in the lake," she answered with a smile. "It will be happy to go back home if enough of us encourage it."

Returning the smile, Jadren brandished his map. "All right then, here's the revised plan."

~ 25 ~

G ABRIEL LOOKED AROUND the gathering of faces, sober in the advent of what they planned to do. "This is not the ending to House Phel that any of us wanted or hoped for," he told them, searching for the right words.

"We didn't want an ending at all," Han, front and center, snarled. "We can't just give up!"

"Right," Iliana agreed from beside him. "For most of us, this is the only place we've found to call home, and now you want us to just scamper off? Lord Phel," she added to the end, with a faint flush."

"We're not asking anyone to die for House Phel," Nic inserted firmly. "All we're doing here is creating an opportuni-ty for our non-combatants to escape. Children, babies, the invalid." Her voice broke a little on the last, and Gabriel set a hand on her back to steady her. Not only had Nic's mother failed to improve, but with Asa so taxed with the flood of wounded, he'd been unable to sustain her previous level of care. The unresponsive woman had begun to deteriorate rapidly. Nic, naturally, blamed herself and couldn't be talked out of it.

"This 'opportunity' of yours will ensure your deaths,"

Wolfgang pointed out, his arm around Costa, who leaned against him unhappily. One of the more malicious spirits had scored Costa's cheek, leaving a furrow from temple to chin, likely forever scarring the handsome man.

Gabriel regarded the wizard soberly, then looked over all the faces listening intently, taking in their varying expressions of fear, stubborn determination, hope, and despair. "That army outside wants one thing: my death and the destruction of House Phel."

"So you'll just hand it to them, Lord Phel?" Sage demanded, holding a wicked looking staff in her capable hands. The glass wizard had commandeered one of the pruning hooks from the garden shed, proving handy with the improvised weapon.

"This is not your fight," he answered simply. "I refuse to take all of you with me."

"With *us*," Nic corrected, sliding him an emerald glare of warning.

Gabriel had turned over and over in his mind how to get Nic out of the house with the others, but every plan he came up with was immediately complicated by the fact that she was on guard for such a maneuver. Nic categorically refused to consider leaving him. It didn't help that she rightfully pointed out that he'd never get off the final blast at the intended power without her assistance.

He held up his hands to silence the murmurs of discontent. "I won't force anyone to leave. But I will give you the option. Here is the plan. I'm going to drop the wards between the manse and the lake. I'll create the appearance of weakening to lure our attackers there, then allow them in. Meanwhile, I'll create an opening at the back, as well. Anyone who chooses to leave can escape that direction and to the river. There are boats moored there or, if you can swim, cross to the other side. With any luck, the hunters will have come around to the front and you won't have many to contend with."

"And if we do?" someone from the back asked, nerves in their voice.

"I'm counting on Han to lead those of you who can fight in covering the others." He caught and held the blond familiar's gaze. "You might have to fight your way free."

Han nodded reluctantly, but with solemn acceptance of the assignment.

"Iliana, Quinn," Nic said, "I'm hoping you two will take charge of the children, injured, and other noncombatants. Many will have to be carried out on stretchers. Asa and his assistants are getting everyone prepped to be moved."

Quinn nodded, weeping openly.

"What about Nathi?" Iliana cried. "She won't be able to escape, especially now that the lake is dry."

"Tell her to go deep," Gabriel answered. "She survived the sinking of the manse before. Tell her to go wherever she went then."

Iliana accepted that with poor grace, her transparent face revealing her doubt. Nic looked up at him, smiling with rueful resignation.

"Lord Phel!" one of the house pages called out as he came running in. He'd been assigned to lookout duty. "There's activity on the far side of the lake."

He repressed a growl of aggravation. Reinforcements, just as they'd been about to act? More terrible luck. "Can you be more specific?"

"We can't tell yet. I was told to come fetch you, Lady Phel, and Commander Han immediately."

"We're coming," Gabriel replied, then raised his voice over the exclamations and murmurs. "Meanwhile, proceed with our plan. I want those noncombatants prepped to move."

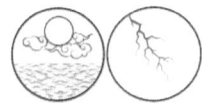

BEING IN WILD cat form was even more fantastic than Selly had anticipated—and she'd anticipated a lot. She hadn't wanted to test out her skills in a situation this dire, but the sleek, inherently lethal body served her well in this instance. It had been great for scouting, especially since the automatons and hunters—even when they did spot her—ignored her as irrelevant and unintelligent wildlife.

Apparently they lacked the ability to discern her magical nature as wizards and other familiars could. Interesting to know.

The form had been less great for, at long last, seeing her parents again. She'd been about to fling herself into a big hug when she remembered she didn't look like their daughter anymore. Jadren had been willing to shift her back to human form any time she signaled her desire, but that hadn't been the moment to introduce them to her new and even more magically bizarre self. Time enough to phase them into another startling change in their children when they won this battle.

Keeping an eye on Jadren for his signal that he needed her, Selly guarded the phalanx of minor water-workers—those expert at wicking moisture out of most anything—led by her own mother. Jadren had simply told them Selly was a magical guardian who'd protect them from the hunters and they'd accepted it with only a bit of jaundiced side-eye. If Daisy gave her a harder, longer look than the others, Selly put it down to her mother's fiercely protective nature, not any kind of maternal instinct. No way could her mother sense Selly inside the body of a big, black marsh cat. Right?

Going with the water-wickers to the point where the attackers had dammed the inlet to the lake went fairly smoothly. As Jadren had observed, the hunters and automatons had no fear of reprisals from the rear. The disadvantage, he'd sardonically observed, of the masterminds absenting themselves from the actual battle and leaving a mindless horde to carry out their evil plans. The horde focused on simple tasks: surrounding the manse, draining the lake, uncovering and penetrating the arcanium. Oh, and killing anything in their way.

Once Daisy marshaled the water-wickers, the lot of them chanting a familiar work tune to stay in sync, encouraging the water to push through the hastily constructed earthen dam, then they attracted the attention of the enemy.

Several hunters and two automatons—one in humanoid shape and the other like a spiky wheel with blades for legs— headed their direction. Selly left the machines to the El-Adrel wizard–familiar pair Jadren had assigned to them and hurled herself at the hunters without waiting for them to get any closer.

In this form, she was far larger than the weaselly canine creatures, and she outweighed them. Three on one didn't give her fair odds, but her fangs outmatched theirs, as did her razor-sharp claws. She didn't need moon-magic silver to slice her way through their foul, yipping flesh, nor did she pause to exchange taunting comments with them. She immersed herself in her hot-blooded predator's mind, giving up all reserve and human niceties. This was the red rage she'd experienced before, when she'd lost her mind to the insane whirl of the need to escape, to fight her way free, but focused like cold silver. She could be the wild cat and not lose herself.

The best of all her selves.

The chanting continued, a rhythmic song of simple home life, of wringing out clothes and cloths, of sending water away from bedding and places meant to be dry, a homey backdrop to her systematic dismemberment of the creatures whose kind had terrorized her and Nic, who'd done their best to kill Jadren. They were no match for her, the last falling to twitching slices of rotten flesh at the same moment the water gladly punched through the dam, gushing into its rightful place.

The lake was big, so the wave didn't overwhelm the hunters guarding the automaton crew noisily banging on the arcanium, but it did get their attention. Long snouts swiveled around and the loose circle of them dropped to all fours. The more distant individuals, the ones on higher ground, began loping toward the group of water-wickers on the high shore of the slowly refilling lake, but others simply forged into the water. Disconcertingly, they didn't swim, not even to dog paddle. Instead, they disappeared beneath the surface as they clawed their way along the muddy bottom in single-minded purpose.

The automatons, on the other hand, bent to their task with intensified purpose, their clanging increasing in speed and volume as they became aware of the changing circumstances. The water-wickers intensified their own efforts, the chanting growing faster and louder also, the water eating away the last of the earthen dam and flowing with renewed force into the basin, becoming a roaring waterfall at the edge of the inlet. Selly herded her mother, and thus the others behind her, back from the ledge, lest it collapse. As waves hit the arcanium, a couple of automatons floated free, waving their arms and legs in futile distress.

Also, she knew those hunters arrowing toward them underwater would arrive sooner than anyone expected. She had experience with the foul creations and could anticipate better than her mother, who remained relatively innocent of encounters with monsters.

On the other side of the lake, her father led a group of workers in employing their digging equipment to fill in the outlet that had been widened to drain the lake. They used a mixture of mix of lime, clay, and sand, a recipe Gabriel had found in the musty old library of the house, using it to reinforce the sides.

Jadren led the El-Adrel wizards in powering down the

automatons, one force focusing on the arcanium, while other wizard–familiar teams burst of the woods, taking on the metallic sentries circling the manse just beyond the silver shimmer of Gabriel's wards. Alise remained with Jadren, a slim, shorter and darker form, the Harahel librarian at her other side as she lanced her magic toward one humanoid automaton after another. In the wake of her magic, released spirits wafted into the air, angry and confused. Some tried to attack the arcanium again, seeming not to understand they lacked any kind of corporeal form anymore to do it with. Other spirits misted toward Alise, vanishing into puffs of nothing if they came too close.

Surprised that she could visualize those spirits so easily, entranced by the magic radiating from Alise and the other wizards, visible to her as never before, Selly nearly forgot about the hunters coming for the group she guarded until they suddenly erupted from the water. The water-wickers behind her screeched in shock, their chanting breaking apart into ragged bits, their magic shattering.

That was all right, as they'd done their job, the water pouring into the lake. It would take time to completely refill, but the scales had been duly tipped, the balance restoring itself. Most of the water-wickers ran—as Jadren had told them to do—but not Daisy. Selly interposed her body between her mother and the oncoming hunters, snarling at her.

"Don't you sass me, Seliah Phel," her mother retorted. "I know perfectly well that's you and I'm not abandoning you to fight these creatures alone.

Selly didn't have time for surprise that her mother had

recognized her in this form, she was too busy taking apart one hunter after another. There were too many, however, and she began to tire, dashing back and forth to keep them off the woman defending herself with a sharp-edged hoe. She needed help.

Just then, magic surged and crashed, accompanied by a roar from many throats. Water from the lake rose into a massive fist and pounded down onto the phalanx of hunters hounding Selly and Daisy, dragging the lot of them into the lake basin.

Gabriel.

~ 26 ~

JADREN PUNCHED A fist in the air at the advent of Gabriel Phel's water magic taking possession of the returning lake and using it to batter the hunters going after Seliah and Daisy. He'd been poised to dash over there, but he'd too easily envisioned a scenario where he'd be too late. Seliah had wanted to remain in her fierce big cat form for these initial sallies, unless and until he needed her magic. But there were limits to what she could do.

He watched with relief as Seliah took advantage of the reprieve to herd her mother back to the safety of their own rear guard. The older woman was fit, jogging easily alongside Seliah, one hand trustingly on the cat's back.

Turning his attention back to the manse, he assessed the current situation. They'd nullified the immediate threat to the arcanium, but all advantage of their surprise attack from the rear had been lost. It had lasted longer than he'd hoped for, frankly, which had preserved their fighting power. Now, however, they faced overwhelming odds, not remotely in their favor.

With the collapsing of his wards, Gabriel had emerged onto the wide, gracious front porch that wrapped around the main section of the manse, his tall, silver-haired form distinctive even from a distance. Nic, in human form, stuck beside him, and a small force of fighters ringed them protectively. Squinting, doing a rough count, Jadren determined that group represented less than a third of everyone who should have been in residence at the time of the attack. Were the rest hiding inside or...

A small falcon came shooting across the lake, backwinging to land on Alise's shoulder. "This is Quinn Byssan!" she gasped in surprise. "She and Sage had just nailed putting her in alternate form when I left. What is she—oh, she's carrying a note."

Quinn chirped in authoritative agreement, folding her wings to her speckled back.

"Nic says they'd already mobilized the noncombatants, including a large number of patients—damn—to escape out the back of the manse with a suitable distraction. We need to do more to pull the bulk of the hunters to the front, just in case we don't carry the day. He's prepared to lay down devastating magic." She looked to Quinn, wizard-black eyes cold. "Maman must be in the group they're taking out the back."

The falcon chirped an affirmative and Alise turned back to Jadren. "I want to go with that group and help."

"Is that wise?" Cillian inserted.

"I can summon defensive spirits if necessary," she said dismissively.

"Cillian is right," Jadren put in, earning a grateful look from the Harahel wizard. "We need you here to deal with the spirits in the automatons. Look—more are coming our way."

"This is my mother we're talking about," Alise spat, lifting her chin in that stubborn defiance that was all Elal. Or, all Phel, as it turned out.

Jadren hated to pull rank, but he had to. "You're under my command Alise Phel, both in this operation and as your senior in the Phel family." He pointed to Seliah, who came loping up just then, tongue lolling as she panted, Daisy Phel a few steps behind. Not far away—much too close—the hunters were massing. "Here's a lesson for you, Baby Elal. Learn to delegate. Trust in other people to handle things for you."

She fumed visibly, yanking her arm away when Cillian tried to take her elbow. "Baby Phel," she spat. "If you're going to condescend to me, Lord Jadren El-Adrel, then get it right."

She handed Quinn to him and stalked stiffly away to the warded staging area where El-Adrel wizards were bringing deactivated, but still spirit-animated automatons, methodically working through ripping the spirits free and sending them into the ether.

"Tell them we understand the plan and will support," he told Quinn, "but we're going to need a lot of magic to deal with this horde."

Experimentally, he grabbed a severed piece of hunter lying nearby, twitching and trying to crawl its way to rejoin another. Drawing Gabriel's original dagger, given to him by Seliah for safekeeping, he stabbed the limb with it. Nothing happened. Looking up, he found a circle of people watching him in puzzlement—except for Seliah managed to make her cat's face grimace—some seeming to think he might've lost his mind. Joke was on them—he had, but not related to this. He pocketed the dagger, knowing Gabriel would want it back. "Assume that every one of these hunters has been proofed against the moon magic that previously melted them. We're going to have to chop, then incinerate. One by one."

"We've got to be outnumbered ten to one," GF said with disbelief.

"More like fifty to one," Jadren replied.

"Correction," Alise said, joining them, looking slightly chastened. "Maybe as much as a hundred to one. I just detected a group of cloaking spirits on some reserves lurking in the eastern marsh. Hunters are on the move this way. I cast about and there's a group approaching from behind us, too. I can rip away the cloaking, but it will tip them off that we're on to them."

Jadren gave her a solemn nod of thanks. "Let's wait until we're in position then. I'm glad you're with us."

She shrugged, unwilling to be that gracious, and returned to her task.

"All right," Jadren said, "let's plan this diversion. Quinn, take the message."

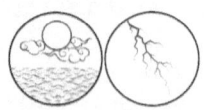

IT WASN'T A brilliant diversion, as such things went. Since Jadren and his small army of magic workers were already sitting ducks with the temerity to threaten to nibble the vast horde of hunters to death, they presented a lovely target. The hunters converged on them from all directions, until they were entirely surrounded.

On the plus side, they did serve as an excellent diversion and Phel sure better be taking advantage and planning how to properly express his gratitude.

On the down side... Well, Phel might not need to award any bonuses as they looked unlikely to survive. Seemed kind of anticlimactic, but then, Jadren had always known being a hero was a fool's game.

They'd retreated to a knot of concentric circles, with their weakest members in the center. Alise had summoned warrior spirits to guard them, though they weren't any more self-directed than the hunters. They also didn't tire, so that was something.

Cillian Harahel had turned out to be more useful in a pitched battle than a librarian ought to be. From his encyclopedic memory, he recalled several enchantments that anyone with sufficient magic could cast, and he deployed those to good effect—freezing groups of hunters in place to be chopped apart or miring them in the plentiful mud with similar results.

The El-Adrel wizards deployed their best devices, discovering that the favored weapon of their burrowing darts didn't affect the hunters they way they did living creatures—no pain, no real effect on their ability to keep going—but that flying disks with serrated edges served well to sever their front and hind legs.

The mundane fighters had to be wary of the snapping jaws and sharp-edged fangs, but they could then follow in a second wave and at least chop the hunters into smaller, less-threatening sections.

Seliah, of course, was a one-woman killing machine, handling the hunters Cillian couldn't immobilize, and he guarded her flank, holding his own with Mr. Machete and such devices as he was able to activate on the fly.

And it still wasn't enough.

The hunters kept coming, mounding around them in twitching, taunting, and writhing piles of rotten malevolence. In places they formed walls that afforded some protection from the onslaught, though one had to be careful of coming too close to claws that swiped of their own accord or disembodied slashing fangs.

Everyone was tiring. The wizards without familiars had pretty well emptied their reserves, retreating gray-faced to manually defend the core of their most vulnerable, which included Gabriel's parents. Those with familiars hung in there, but the familiars were starting to run low. And physical bodies could only sustain so much. They were wearying, hungry, and thirsty. It showed, too, more hunters getting through the outer ring of their defenses, more people crying out in shocked pain as fangs and claws slashed through to injure them.

"Phel had better do whatever splashy magic he has in mind," Jadren gritted out to Seliah during a rare break in the constant effort. "We can't hold out much longer."

As if summoned, Quinn arrived in falcon form, bearing another message. "This better be the news we're looking for. Cover me," Jadren told Seliah, able to smile a little in memory of the first time the pair of them had fought a horde of hunters. Her jaw fell open in a feline grin, clearly remembering, too, how he'd told her to cover him—having no idea what that actually meant—and then run willy-nilly into the fight. They'd come a long way since then.

Tail lashing, Seliah turned her back, ready to defend him against all comers while he read the disheartening news. "Phel can't unleash anything devastating on the hunters with us in the middle of them. He's picking off the edges, but the moon silver isn't working to melt them—we knew that—so it's slow going. Good news is they've evacuated everyone they needed to, but we're at a stalemate. He wants to know how long we can hold out." He laughed bleakly. "Or if we can extract ourselves from the line of fire."

He looked around, as if their situation might have changed. "Extract how and to where? No, Lord Phel, we can't."

Quinn took wing, though he hadn't meant for that to be his reply. Still, it was the definitive answer. Seliah dismembered a hunter, then looked over her shoulder at him with a bloody mouth. "Yeah," he told her. "It's time for the desperation move. Let's just hope this works."

She came to him and he brought her back to human form, the effort surprisingly easy. Which was good, as he was running low on magic. They'd made that deliberate decision, for her to remain in alternate form as long as possible, to reserve her potent reservoir of magic for the desperation move, figuring it would likely come to this. Seliah spat a bloody gobbet of spit to the ground, then wiped her mouth with the back of her hand.

"There's my lovely Lady El-Adrel," he drawled.

She made a face at him. "That stuff tastes foul. You have

no idea."

He chuckled at the old joke and took her hand, fishing the widget out from under his shirt. "Your folks likely witnessed that transformation," he warned her, wishing they'd had time to ease them into the concept of their daughter becoming one of the ferocious wild cats that haunted the western marshes.

"I think they knew already. Mom seemed to, anyway."

"Interesting. You would be a good mother," he observed.

"Then this better work," she replied with a cheeky grin, "as I'd love a bumper crop of El-Adrel babies."

"Am I to live with farmer metaphors all my life?" he complained.

"You love it. You love me."

"I do, it's true." He paused, gazing at her with all the love in his heart. "If this doesn't work, it's been a real privilege, Seliah."

"Yes. I wouldn't trade any of this." She leaned in to kiss him.

"With that mouth?" he exclaimed, rearing back.

"Hey, I rinsed, but fine." She gave him a black scowl, then gasped as he dragged her to him and kissed her as if it might be the last time.

"Delicious," he told her in all sincerity. "Are you ready?"

"Let's do this."

~ 27 ~

GABRIEL PACED THE porch, full of magic for their final strike and impotent to use it. A few of the faithful remained with them. Han, who'd returned after seeing the non-combatants safely away, Wolfgang, Costa, and a very stubborn trio of Sage, Quinn and Iliana. Everyone else had made it safely out the back. Jadren, Seliah, and the others had done a great job of drawing the hunter horde to them.

Too good of a job, as the group on the porch of the manse could only stand by helplessly and watch the thronging mass of unnatural creatures surge and heave over the diminishing group of their rescuers. The once beautiful lake roiled with mud, thrashing hunters, and broken automatons, the dome of the arcanium—ironically and miraculously still intact—barely peeked above the surface now as water continued to pour in, no longer with his assistance. He'd sacrifice the arcanium in a heartbeat to help their people on the other side of the lake, those heroic rescuers who'd arrived in the nick of time, likely sacrificing themselves in the effort.

"Jadren didn't say what they planned to do?" he demanded of Quinn, yet again.

"Gabriel," Nic said soothingly from her perch on the white-painted rail. "Quinn has already told you everything she knows."

"I know, I know." He held up a hand in apology, but Quinn only looked away unhappily.

She was berating herself for not lingering to get more than that single reply. "I heard something about a desperation move as I flew away," she repeated. "I know I should have gone back to find out more."

"Well," said her sister and wizard, Sage, in her frank fashion, "the next time we're transforming you rapidly in and out of your alternate form to use you as a messenger in a pitched battle, you'll know better."

"If there *is* a next time," Quinn said, and burst into tears.

Nic gave him a mildly accusing glare and Gabriel raked a hand through his hair. "Quinn," he started say, wanting to apologize and realizing in the same moment that promising her there would be a next time was absurd and not what any of them wanted.

"Look!" Nic exclaimed, hopping off the rail and pointing across the lake. "Magic. Big magic."

He squinted unnecessarily, as extending his wizard's senses told him much more, Nic's acuity for sensing magic as always well ahead of his. "What magic is that?" he asked of no one, completely befuddled.

"It feels like healing and… yet not," Nic answered, sounding similarly confused. "Wait, look at the hunters. What are they—" She broke off on a choking sound of surprise.

"They're multiplying," Gabriel said grimly.

"No." Nic laughed, a shockingly joyous sound, one he

hadn't heard from her in what felt like forever. "They're reverting to their composite parts. That's a gang of weasels scurrying for the deeper underbrush."

"And jackals," Costa exclaimed. "We have those back home. I'd recognize them anywhere."

"Are those rabbits?" Sage asked in disbelief, and Iliana laughed.

"Jack rabbits," she confirmed.

"What a strange mélange of creatures," Nic marveled.

"And not a one interested in attacking anyone," Han observed with satisfaction. He slid a look to Gabriel, who stared at the chaotic scene in disbelief. "Though we may have a critter problem in the woods around here for a while, Lord Phel."

Gabriel tore his gaze from the jumble of animals scampering as fast as they could for cover, finding the blond familiar grinning from ear to ear. Slowly, Gabriel shook his head, a smile of his own stretching lips that had been pressed in a flat line of despair for so long that it felt as if they might crack. "I'll take that problem."

"Yes, we will," Nic declared, threading her arm through his, and beaming up at him. "It's going to take a bit to process, but I think we may have survived."

He covered her hand with his. "Maybe so. I don't want to be hasty, but...." He gazed out at the area on the other side of the lake, rapidly clearing of animals, more of various species swimming to the banks of the lake and dashing away. "I don't understand how they did it."

"We'll find out," she assured him. "Meanwhile, we need to

muster to deal with the injured."

"Perhaps we can help with that." A tall, dark-skinned man emerged from the side of the porch, followed by a considerable group of others, all wizards, all wearing long robes. "Lord and Lady Phel, I'm Lord Chaim Refoel. We've come to your assistance."

"A bit late," the dark-skinned woman just behind him said with a rueful smile. Both had the look of Asa, a distinct family resemblance. "I am Liat Refoel."

Gabriel managed to recover from his surprise more quickly. It had been a day of turnabouts. "We'll take all the assistance anyone is willing to offer," he assured them, aware of Nic's bemusement beside him. "But... House Refoel? I understood you would not violate your ethical code by taking sides."

Liat and Chaim exchanged opaque glances, and Chaim cleared his throat, looking somewhat chagrined despite his cool ascetic demeanor. "It's been pointed out to us—to me— that choosing not to interfere is also a choice. In standing back, we allow evil and injustice to flourish. As the new head of House Refoel, I am officially amending our policy. We will continue to offer aid and healing to any who need it, but we will also take a stand."

"Upon careful consideration of all sides," Liat amended with a ghost of a smile. "Now, it seems we have wounded to tend."

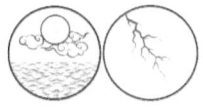

ALISE HAD NEVER been so exhausted in all her life. It was enough to make her long for the crushing schedule of Convocation Academy. Utterly depleted of magic, injured in half a dozen places, and tired to her bones to the point she didn't think she could so much as stand upright, she nevertheless found renewed energy at the sight of the group cruising toward them in a cadre of elemental carriages bearing the sigil of House Refoel.

Han and Iliana were the first to disembark, both showing signs of exhaustion and battle, but also laughing and shouting with joy at the sight of her. They raced to embrace her, seizing her in a three-way hug that solidified the lasting truth that *this* was her real home. She finally broke away to introduce them to a weary Cillian, who looked less like a librarian and Convocation Faculty than like some sort of mud-encrusted forest creature. The three of them already knew each other, it turned out, from Convocation Academy, since everyone else in the world was apparently more social than Alise.

Nic arrived on their heels, embracing her fervently, then taking her by the shoulders with a ferocious glare. "I clearly told you to stay put," she said, shaking Alise a little. "You could've been killed!"

"You're welcome," Alise replied drily, then gave Nic's protruding belly a long look. "Should you be out, running around and fighting beasties in your condition?"

"I'm pregnant, not an invalid," Nic answered tartly. "Don't you start with me too. Besides, it's not my fault that said beasties came to me." She seized Alise in another fierce hug. "I missed you. If you'd been here, you would have told us about the cloaking."

"Maybe," Alise conceded. "It took me a while to notice it on the reserve forces. Nic—it's definitely Papa's work. I recognize the signature."

Her elder sister nodded grimly. "I'm not surprised, much as I'd rather it be otherwise. He won't ever let this go. And Nander?"

Alise grimaced. "Solidly under Papa's thumb. I think we have to treat him as the enemy. Certainly not an ally."

"All right then." Nic squeezed her arm. "Just you and me then, the black sheep on our own against House Elal."

"The good news," Jadren said, joining them with his arm around Seliah, Gabriel flanking them after having assured himself of his parents' wellbeing, "is that you *can* count House El-Adrel as your ally now."

"Yes," Seliah said with a delighted smile. "So, not entirely on your own."

While Nic gaped, Alise and Gabriel demanded how that had come to be. Seliah's smile turned conspiratorial. "It's a long story, but Katica El-Adrel is dead. You're looking at the new Lord and Lady El-Adrel."

Recovering quickly, Nic congratulated them both. "That explains the presence of all these El-Adrel wizards and familiars. Beyond that, you also somehow convinced House Refoel to come to our aid."

"I blame Seliah," Jadren said with a snide grin, "and her seductive powers." She elbowed him in the side, glancing nervously in the direction of her parents, who were fortunately not paying attention.

"Regardless," Gabriel said, clearing his throat manfully, "I'm glad the healers are here. I have to ask you, Jadren, as we're all dying to know—what in the Dark Arts did you do to those hunters?"

"It's his magic," Seliah said proudly.

"Being able to heal?" Alise asked, looking back and forth among them. Cillian, stepping up to join them, shrugged his own ignorance. Neither of them had been able to make out what Jadren had done either, and hadn't had the opportunity to ask.

"Not exactly," Jadren temporized, exchanging a look with Seliah, who nodded encouragingly. "I put them back to their original state. It seems that's my ability, more than healing. It's a variation on El-Adrel enchantment, but on living things. I can make them work the way they're supposed to."

"So you returned them to their component parts," Nic said with obvious fascination. "And not dead."

Jadren stroked his beard thoughtfully, nodding. "It seems so. I still have a lot to discover about how it works."

Alise noticed Cillian's avid interest also, certain he was using his own magic to record mental notes.

"We have time later," Gabriel said by way of agreement. "Make sure you all get treated by a healer and let's retire to the manse. We're having the non-combatants brought back home, so let's convene there to trade stories." He tugged Nic against him. "We have allies," he informed her. "And you said it couldn't be done."

"We still have Elal and Sammael against us," she replied darkly.

"Yes," Cillian said, "but indications are that you might have House Uriel in your corner, and possibly soon, House Harahel. Particularly if House Hanneil is truly involved."

Alise belatedly introduced Cillian to Nic and Gabriel, adding, "It's another long story."

At that point, they all agreed to wait until everyone was healed and they had food, rest, and plenty of wine on hand to catch each other up on everything that had happened.

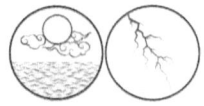

"I DIDN'T EXPECT House Phel to be so beautiful," Cillian commented as they climbed the steps of the broad front porch, both of them feeling much better for Refoel healing.

She slid him a dubious glance. "You thought it would be a hut on stilts surrounded by bog water?"

"Not quite that bad," he replied, flushing.

"That's *exactly* what I expected," Nic piped in from behind them, giggling at Gabriel's sour grunt in response.

"Apologies, Lord Phel," Cillian said over his shoulder.

"None needed, Wizard Cillian," Gabriel replied. "As you perceive, even my nearest and dearest amuse themselves with swamp jokes."

"I know I do," Jadren put in easily.

"Perhaps you can give me a tour of the manse," Cillian suggested to Alise as they all entered the main hallway.

"I'd be happy to—though first I want to go visit Maman. I understand they've put her in the infirmary with everyone else."

"Lady Elal," he mused. "I recall her visiting Convocation Center with Lord Elal. Is she unwell?"

"In a word, yes. She was our father's familiar until—" Alise broke off, realizing what she'd nearly spilled in her brain-fogged weariness.

"Until what?" Cillian asked, curiosity clearly piqued. "I've never heard of a familiar separated so long from their wizard and still alive."

Jadren frowned. "That's an excellent question. How has that been possible?"

Out of Jadren's line of sight, Seliah was giving Alise a wide-eyed, panicked shake of the head. So she'd never told Jadren the truth? Well she was safe for the moment, because— whether Cillian was friend or not—no way was Alise handing House Harahel the information on what she'd done. She shrugged. "The wizards have been bleeding off her magic and our resident Refoel healer, Asa, has been keeping her alive with his wizardry. He's very good," she added in the face of Cillian's patent disbelief.

"I find it extremely difficult to believe that would work for any length of time," he said.

"It hasn't," Nic inserted, coming to the rescue. "In truth," and now she turned to Alise, grief in her eyes, "I should warn you that you'll find Maman much deteriorated from when last you saw her."

Apprehension stabbed at Alise. "How much?"

"You should see for yourself, but…" Nic's emerald eyes filled with tears and she looked away, blinking rapidly to clear them.

"I'll go now," Alise said. Then, remembering her manners, she turned to Cillian. "Ah…"

"I'll give Wizard Cillian the tour," Gabriel offered with gentle compassion, "while you all pay a visit to the infirmary. I know Jadren and Seliah have people they'd like to see and Nic will want to be with you." She gave him a grateful smile, while Seliah looked decidedly unhappy with the arrangement. "This way, Wizard Cillian," Gabriel said graciously. "Perhaps I can convince you to abandon Convocation Center and become our resident Harahel wizard."

"Thank you, Lord Phel." Cillian flashed her an astounded look. "But very rarely do houses keep Harahel wizards on staff. We're not considered to be all that valuable. And, please, just 'Cillian' is fine."

"Then you must call me Gabriel. And that surprises me. I confess our library is in dreadful condition and desperately needs any magical assistance you can provide."

"I understand there may be books in the Phel library never before catalogued," Cillian replied eagerly, as they wandered off.

"Gabriel has found a new friend, it appears," Nic said in Alise's ear. "A cute one, too."

"Just a friend," she hissed back reprovingly. "Now, how much should I brace myself for seeing Maman."

Nic's face fell. "As much as possible, baby sister."

~ 28 ~

THIS IS IT, Selly thought to herself glumly. All her pigeons—or Ratsiel couriers, to use a Convocation analogy, rather than a farmer one—were coming home to roost. And Jadren was so up, so jubilant over his incredible feat, winning that battle with his newly discovered skills. They were in harmony, at the height of their partnership, and now he'd find out that she'd withheld vital information about Alise being able to sever their bond.

Why, oh why, hadn't she told him the truth before this? Her mother always said it never paid to put off difficult tasks, they only grew harder for the waiting.

The infirmary boiled with barely contained chaos. Asa stood in the middle, directing the positioning of patients, assessing those as they were brought in, and making determinations for prioritization—all while cuddling the sleeping baby Cornelis in the crook of one arm. His professional gaze raked the four of them, face relaxing as he took in their relative good health.

Selly recognized a number of the healers she'd known at House Refoel, busily assisting, and waved to Maya and Liat. They'd catch up later. Chaim was still out at the erstwhile battlefield, which was just as well. He and Jadren did better apart, especially if Jadren would soon insist on severing their bond. She didn't need Chaim crawling all over her with his invitations. Jadren wouldn't do that, though. Not now, after all they'd been through, all the promises they'd made each other. Would he?

Catching her unhappy thoughts, Jadren glanced at her. "You all right?"

"So many injured," she said, gesturing vaguely. It wasn't fully a lie.

"They're getting the best care. Look, Asa's baby was born. Life goes on. Congratulations," he said to Asa, who returned the grin, looking fondly down at his son. "Would you like to hold him?"

"I'd love to," Jadren answered, taking the infant with care, surprising Selly with both his lack of hesitation and skill. "Look how tiny," he said to Selly, chuckling as Cornelis woke and sleepily grabbed for Jadren's fiery beard. "I want one."

She brushed a fingertip against the little fist, moved when Cornelis wrapped his hand around it. "Me, too," she told Jadren.

"Then why do you sound so sad?" His brow creased with concern. "It doesn't have to be right away. We can wait."

"Let's talk about it later," she said, and he frowned more deeply at the edge of desperation in her voice. "I have something I have to tell you."

"Jadren, Seliah," Alise said, breaking into the conversation, "Maman is in a private room. I didn't know if you wanted to come with us…"

Alise looked so broken and weary, and Selly really didn't want Jadren to find out this way.

"We'll come with you," Jadren said before she could think of an excuse. "Stronger together," he reminded Selly with an intimate smile. "Asa, do you want your baby back or can I keep him a while?"

"Keep him as long as you like," Asa said fervently. "You'll be back when he starts wailing."

"Good lungs," Jadren said to Cornelis with satisfaction. "Well done."

Nic raised her brows behind Jadren's back. "This is a side of him I never expected."

"He has a soft heart, under the caustic surface," Selly replied, hoping she wasn't about to break that soft heart. She trailed behind, dragging her feet, reminding herself that Nic and Alise were facing something far worse.

Selly had seen the former Lady Elal before, but it had been months ago and she'd looked relatively healthy, save for being non-responsive and staring at the ceiling with feline eyes that saw nothing. Her much-changed appearance shocked Selly, even with the warning, and her heart broke for the sisters. One of the new Refoel healers had been sitting with her, and he rose at their entry. "Lady Phel," he said, bowing. "I'm afraid I've done all I could."

Nic sucked in a ragged breath, moving to take her mother's hand. "Is she dying?"

"Not yet, but it seems inevitable." He shook his head. "I'm not sure how it happened, but it seems the bond with her wizard attenuated so much that it snapped. Oddly enough, the same problem seems to have occurred with Asa's familiar, Laryn." He left it there, inviting explanation, but not requiring it.

"If you knew how it happened," Alise said slowly, her gaze on her mother, "would you be able to repair the damage?"

The healing wizard shook his head. "No, it seems that—however it occurred—for both women, the breaking of the wizard–familiar bond created a backlash effect. Probably it was contained in the magic of the bond itself, as a deterrent to any attempt to manipulate the bond."

Jadren was no fool. His gaze rested on the side of Selly's face with palpable heat. "Manipulate the bond?" he asked with deceptive mildness. "I didn't think that was possible."

"It shouldn't be," the Refoel wizard agreed, "but something has happened to create that effect in these two cases. I'll leave you all with her. Summon me when you're ready for me to return."

"Thank you," Nic murmured. Once the healer left, closing the door behind him, Nic pinned Alise with a stern, green-eyed gaze. "It's not your fault, Alise."

"It *is* my fault," Alise replied woodenly, sounding devastated and bitter. "I'm the one who severed the bonds, for both of them. Who else's fault could it possibly be?"

"You…" Jadren trailed off, sharp, wizard-black gaze traveling between the three women. "Severed the wizard–familiar bond. Of course you did." He laughed. "I'm an idiot."

Nic closed her eyes briefly, then met Selly's gaze. "I'm sorry, Seliah. I didn't realize you hadn't told him."

"Tell me?" Jadren cut in before Selly could say anything,

drilling her with a black glare. "No, she didn't. But then, why would she? This is the secret. I see now."

"Jadren, I..." Selly didn't know what to say. There were no words.

"Wizard Alise, Lady Phel," Jadren said with cool formality. "Please accept my sympathies and those of House El-Adrel. If there is anything I can do to assist, it's yours." He glanced down when Cornelis cooed, seeming surprised to be holding the baby still. Handing the infant to Selly, he searched her face. Then spun on his heel and left. The carefully controlled precision he used to close the door behind him spoke volumes.

Selly stood there, rootless, unmoored, holding a child that wasn't hers, in the room of a dying familiar who could have been herself. Nic met her gaze, seeming to understand it all. "Go to him," she urged softly. "Explain."

Woodenly, Selly nodded, not yet moving. Alise seemed to be off in a world of her own, so likely it was better for them to be alone. "Do you want to hold Cornelis?" she offered, and Nic stretched out her arms in welcome, taking the baby.

"Maman always did love babies," she said in a watery voice. "She once told me that we—Alise, Nander, and I—had been the best part of her life."

Not knowing what to say, Selly eased out of the room, then hurried through the subsiding chaos of the infirmary, looking around for Jadren. Maya, always the most empathetic of people, waved to Selly, then pointed out the big bay windows. With a grateful smile, Selly ran out the back door, spotting Jadren standing on the bank of the lazily flowing Dubhglas River, the set of his shoulders rigid. The trees on the rising hills beyond had begun to take on autumn color, shining a brilliant golden green, in contrast to the bloody evidence of the battle scattered all around.

Picking her way to him, she came up beside her lover, her friend, her wizard. He said nothing, though he was obviously aware of her presence.

"I'm sorry," she said softly, not knowing where else to start.

"I assume you've known for a long time," he finally said, his voice uncannily neutral. "Since before I left you here."

"After you left," she corrected, wanting him to know that much, "but yes, I knew before I came after you."

He turned to face her, hands jammed deep in his pockets, expression stark. "Why didn't you tell me?"

She took a deep breath. "I should have."

"Yes, you should have," he spat back. "I thought you trusted me, Seliah."

"I do trust you," she protested.

"This isn't trust. Don't *lie* to me." He snarled the word.

"Fine," she snarled back. "I trust you now, but I didn't then. You *left* me, Jadren. You abandoned me and made it clear that you'd take any opportunity, however slim, to dissolve the bond between us."

"For your own good!"

"I didn't care!" she nearly wailed it. "I loved you. I loved you then. I loved you at Refoel. I love you now. And you can call me selfish and a liar and a terrible human being if you want to—and I'll accept that, because it's all true. But I was so afraid that you would have Alise severe our bond that—"

"You think I would have done *that* to you?" He stabbed a finger in the direction of the infirmary, incredulous. "How can you imagine I would want that fate for you?"

"We didn't know that part then," she countered. "If I had told you that Alise could do this and I would be perfectly fine and free and happy, are you saying that you would not have wanted to do it?"

He stared at her, his face a rictus of emotions. At last he sagged. "No, I can't say that."

And there it was.

She nodded, holding back the tears. "I'm sorry I didn't tell you and that I deprived you of that opportunity."

"The opportunity to have you wasting away like that?" he sneered. "How little you think of me."

"Oh, stop it," she snapped, anger rising. "You know I think the world of you. I never wanted to lie to you, to withhold secrets from you. All I wanted was for you to let me love you. Nothing else matters to me, but you. I would do far worse to keep you, so if you think I'm letting this break us up, then you have another think coming!"

He blinked at her. "Another think coming?" he repeated. "Is that a farmer saying?"

"Don't make fun of me, Jadren," she warned. "I am not in the mood."

"No?" He caught her around the waist and drew her close, ignoring her struggles as he nibbled on her neck. "What are you in the mood for?"

"Taking you apart piece by piece," she raged at him.

"That's my girl," he said with abiding affection. "My wild cat."

She slowly ceased fighting him, sense penetrating—along with the realization that he wasn't angry with her anymore.

Easing back, she studied his face, and he returned her regard seriously, with just a hint of wicked mischief quirking his lips. "You forgive me?"

"I forgive you," he said solemnly. "Especially as your self-ishness, as you call it, saved your life. And saved us from my foolishness. I'm a lucky wizard."

"Yes," she sniffed. "You are."

He laughed and lifted her off her feet, kissing her soundly before setting her down again and tapping her on the nose. "No more secrets between us. No more lies."

"No more leaving," she specified sternly, and he inclined his head in agreement.

"There is one small thing, however," he said, looking so serious that her heart clenched.

"What?"

"You'll need to be punished," he answered in a sensuous purr.

Oh yes, she certainly hoped so.

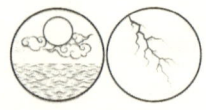

Look for Alise's trilogy, coming in 2024!

Follow Jeffe on social media for updates—options at www.JeffeKennedy.com—or subscribe to her newsletter.

We only send one when there's news to share.

TITLES BY JEFFE KENNEDY

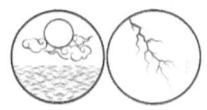

FANTASY ROMANCES

BONDS OF MAGIC
Dark Wizard
Bright Familiar
Grey Magic
Familiar Winter Magic
(Also Available in Fire of the Frost)

RENEGADES OF MAGIC
Shadow Wizard
Rogue Familiar
Twisted Magic

HEIRS OF MAGIC
The Long Night of the Crystalline Moon
(also available in *Under a Winter Sky*)
The Golden Gryphon and the Bear Prince
The Sorceress Queen and the Pirate Rogue
The Dragon's Daughter and the Winter Mage

SORCEROUS MOONS

Lonen's War

Oria's Gambit

The Tides of Bára

The Forests of Dru

Oria's Enchantment

Lonen's Reign

A COVENANT OF THORNS

Rogue's Pawn

Rogue's Possession

Rogue's Paradise

CONTEMPORARY ROMANCES

Shooting Star

MISSED CONNECTIONS

Last Dance

With a Prince

Since Last Christmas

CONTEMPORARY EROTIC ROMANCES

Exact Warm Unholy

The Devil's Doorbell

FACETS OF PASSION

Sapphire

Platinum

Ruby

Five Golden Rings

FALLING UNDER
Going Under
Under His Touch
Under Contract

EROTIC PARANORMAL

MASTER OF THE OPERA E-SERIAL
Master of the Opera, Act 1: Passionate Overture
Master of the Opera, Act 2: Ghost Aria
Master of the Opera, Act 3: Phantom Serenade
Master of the Opera, Act 4: Dark Interlude
Master of the Opera, Act 5: A Haunting Duet
Master of the Opera, Act 6: Crescendo
Master of the Opera

BLOOD CURRENCY
Blood Currency

BDSM FAIRYTALE ROMANCE
Petals and Thorns

Thank you for reading!

ABOUT JEFFE KENNEDY

Jeffe Kennedy is a multi-award-winning and best-selling author of epic fantasy romance. She is the current president of the Science Fiction and Fantasy Writers Association (SFWA) and is a member of Romance Writers of America (RWA), and Novelists, Inc. (NINC). She is best known for her RITA® Award-winning novel, *The Pages of the Mind*, the recent trilogy, *The Forgotten Empires*, and the wildly popular, *Dark Wizard*. Jeffe lives in Santa Fe, New Mexico.

Jeffe can be found online at her website: JeffeKennedy.com, every Wednesday at the popular SFF Seven blog, Facebook, Goodreads, BookBub, Twitter, YouTube, Instagram, and—just like all the kids these days—TikTok. She is represented by Sarah Younger of Nancy Yost Literary Agency.

jeffekennedy.com

facebook.com/Author.Jeffe.Kennedy

twitter.com/jeffekennedy

goodreads.com/author/show/1014374.Jeffe_Kennedy

bookbub.com/profile/jeffe-kennedy

Sign up for her newsletter here.

jeffekennedy.com/sign-up-for-my-newsletter

www.ingramcontent.com/pod-product-compliance
Lightning Source LLC
Chambersburg PA
CBHW031032030726
47497CB00004B/1101